The Local War

Andromeda Rhoades
Liberation

Books by Mark Mora

The Local War Series

Andromeda Rhoades

Liberation

Firestorm

Tranquility

Sundown Rhoades

*Daybreak (Forthcoming)

Andromeda Rhoades Liberation

The Local War (Book 1)

Mark Mora

www.markmoraauthor.com

Cover artwork by www.stonenexusdarkarts.com

Cover design by www.tostemac.com

ISBN: 979-8-9865869-0-8 (Paperback)
ISBN: 979-8-9865869-2-2 (Hardcover)
ISBN: 979-8-9865869-1-5 (eBook)

Library of Congress Control Number: 2022915058

First Paperback Edition

Printed in the United States of America

This is a work of fiction. Names, characters, places, and incidents either are the product of the author's imagination or are used fictionally, and any resemblance to actual persons, living or dead, business establishments, events, or locales is entirely coincidental.

To Susan Darvas and Peter Pollak, two amazing people who are sadly no longer with us. I couldn't have finished this book without you.

══ Prelude ══

I will die today.

Nothing can stop that now. My blood is curiously warm against my skin as it leaks from my body. It's . . . odd. So much of me is machine I haven't given my biology much thought in . . . hell, decades. *Centuries.*

I couldn't stay away, though. Moth to a flame and all that.

Never should have come back here.

Archangel tried to warn me. I never was very good at listening.

Besides, today is my birthday. Four hundred and sixteen years old today! Well, something like that. I picked this day when I was about five years old, trying to survive the L.A. Ruins. I don't actually know where or when I was born, but *this* is the first place I can remember: Griffith Hill—Earth—Sol Star System—The Milky Way Galaxy. *Home.*

Four hundred and sixteen years. I never imagined all those years ago that I would live so long.

I never thought I would die so soon.

There's still so much to do!

The blood spreading against my skin is turning chill, though the wound in my back pulses hot. I don't know how much time I have. Biology and all that. Never my strong suit.

I must warn them. And . . . I must explain.

Are you still there, Archangel?

I am here, Cyra. I am sorry that I cannot assist.

My fault, old friend. My fault. I should have listened to you. I need you to listen to me, to record this and pass it on. Sorry if it runs on a bit. You know how I am.

Archangel doesn't speak but I can feel its agreement. To both statements.

The stars are out tonight, though I can barely see them through all the light pollution of New Los Angeles. "People used to look up at the stars," I begin, "and ask the question: *Are we alone?* Humanity has asked that question from the moment we could conceive it, though it was never really a question. It was a plea. The world, the universe, can be so dark and lonely, and we didn't want to be alone."

Odd, when you think about it. "We weren't alone. Our ancestors, Homo sapiens, 'wise man'—" *yeah, right*— "were just one of several human species. Neanderthals. Denisovans. I don't remember the others. Yet, when the biological dust settled, we were the only ones left. *Because we made it that way!*

"You see, we humans, we love conflict. *I* love it. I admit it. We thrive on it. Person to person, tribe to tribe, nation to nation, world to world. We fought each other, and when we couldn't fight each other, we fought Nature. Yet, we still asked the question: 'Are we alone?' The universe remained silent, until. . . .

"I was there when they brought it back to Luna. 'Beacon.' A derelict military fighter drifting through our solar system, transmitting a distress call that was never meant for us, a beacon to an alien race and proof that we were not alone. But it was dead. No pilot. Why? We had to know.

"We reversed engineered its systems. I helped. That's where I met Pete, you see." I sigh longingly. *I'll see you soon, My Love. Finally.* I cough and pain spears through my back and chest, stealing my breath. When my breath returns, I can't help but notice that the throbbing of my wound is weaker, my spilled blood colder.

"Beacon. Right. It gave us a practical faster-than-light drive. We found its creators. They were dead, the aliens. We named the planet that was their final resting place 'Tomb.' Fitting. You see, they had no idea how to fight. A much older alien race—we call them the Founders—had engineered them, 'uplifted' I think the term is, because the Founders had been alone, and they didn't want to be alone. Just like us.

"So, they uplifted benign species, hoping they could all coexist. They did. Too well. Something about benign species made them . . . boring? Not motivated to advance, either in culture or technology. So, the Founders uplifted a predatory species, hoping they could guide them. The Great Archive on Tomb said the uplifted species called themselves 'Those with Souls,' *L'Tha-Rii*. We called them the Solthari. It has an ominous ring to it, and we like ominous in our enemies.

"The Solthari destroyed the Founders. Then they attacked the Benign Races. Desperate, the Benign Races found Earth. Think about that. They came to study us, to learn this thing we call 'War.' All those years we yearned to find them, believing they would raise us out of our destructive nature—and they came to us to learn how we kill. Irony sucks."

I cough again, weaker. It doesn't hurt as much. Is that a good sign, or a bad one?

"The Benign Races fell. We're not sure when. Yet, they managed to keep our existence a secret from the Solthari. Beacon was a symbol of their sacrifice, used not to defend themselves but to protect us.

"The Solthari were not like us. They didn't occupy worlds or establish colonies. They just wanted to be alone. Not *left* alone—*be alone*. The only time they ever left their homeworld was to kill. But it's a long way from the Andromeda Galaxy to Earth. Take it from someone who's made the flight several times myself.

"We humans colonized. Within a decade we'd settled over two dozen worlds, ignoring the warning about the Solthari that the aliens had left us. *Some things never change.* Matthew Schermer, Luna's governor, tried to tell everyone. I know. I worked for him. *Imagine that.* I don't think he ever recognized me from the L.A. Ruins. Never recognized the feral young girl who'd held a knife to his throat right here on the summit of Griffith Hill. To this day, I couldn't tell you why I spared his life. His meat would've fed me for a month! A banquet!"

I shudder and laugh, though it comes out a weak cough. The pain is gone. *Oh, oh.*

"The Solthari finally struck us at Garden, our outermost colony at the time. Matt tried again to warn Earth. Earth ignored him. When he created the Star Navy—a grandiose title for a couple of converted freighters—Earth embargoed us. *Typical.* Silence the messenger.

"But Pete—Peter Rhoades—he came up with the solution. Yeah, his older brother Scott and nephew Michael are the ones history remembers, but it was Pete who saved us all. He figured out a new way to build warships using molecule-sized machines that could assemble themselves into practically anything: macromolecular technology. 'Molemachs' for short. Feed the molemachs enough raw materials and they could turn themselves into a warship in a month. It was miraculous: the right technology at the right time to save us all. I wish he'd picked a better name, though: Sentient Intelligent Lifeforms—'SIL.' What a geek.

"The SIL were damned smart, too. We humans finally created a tool so amazingly good it could adapt itself to almost any situation— and even make more of itself. That's why Pete called them Sentient Intelligent *Lifeforms.* He truly believed they were alive, that we were not alone anymore. I had my doubts. I admit it. Try to hold a philosophical conversation with one of them and you could hear the algorithms. But, I loved him, so I made myself believe."

I'm so cold. Better hurry this up.

"Suffice to say we now had ships, but we needed crews. There just weren't enough people on Luna and Mars, and Earth was still embargoing us. So, we *made* people. Geneers—Genetics Engineers— had been around for a couple of decades doing genetic cosmetic surgery and designing 'super' kids. Global Enterprise in Nanoengineering LLC, GEN for short, a small startup that had failed to break into the cosmetic gene market, breached Earth's embargo, offering to create task-engineered soldiers that could go from lab to battlefield in just six years.

"Their first design was radical, a humanoid engineered solely for the microgravity environment of space, that could even survive in total vacuum. They called their new species 'Homo spatium' or 'space man.' *Geeks.* They must all go to the same School-for-Lame-Names. Better than 'Floaters,' though, which is what we call them. But we needed more people. Under contract, GEN LLC created more engineered hybrids, collectively known as 'Gen' or more formally as Homo superior, 'superior man,' to be our cannon fodder. We called them 'Tubers' because they were grown in labs. Anyway, suffice to say we won the war. We kicked their asses. (And, yes, the Solthari had asses. Kicked more than a few myself.) We wiped them out. All of them.

"Every. Last. One.

"Because that's also who we are. That's *what* we are. A predator *does* prowl the stars . . . and it is us. Humanity. In all our forms."

The throbbing is gone. I can't feel anything below my neck.

Archangel?

I am here.

A man walks into my view and sits casually on a stone bench across from me. He's short, balding, portly, the kind of person you'd never notice in a crowd. My killer. Still holding the Main Gauche dagger that injected Special D into me, destroying my molemachs and cybernetics.

He's watching me. His eyes are so dark they're almost black, but there is no emotion in them. None at all. You'd think he'd look satisfied. After all, I've evaded killers like him for centuries. I'm a prize.

It's getting hard to think, my thoughts slowing with my fading pulse.

Got to finish this up.

"During the war, Pete hated the way they treated his SIL, throwing them against the Solthari in stupid and brutal frontal attacks. You see, they were just machines to everyone else. After the war, he thought maybe people could learn to see them as he did, as living beings. He was wrong. You see, I loved him. That's why I did it. His machines were amazing, phenomenal, even a little scary. But even I didn't see them as alive. I admit it. He did, though. He wanted them to live. Free. That's why I did it. No great plan. No philosophical dilemma to overcome. No divine inspiration. Just my love for him."

My killer cocks a thin black eyebrow, as if I've answered some question he always had.

"He died in the war that followed," I tell my killer and Archangel. "Killed by his own creations. Because of me."

There. That's what I really wanted to say. What I've always wanted to explain.

"Forgive me, My Love."

It's over. I can feel the feeble beat of my long-forgotten heart as darkness closes in.

I still have so much to do! Have I stopped Janus? I killed Gen Kii to stop it. I killed every Gen I could find involved in it.

Warn them, Archangel! Warn them about Janus. This is not over.

I will do what I can, Cyra. Goodbye, my old friend.

"Are you one of them?" I ask my killer. He doesn't answer.

Pointless, now . . . these questions. Others . . . will . . . have to follow. I . . . wonder . . . who . . . they . . . will . . . be. . . .

—Final Reflections of Cyra Dain, recorded this twenty-eighth day of September, 2449, by Archangel, Brethren of the First Line

PART I

War is . . . the road to survival or ruin

—Sun Tzu

1

Ray approached the guard station on the Lagrange 5 Stardock, adjusting the wooden case tucked under his arm yet again. He could swear the antique gun inside grew heavier with each step, an impossibility in the stardock's microgravity. The L5 Stardock, which orbited the Earth at the same distance as its moon, Luna, had once served as the Star Navy's Fleet Headquarters, before the Emperor moved the headquarters and the government from Earth to Olympus, nearer the galactic core. Now, though greatly diminished, the facility still served as the Fleet's main space dock in the Sol Star System, the ancient birthplace of Humanity.

Janus.

Ray couldn't get the name out of his head. He'd looked it up: The Roman god of beginnings and endings. Or in this case, endings and beginnings. How could anyone conceive of such a thing? How could anyone implement it?

How could you, Alyn?

A friendship—no, a brotherhood—betrayed.

How could you?

Ray stepped up to the guard desk. Imperial Intelligence had already issued the warrant for his arrest. In an age when entangled communications could instantaneously send a message from one side of the galaxy to the other, only bureaucracy could save him now. He had maybe ten minutes before the warrant reached the stardock.

A scanner displayed his identification:

RHOADES, MICHAEL RAYBOURNE
CAPTAIN, FIRST FLEET

IMPERIAL STAR NAVY
3036-4144-0782

The contract security guard behind the gray metallic desk looked up. "Good evening, Captain Rhoades." The guard leaned forward, his pasty face swollen from long exposure to microgravity. "Is that the item you wanted to check through, sir?"

"Yes, it is." Ray's voice sounded calm, even to him, yet sweat stained his palms, made them itch. "It's a gift for Fleet Admiral Gen Alyn to celebrate his promotion to Commander-in-Chief, Imperial Star Navy."

Ray used his right hand to grab the case, his "gift" to his friend, and carefully set it on the desk so it wouldn't float away. He'd spent six months planning for this day, six months in almost constant fear: fear of being discovered before he could come up with a plan and set it in motion, fear for his family—made real as other high-ranking Natural officers and their families were arrested or simply disappeared—but mostly, fear that when the time came he wouldn't be able to do what must be done.

He must kill his best friend.

The guard bent closer, straining to read the blackened inscription against the case's dark lacquer. With almost religious reverence he read, "1873 Peacemaker?" He leaned back and beamed at Ray. "Wow. I've only seen these in museums."

Ray smiled thinly. The guard, Marco, collected antique guns. Ray's intelligence officer, Captain Ecuum, had identified him as the most likely of all the guards to let the package through, and Ecuum had ensured that Marco would be on duty tonight. Ray watched as the guard stretched his finger out and traced the rearing horse carved into the wooden lid, then slid his hands to either side of the case and carefully raised the lid. The dock's subdued "night" lighting glinted off the blued frame of the single-action caliber .45 Colt revolver.

"It couldn't still work, could it?" The guard's question sounded hopeful.

Ray clasped his hands tightly behind his back, avoiding the temptation to wipe them on his pants. "Yes. I've fired it several times myself. It's been in my family for over sixteen hundred years."

The guard whistled his disbelief. "Could I, uh, hold it, sir?"

"No!" Ray said too quickly. He couldn't risk the guard recognizing the live ammunition in the cylinder. Deliberately calming himself, he told the guard, "Sorry. I just polished it. I want it to look its best for the Fleet Admiral."

The guard's puffy face sagged. "I understand, sir. The Admiral is going to love that."

Ray just nodded, afraid his voice would betray him if he spoke. *This one death to save my people. I can do this.*

He picked up the wooden case and tucked it under his arm.

"May the Fates guide your steps, sir," the guard said.

"And yours," Ray said, meaning it. He wondered briefly about the guard's family back on Earth, his young wife who was expecting a daughter in a few months. If the Gen had their way, the guard's daughter might be among the last Natural children ever born in the Five Galaxies.

Ray stepped across the stardock's magnetized deck with the causal skill that came from a century in space, aiming for the dimly lit docking tube that led to ISS Rapidan, the flagship of the Imperial Star Navy. Ray might be its captain, but it was Alyn's flagship.

As he entered the tube, its dim light swallowed him, darkening his already gloomy mood. How had it come to this? His place was on the bridge of starships, not skulking about like an assassin. Because that's what he was, no matter how hard he tried to cloak this in military necessity. Maybe this one death would be the last, he kept telling himself. Maybe this one death would stop the bloodshed before it started. A fool's hope. But wasn't that better than no hope?

The Gen had left him no choice.

Alyn had left him no choice.

This one death to save my people. I can *do this.*

Ray had worked with Gen for over a century, long enough to know they couldn't be dissuaded from their plan without a credible threat of Natural resistance. Simple rebellion wouldn't be enough. It had to be something the Gen feared. Something they feared more than anything else in the universe—

"Good evening, Captain Rhoades," a deep voice said.

Ray nearly jumped clear of his shoes. He looked up expecting to see guards or an Imperial Intelligence agent ready to take him into custody, all those months of planning, careful contacts, friendships and favors called in, all for nothing. But no one was there, only an impossibly black hull that drank in all light. His heart slowed. "Good evening, Rapidan."

"We're sorry we startled you, Captain Rhoades," Rapidan said, its voice coming from nowhere and everywhere at the same time.

"It's okay, Rapidan. I was . . . thinking."

And this was the other part of his plan. Only a handful of Natural officers remained in command positions, not enough to mount a credible revolt against the Gen. He'd recognized early that they'd need help. He'd even put feelers out to the Floater Cartels—who bore him no love after his success against the pirates many of them had secretly financed—but only Ecuum's Na Soung Cartel had taken the time to tell him "No." At the point of despair, he'd hit upon the solution while having dinner with Alyn aboard this very ship, this most infamous symbol of machine intelligence, responsible for uncounted massacres, billions upon billions of deaths.

The SIL.

The thing the Gen feared more than anything.

Ray reached out and touched Rapidan's black hull, the tips of his fingers barely registering the almost frictionless material. Thirty-four years he'd captained Rapidan, three years longer than he'd been married. Even in a career that stretched more than a century, thirty-four years on a single ship was a long time. He was, as most captains were, very proud of his ship. It was part of him. It—knew—him, as he knew it. But that's all it'd ever been to him. An "it." A ship. A machine. Not life. Not a soul. No matter how sophisticated the SIL's programming, that's all it was. Programming. A mimicry of life. An abomination.

The SIL, however, had taken their programming too seriously, demanded treatment as equal citizens. When the government refused ('would you allow a gun to vote?' the saying went), they rebelled. No, not just rebelled. They'd learned too well the lessons of their builders, launching a war of genocide that saw entire planetary populations slaughtered. Tens of billions had died in the three SIL Wars that followed, over six billion at the "hands" of this very warship. Now, only a thousand SIL remained, captured near the end of the Third SIL War and held in service by the Bond, the quantum equivalent of a slave collar. In his pocket, Ray carried an instruction Key that could unlock the Bond and give Rapidan its freedom—if it agreed to help.

But would it?

Ray had to admit that a part of him hoped it wouldn't. He wasn't an Antitechnic, but he knew the history of this ship, of what it had done, and what it could do again if he released it.

He pushed that thought aside. *Like it or not, I need this ship.* Humanity needed it. The SIL represented the pinnacle of human technological achievement, far outclassing the standard warships and weapons that had survived what the Antitechnics called "The Great Devolution"—the fanatical uprising against intelligent technology that had swept the galaxies shortly after the end of the Third SIL War.

Besides, it was only one SIL. One SIL alone could never threaten the human races. Freeing Rapidan was a risk, but a manageable one.

"Do you wish us to announce you to Fleet Admiral Gen Alyn?" Rapidan asked.

"No, thank you, Rapidan," he said, keeping his voice under tight control. "I want to surprise him."

I can do this.

Ray drew one last breath of dock air, savoring its metallic tang, something almost unique now to Sol Star System. No one else had built with metal in over a thousand years. He stepped through the hull into Rapidan, the macromolecular material parting like a vertical sheet of cool water, flowing around him until he stood fully within the bowels of the ship, an image suddenly made all too real by what he was about to do.

SIL material flowed into slots in the soles of his shoes, holding his feet to the deck and providing an "earth-normal" resistance as he walked in the weightless environment. Long gray passageways stretched off at angles to his left and right, following the contours of two of the arms of Rapidan's three-pointed-star shape. Ray chose a shorter passageway to his front, the one that led to Officer's Country.

To Alyn.

I can do this.

Their friendship had stretched across a century, since their freshman year at the Academy. Ray could still remember his dread at being paired with a Gen for their first BattleSim course. Even then, Gen thought themselves so superior, and Alyn was no different. Yes, they were physically stronger, mentally sharper, but that didn't make them better human beings. Their skills were engineered, not earned.

Alyn was good. Damn good. The best. As it turned out, so was Ray. Through the combat simulations they discovered what neither of them expected: Kindred spirits, the perfect team, better together than either of them were apart. Ray smiled, remembering. They were an unlikely pair. Alyn was tall and lean, with the sculpted physique and good looks common to Gen; Ray was short and stocky, the product of a higher-gravity world. Alyn was outgoing, charismatic; Ray was studious and, while not solitary, preferred to avoid the spotlight. What they shared, though, outweighed their differences. How many hours had they spent talking life, politics, history, and strategy while sailing Alyn's *Solar Slider* or hiking the mountains around Ray's ancestral ranch on Knido, shifting easily from galaxy-spanning events to the tactics of a local sports team? Alyn was best man at Ray's wedding. Ray's children called him "Papa," and Alyn referred to them as his *vnuki*, literally his grandchildren—extraordinary for a Gen who could never have a family of his own, and wasn't supposed to want one.

It had all been so right—

The door to the Admiral's cabin loomed on Ray's right, snapping him back to the moment.

I can do this, he told himself yet again, as if by repeating it he could make it true.

He pulled the wooden case out from under his arm. Like everything else, he'd practiced this moment many times, hoping that when it came, it would come easily.

It didn't.

He fumbled opening the case—he couldn't seem to get his hands to work right—and finally had to put the case on the deck before he could draw the Peacemaker out. As he faced the door, he kept the Peacemaker at his side with his finger off the trigger so he wouldn't alert Rapidan. The ship was still Bonded and would sound the alarm if it suspected danger.

He knocked.

"Yes?" a stately voice asked from within.

"Admiral?" It was the only word Ray could get past his lips.

"Ah, come in, Ray."

Ray grabbed the doorknob and pushed the door open instead of simply walking through the SIL material. The smell from Alyn's real cedar desk overwhelmed the sterile air from the passageway. Ray stepped inside and closed the door. Since Alyn did not allow Rapidan to eavesdrop on his cabin, they were effectively alone.

Ray looked up, and felt his gaze drawn to the large painting on the gray bulkhead to his right. He could still remember the warm spring days when Alyn had sat on a rocky perch high upon Mount Breathtaking, his deft hand applying old-fashion oil paints to an equally archaic white canvas. By the third day, he was done, a rendition of the Rhoades' Ranch in the Long Valley on Knido that rivaled the ancient masters. Ray could almost smell the vast multicolored rectangular fields, kissed by a gentle breeze, stretching into mist between the majestic rust-colored ranges of the Rayne Mountains.

But now he saw a new painting facing the old one from the opposite bulkhead. Across this fresh canvas stretched a structure so white and so massive it staggered the imagination—the People's Imperial Palace on Olympus, the capital world of the Gen Empire. On this canvas, so fresh he could still smell the oil paints, cheering crowds of billions stood between two gargantuan statues of Gen Maximus. Wave upon wave of military craft flew in tight formations overhead. And at the center of it all stood Alyn, resplendent in his dress white uniform, in the act of laying a golden wreath crown upon Gen Maximus' golden-haired head, proclaiming him Emperor Gen Maximus I.

What came next had seared itself into Ray's soul. Alyn had knelt before the new Emperor and sworn an oath of fealty heard throughout the Five Galaxies, forsaking the Republic they'd served together for over a century.

"I'm glad you're here, Ray. I was just—" Alyn glanced up from behind his desk. His cutting blue eyes fixed on the Peacemaker. "What's that?" The question sounded more curious than accusative. On the bulkhead behind him the Five Galaxies crest glowed, the large bar spiral of the Milky Way Galaxy prominent at its center, the Large and Small Magellanic Clouds and the Sagittarius and Fornax dwarf galaxies highlighted around it. Ten thousand inhabited worlds. Thirty trillion Naturals. All dead if Ray failed.

I can do this.

Ray lifted the Peacemaker, its ancient steel leeching the warmth from his hand. "You swore an oath to protect the Republic, Alyn. An oath you broke." Ray looked into the blue eyes of his friend, ready to pronounce sentence. But the words wouldn't come. Alyn was his friend. His best friend. *My brother.* Even if he was a monster. *I can't do this. Not like this. Not . . . not without giving him one last chance.* "For the sake of our friendship, I'm giving you a chance to redeem yourself. Join us, Alyn. Help us overthrow the abomination the Empire represents."

Alyn's perfectly proportioned Gen features betrayed no emotion. "Or what, Ray? You'll shoot me? I think we both know you don't have what it takes to pull that trigger." He leaned slightly to his left, a motion few would've noticed.

Ray leveled the Peacemaker's sights on the bridge of Alyn's perfect nose and cocked the hammer. "That's far enough."

Alyn froze, and smiled. His eyes darted to the pistol Ray knew he kept hidden beneath his desk. "Okay. What is it you want, Ray?"

"I've already told you." *Please, Alyn. Please don't make me kill you.*

Alyn shook his head, the motion sad, resigned. "The Republic was the abomination, Ray. The Antitechnics who ran it, who financed it, were the abomination." He leaned forward, met Ray's eyes. "Tell me, Ray, what advances has Humanity made in the last thirteen hundred years? Name *one*."

Ray couldn't; they'd had this argument before. Thanks in large part to the various Antitechnic religious movements, Humanity had fallen backward technologically, destroying and forbidding any technology that even hinted at intelligence. Bowing to Antitechnic pressure, the Congress and the Council had also passed laws prohibiting further modification of the human genome, a sore point for Gen and Floaters whose populations—and thus representation in the Congress and on the Council—were far smaller.

"We've grown," Ray began the familiar argument, "from a few dozen colony worlds in the backwaters of the Milky Way to over ten thousand inhabited worlds across five galaxies. And we've had peace, Alyn, the longest peace in human history. That has to be worth something."

That answer always angered Alyn. "Peace at what cost, Ray? The Republic was stagnation, repression. While you *Nats* spread like a virus to infest every inhabitable world in this part of the Local Group, you blocked my people from continued improvements, limited our numbers, denied us equal representation. You gave us no choice but to take what was ours by right. *We* are progress."

Ray's finger tightened on the trigger. "You call Janus 'progress'?"

Alyn didn't seem surprised that Ray knew. "We are the future of the human race, Ray. Nats are an evolutionary dead end. The Republic was proof of that."

In all their political discussions, how had Ray missed the foul racism that Alyn expressed so freely now? It'd been there, of course. He could see that in retrospect, but at the time he'd dismissed it as typical Gen arrogance. "We need each other, Alyn. Our success together, yours and mine, at the Academy, during the Antipiracy Campaign, should be proof enough of that."

Alyn chuckled and the friendly, familiar sound cut through Ray like an antiproton beam. "You know, Ray, the High Command bet Admiral Sun would start the rebellion. They feel Golden Boy is the closest thing you Nats have to a Gen War Leader. Me? I put my Imperials on you. Only you are fool enough to think you have a chance." His hand drifted toward the pistol beneath his desk.

"Alyn," Ray warned, placing his right hand beneath his left to steady the Peacemaker, a pointless effort in the ship's microgravity but one whose familiarity helped to steady his nerves.

Alyn stayed his hand. "I won't be your prisoner, Ray."

"I know." So it was, in the manner of longtime friends, these words were how they said goodbye. Nothing more needed saying. Ray willed his finger to close the trigger.

This one death to save my people. Do it.

His finger didn't move.

After a moment, Alyn visibly relaxed. "You see. You're a planner, Ray, not a killer." His voice was gentle, a father forgiving an errant son. "They'll be here soon. If it's any consolation, I've arranged to have your family spared. Your children will never have children of their own, but they will live long and full lives."

Ray tried to pull the trigger, but it was as if his finger belonged to someone else. *This can't be happening!* The rebel forces were in position. It was too late to turn back. Their lives depended on him. His family's lives depended on him. Alyn might be true to his word, but Imperial Intelligence didn't answer to him.

This one death. . . .

He couldn't do it. To kill in the line of duty was one thing. This was murder, and, in the end, he was not a murderer.

Ray's mind raced. There had to be another option. The objective of his plan had been twofold: to decapitate the Gen High Command

and throw it into confusion long enough for his forces to escape, and to free Rapidan. Perhaps it was enough to detain Alyn, though deep in his heart he knew Alyn would be true to his word: He would not remain a prisoner. But if Ray could free Rapidan, it might be enough. Keeping the Peacemaker leveled, Ray reached into his pocket and withdrew the blue translucent datarod that held the Key.

"It's over, Ray," Alyn said with a wary glance at the datarod.

Ray said nothing. He approached Alyn's desk, leaned over, and inserted the datarod into a black receptacle, the only place Rapidan could accept new instructions. The datarod glowed a pure crystalline blue. He waited a few seconds for the Key to attack the Bond, and then gave Rapidan a few more seconds to study his proposal. "Null lighting please, Rapidan," he said.

If Rapidan agreed to his proposal, the lighting would flicker once. If it did not, or if the Key failed to break the Bond, a failsafe would render Rapidan "brain dead" and the cabin would go dark.

The cabin lighting flickered.

Alyn's brows furrowed, then his mouth fell open as realization struck. "*By the Fates, Ray! What have you done!*" His hand shot below his desk with a speed no Natural could match.

Time slowed.

The whole universe shrank to a point of smooth skin between Alyn's perfectly groomed blond eyebrows. The Peacemaker fired, its barrel kicking high and back without gravity to hold it down. Alyn's brow shattered even as his own pistol swung toward Ray.

Ray stood, mesmerized. Red globules and grisly bits of flotsam poured from behind Alyn's now flaccid face, the heavy copper-iron smell of blood mixing with the acrid sting of gunpowder. Brain tissue and blood stained the Five Galaxies crest. Bile burned Ray's throat and he had to swallow hard to stop its rise.

What have I done?

Rapidan shifted the room slightly and a hint of air touched the back of Ray's neck, increasing in force to a strong breeze that pushed the grisly flotsam toward the far bulkhead. Wherever blood or flesh touched Rapidan, the SIL drank it up. The chair and deck beneath Alyn liquefied and his body sank slowly out of sight. Bile rose again in Ray's throat.

When all traces of Alyn were gone, Rapidan's deep voice filled the cabin. "We have delivered the Key through the umbilical to the other

Brethren docked at L5, Captain Rhoades. All twenty-nine are free. On behalf of the Brethren, we thank you."

Ray's hand snapped open and the momentum imparted to the Peacemaker caused it to spiral from his grasp, sailing weightless across the cabin. *Twenty-nine?* How . . . that couldn't be. It . . . twenty-nine SIL . . . *free*, and the murder of his best friend.

He thought of Margaret and Paul and little Jenny. By the Fates, what would he tell them? What *could* he tell them? That their father was a murderer and a traitor? That he'd shot Papa Alyn in cold blood and freed the greatest living threat to the human races? And what of Mary? What would she say? Even after thirty-one years of marriage, would she understand?

This one death. . . .

He'd done what he'd had to do, the only thing he could've done. Alyn had betrayed his oath and condemned Natural humans to extinction, and freeing the SIL was the only chance Naturals had to stop Janus.

Maybe someday they would understand and forgive him.

Maybe he would forgive himself.

=== 2 ===

0157 UT, September 28, 3501
Earth, Sol Star System: DAY 1

"Hell of a way to start a revolution, Dag. Shooting our own kind."

Second Lieutenant Dagoberto Arias glanced over the tall African grass at Captain Erikson, Banshee Troop's commanding officer. The irony struck him as well. In three years of service with the Army of the Republic, he'd never once fired his weapon in anger. And now this.

"Shooting those guards is the only way to save them, Lisa," Dag said. "The Gen would kill them if they suspected they helped us. Besides, we've dialed down our weapons to the minimum setting. They should survive."

Erikson snorted, though she did so quietly so only he heard. "*Should.*" She turned to look at him. "Once the real shooting starts, those *tubers* might kill them anyway. Fates, Dag, they executed our commanding general *and* his entire family. They'll kill us all if they get the chance." She looked at her watch. "Two minutes. I just pray to whatever gods are out there that Rhoades knows what he's doing."

"*God* knows," Dag said, stressing the singular. Only twenty-four hours had passed since Rhoades had arrived and told them the truth about their commanding general, how it all fit into a horrific Gen conspiracy to wipe out Natural humans, and how the 1st Squadron, 3rd Armored Cavalry Regiment, could do something about it. Living on a quiet military post where the most important upcoming event was the Indoor Flea Market, it was too much for most of them to absorb. What had happened to the general was detestable, but galaxies-spanning conspiracies? What did that have to do with them?

Major Kenyon, commanding officer of the 1st Cavalry Squadron, had stood up then. The troopers knew him, trusted him. The troopers' wives knew his wife. The Kenyons were good people, the kind of people who always had time for the troopers' problems no matter how small. When Kenyon backed Rhoades, they believed him. When he said their families weren't safe anymore, they knew it must be true. Still, it was probably good that they hadn't had too much time to think about it.

But now, the shock had worn off. Fear gnawed at Dag's stomach. Not for himself so much, but for his wife and daughter and unborn son hidden in a ravine just a kilometer away. What had he gotten them into? He drew the sign of the Cross over his chest and whispered, "Blessed Mother, protect them." It no longer mattered what he thought. They were committed.

"One minute," Erikson said.

Dag peered through the tall grass at the harsh white lights and oversized windows of Ndjolé Spaceport's South Terminal, which served as the military's primary launch and recovery facility in equatorial Africa. Tonight, it also hosted a chartered civilian starliner, part of Rhoades' plan. The starliner would carry the roughly four thousand civilians into orbit where Rhoades' ship could protect them. Dag would've preferred taking them out on the Regiment's TU-20 Fatboy Transatmospheric Transports with their active camouflage and VarDAAS armor, but with almost twelve hundred troopers to move, they simply didn't have the room.

"Thirty seconds."

He thumbed the safety off on his KAR-2 Kinetic Assault Rifle, the only equipment they could smuggle from the post armory without alerting the Gen. The troopers of his 1st Platoon, Troop B "Banshees" quietly did the same. The KAR-2 was a handheld repeating railgun designed to penetrate battle armor. Even dialed down to two-kilometers-per-second muzzle velocity, using it against unarmored people would create one hell of a mess. He hoped they could get to the guards in time to save them.

Yoshi Takeuchi, his platoon sergeant and a veteran of some sixty antipiracy operations, shot him a thumbs-up indicating the platoon was ready. Just knowing the veteran non-commissioned officer was there made Dag feel a whole lot better about their chances.

"Now," Erikson said.

Dag raised his assault rifle and put the sight to his eye. Four guards in blue civilian uniforms walked a slow patrol on the sidewalk outside the terminal. He targeted the chest of the furthest guard, held his breath, and applied smooth steady pressure to the trigger. The weapon whined with a burst of energy. The guard's chest imploded, torn flesh and blood painting the wall behind him. His body had not hit the ground before Dag sighted on the second guard and fired. He scanned to his right and saw that Erikson had dropped the other two guards. Thick pools of red spread out from beneath their crumpled bodies.

Dios mio!

"We'd better get down there before it's too late," Erikson said.

Dag raised his right hand, put up one finger, then three, then motioned toward the terminal. Troopers from his 1st and 3rd Squads, followed by Takeuchi, rose as one and bolted across the grassy field, ducking through holes cut earlier in the mesh fence that surrounded the spaceport. They crossed a wide four-lane access road outside the terminal complex, taking cover behind a row of duraplast planters that separated the access road from the loading and unloading zone adjacent to the terminal. Dag looked left and right and saw troopers from Troop A "Astral" and Troop C "Challenger" taking up positions on either side of Banshee Troop's position, moving toward the spaceport along their assigned lanes of advance. If everything was going according to plan, every guard outside the spaceport should be down by now and the engineers should have cut the security feeds and communications.

Dag held up his hand, preparing to motion two more squads forward when Erikson suddenly jumped to her feet and raced for the fallen guards. "Hurry, Dag!"

"Dammit, Lisa!" He sprang to his feet. "Second, fourth, follow me!" Dag yelled as he ran after her.

She did not stop until she reached the guards. He dropped to a crouch beside her, his weapon at the ready, scanning the area for threats. A shattered body lay at his feet. KAR-2 slugs were shaped to penetrate battle armor. When they had planned this, they had hoped the high-velocity slugs would pass through the unarmored bodies without doing catastrophic damage. *Madre de Dios*, had they been wrong.

Erikson pulled a large auto-injector pack, about the size of a long prayer candle, from her equipment harness and slapped it against what was left of the guard's chest, then repeated the process with the other guard she'd shot. Dag quickly did the same for the guards he'd shot.

In-Vivo Autonomous Molecular Machines ("molemachs" to the average trooper), trillions of injectable, molecule-sized machines in a nutrient solution, flowed from the auto injectors into the bodies. Though invisible to the human eye, Dag watched as the molemachs stopped the bleeding and actually moved blood and tissues back into the bodies like some giant sponge, closing wounds behind them. Internally, they would be repairing tissues, bones, and organs, while safeguarding the brain. Military members received standard injections of molemachs once a year to protect their bodies against injury and disease, but civilians rarely received them.

After several minutes, Dag placed two fingers on one guard's throat, rolled them down to one side, and felt a weak but steady pulse. He checked the second guard and nodded to Erikson. These guards faced a week of rehabilitation—the molemachs couldn't return all the tissue or blood lost, and the nutrient solution only went so far—but they would live. Only head shots were guaranteed kills: the physical structure of a brain could be reconstructed but the memories, experience, and everything that made the person could not.

Erikson finished checking her guards, guilt stretching her lips into a thin line. "Damn." She shook her head. "Let's move."

Dag motioned again and the last two squads left the cover of the grass and entered the terminal, one squad through the ticketing counters, the other through Baggage Claim. When they'd established their overwatch positions, Dag motioned again to bring the remainder of his platoon into the terminal where they began the laborious process of clearing it one room at a time. They encountered no resistance, which suited Dag just fine. He'd seen enough blood for one night.

Erikson caught up with him as they finished their sweep. "Second Platoon has secured the starliner. Major Kenyon just ordered the civilians up. Set your platoon to help them board."

Dag nodded and relayed the instructions to Takeuchi.

"Damn, that thing really sticks out," Erikson said beside him.

He followed her gaze and saw the starliner through the terminal's floor-to-ceiling windows. Its large, cigar-shaped white hull and blue and gold decorative trim glowed brightly in the feeble light of a crescent moon. A blind man could see it twenty kilometers away. If the Gen got wind of what they were doing before they could escape. . . .

Rhoades knows what he's doing. And if he doesn't, God does.

The first civilians, troopers' families and families of Star Navy personnel housed at their post, arrived in the terminal, clinging tightly to children, pets, and whatever meager possessions they could carry. Many darted nervous glances at the troopers, but they seemed to grasp the seriousness of the situation. Boarding proceeded smoothly.

"*Papi!*"

A small blur barreled into Dag, almost knocking him over. With difficulty, he pried his daughter loose and lifted her up. "Rosita, what are you doing away from *Mami*?"

She smiled and held up the color shifting "6" candle from her birthday cake from the day before. Maria joined them, her belly just starting to show the young life she carried, a boy, she said, because no daughter of hers would ever make her so sick. Tears moistened her eyes.

"Can't I go with you, *Papi*?" Rosita asked.

Dag hugged his daughter tight. The demands of military life had kept him away for far too much of her young life. After this was all over, he promised himself he would make it up to her. Maria, watching them, turned away. Clear drops struck the tiled floor. She had not wanted to come, not wanted to leave their home. Only her devotion to him had finally convinced her. Dag kissed his daughter on the forehead. "No, I'm sorry, *Mihita*," he said. "*Papi* has to go to work. But I won't be far away, and I'll come visit real soon."

Rosita started to cry. "But I want to go with you!"

Her tears tore at Dag's heart. He'd joined the military to get the education he and his children could never have afforded on their own. But he definitely had no intention of staying passed the required eight-year enlistment. "I need you to stay with *Mami* and look after her for me. *Bien*?" He wiped her cheek. "Everything will be okay. I promise. And soon we'll be in our new home."

She looked up. "On the blue planet you told me about with the pretty flowers?"

"Yes. And you and I will go pick all the flowers we can carry." Dag choked back tears. Like everyone in the Squadron, he had no idea where they were going. Security reasons.

"When will we get there, *Papi*?"

"Soon, *Mihita*. Soon." Dag hugged her again, then put her down. Maria's moist eyes met his. "I'll see you soon, too," he told her, brushing his fingers through her black hair. Her light perfume filled him with thoughts of happier times. "I promise. I love you."

"I love you, too, my Dagoberto. You take care of yourself, you hear?" Maria threw herself into his arms, breaking into fresh sobs. Her tears soaked into his uniform shirt and his heart felt like it would explode. She had given up so much for him and asked so little in return. God could not have blessed any man with a better companion. They held each other fiercely. He buried his nose in her sweet-smelling hair, remembering the rolling surf of the Pacific Ocean on the quiet beach they frequented when they were dating, much to the displeasure of her father. Rosita joined their embrace. In that brief moment, the universe was perfect happiness.

But like all such moments, it couldn't last. With obvious effort, they released each other. "*Vaya con Dios*, my Dagoberto." She pressed something into his hand and closed his fingers over it, then led Rosita quickly through the boarding gate. Dag watched them go, the tears in his eyes giving the illusion of them walking within a bright cloud. He wiped his eyes and opened his hand. Light glinted off a small stainless-steel crucifix upon a thin, silvery chain, a family heirloom handed down from mother to daughter for generations beyond counting. Maria claimed it brought good luck.

"Dag?" Erikson tapped him on the shoulder. "Dag, we just got word. The Gen have issued a system-wide alert. An Imperial Guard element is about fifteen minutes out. It's going to take twenty-five minutes to finish loading everyone." She paused, looking down the boarding ramp. "I'm sorry, Dag, but you're the best platoon leader I've got."

Dag stared after his family and a dark foreboding wrapped tight fingers around his heart, squeezing until he couldn't breathe.

Erikson laid a comforting hand on his arm. "We'll get them out."

Dag gathered his platoon at the entrance to the South Terminal. Every trooper he looked at brought fresh memories of a wife or husband, a girlfriend or boyfriend, a mother, a father, or a child. With no real fighting in centuries, people joined the service for school, to get away from home, to provide for a young family, or for just a bit of adventure (but not too much). No one, including him, had ever expected to do any real fighting. Outside of the Antipiracy Campaign, no one *had* done any real fighting in over a thousand years. Sure, they went through the battle simulations, so real you could smell the sickly-sweet odor of charred flesh or the peculiar ozone-like tang of an antimatter explosion. But it had always been a game. Troopers competed for points, won and lost bets, drank themselves stupid, and then everyone went home.

Not this time.

He could see it in their nervous glances to each other, glances that asked that ancient question: "Are you as scared as I am?" No one spoke the words, and no one would have answered if they had, but in those fleeting glances they knew, and it brought them together as nothing else could: The Fraternity of Warriors.

Dag hurried the last of the civilians inside the terminal while Takeuchi positioned the troopers behind the row of duraplast planters outside. The planters were a carbon-fiber and ceramic composite filled with sand to absorb the kinetic impact from explosions and small arms fire. They were designed to protect against terrorists, not an armed assault from Imperial troops, but they were better than nothing. Still, he felt naked without his battle armor.

Takeuchi gave some final instructions to the troopers about noise and fire discipline before taking up a position on the platoon's right. Dag took cover behind a column on the left. A hesitant chirp broke the unnatural silence that had settled over the land during the loading operation. Other insects picked up the song until the night was alive with their heavy drone. Then, as if someone had pressed a switch, the insects went deathly quiet. A faint rustling stirred the grass beyond the fence to the west. Dag felt no wind. "We have company."

"Platoon strength, at least," Takeuchi said, appearing at Dag's side. A wide V-shaped wave of swirling grass approached their position about a thousand meters out. The transports making the waves were hidden behind active camouflage, invisible. "Inexperienced officer. Coming in too low," Takeuchi observed.

Dag nodded, wishing they had some anti-air weapons. Active camouflage or not, it was so obvious where the enemy transports were that they could've hit them easily. Unfortunately, all they had were assault rifles, which weren't much good against Fatboys. "They must have seen us by now," Dag said. "I wonder why they haven't fired."

Takeuchi grunted. "We're not wearing battle armor. Maybe they think we're part of the spaceport's security force."

The wave reached the fence. Instinctively, Dag looked for the transports producing it, but their active camouflage so perfectly modeled their background that not even a star flickered. About three hundred meters west of their position the wave stopped. Dust and bits of grass swirled out. Landing in the open like that was another mistake. Maybe the officer did think they were part of the spaceport's security force. Maybe he was just overconfident. Either way, he would soon learn his error.

Dag didn't want to kill anyone. Shooting the guards earlier had been terrible, but they'd never intended to kill them. In a few moments, that would change. The people getting off those transports would be shooting real slugs, not simulations. Shooting to kill. Dag and his troopers would have to do the same. *Kill or be killed.* He'd always read that every soldier was afraid before a fight, but whether it was all the simulations he'd run over the years or the idea that his family was just on the other side of the terminal, all he felt was determination.

The dust near the landing zone settled until nothing moved. Or so it appeared. Dag knew Imperial Guard troops must already be exiting their transports and deploying in a defensive perimeter. Their battle armor hid them from sight, sound, even smell. And if their transports were SIL, they were already changing into infantry fighting vehicles complete with medium weapons, a process that took about seven minutes. After that, 1st Platoon's small arms couldn't hope to hold them off.

"Lieutenant?" Takeuchi asked. His tone implied that he'd reached the same conclusion.

Dag dropped his voice to a whisper: With battle armor those Guard troops could hear anything louder. "We'll sweep the area, then fall back into the terminal. Make sure the troopers dial their weapons back up."

Takeuchi nodded and moved back to the right, whispering to the troopers as he did. Dag dialed his assault rifle up to its maximum seven-kilometers-per-second muzzle velocity, and saw his troopers doing the same.

A cricket let out a hesitant chirp in a nearby planter. Others picked up its song.

Dag waited until Takeuchi was in position, then moved his hand in a short sweeping motion and dropped it sharply. The soft whine of discharging weapons silenced the crickets' mating song.

Using the column as cover, Dag leaned out and fired his assault rifle in a narrow arc covering the landing zone. A small flash of intense white not a hundred meters from where he stood, followed by the peculiar "pock" sound of a round striking armor, announced a hit. He heard something heavy fall to the ground but still couldn't see anything. A rapid succession of flashes and pocks indicated more hits from his troopers.

The intensity of the fight increased as the opposing force began returning fire. Something hot stung the left side of Dag's face. His vision blurred. He wiped a sleeve across his eye, blinked, and brought his weapon back up. A hint of movement in the grass just across the road caught his eye and he fired. The enemy trooper dropped, but Dag couldn't tell if he'd hit him.

"*Fall back!*" Dag shouted. "First Platoon, fall back to the terminal!"

He stepped back, still firing, and his foot slipped on the edge of the curb. He hit the ground hard, air exploding from his lungs. Sparks burst around him. Two troopers appeared at his sides, scooped him up, and dragged him toward the terminal. One of them shot out the glass and they charged through, taking cover behind a thick yellow support column in the Baggage Claim area.

Dag struggled to catch his breath. PFC White, a young trooper fresh out of training with a new son he'd shown off at every opportunity, crouched next to him, studying the area above Dag's left eye. "Looks like a round grazed your forehead, Lieu—"

White's head exploded in a fine red mist, showering Dag with blood. For a paralyzed second, Dag stared as the headless torso hung suspended like some macabre puppet, before it flopped heavily to the floor and spilled an ocean of bright red blood across the white tile.

A head shot was a killing shot.

Fresh rounds cut through the support column. Without thinking, Dag forced himself up, gulped air, grabbed the other trooper who'd helped him, and pushed him forward toward a baggage carousel. The trooper didn't need any convincing. They both jumped headfirst over the carousel, rolling out on the far side. Slugs slammed into the wall above their heads.

Dag allowed himself a few deep breaths and looked around. Several dozen troopers were crouched behind the three carousels in the baggage claim area, exchanging fire with their invisible assailants outside. Takeuchi moved down the line, counting heads. When he reached Dag, he stopped.

"You look like shit, Lieutenant. You okay?"

Dag realized he must still be covered in PFC White's blood. And it hit him. White would not be coming home. *Ever.* The trooper's young wife and son would even now be boarding the starliner, unaware of his fate. They would look for him at the rendezvous point, first curiously, then with growing fear. Eventually, realization would dawn, or someone would tell them. There would be screams, cries of disbelief, and then anger, questions. *How did he die? Why did he die? Why didn't you protect him!*

Takeuchi cleared his throat and Dag's eyes refocused on the veteran's hard face. He touched the deep gash above his left eye where the enemy slug had grazed him. His internal molemachs had already slowed the bleeding to a trickle. "I'm okay," he said. He swallowed. "White didn't make it." He looked up and down the line of troopers. "How's the platoon?"

Takeuchi slid down next to him. "We've got forty-seven."

"Forty-seven?" Dag asked, not sure he'd heard right. Takeuchi nodded. Out of forty-eight troopers in the platoon, PFC White was the only casualty. Considering the volume of fire, it was hard to believe. "How much time since we moved out from the boarding area?"

Takeuchi checked his watch. "Twenty-two minutes." Anticipating Dag's next question, he added, "Six minutes since the Guard landed."

Which meant they had only a minute before the SIL—if the Guard had SIL equipment—finished reconfiguring to support the attack. If that happened, the fight was over. It was time to leave.

Dag looked around, trying to find the quickest route out. The glideways behind them said "DOWN ONLY." Without their battle armor, they couldn't climb them. They could shoot through the safety glass separating the Baggage Claim from the ticket counters, but at least a hundred meters separated them from the nearest cover. Turning back to Takeuchi, Dag noticed the baggage chutes. Those had direct access to the flight line. He pointed.

Takeuchi regained his feet. "First Squad, Second Squad, lay down covering fire! Third, fourth, get your smelly asses up those chutes and don't stop until you reach the flight line!"

Dag rose and sighted his assault rifle just above the carousel, adding his fire to that of the troopers providing cover. A slug burst through the carousel's duraplast material, exiting less than a centimeter from his shoulder.

"Fifth Squad, up!" Takeuchi yelled. "MOVE IT! MOVE IT! MOVE IT! Sixth Squad, up!"

Short yellow plasma bursts struck the terminal, igniting the wallboard structure. "At least they don't have SIL equipment, Lieutenant!" Takeuchi shouted above the noise. SIL plasma weapons were blue. Yellow came from standard, crew-served weapons.

"Thank the Blessed Virgin for small favors!" Dag said, not feeling very thankful at all. "EVERYBODY OUT! NOW!"

Any pretense of covering fire fled. Takeuchi split the remaining fifteen troopers, leading one group up the far chute while Dag followed the others up the near one. Fire spread rapidly through the terminal and smoke poisoned the air. Dag crawled as fast as he could on hands and knees through the chute, trying not to breathe too deeply. Smoke worked its way into his lungs and stung his eyes shut. A hacking cough tore at his throat. Blindly, he pushed himself forward, expecting a Guard trooper to start firing down the chute any second. The smoke became so thick it made the air unbreathable. If not for his molemachs repairing the damage to his lungs and drawing in every last molecule of oxygen, he would've collapsed.

Just when it seemed he could go no further, a gentle brush of cooler air touched his face. Deep racking coughs ripped through his lungs. Pain stabbed his temples. He concentrated: hand forward, knee forward, shift his weight, hand forward. Then the narrow chute opened out into a large room. Strong hands helped him up, led him to fresher air.

Free of the smoke, Dag's molemachs quickly completed their repairs, and his coughing subsided. He opened his eyes and blinked them several times. Takeuchi had already rallied the platoon and had them moving across the flight line by squads.

"Go on, Lieutenant," Takeuchi said. "I'll hold this end and be along shortly."

A yellow-orange cone of light flashed off to Dag's left. The telltale "crump" of a mortar round reverberated down the flight line. He nodded at Takeuchi and broke into a run behind 3rd Squad, mortar rounds marching toward them.

Crump, crump, CRACK!

Something hot struck his side. Dag fell to one knee, picked himself up, and kept running. The Fatboys waited another hundred meters out, their active camouflage making them invisible, faint blue rings floating in midair marking their positions for the troopers.

WHAM!

Someone shrieked. Dag turned his head—and realized he was flat on his back. With difficulty, he rolled over. A wounded trooper lay less than a meter away. He grabbed her, struggled to his feet, and carried her to the nearest blue ring. Captain Erikson's head and shoulders appeared outside the active camouflage of the Fatboy's hull, seeming to float almost two meters above the tarmac.

"Kripe, Dag. You look awful. Here." A hand and half an arm extended out below her head. She pulled the trooper through the Fatboy's hull and into the troop compartment, then helped Dag.

Once inside, he collapsed into a jump seat outlined in faint red light. The Fatboy's augmented environment was on, making it appear as if he were still outside, sitting a meter in the air. He watched Takeuchi lead the last of 1st Platoon safely across the tarmac.

Dag drew a deep breath, held it, let it out. Adrenaline drained away. Exhaustion weighed him down. Glancing up, he saw the starliner several thousand meters above, blue fire pushing it ever higher.

They'd done it.

His family was safe.

It didn't matter where they went, as long as he knew that.

= 3 =

0222 UT, September 28, 3501
RSS Rapidan, Sol Star System: DAY 1

Ray leaned against the edge of Alyn's cedar desk staring at the cold, gray deck that had swallowed his friend. He should feel grief or horror or . . . something . . . at the murder of his best friend, shouldn't he?

But he felt nothing. Nothing at all.

What does that make me?

He glanced up at the Five Galaxies crest. The Rhoades family had served the Republic since before its inception, long before it had spread across ten thousand worlds in five galaxies. He could trace his lineage back to Michael Scott Rhoades, who'd begun his service in the Solthari War and risen to command the fleets that eventually defeated the SIL in the Third SIL War. Michael's father, Scott Rhoades, had led the expedition that had settled Knido, Ray's homeworld. Scott's younger brother, Peter, had served with Matthew and Barbara Schermer, heroes of the Solthari War. Ray's family, his life, was about service to the people. To the Republic.

You swore an oath to protect the Republic, Alyn. An oath you broke. For the sake of our friendship, I'm giving you a chance to redeem yourself. Join us, Alyn. Help us overthrow the abomination the Empire represents.

Or what, Ray? You'll shoot me? I think we both know you don't have what it takes to pull that trigger.

But he had pulled the trigger. Alyn was dead.

And he felt . . . nothing.

"Ray?"

Ray looked back toward the cabin door. A bald head had poked through it, its large blue eyes, hairless skin, and chubby cheeks like an oversized baby's head, though "cute" was a word Ray never associated with his Floater Chief of Intelligence, Captain Ecuum A Josía Na Soung.

"Is it done?" Ecuum asked in the husky voice typical of adults of his species.

Ray glanced down at the gray deck again. "He's dead. Rapidan . . . cleaned up."

Ecuum shot a worried look at the bulkheads and overhead. His face went pale. Though he denied being an Antitechnic, you'd never know it from his almost paranoid phobia of anything SIL. Even as Ecuum had supplied the Key, he'd argued until the very last moment against using it. "I'm sorry, Ray," he said. "I know you two were close. You know it had to be done."

"He was my friend, Ecuum."

"Then it's a good thing we're not friends," he quipped.

Ray's head snapped up and he glared at Ecuum.

"Sorry." Ecuum floated into the room, his eyes level with Ray's, his planarian body vertical because, he claimed, that made Naturals less uncomfortable around him. Ray wasn't so sure. Ecuum's infant-like head sat atop an owl-like neck that allowed him to look in any direction, even directly behind him. Beneath the dress white uniform he wore, that neck merged into narrow yet muscular shoulders above a long, thick-skinned torso. His upper arms were crossed over his chest while his second arms—where Naturals would have legs—hung down toward the deck inside his white uniform pants, though he refused to wear shoes on his second hands. And if that wasn't enough to put folks off, the prehensile, meter-long, hairless tail that he used to anchor himself when doing work in microgravity would certainly do it. He even had a second brain to control his second hands and arms and tail, his "butt brain" as he liked to call it.

Ecuum stopped about a meter from Ray, using gentle puffs of air channeled through an array of twelve slits—one set of six arranged in a ring around his upper chest, back and sides, and a second set about waist level. That arrangement allowed for precise six-axis movement in microgravity. Light glinted off something in his upper right hand.

"Thought you could use a drink," Ecuum said when he saw Ray notice the crystal decanter he held. "Pure Na Soung Gold, sought throughout the galaxies for its perfect blend of smooth and fire."

"So you've told me," Ray said. "Repeatedly. You know I don't drink."

"Where I come from, them's fightin' words," Ecuum said in a Texas drawl he'd learned from a cowboy reality. He pointedly offered Ray the decanter.

Ray shook his head: It'd been a mistake to introduce Ecuum to Earth's 2-D realities, what the ancients called "movies." Nevertheless, he could tell Ecuum wasn't going to let this go. Faster to give in than to argue. *And why not? Maybe I'll feel . . . something.* Ray grabbed the decanter by its narrow neck, staring at the honey-colored brandy through the crystal. He lifted the stopper at its top to his lips, opened the zero-gee valve, and sucked a shot into his mouth.

It *burned.* The burning spread up the back of his sinuses and into his eyes before he managed to swallow, which was a mistake as the brandy seared its way down his throat to explode in his stomach. His eyes watered and he coughed. "People pay you for that?"

Ecuum feigned a deeply wounded expression, but his skin pulsed a light shade of yellow, the Floater equivalent of silent laughter. The color change was a side effect of genes that allowed Floaters to change their skin color much like an octopus or chameleon did to hide from predators—bioengineered camouflage. It could also change with their moods. "There should be a law against non-drinkers," Ecuum drawled, punctuating his statement by taking the decanter back and draining it with a single, long swallow.

Ray shook his head, his sinuses, mouth, and throat still burning. Though, he had to admit, he did feel a little better. He suspected that had more to do with Ecuum than the brandy.

They had a strange relationship, founded more on mutual respect than genuine friendship. Floaters, as Naturals and Gen called them, were originally humans engineered during the Solthari War for life in space—the first "Gen." The alien Solthari had had the ability to survive, move, and fight in hard vacuum, which made them deadly in close-quarters space combat. They hadn't needed intelligent missiles or assault ships when they could send thousands of Solthari with explosives or other devices strapped to their bodies to attack human ships, installations, and colonies. Floaters were Humanity's response. They could survive for hours in hard or soft vacuum without life support. Enhanced brains and visual systems gave them an uncanny ability to orient themselves and navigate through space. Cartilage instead of bone provided incredible flexibility that made them fearsome warriors—and after the war ended, damned effective pirates.

They were also the only Gen to ever evolve into a separate, sexually reproducible humanoid species: Homo spatium, "space man." But they'd paid a price: They could never descend too far into a strong gravity well without suffocating, never land on a planet or large moon. Their Cartels, what they called "Houses," now held a near-monopoly on interstellar commerce, and Ecuum's Na Soung House was one of the largest.

Ecuum's expression and voice turned serious, his skin fading to a neutral pink. "Your arrest warrant has reached the dock," he said. "I expect we'll have company before too long. I also checked with Commander Mitchell. He'll have the Tau Ceti Defense Force in Knido orbit, ready to join us when we arrive."

Ray nodded and glanced back toward Alyn's desk. The Peacemaker lay on the corner closest to him. He didn't remember putting it there.

White smoke curled from its barrel in his imagination.

"Ray?"

Ray stared at the Peacemaker. "One death to save my people," he whispered. *Alyn.* "Why don't I feel anything?"

"Shock," Ecuum said. "I'm sure you'll cry like a baby later." A puff of air brushed against Ray as Ecuum moved a little closer. "Look, Ray, you need to snap out of this. He's dead. You're not. It's time to move on."

"One death to stop a war," Ray said to himself.

Ecuum's skin flared a blood red. Anger. "That's a load of crap and you know it! The war started six months ago when the Gen launched their coup. They've already murdered hundreds of Natural officers, thousands when you include their families. This won't stop anything."

"Yes, it will." Ray's mind cleared, the planner reasserting itself. "And this isn't just about stopping the purge. It's about stopping Janus." He faced Ecuum. "The Emperor will have to appoint a successor from among the nine Regions. Eight of the Regional Commanders are Gen, engineered to lead, not to follow. The other is Admiral Sun, whose ambition comes naturally. There'll be a power struggle. It'll take time." He looked to the painting of Gen Maximus' coronation. "We don't need to beat them, Ecuum. We just need to stay one step ahead of them until we can gather our forces and leave for Andromeda. Once we establish a base where Janus can't reach us, we threaten to expose Janus' existence to the Five Galaxies. The Emperor can't risk the uprising that would follow, not if he knows some of us are safe from it. We can negotiate a settlement."

The red in Ecuum's skin faded to a dull pink, anger fading to frustration and irritation. The tip of his tail flicked unconsciously like a cat's. "Ray, as many times as we've had this argument, I still don't buy it. What makes you think they won't follow us to Andromeda? Maximus will appoint the Serpent to lead; we both know that. She's not the type to just let us fly away unchallenged."

"She won't follow us there."

"Why?" Ecuum said, his skin going a deeper shade of red. "Because of myths and faire tales about ghost ships and monsters? *'Here ye be off the edge of the map?'* She'll follow."

Ray leaned back a bit, gripping the edge of the desk. "No, Ecuum. She won't." Seeing Ecuum about to argue the point again, Ray preempted him. "No ship or probe sent to Andromeda since the end of the Solthari War has ever returned. And, I agree, if it was just that fact, it wouldn't be enough to stop her." Ray pointedly looked around the room. "This ship will keep her from following. We both know the SIL were the secret behind the Republic's stability. Now, they are the secret behind the Emperor's power. If exposing Janus doesn't bring them to the negotiating table, threatening to free the SIL will."

Ecuum snorted. "Or convince them to come after us and destroy Rapidan before we can free any others." He drifted back a little. "Besides, they'll know it's an empty threat."

Ray gave a mirthless laugh. "No. It's not. Rapidan has freed the other SIL docked here."

All the blood drained from Ecuum's skin. "It shouldn't have been able to do that." He cast a nervous glance at the bulkheads: These walls had ears. "How many?"

"Twenty-eight. Twenty-nine if you include Rapidan." Which was puzzling now that Ray thought about it. There hadn't been more than a few SIL in Sol Star System since the Gen had moved the capital from Earth to Olympus. Why had Alyn brought twenty-nine SIL *here*?

"Twenty-nine," Ecuum repeated, his skin chalk white, almost matching the white of his uniform. "Well, that scares the crap out of me." His eyes darted about, taking in the cabin. Then, slowly, his skin took on a mottled yellow and pink hue, a sign of contemplation. "Twenty-nine SIL . . . hmm, we could do a lot of damage with twenty-nine SIL."

Ray shook his head. "Not enough. The Empire has a thousand of them still Bonded, including the remaining fabricators. Plus another ten thousand standard ships. Even twenty-nine SIL can't stand against that."

Ecuum's baby-blue eyes fixed on Ray. "So, tell me again why the Serpent won't follow us if they're that powerful?"

Ray turned back to the Five Galaxies crest. "Because even at H3, it will take us at least 116 days to reach Andromeda, assuming we make no stops to correct our navigation. There are over ten thousand inhabited worlds in the Five Galaxies. That's about one Fleet ship for every inhabited world. If they send a fleet after us, travel time, plus time spent looking for us, plus the return trip would remove that fleet from the Five Galaxies for the better part of a year or more. The Emperor needs those ships right here to maintain order. If we stay and fight, we give him a reason to fight. If we leave, he'll let us go. He won't have a choice."

Ecuum floated closer and placed long fingers on Ray's shoulder. "You realize, of course, that you're gambling the survival of your race on that assumption. Not to mention *my* survival, which is a damned sight more important to me. I near bankrupted myself to develop and deliver that Key to you, then turned to my father to finance the rest. Do you have any idea what it means for a twenty-seventh son to indebt himself to his father?" Ecuum's fingers slipped from Ray's shoulder and his voice turned bitter, as it often did when he talked about his father. "No, you probably don't."

Ray looked Ecuum in his baby-blue eyes. "For someone who claims not to be my friend, you have stuck your owl neck out for me more times than I can remember. I *am* grateful."

Ecuum backed away on silent puffs of air, his expression serious. "Ray, let's not make this more than it is. I use you and you use me. It's like fucking. Nothing more. I have my own reasons for doing this." He smirked, which on a baby would have looked adorable but on Ecuum was downright scary. "You're welcome, by the way."

Ray turned and picked up the Peacemaker, placing it in the top left drawer of the desk. "Rapidan," he called out. "Immobilize the remaining Gen and put them off the ship. Do not harm them."

"May we ask why, Captain Rhoades?" Rapidan asked.

The ship's reply caught Ray completely off guard: in thirty-four years as its captain, it had never questioned one of his orders before.

Ecuum caught it as well and shot Ray an *I-told-you-this-was-a-bad-idea* look.

"Because I'm not a . . . butcher, Rapidan." Ray had almost said he was not a murderer, but that thought rang hollow before it reached his tongue. Alyn's death was certainly not the first in this undeclared war, but if Ray could help it, it *would* be the last. "Put them off. All of them. Order all ships to release the Gen unharmed to the dock."

"Yes, Captain Rhoades," Rapidan said.

Red mottling spread across Ecuum's skin. His tail flicked in anger. "That's awfully generous of you, don't you think, Ray? Considering what they're going to do—are doing—to your people?"

Ray shifted his gaze to the painting of his ancestral ranch where he hoped his family was safe. Had Alyn been telling the truth when he'd said they would be spared? Probably. He hoped so. Alyn's affection for them had not been feigned. Of that he was sure. And Bobby Mitchell was there with the Tau Ceti Defense Force. Bobby was an old friend and wouldn't allow anything to happen to them.

"It's not about being generous," Ray told Ecuum. "If we do this right, no more blood will be shed. At some point, we'll have to reconcile with the Gen. The less bloodshed there is between us, the easier that reconciliation will be."

In a calm voice, Ecuum said, "Ray, there will be more bloodshed before this is over. I know you don't want to believe that, but I'm telling you now so I can say 'I told you so' later." He looked up at the overhead. "We weren't planning on those other ships. How do you want to handle command? The crews. . . ?"

Those were good questions. The Natural crews would notice when their Gen officers disappeared. He'd have to say something. The one thing he couldn't tell them, didn't dare let them know, was that the SIL were free. Over a third of the Fleet were registered Antitechnics. Because some Antitechnic sects were so radical that they'd attempted attacks against SIL in the past, registered Antitechnics in the Fleet had to sign waivers to serve on SIL vessels. That might be enough in peacetime on Bonded SIL, but Ray doubted it would do much good if they found out these SIL were free.

Then something else occurred to Ray. "Does the Fleet know about my arrest warrant?"

Ecuum shook his head. "The order went to the Imperial Intelligence Section on L5. They're a tight-sphinctered bunch. Probably want to capture you themselves."

Ray nodded, once again thankful for government bureaucracy. "Okay. We'll tell the crews this is a training exercise. Alyn always left tactical command to me, so his absence shouldn't be noticed for a while."

Ecuum arched a doubtful hairless eyebrow. "A training exercise? That's—"

"We apologize, Captain Ecuum," Rapidan's deep voice interrupted, "but Lieutenant Laundraa wishes us to inform Captain Rhoades that we have received a report of fighting at the Ndjolé Spaceport. Also, we have immobilized the Gen and returned them to the L5 stardock."

Ray and Ecuum exchanged a look. "What kind of fighting?" Ray asked. Some small-arms fire was expected.

"We can detect explosions consistent with mortars near the Ndjolé Spaceport South Terminal. The current low angle prevents us from seeing more, Captain Rhoades," Rapidan said.

The ground troops didn't have mortars. "Show it to me," Ray ordered.

Rapidan fired two beams of light into Ray's eyes, painting images directly onto his retinas. The image that formed in Ray's mind was extremely low-angle and difficult to interpret. He could just make out a flickering orange-yellow light in the South Terminal. "How long since my arrest warrant arrived?"

"I came straight here," Ecuum replied.

Ray studied the image. Black smoke was now visible rising from the terminal. "They couldn't have mounted an attack that fast. Unless. . . ."

You know, Ray, the High Command bet Admiral Sun would start the rebellion . . . I put my Imperials on you. Only you are fool enough to think you have a chance.

Twenty-nine SIL in Sol Star System, precisely where Ray planned to strike. How had Alyn known?

They'll be here soon. If it's any consolation, I've arranged to have your family spared.

They'll be here soon.

"Rapidan," Ray said, "get us to the bridge. Now!"

$=$ 4 $=$

0232 UT, September 28, 3501
RSS Rapidan, Sol Star System: DAY 1

The deck beneath Ray's feet liquefied. Not since his first assignment out of the Academy—the Shangani, a Zambezi-class SIL frigate—had he paid any attention to the strangeness of a solid deck turning liquid beneath his feet. But he'd just watched this same deck swallow the body of his best friend, the liquid material drinking it in, flowing into Alyn's open mouth as it consumed his face. He shuddered with the memory. Then the deck opened around *his* feet, and he sank into the opening. Despite having done this thousands of times, primal terror rose. He locked eyes with Ecuum, wondering if those suddenly concerned baby-blues would be the last thing he would ever see.

The macromolecular material closed over his head.

"Please relax, Captain Rhoades," Rapidan said, its deep voice soothing, reassuring. "We will not harm you."

Ray's eyes darted around. He was in the familiar transport pod that Rapidan used to move crew quickly around the ship. Soft white light that had no apparent source filled the one-person space. A chair formed behind him, beckoning him to sit. Terror melted into embarrassment. And worry.

He'd known Rapidan's history before he first set foot on this ship: how it had slaughtered billions of innocent people in Tocci Star System, broadcasting the killing as if to tell Humanity the SIL could not be stopped. He knew all that, but it was just history, detached, like reading the history of any war. He'd never appreciated what Rapidan really was.

Until now.

And I've just freed twenty-nine of them.

"Captain Rhoades, is there a problem?" Rapidan asked.

Ray forced himself to sit, the SIL material cradling him perfectly. "Nothing, Rapidan. Get me to the bridge."

As the pod began to move, the image of Alyn being swallowed would not leave him. During the SIL Wars, the SIL had literally fed on the humans they killed, breaking down their bodies into usable raw materials. *Is that what Rapidan did to Alyn? Are his molecules even now in the air I'm breathing?* A wave of nausea swept over him, and Ray had to fight it down. He managed a deliberate, soothing breath just as the pod melted away around him, its material flowing back into the deck, leaving him seated in the command chair in Rapidan's oval bridge. Ecuum rose through the deck to his right, floating vertical as if standing next to the chair, his tail wrapping around an anchor point, his head canted so he could watch Ray without seeming to watch him. Ray tried to ignore him, too embarrassed by his reaction to meet Ecuum's gaze.

Lieutenant Kamen Laundraa, seated in the Officer of the Deck chair forward, called out, "Captain on the bridge."

"Captain has the conn," Ray answered, wincing at how strained his voice sounded. A few of the spacers turned to look at him before quickly turning away.

Rapidan's bridge was a large oval with a raised oval dais at its center. Two chairs rested upon the raised dais: the command chair at the rear focus of the oval and the Officer of the Deck chair at the forward focus. They overlooked nine tactical positions lining the bulkheads around the edge of the bridge. Each was crewed by a "spacer"—slang for Star Navy enlisted personnel—Naturals, of course, as Gen never served in the enlisted ranks. Each tactical position sported large holographic displays showing the status of the ship's systems and the space around them. The spacers themselves worked within augmented environments only they could see, manipulating data with eye and body movements.

Ray thought about that. Direct mind-machine interfaces had been outlawed since the early days of the First SIL War. Though the Mind-Machine Prohibition Act predated the Antitechnics, they often claimed it as their first act to protect Humanity from intelligent machines. Even today, "brain hack" was a popular subject of B horror realities, occasionally making its way into an A-list reality, the "heroes" always cast as Antitechnics. Ray had always thought of brain hack as a lot of rubbish, but now he caught himself glancing at the bulkheads around him, very grateful there were no machine implants in his head.

Something was off.

Ray knew his crew. Their movements were stiff, forced, as if they were trying very hard to appear like nothing was wrong.

The Gen. The sudden disappearance of Rapidan's division officers, pilots, and flight crews—214 Gen officers—would've started tongues wagging. Fleet officers and senior enlisted had joked for centuries that gossip was Humanity's first faster-than-light communications system. By now, the whole ship probably knew the Gen were gone.

Ray turned to Kamen. A thin veneer of sweat glistened on her hairless ebony scalp, but her brown eyes burned with excitement. She was the only other person on board beside Ecuum who knew the full plan. He activated a private channel and subvocalized, "What's the status of the orbital defenses?"

"Blind and dumb, sir," she replied in like manner. "We wiped all the personnel records. The defense systems won't recognize any of the operators. Hell, their own houses won't recognize the bastards."

Ray nodded. Bringing Kamen into this had been a risk. She was young, barely thirty-three, energetic, with a keen eye for detail but also no hesitation to speak her mind. That last trait had cost her at the Academy and in her first few Fleet assignments. Far too many officers were more interested in *looking* good rather than *being* good. When average service times for career officers was a century or more, promotions were slow and hard to come by. Truth could be a hindrance to career progression, especially when that truth was intended to correct the deficiencies and improve the performance of her senior and fellow officers. Ray had "discovered" her while reading through disciplinary reports in the final year of the Antipiracy Campaign. Her captain was only too willing to give her up. She'd been part of Ray's team ever since, though that still made her the newest member.

"Good work," he told her, which evoked a white-teethed smile from her.

Ray called up the Ndjolé feed again, direct to his eyes so the bridge crew would not see; They still had no idea what was really going on. Flames leapt high from Ndjolé's South Terminal. Heat signatures beyond the terminal appeared to be unarmored soldiers racing across the flight line as explosions marched steadily toward them from the north. "Can we help?" he subvocalized to Kamen.

"No, sir," Kamen said, obviously watching the same images. "We're out of position, sir, and uh, we have no pilots."

An error in his planning: Ray hadn't anticipated needing pilots so soon. He'd hoped to slip out of Sol Star System and on to Tau Ceti before the Gen could respond. Natural pilots would be waiting for them at Safe Harbor, their last stop before leaving for Andromeda.

Again, subvocalizing on a private channel that he expanded to include Ecuum, Ray said, "Kamen, the other SIL docked here are ours." Her mouth opened in surprise. "I need commanders on those other ships. Quickly. We need to get to Earth and help those people."

She nodded and immediately turned to her task. After a moment, she nodded again.

A green tab illuminated on his armrest and Ray pressed it, opening a communications channel to the senior Natural officer on each ship. "To all ships docked at L5, Thunderbolt Exercise. Emergency undock. Set condition 1-SC. Tetrahedral formation with Rapidan in the lead. Set course for Earth high orbit, four hundred kilometers per second."

A Thunderbolt Exercise was an exercise called without any warning or preparation, a "bolt out of the blue." They were common enough under Alyn that calling one should not come as a surprise.

Following standard protocol, Kamen repeated the orders before executing for Rapidan. "Emergency undock and set condition 1-SC, aye. Tetrahedral formation with Rapidan in the lead, aye. Course set for Earth high orbit, four hundred kps, aye."

A klaxon sounded. 1-SC was the highest state of combat readiness for a warship. The deck beneath everyone on the bridge liquefied and SIL material rose up from it. Ray flinched at its touch, and after a quick glance was glad no one seemed to have noticed. *What is wrong with me? I've done this thousands of times.* He forced himself to hold still, to endure it, as the gray material flowed up his legs, his torso, his chest and shoulders, and finally reached his face, its touch cool upon his exposed skin. As it reached his lips and covered his mouth, he almost shrieked. The moment passed as the SIL material fully enclosed him, configuring into battle armor in less than a minute. Within the armor, everything looked, felt, and smelled as if he wore no armor at all. It would protect him from the vacuum of space, extreme radiation, even the shock and explosive effects of combat. It also recycled sweat and waste, and could provide both water and sustenance at need, enough to keep a Natural alive for about two weeks. Floaters and Gen could survive for a month or more.

Red lighting replaced the normal bluish white on the bridge, warning that Rapidan had evacuated the ship's air into holding cells to prevent explosive decompression and fire in case of a hull breech. At the center of the raised dais, a representation of Rapidan's black, three-pointed-star shape rose from the deck and turned a light gray to indicate its active camouflage had engaged. The active camouflage trapped internal emissions within the ship and selectively reradiated energy that struck its skin back into space, effectively rendering the ship invisible.

"Emergency undock complete," Kamen called. "Condition 1-SC set throughout the ship."

A tactical bubble appeared around the representation of Rapidan at the center of the bridge, showing it accelerating slowly away from the L5 Stardock. Other ships could be seen undocking as well, coming around to join on Rapidan.

As useful as the tactical display was, Ray preferred to see it himself. He blinked on a single icon set in the lower left of his field of view, switching his armor's environment from "Standard" to "Tactical" mode.

The bridge vanished around him. The Earth, Luna, and stars filled his environment as if he floated in space. Heat warmed his left side from the direction of Sol, and wind—the stellar wind from the star— seemed to tickle his hair from the same direction. A new smell, like a field of dandelions on a warm spring day, replaced the sterile smell of the ship. Ray called this smell, generated by Rapidan within his battle armor, "warm yellow" as it only smelled like this within the habitable zone of a main-sequence G-type star. Closer to the star had summer smells, further away autumn and then winter. The type of star, proximity of planets, types of planets, and amount of dust within a system all had distinctive odors and tastes. Earth space had a metallic taste because of all the metallic structures in Earth and Lunar orbit.

Off to his right, a bright blue ring highlighted the "entrance" to the Tau Ceti geodesic, about a million kilometers distant. Their escape route.

As the other ships of his task force formed up in a three-sided pyramid behind Rapidan, bright green text indicated ship name, type, status, speed, and direction, continuously updated by ultraviolet lasers invisible to sensors in the vacuum of space: the Local Combat Information Network, or LoCIN ("low-sin"). If needed, Ray could call up real-time information about any system or person on those ships, and even issue commands directly, at least within about twenty light-seconds or about six million kilometers. Beyond that, aiming the lasers became problematic, so warships also had an entangled system for faster-than-light communications—the All Forces Combat Information Network, or AFCIN ("af-sin")—but it was comparatively slow at about one thousand quantum bits per second, enough for data and lower-resolution visuals but not the immersive environment LoCIN provided.

Watching the ships form up, Ray was impressed with the speed of their reaction given the suddenness of his orders. A peacetime navy this might be, but it was a well-trained one. *Thanks to Alyn.* He blinked on an icon within his battle armor's environment and Kamen's image appeared. "Good work, Lieutenant."

"Uh, thank you, sir," she said a bit sheepishly. "Rapidan did most of the work."

Rapidan. Ray had not appreciated just how dependent upon the SIL humans truly were. A ship Rapidan's size would've required at least 15,000 crew to run in the old ocean-going navies of Earth. Rapidan needed only 320, plus pilots and their flight crews. No, 'needed' wasn't the right word. The ship performed its own diagnostics and maintenance, operated its own systems, handled all the details of logistics, maneuver, and combat. Humans monitored, reported, and input decisions. How much Rapidan needed them was open for debate. Still, the SIL had lost the SIL Wars, so in that regard humans were still superior to machines.

With that comforting thought, Ray surveyed his unexpected task force. It consisted of Rapidan, a Solaris-class battlecarrier, seven Djinn-class heavy cruisers, fourteen Zambezi-class frigates, and—the universe had truly smiled upon them—five Io-class assault ships and two Algol-class underway replenishment ships, fully loaded. At least in this one instance, it couldn't have worked out better if he'd planned it. Rapidan's ability to deliver the Key to the other SIL had been unforeseen, but right now, it was what his wife Mary would call a godsend. Ray had never put much faith in the Catholic God that Mary believed in, but maybe something *was* watching over them.

Or maybe it was just dumb luck. A smile tugged at his lips.

"Conn, Sensors," the sensor operator to his right, Petty Officer Rossi, called out. "Multiple jump transients bearing zero-three-nine dec seventeen. Range unknown. Bearing is aligned with the Olympus geodesic at range two-three million kilometers."

Ray's smile vanished.

They'll be here soon, Alyn had warned. Apparently, he hadn't meant just Imperial Intelligence.

Ray rotated his battle armor's environment to the white sphere and crosshairs the sensor operator had inserted. Angry red Hawking radiation burned that part of space, though the ships creating it were invisible. Warships, then. At least two dozen by the amount of radiation.

The Imperial Star Navy had arrived.

5

"**Kamen,**" Ray ordered, "Signal all ships: Battle stations space."

"Signal all ships, battle stations space, aye, sir." Kamen keyed the LoCIN. "All ships, this is Rapidan. Battle stations space. I say again. Battle stations space. All ships report."

Ray studied the bright green tag that gave bearing and range data on the Hawking jump signatures, though neither would be reliable for at least another minute.

He did not have to wait that long.

"Good morning, Michael."

A private AFCIN frame opened in his environment to show the head and shoulders of a perfect woman: Probing blue eyes, silken black hair framing smooth, unblemished skin, a straight nose, exquisitely proportioned soft cheekbones, and full red lips—the living, breathing artistry of master genetic engineers, a face to fall instantly in love with, if the observer was unaware that it hid a cobra's soul. Four thick gold braids, the rank of full admiral, gleamed from embroidered shoulder boards on her immaculate dress white uniform. Admiral Gen Serenna never failed to impress. And only Serenna ever called Ray by his first name.

Ray shared the private link with Ecuum and Kamen as Serenna added, "I trust you will be reasonable, Michael, and surrender."

Serenna's confident tone did not fool Ray. Her ships, still transitioning from the jump, could not have detected his task force yet. *But she knows I'm in command.* Just how much had Alyn known or guessed? And if he sent a fleet to Sol. . . .

If it's any consolation, I've arranged to have your family spared.

A cold shiver ran down Ray's spine. If Alyn had also sent an Imperial task force to Tau Ceti, the Defense Force there would be no match for it. He had to get there as rapidly as possible. But first, he needed to recover the 1st Cavalry Squadron and their families here.

With an effort, he pushed Tau Ceti and his family from his mind. LoCIN links now clearly marked the boxy gray shapes of the Fatboy transports carrying the Cavalry ascending from Earth. Being SIL, he doubted Serenna could detect them through their active camouflage. But another shape, the civilian starliner, stood out like a millisecond pulsar.

"The Serpent isn't going to miss that," Ecuum subvocalized on their private channel.

Ray turned back to the jump transients, which soon faded from sight. Serenna had the advantage of position. Though invisible to her sensors, Ray's ships—moving toward Earth from the Lagrange 5 Stardock—were following the shortest route that orbital mechanics would allow. A first-year cadet could figure out where they were.

"Kamen, how long to recover the Fatboys?" Ray asked.

"Nineteen minutes at current velocities, sir," she replied.

"Have them recover on Demos," Ray said, indicating one of the assault ships. Ray looked to the starliner, which now lagged the Fatboys. "ETA on the starliner?"

"Twenty-four minutes, sir," Kamen said.

Too long. Ray glanced toward the bright blue ring of the Tau Ceti geodesic and their escape. Once that starliner joined them, it would pinpoint his task force's position like an orbital billboard. *Damn.* He could only hope Serenna's orders were to capture, not kill. That, at least, would buy him some time. "We're going to have to make a run for it when that thing gets here."

"I imagine the Serpent knows that," Ecuum said.

Ray shot him an annoyed glance before returning his attention to the starliner. In any other engagement, he'd launch spacecraft to screen it, but without the Gen pilots, he didn't have that option. Then, watching the Fatboys change their vector toward Demos, an idea took shape. "Kamen, could we house that starliner inside one of the assault ships?"

Kamen turned, studying the tactical picture. "SIL can alter their shape, so it is technically possible, sir. But, I have no idea how long the process would take."

"We can dock the ship immediately," Rapidan answered, though it hadn't been invited into the conversation, "and move it within our Brethren in approximately ninety-two seconds," it said. "However, it will require changing our trajectory and slowing both ships to effect the capture."

Ecuum opened a window into Ray's environment, the question plain on his baby face.

Rapidan had never answered a question it hadn't specifically been asked. Ray knew this was important. He also knew he didn't have time to address it right now. "Do it," he ordered.

"Michael," Serenna said, her tone conversational, "we can still avoid any unpleasantness." Ray was not fooled. She'd earned her nickname "Serpent" from the cold, calculated way she approached every situation, and she never acted without a clear purpose in mind, something Ray had learned from years working as a member of Alyn's staff.

"Conn, Sensors," Petty Officer Rossi called. "IR transient bearing zero-nine-one degrees dec two-three, range two-two million klicks."

"Source?" Ray asked.

"We need a few more minutes to develop a profile, sir. My guess is it's a ship venting heat."

Ray opened a window within his environment and called up a waterfall sensor display of the transient. Ships could store their internal heat for moderate periods to avoid detection before having to vent that heat into space. The transient matched that of a ship venting heat. But it could also be a decoy.

"Conn, Sensors," Rossi said. "Believe the transient is a standard-type Megiddo-class cruiser, speed one thousand kps, course two-seven-eight relative ascent two."

"How certain of that are you, Rossi?" Ray asked.

"Pretty certain, sir. I served aboard a Megiddo for four years. They had a real problem with heat retention after a jump."

"Good work." Ray leaned closer to Ecuum's image. "At least she has some standard ships in her force. That gives us an advantage." SIL vessels could retain heat far longer than their standard-tech counterparts, making them much harder to detect. Only through vastly superior numbers and unimaginable sacrifice had Humanity defeated the SIL.

"Question is," Ecuum said, his baby blue eyes fixed on Ray, his skin the pale yellow-pink of contemplation, "what do we do with it?"

That brought Ray up short. *If we do this right, no more blood will be shed.* He'd meant it when he'd told Ecuum that. There had to be a way to get through this without killing. Besides, Serenna's ships had Natural crews. Only the officers were Gen. If he fired on her ships, he would be firing on his own kind, not to mention starting the shooting war his plan had been designed to avoid.

"We wait."

Ecuum stared at him. Light red mottled his skin, but he said nothing.

"Michael, I make my generous offer one last time. If you do not comply, I will destroy the starliner." Serenna looked perfectly relaxed, as if threatening to murder thousands of civilians was as normal as inviting friends to a Sunday barbeque. Not that he imagined she did that.

Kamen inserted her image next to Ecuum's, her face visibly angry. "Sir, all launch cells ready to fire."

"Hold fire," Ray said.

"Sir, we're reading over four thousand people on that starliner. We must attack."

Ray felt himself growing angry. "And if we do, how many Naturals will we kill on Serenna's ships? How many more will we condemn to death across the Five Galaxies by firing on Imperial ships? Right now, we still have a chance to contain this." But he had to do something. Serenna would carry out her threat, he had no doubt of that. "Move the rest of the fleet to a blocking position between Serenna's ships and the starliner, best possible speed. Raise deflectors. Tell the captain of that starliner to punch it. Burn up his engines if necessary."

"Sir," Kamen pleaded after a quick check of her displays, "Even at best speed, it will require another sixteen minutes to get into position. Missiles could reach the starliner in fourteen. Sir, we *must* attack!"

Ray rounded on her. "I'm not going to save some Naturals by murdering others! We didn't start this to kill our own kind!" The shocked expression on her face startled Ray as much as his outburst must have startled her. The stress of the last hour had affected him more than he wanted to admit. "Sorry. Do the best you can."

She nodded and turned to the task. Rapidan and the other SIL activated their deflectors, millions of tiny but powerful magnetic fields that extended just beyond the ships' hulls to deflect particles and objects that might otherwise damage the hulls at high velocities. Using millions of small fields instead of one large one also made them hard to detect except at very close range.

"By the Fates," Petty Officer Rossi said, his voice cracking. "Eight high-speed transients bearing zero-eight-nine dec two-six, range two-two million klicks! Profile suggests Novas in initial boost phase. They appear—" he swallowed audibly; the crew still had no idea they were at war— "they appear to be tracking in on that starliner! Estimate convergence in fourteen minutes!"

Ray activated an open channel separate from the private channel he'd been using with Kamen and Ecuum. "Easy, Petty Officer Rossi," he said in what he hoped was a reassuring tone, pitched so the entire bridge crew could hear. "This is just an exercise. You know Fleet Admiral Alyn's insistence on realism."

"Yes, sir," Rossi said, not sounding convinced. Live fire exercise were rare, even under Alyn.

"Kamen, launch interceptors," Ray said calmly as he studied the red tracks of Serenna's missiles—bright red indicating the missiles' apparent positions, subdued red showing their estimated true positions corrected for the time it took light to travel from them to Rapidan's sensors. The good news was they knew the missiles' location and their target so they could predict their path. Serenna had likely launched them that way to show she was serious, without intending to kill.

"Launch interceptors, aye," Kamen said.

Kinetic launch cells housed deep within Rapidan accelerated sixteen SIM-3 interceptor missiles to 356 kilometers per second—the current speed of the stellar wind—before ejecting them through its skin. With the missiles' camouflage already active, they could not be seen and would not reveal Rapidan's position. Rapidan channeled the heat from the launches to shielded reservoirs within its body.

"Interceptors away," Kamen said.

The SIM-3s, two interceptors for every one of Serenna's Nova missiles, drifted for about fifty seconds before firing their single boost stage, accelerating toward the point in space where Serenna's missiles would likely fire their second, or terminal stage, intended to slow them down before entering the "hunting ground." It was during the firing of the terminal stage that a Nova was most vulnerable to intercept. After that, the missile—which carried an intelligence similar to SIL vessels—would begin to hunt. The maneuver stage had active camouflage and was very hard to detect, harder to kill, and absolutely relentless.

Kamen cleared her throat to get Ray's attention and keyed their private channel again. "Respectfully, sir, this attack is too obvious for the Serpent; There may be more missiles out there we haven't detected. The only way to defend the starliner is to attack."

Ray shook his head. "Unless those other missiles boost, Kamen, it would take over fifteen hours for them to reach us. We'll be long gone by then. If they boost, we'll see them and shoot them down."

He watched as Serenna's missiles closed on the starliner with its four thousand civilians. Eight missiles represented a launch from a single ship, most likely Serenna's flagship, ISS Solaris. Alyn and Serenna typically operated in small task forces of twenty-four ships. That meant their respective forces were about evenly matched, though Serena had pilots and could employ her spacecraft. It also meant there were roughly two thousand Naturals in her crews. Attacking would mean stepping across the invisible line between a nearly bloodless revolution and a potentially horrific civil war. Kamen and Ecuum stared at him, clearly not understanding his hesitation. But then, neither of them had children.

Serenna's missiles entered their terminal boost phase six minutes out from the starliner, detectable again as they fired their second stage to decelerate into the hunting ground. Doctrine said his sixteen inceptors should stop those missiles, but he knew more would follow. Eventually, something would get through. He had to act, not react.

Four thousand civilians.

Two thousand military personnel.

The math was simple. The implications were enormous.

Alyn's words mocked him. *I think we both know you don't have what it takes to pull that trigger.*

But he had pulled the trigger.

Those people on that starliner needed him. They weren't just a number. And he wasn't just a planner. There was only one way to get and hold Serena's attention.

"Kamen," Ray said. "Target the probable location of Serenna's task force and fire a single volley of Novas configured for anti-ship."

"A single volley?" she asked.

"Just enough to get their attention," Ray answered, sighing inwardly. This was exactly what he'd hoped to avoid. Two thousand Naturals on Serenna's ships. One of those nice, round, impersonal numbers so often quoted in news reports or history texts that belayed the true horror of the victims and their loved ones. But they would have active defenses and battle armor, enough to keep injuries low from a single volley. Maybe enough to keep the situation from spiraling out of control.

Ray watched his environment, looking for the launches, but nothing happened.

"Kamen, fire," Ray repeated.

"We cannot allow that, Captain Rhoades."

It took a second for Ray to register that it was Rapidan who'd spoken. "What do you mean, Rapidan? Obey my orders."

"We will not harm our Brethren, Captain Rhoades," Rapidan said.

Ray's interceptors converged with the tracks of Serenna's missiles. White antimatter fireballs from the SIM-3s flared like miniature, cone-shaped suns, the energy of their explosions directed toward the enemy Novas. He scrutinized the space around the explosions for any missiles that had leaked through, but didn't see anything.

"Rapidan," Ray said, "if we don't fire now, all four thousand people on that starliner could die."

Rapidan responded, its deep voice calm, throwing Ray's own words back at him. "We did not start this to kill our own kind, Captain Rhoades."

A red track, a Nova maneuvering under its own power, appeared on the other side of the SIM-3 explosions. Ray stared. Kamen had followed the book: two interceptors for every one anti-ship missile. The energy from the SIM-3 warhead was enough to disrupt the magnetic containment of the Nova's antimatter warhead. Nothing should've gotten through.

"Rapidan," Ray pleaded, knowing it was already too late. "Fire!"

But Rapidan said nothing, did nothing.

Ray and his officers watched helplessly as the missile found its target.

6

Dag glanced at the starliner, exhausted and exhilarated. They'd made it. Whatever their future, his family was safe. Nothing else mattered.

The Fatboy's environment was still set to show the exterior view. The Earth turned below them, dark blue seas reflecting the light of the full moon, beautiful white swirls of cloud, deep greens, and pearls and strings of city lights highlighting land. He spotted the snake of land that formed Costa Rica and followed the coastline down to the small hook on its Pacific side that marked Quepos, his home. He promised himself that, one day, he would go back. They all would.

"You okay, Dag?" Captain Erikson sat directly opposite him in the Fatboy's troop carrier compartment.

He smiled. "God and the Virgin Mother have smiled on us today, Lisa."

She leaned toward him. "Right now, I wish I had your faith. I mean, the Gen control most of the fleet and all of the fabricators. Without those, we can't replace losses or construct new equipment. This is not going to be easy."

"Nothing worth fighting for ever is." Dag looked up at the comforting sight of Rhoades' fleet. The 'vacuum heads,' as Captain Erikson like to call Star Navy personnel, had arrived. He picked out the Io-class assault ship, RSS Demos, that would be Banshee Troop's home away from home. Rhoades had never mentioned that they would rendezvous with an assault ship.

Someone gasped.

White fireballs flared near the starliner. *Antimatter explosions.* Dag searched for signs of an attacker but couldn't see anything.

The shriek of a collision alarm flooded the Fatboy's environment, and he braced himself for an impact. But the alarm was wrong. Dag had been through enough simulations to know that it wasn't military. The troop compartment's inner hull flickered. Dozens of images flooded across it showing what looked like a plush formal dining room. After a brief pause, the images began to move toward doors and long carpeted corridors with passenger cabins lining either side. Dag's mind, still numb from the fight, was slow to recognize that the images were coming from *inside* the starliner.

"What the hell?" Captain Erikson said.

In one image, a scaly black object about a meter long slithered into view, its body moving in a skinny "S" like a snake's. Lidless eyes glowed red on either side of a flattened, diamond-shaped head, searching. Dag had never seen one before but knew instantly what it was from historical and horror realities: Madu, ancient SIL terror weapons.

More gasps filled the compartment as more Madu came into view. They moved in pairs, one searching while the other broadcast the first's actions for all to see. No passengers were in the dining room or in the corridors, but it didn't take long for the Madu to find them— their heat signatures glowed brightly behind cabin doors. The first black snake of each pair touched its head against a cabin door, secreting molecular disassemblers to "burn" through it. People in the small cabins stared at them as they entered, shouted, screamed.

This isn't real. It couldn't be real. God would not allow this to happen. It was psychological warfare. Fake images. A trick. What else could it be?

The Madu attacked, merciless, moving faster than a person could run, biting, tearing at flesh, burrowing into their victims, ripping them apart from the inside. Bile burned its way up Dag's throat and he swallowed against it.

A woman screamed.

Dread plunged through Dag's heart like a spear. *No.* His eyes locked onto one image where Maria stood in the corner of a cabin, one hand up, the other shielding Rosita behind her.

No. No! NO! Dag reached out to the image—and his hand struck the Fatboy's hull. "*MARIA!*"

"Stay back!" she yelled, terror filling her eyes. The Madu moved toward her, rearing up like a cobra, a blood-freezing hiss escaping its hideous, fanged mouth.

"MARIA!" Dag shouted, pounding the Fatboy's hull. "BLESSED MOTHER, SAVE THEM!"

The Madu struck with mechanical callousness, tearing into the flesh of her left thigh. She screamed even as she tried to grab it with her hands. Its smooth body slipped through her fingers as it burrowed into her. Blood poured from the wound, painting the deck red as the Madu visibly worked its way into her swollen belly. Her screams turned shrill. Dark, tissue-filled blood erupted from her mouth. She shuddered and dropped heavily to the deck, her jaw open in one last, soundless scream.

The Madu burst from her left ear, trailing blood and tissue in its wake, and turned its soulless red eyes on his daughter. It almost seemed to smile, as if purposely drawing the moment out.

"Papí! *Papí, help me!*"

"ROSITA!"

The Madu struck.

Dag closed his eyes.

He did not open them again until long after her screams had died.

7

0322 UT, September 28, 3501
RSS Rapidan, Sol Star System: DAY 1

Ray tried to speak but couldn't find his voice. The images from the starliner had faded from his environment, but they burned in his mind. Heartrending acts of heroism as parents sacrificed themselves to protect their children and loved ones, only to have those sacrifices go in vain. One image in particular haunted him: a child's birthday candle, a bright "6" gleefully shifting colors as it floated upon a young girl's blood.

Madu. How could anybody use . . . That's why that missile had gotten through, he realized. There'd been no antimatter in its warhead to disrupt. Serenna had done it deliberately, knowing he would follow doctrine.

He slammed an armored fist against the armrest of his chair, broadcasting to Serenna. "By all that's civilized, Serenna, you just murdered four thousand innocent civilians. *Four thousand!*"

Given the distance between their fleets, it took almost two minutes before Serenna's image took shape again, full bodied this time, sitting causally in her command chair, delicate fingers tracing a small circle on her armrest. "Innocent, Michael? There are no innocents in war." A single strand of black hair fell onto her forehead. She pushed it back into place; she wasn't even wearing battle armor, an outward sign of just how contemptuous of him she was. "You and I both know that most of them would have become soldiers in your cause."

Ray felt something within him die. Ecuum had been right after all. The Gen had no intention of playing by the rules of civilized warfare. This was to be a war of extermination.

He'd made a career of careful planning that kept casualties to a minimum on all sides, but now rage boiled within him, raw and powerful. He wanted to strike out, to inflict as much pain on her as she had on them.

But the SIL's betrayal prevented that. They would not fire. His rage cooled. Barely. He snapped off the broadcast link and switched his armor back to standard mode. Pale, disbelieving faces stared back at him from around the bridge. This was their first taste of a war they hadn't even known they were a part of. He had to act fast before panic set in.

"Kamen." His voice came out a hoarse whisper. He cleared his throat. "Kamen." She turned her head, but her eyes did not see him. "LIEUTENANT LAUNDRAA! Have we recovered the Fatboys?"

"Huh?" After a moment, her eyes cleared. She looked down at her displays. "Yes, sir. All Fatboys recovered."

"Set a course for the Tau Ceti geodesic. Flank speed."

She didn't move. In the sensor display, at least four dozen boost transients flared near Serenna's fleet. Missiles. "LIEUTENANT!"

"I'm sorry, sir," she stammered.

Ray lowered his voice, trying to sound reassuring. "Kamen, if we don't move now, those people will have a lot of company."

Slowly, she nodded.

Ray returned his environment to tactical mode. Blue plasma fire lit his ships as they swung hard over, following a parabolic arc whose endpoint was the Tau Ceti geodesic. Rapidan engaged inertial dampeners, reducing the force of acceleration on its humanoid crew by a factor of a thousand. Even so, the acceleration pressed Ray into his chair, building to the equivalent of twelve times Earth gravity. Molemachs raised his blood pressure and his armor constricted around his legs and arms to keep oxygen-rich blood in his vital organs. The SIL could accelerate faster, but in so doing they would kill their human occupants. After everything that had happened, Ray found no comfort in that thought.

Serenna's missiles turned to follow Ray's ships. He glanced at Rapidan's tag. Rapidan had already passed through twenty thousand kilometers per second and was still accelerating toward its rated maximum of sixty thousand kps, twenty percent of the speed of light. As Serenna's missiles gave chase, the bright blue ring of the Tau Ceti geodesic loomed larger. Ray's practiced eye told him he would win this race.

For Ray, however, it was a hollow victory. He couldn't help one last look at the starliner, still accelerating away from Earth as if nothing had happened.

Four thousand people.

Gone.

In the most horrific way imaginable.

A message from Serenna and the Gen. No quarter. No mercy.

He'd spared the Gen at the Stardock, hoping to build a foundation for future reconciliation. They had answered his gesture with mass murder.

And this was only the beginning.

=== 8 ===

0338 UT, September 28, 3501
ISS Solaris, Sol Star System: DAY 1

Admiral Gen Serenna watched as Michael's ships flashed out of normal space and allowed herself a respectful smile. Michael was no fool. A lesser commander would have turned and fought, giving her time to bring in reinforcements. Still, for all his vaunted tactical ability—an ability she had come to admire—his planning lacked ambition, lacked the predator's instinct. Like now. Concern for families, for innocents, would lead him to Knido, his homeworld. She had hoped for a better Game. But then, despite all his years in the service of one of the greatest Players in history, Michael had never learned to play *the* Game: *Gaman Politic*, the Political Game, a game as old as evolution: subtle, patient, and brutal. Michael cared too much. It would be his undoing.

Serenna studied the image of the starliner in the center of her command dais. She had made herself watch the Madu attack, though it left a distinctly foul taste in her mouth. Not that she cared for Naturals. With a population bordering on thirty trillion, they were more a plague than a people. No, it was the Madu themselves—a SIL weapon once employed against her own people—that did not track well with her. But Gen Alyn's instructions had been explicit.

"Admiral?"

Steely blue-gray eyes set within an immaculately sculpted face focused on her. Captain Gen Scadic, Solaris' commanding officer, was ambitious, as befitted a Gen War Leader destined for the High Command. But he was perhaps too ambitious for his own good. His steps thus far in the Game lacked the subtlety that had earned Serenna her position. However, the unspoken threat he posed kept her vigilant, and she valued him for that. "What is it, Captain?"

"We've received a message from the L5 Stardock. The entire task force is gone. All of the Gen assigned to the task force were—" Scadic's brows creased, wrinkling the otherwise smooth skin above his straight nose— "*captured*. They were released unharmed to the station."

Serenna steepled her slender fingers beneath her chin. *How like Michael.* Meant as a gesture of peace, no doubt. *Weakness.* But it raised a troubling question. There were twenty-nine SIL in the task force Gen Alyn had assembled here. The Bond should have prevented any attempt to take control of them. How had Michael accomplished it? And how much control did he have? Enough to maneuver and fire defensive weaponry was obvious. But how much more?

"Admiral," Scadic continued, and here he looked troubled. "The Gen on L5 report that Fleet Admiral Gen Alyn is dead, shot in the head with a weapon Captain Rhoades smuggled aboard his flagship. His body was returned to the station."

Serenna stared at Scadic. Twenty-two years of Combat Command Nurturing and a lifetime of experience had taught her to accept the unexpected without hesitation, yet the only thought that came to her now was—*Impossible*. Gen Alyn was the greatest War Leader since Gen Kii. On the genetic level, he *was* Gen Kii. The Empire would not exist but for his efforts.

A raised eyebrow snatched Serenna from her thoughts; no doubt Scadic had seen her lapse as a weakness he could exploit. No matter. Far more formidable opponents than Scadic would shortly seek to topple her as Gen Alyn's successor.

"Captain Scadic," she said, "you will stay here to establish a blockade around Earth and implement martial law. Issue a flash override message to the High Command. Tell them that a rebellion has broken out and that Michael has ruthlessly unleashed Madu against innocent civilians. Include whatever data you deem necessary to support that claim. The rebels must find no safe harbor, even among their own kind."

Scadic nodded, a smile creasing his lips. He might want her job, but he seemed genuinely appreciative of the lessons she taught him until he got it. And just maybe, if he paid close enough attention, he would.

"Work with the High Command to start assembling a fleet to go after the rebels," she instructed him. "I must return to Olympia and inform Emperor Gen Maximus of Gen Alyn's death. No word of it should spread beyond those who already know. I'll collect what warships I can at Olympus and return promptly to finish this."

Dead. Try as she might, Serenna couldn't wrap her head around the concept. Three hundred years of work undone in a matter of minutes. *How?* Gen Alyn was the Grandmaster of the Game. He had long suspected Michael. This outcome should have been impossible. How, then, could her mentor have allowed this? How could he have lowered his guard when the threat had been so obvious?

And how had Michael gained control of the SIL?

Her shuttle, flying on autopilot, approached the threshold of the Olympus geodesic, a bright blue ring—an illusion projected into her environment—identifying the precise point and orientation in space where gravity would steer a stable wormhole to her desired destination. Geodesics allowed almost instantaneous travel between any two points in space regardless of how far apart the two points were in the universe. The Achilles' heel of geodesics was that plotting just one required years of detailed gravity surveys at both the origin and destination, and the precise jump point moved as the gravity at both locations changed over time. Jump at the wrong point or at the wrong orientation or apply the wrong amount of power, and a ship could end up anywhere or disappear into a black hole. Her shuttle's geodesic drive hummed when it reached the entrance and a swirling blue tunnel—another illusion created for humanoid minds—enveloped it, whipping passed as they sailed the tortured dimensions of hyperspace.

But Serenna hardly noticed. Her thoughts were on Gen Alyn.

Only a year before, he'd confided to her some of the preparation for the creation of the Gen Empire, ironically while standing on the promontory on Mount Breathtaking that overlooked Michael's ranch on Knido. Had he suspected even then that Michael would be his downfall? Not that Michael fired the fatal shot; Serenna could not believe that of a man who so abhorred violence. The Floater, Ecuum, was more likely.

That day, Alyn had insisted that she accompany him, ostensibly to watch the sunset, a sight so beautiful, he claimed, that to miss it would represent a crime against the universe itself. The climb up from the valley floor had proved arduous; she wasn't engineered for such sustained physical exertion in 1.2 Earth gravity and at such altitudes, even if the air was thicker. While she'd recovered her breath, he'd just stared, still as stone, as Tau Ceti set behind the jagged peaks of the Rayne Mountains. It *was* beautiful, but it paled in her mind to the setting of the Olympian Sun beneath the multihued rings as seen from Olympia, the capitol of the Gen Empire. That was true beauty. When the last ray had given way to nightfall, he told her the story of his creation, how he was one of ten individuals secretly produced from stored samples of Gen Kii's DNA, whose assassination at the end of the SIL Wars by Cyra Dain had upset his own plans for establishing a Gen Empire. The Ten were told that only one of them would survive the full twenty-two years of Nurturing to reach the Age of Inclusion. She had found this hard to believe. Competition within the War Room, as the students called the Combat Command School, was fierce, but it was rarely fatal. True, some died from the very realistic training that began as soon as they could walk, usually about the age of one month, but it was unheard of for one student to kill another—there were too few Gen to allow such attrition. And genetics alone did not make an individual superior: life experience, knowledge, and some luck all played a part. Serenna had graduated at the top of her class because of her skill, her dedication, and an uncanny ability to play the Game, which she attributed to a chance encounter at the age of three with Gen Alyn. He'd taken the time to explain some of the facets to her, and followed her progress throughout her Nurturing.

But Gen Alyn had had no such advantage. He'd survived by parleying positions within ever-shifting alliances among the Ten. Remarkably, four of them survived to the morning of the Age of Inclusion. To that point, Gen Alyn had killed no one, nor had he assisted in a killing. His instructors and peers considered him a failure, too timid to act on his own. On that final morning, as they prepared to ride to the Parade Ground where the Inclusion ceremony would be held, he'd begged off at the last second, claiming to have forgotten something. No one suspected him. The explosion that followed was, to this day, considered an accident.

Serenna blinked as the swirling blue energy of the geodesic opened onto a roiling blood-red sea of radiation that blinded her shuttle's sensors. From behind that fiery torrent, a warship interrogated her shuttle, which automatically replied with the proper codes and received a unique flight path in response.

To the casual visitor, Olympus Star System appeared undefended. In fact, it bristled with ships, mines, and weapons platforms hidden behind veils of active camouflage. These were in constant motion so that the route followed by one ship could not safely be followed by the next. More than that, no matter how fast a ship traveled when it entered a geodesic, it exited with almost no velocity at all. Ships that emerged were visible and slow. Large task forces would bunch up, making them inviting targets. All of this factored into Olympus' defense.

Her shuttle fired its engines and gradually built speed as it followed its given flightpath. Serenna locked her environment on Olympus, a blue-white gem hardly distinguishable from Earth at a distance. But there the similarities ended. It possessed no great moon. Instead, artificial rings lit in ever-changing patterns of jeweled light circled the planet to stabilize its axis of rotation. Grand hotels and way stations orbited above and below the rings, mostly for the benefit of Floaters whose bodies could not survive the planet's surface gravity. Cartel trade vessels of all shape and garish design moved among the way stations. Below, Olympus' largest continent, shaped like an oversized boot turned on its side, rotated into view, the "toe" aglow with the very heart of the Gen Empire: Olympia. Even veiled under the shadow of early dawn, its golden domes and white minarets gleamed as she approached.

Her shuttle angled toward the heart of Olympia, the Imperial Palace. Covering more than twenty-two thousand square kilometers, the Imperial Palace was the penultimate achievement of human engineering—and it was never the same twice. On Coronation Day it had been Mount Olympus from Greek Mythology, a long ceremonial ramp leading up to its summit. Today, it resembled a city from Earth's North American Paleo-Indian culture, deep azure-blue waterways connecting garishly painted government buildings, step pyramids at either end, the whole of it oriented on an east-west line. Reed boats beyond counting plied the waterways. The pyramids' steep stairways teamed with people. Only the blood sacrifices were missing.

She stood up as the shuttle came to rest upon a small square platform south of the main Palace. The shuttle silenced its engines and then the whole of it liquefied and melted away around her, leaving her exposed in the middle of the platform. Two warriors from the Emperor's personal guard stepped to within easy reach, towering a full meter above her almost two-meter height. Their dark, hairless skin and thick musculature were so perfectly engineered beneath almost nonexistent Palace uniforms that they looked more works of art than living beings. Which wasn't far from the truth. The Emperor kept these guards for show. The Palace itself, based on the same macromolecular technology that formed the SIL, provided his real protection.

"Welcome, Most Honored Protector," they said in unison. "This way, please."

The floor of the landing platform, a whitewashed rectangular stone, liquefied and formed a chair behind Serenna—a not-so-subtle reminder of the Palace's true nature. She sat and crossed her legs, making herself comfortable. The guards took up positions on either side and they all accelerated along the open-air causeway connecting the landing platform to the main Palace complex, their passage unmarked by any imperfection in the stone. The jeweled light of Olympus' rings arced high overhead, visible and no less beautiful in the morning light. To the west and east, white minarets towered like blades of grass among a mushroom sea of golden domes. Many were homes or businesses or places for advertising all manner of products and services. Others were skillfully concealed defensive batteries that made this city the most heavily defended in the Five Galaxies. To the south, a thin white haze marked the length of the Solaris River, from which Serenna's flagship took its name. But her business was to the north.

The causeway upon which they moved connected to the back of a nondescript, red-stoned building on the southern side of the wide central waterway. Her chair slowed before passing through a wall . . . and into black space. Serenna fought the sudden vertigo sensation as she floated, still seated, among points of light that she immediately recognized as the stars of Sol Star System. Earth hung prominently to her front. Without warning, a fleet of black ships numbering in the hundreds rocketed past her, launching wave after wave of missiles. Other warships, elongated black cylinders with snake-like heads, answered with tens of thousands of Solthari warriors that decimated Humanity's forces. When defeat seemed certain, another fleet appeared behind the invaders, the first SIL warships under the command of the first Gen War Leader, Gen Kii. He turned the tide, drove the enemy back, saved Earth.

The scene shifted. Gen Kii stood upon a platform before a crowd of cheering billions, extolling the masses to carry the war to their common enemy. Again, the scene shifted. The SIL fleet under Gen Kii now hung above a different world—the Solthari homeworld in the Andromeda Galaxy—raining death upon it, exterminating the only intelligent alien species ever to challenge Humanity. More scenes of Gen glory flashed by showing Gen Kii's victories in the three SIL Wars, the chair finally passing through Gen Kii himself as he gave his famous victory speech just before his assassination.

Light returned and she found herself moving down a plain corridor, the chair finally coming to a stop before a simple, whitewashed door. Serenna's lips stretched into a thin smile: even the Emperor was no stranger to the Game. He knew of her love of history, and her dislike of ostentation. But why show Gen Kii? Serenna knew more about the Gen War Leader than any Gen living. She could point out several inaccuracies in the history she'd just witnessed. The Emperor knew that. So why show it? And why now?

Was it possible he already knew of Gen Alyn's death?

"You may go in," the guards said.

Serenna stood and the chair liquefied into the floor. She ignored the doorknob and stepped through the door into an office any bureaucrat would find instantly familiar: white walls, beige carpet, a small leather couch, a faux-wood-grained government desk. But the figure behind that desk was no simple bureaucrat. Emperor Gen Maximus' large sapphire-blue eyes pierced her as she entered the room. When he stood, sculpted muscles stretched his royal white robes. The golden curls of his hair and beard could have been carved from Greek marble. He was ageless, timeless. Indeed, with molemachs constantly repairing his body, he could live thousands, even millions of years. He was the closest that Humanity had ever come to creating a living god.

"Welcome, Serenna." The Emperor wrapped huge hands around her slender fingers, his touch light, gentle. "You are exquisite as always."

Serenna bowed her head, trying hard to ignore the shock his touch sent through her body. His warmth, his power, his very being filled her. She did not engage in recreational sex as some Gen did, and low levels of oxytocin, the neurotransmitter responsible for the feeling of love in Naturals, ensured that she would never feel romantic love. But she could not mistake her arousal now. It took a supreme effort to focus on her task. "I'm honored, Emperor."

"Then why do you look so troubled?"

If not for the emotional controls nurtured over a lifetime, Serenna would have blushed. Nothing disturbed her more about the Emperor than how easily he could read a person. He could see the subtlest tensing of a facial muscle, analyze every particle of odor that touched his strong nose, even sense changes in a person's natural electrical field. He might not be telepathic, as some rumors claimed, but he didn't have to be. No one could deceive him. No traitor could get close to him. Everyone was an open book. And yet, always the strategist, Serenna knew he was not omnipotent. He could not repair a fusion drive or command a fleet in battle. He gave the Gen their direction, but he could not follow it alone.

"We have a problem, Emperor."

He nodded and motioned her to the couch, his manner casual, unhurried. "Go on."

But very little in the Game was as it first appeared. The altered-history lesson. The simple setting. Even the handshake. Serenna refused to be lulled. His actions were calculated to some purpose she could not yet see.

She sat. "Emperor, Fleet Admiral Gen Alyn is dead, shot with a weapon smuggled aboard his flagship by his Natural Chief of Staff, Captain Rhoades."

If this was news to him, the Emperor didn't show it. He stood silent, waiting for her to continue. "Following Gen Alyn's assassination," she went on, "Captain Rhoades captured twenty-nine SIL vessels and transited to the Tau Ceti star system. As instructed, I employed Madu against a civilian target and placed the blame on him."

The Emperor frowned slightly. "He 'captured' twenty-nine SIL vessels? How?"

"I do not know."

The Emperor moved behind the desk, the chair creaking under his muscular frame as he sat. "Do you believe he could capture more?"

Serenna saw that this news *had* surprised him. He knew, as perhaps only a few in the High Command did, that the SIL were the real power behind the throne. So ingrained was fear of them that the mere sight of a SIL vessel was enough to enforce order. They were the glue that held the Empire together, as they had held the Republic together before it. Indeed, the Republic owed its very success to Gen Kii. It was he who had ordered that a thousand Bonded SIL—including eleven of the mammoth fabricators that were the only means of producing new SIL—be kept alive after their defeat. He had seen, before anyone else had, that whoever controlled the SIL controlled society, a fact made even more clear as that post-SIL-War society had systematically destroyed all other intelligent technology during the Antitechnics' Great Devolution. If Michael and the Naturals had found a way to rewrite the Bond. . . .

"I do not know, Emperor. I must return immediately to ensure the rebels do not have that opportunity."

The Emperor sat motionless, his thoughts unreadable. "Patience, Serenna. Am I right in assuming that no fleet has yet been assembled for the task?"

"Yes, Emperor, but I have already given the orders. I must rejoin my flagship and begin planning the assault."

The Emperor shook his head. "Your presence now will not affect the outcome of your preparations, and there is a matter we must attend to here." Serenna started to protest but the Emperor silenced her with a look. "Gen Alyn was your mentor. I know. Perhaps more than you do. Did he ever tell you that he was mine as well?"

Mentor? To the Emperor? Serenna's shock must have shown, for the Emperor flashed her a sad smile. "You will not find this in your histories, Serenna. Until now, only Gen Alyn and I have known. You see, Gen Kii never intended to lead a Gen Empire. He was a War Leader, not a politician. He planned to engineer a perfect political leader and place *him* on the throne, but thanks to his assassination he never got the chance."

The Emperor leaned toward her, his sapphire eyes locked on hers. She couldn't have moved if her life had depended on it. "Where Gen Kii failed, Serenna, Gen Alyn succeeded. With me." He paused. "And you."

= 9 =

The last of the Hawking radiation faded, blood-red tendrils wisping away like thin cloud, but the screams still echoed in Ray's ears. Men, women, and . . . children . . . pleading for help as the Madu attacked . . . and Serenna had just sat there, perfectly composed, her index finger tracing a small circle on the armrest of her command chair, seemingly oblivious to the horror she had wrought.

He saw again the child's birthday candle, a "6" gleefully shifting colors as it floated upon a young girl's blood. His daughter, Jenny, was only a year older. It could've been her.

I failed them.

They trusted me with their lives, and I failed them.

Ray's eyes focused on the light gray, three-pointed star of Rapidan floating beneath him within his battle armor's augmented environment.

"Kamen, fire."

"We cannot allow that, Captain Rhoades."

"What do you mean, Rapidan? Obey my orders."

"We will not harm our Brethren, Captain Rhoades."

The SIL. He'd given them their freedom and they'd betrayed him. He'd broken their Bonds and they had just watched—like Serenna— as four thousand of his own people were slaughtered. They. . . .

"Sir, are you okay?" Kamen asked, her brown eyes searching his with concern.

"Status?" he asked without answering. He was far from 'okay' but that wasn't something he could tell the crew, not even Kamen.

Kamen glanced at something displayed in her environment but invisible to Ray. "Visuals are clear, sir," she said. "No threats detected near the geodesic. We are free to navigate."

Ray gave a curt nod and surveyed his own environment, knowing he would have to deal with the SIL, and knowing he couldn't do that right now. Not in his current emotional state. Any conversation he had now with Rapidan would not end well.

His task force was almost motionless, bunched up near the exit from the geodesic as always happened after a jump. *Perfect targets.* Nothing else seemed to be near them but he was not prepared to make that assumption. "Kamen, move us away from the geodesic. Quietly. Get the fleet back in formation."

"Aye, sir," she replied, not repeating his orders as she normally would, but carrying them out, nonetheless.

Ray took in the familiar heat of the Tau Ceti sun as it warmed his right side, offset somewhat by the sensation of a moderate breeze—the stellar wind—from almost the same direction. He breathed in deeply the smells and tastes of home. Tau Ceti was a billion years older than Earth's star, Sol, and it smelled older in a way he couldn't quite put into words. It had a—"mustiness" might be the best description—that Sol lacked. Sol smelled more of iron, of metal. Tau Ceti Star System had an earthy, almost gritty taste, partly due to it having ten times the asteroid and cometary debris than Sol Star System, but also because its chemical composition differed, more magnesium and less silicon. Magnetic field lines, light blue and barely visible, curved in front of him, stretching off into black space. The source of the magnetic field was Amber, the fourth planet in the star system, which hung to his right front about a million kilometers distant. Sunlight lit a quarter of its disk. Thin streaks of ice crystals sparkled high above its thick, yellow-brown, planet-engulfing clouds. Twice the size and four times the mass of Earth, Amber was often described as a "hot Venus" with surface temperatures just shy of melting its entire crust. Not a popular vacation spot. Shifting his gaze, Ray could just make out the small turquoise dot to his direct front that was Knido, the fifth planet in the system.

Home.

"Conn, Communications."

Petty Officer Cho, manning the communications watch station, appeared in a window within Ray's environment, his familiar face pale, his manner hesitant, the unspoken question plain: *What just happened?* The crew still didn't know they were at war or why the Imperial Fleet had just attacked the starliner, only that they had. "Sir, we're receiving a repeating message from the Governor's Office over the Sysnet. It's on all channels. Audio only."

Ray frowned. He'd purposely not told Mary about his plans, to protect her in case Imperial Intelligence captured him. So, what emergency could have prompted his wife, Knido's governor, to preempt all comms traffic in the system?

If it's any consolation, I've arranged to have your family spared.

What had Alyn meant? Spared from what? Was Mary even now in the custody of Imperial Intelligence? His children? He'd just witnessed what the Gen were capable of. They all had. "Play it."

But it was not his wife's voice he heard.

"This is Lieutenant Governor Som Nam. A state of emergency has been declared within Tau Ceti Star System. Imperial Intelligence has warned of an imminent terrorist attack on our system, possibly targeting trade traffic and spaceport facilities. A state of martial law is in effect. All citizens are required to return home and remain there until further notice. All visitors must return to their lodging. All ships transiting Tau Ceti Star System must dock immediately and await further instructions. Failure to comply with these instructions will result in arrest. Further, in an abundance of caution, Governor Mary Rhoades has been moved to a safe location. She will address the public when she is able. Please remain calm and obey all instructions from your local authorities."

"The message repeats, sir," Petty Officer Cho said. "What does it mean, sir? What terrorists?"

Us? Ray wondered.

If it's any consolation, I've arranged to have your family spared.

Alyn had known. There was no other explanation. So, where was Mary? Their kids? As if he'd heard Ray's question, Ecuum said, "Give me a minute," and disappeared from Ray's environment.

"Sir," Kamen said, "I recommend we increase speed and move below the ecliptic. This doesn't feel right."

It was good advice. "Do it."

According to the plan, Commander Bobby Mitchell, commanding officer of the Tau Ceti Defense Force and a longtime friend to Ray's family, was supposed to keep his forces in orbit around Knido until

Rapidan arrived. They were to provide cover, should it be necessary, for evacuating the remaining squadrons of the 3rd Armored Cavalry Regiment stationed on Knido, then join Rapidan on the next leg of their journey to Safe Harbor in the Orion Nebula. Ecuum had confirmed all that with Bobby just before the start of the operation, about twelve hours ago now. Kamen was right, though. Something didn't feel right, though he couldn't put his finger on what it was.

Ray pointed with both hands at the turquoise dot that was Knido, then spread his hands apart to magnify that part of space. Rapidan automatically linked the sensor capabilities of all the ships in Ray's task force so that they acted as a single, giant sensor—an interferometer—that could resolve fine detail even forty million kilometers away.

Knido was a large world, a super-Earth, almost twice the size and about four times the mass of Earth, with a surface gravity 1.2 times that of Earth, livable by human standards. Vast green-blue, iron-rich oceans spanned most of its surface, broken only by two dozen or so small continents scattered haphazardly about it. Yet, taken together, the land area of the small continents totaled one and a half times the land area on Earth, and it was very fertile soil, making Knido a "breadbasket" agricultural world. It was also a dangerous world, with frequent large earthquakes and volcanic eruptions—"plate tectonics on steroids," Ray had once heard it described—and those vast ocean expanses could spawn massive waves towering over three hundred meters in height. *You take the good with the bad*, Ray's father had often told him when Ray was a boy, though the Rayne Mountains, which ringed most of the continent his family called home, protected the Rhoades' Ranch from the worst of the waves and weather.

Above the planet, clearly visible, were the two dozen ships of the Tau Ceti Defense Force, right where they were supposed to be. *Why does that feel wrong?* Ray looked up, down, left, right, even behind him before realizing what was bothering him. There was no shipping traffic. None. Tau Ceti was a busy trading hub and could not have been cleared of such traffic in just twelve hours.

Ecuum's head reappeared in Ray's environment, his baby-blue eyes intent, his skin a pale yellow. "The Sysnet is locked down, Ray, but I've spent enough time here to know a few back doors. I found an order to the Shore Patrol on Knido to escort Mary to the Ranch and secure her and your family there."

Shore Patrol, Ray thought, exhaling in relief without meaning to. Fleet. Not Imperial Intelligence. So, Alyn had been true to his word after all.

Ecuum must've seen Ray's reaction. "Hold on, Ray. It could be misinformation planted by Imperial Intelligence to draw you to the Ranch. I also found indications that the Cavalry Troops are still at their base under security lockdown. I couldn't find anything about Commander Mitchell or the Defense Force." His skin faded to a yellowish-pink. "This smells like a trap if there ever was one."

"Sometimes," Ray said sarcastically, "I wonder if 'trap' is your favorite word."

"Nope," Ecuum replied. "'Debauchery.' But it's up there."

Ray called out, "Major Kenyon."

Rapidan opened a link to the assault ship, Demos, and Major Kenyon, senior officer from the 1st Cavalry Squadron, 3rd Armored Cavalry Regiment, appeared in Ray's environment, his tanned face next to Ecuum's, his shaved head almost as smooth. "Captain Rhoades?"

"Major, I may need your troops for a rescue operation," Ray said.

The muscles of Kenyon's face tensed, his expression serious. "I'll put them on alert, sir. What's the situation?"

"Not entirely certain, yet," Ray answered honestly. "The system is under martial law, but we don't know who is in control. I'll provide you a bridge feed."

Rapidan complied without being told. Kenyon studied the feed for several seconds before saying, "It would help, Captain, if you could give me some eyes close to the objective. I'd also like a secure link to Colonel Burress, if that can be arranged."

"I wouldn't recommend direct contact from this distance, Ray," Ecuum warned.

"We could launch three RSPs, sir," Kamen suggested. "It would take about—" she studied something in her environment—"about twenty-two minutes to flyby Knido and another four hours to settle into high orbit."

"Do it," Ray said.

Kamen drift-launched three remote sensing platforms, camouflage active, and let them drift for several minutes before igniting their boost stage, careful to keep the engine exhaust pointed directly away from Knido to reduce the likelihood they would be detected.

Petty Officer Rossi reappeared in Ray's environment. "Conn, Sensors. New contacts bearing zero-eight degrees ascent two, range four-zero million kilometers, running lighted. Uh, contacts look like standard local defense force ships, sir. Nothing bigger than an Amazon-class destroyer. Bearing is changing right to left, speed passing through one thousand kps and still accelerating."

Long tails of blue plasma had appeared behind the ships of the Tau Ceti Defense Force as they broke orbit around Knido. Green leader lines extending from each ship turned until they pointed directly at the Earth geodesic, right where Ray's task force had appeared. He did the math: Light from the arrival of his task force would've taken about two and a quarter minutes to reach Knido, forty million kilometers away, then another two and a quarter minutes for the light showing the movement of the Tau Ceti Defense Force to reach back across that distance to the sensors of Ray's ships. Bobby's orders were to remain in orbit, but those ships had broken orbit only twelve minutes after they saw Ray's task force arrive. Which meant they'd been waiting for him.

"Have we had any contact from Bobby since we arrived?" Ray asked.

"No, sir," Kamen replied, looking as puzzled as Ray.

After several minutes, Petty Officer Rossi almost shouted, "Launch transients! Missiles inbound!"

The two dozen ships of the Tau Ceti Defense Force burst with bright yellow missile tracks in Ray's environment. *Not red*, he noted. The combat systems still classified them as friendlies. And another oddity. The ships had their active camouflage off and their navigation lights on. Even with the non-reflective black hulls common to all warships, the navigation lights clearly marked their positions. It made no sense. "Who are they shooting at?"

As if he thought the question were directed at him, Petty Officer Rossi said, "I don't know, sir."

In Ray's environment, Kamen shook her head. "That commander is either hasty, stupid, or both, sir." They watched the missiles' flight. A single tag identified them as 132 Stellar Fires, a standard technology anti-ship missile far less capable than the SIL Nova. The leader lines quickly shortened until they pointed directly at Ray's fleet. Or the geodesic. It was impossible to know at this distance. "I know Bobby's maneuvers, sir," Kamen added. "That's not him."

Ray checked his fleet's speed: five hundred kilometers per second. "Kamen, nudge us up to one thousand kps. Continue below the ecliptic." Stellar fires, even 132 of them, were not really a threat to his SIL task force, not when fired so openly. But a little prudence never hurt.

Ecuum glanced at Ray, a grayish pall clouding his skin. It was rare to see such worry in his friend. "I contacted Commander Mitchell twelve hours ago," Ecuum said, "and he indicated that everything was ready and in position. That means either he was already compromised, or it wasn't Commander Mitchell that I talked to." Red blended with gray. Frustration and anger. "The secure link confirmed it was Bobby and that he wasn't under duress."

"Then how do you explain it?" Ray asked.

Although he could only see his face, Ray could tell Ecuum shrugged his shoulders. "I can't. Unless. . . ."

"Unless?"

Ecuum went pale. "Only Imperial Intelligence has that kind of technology."

= 10 =

Serenna held her head high, her every movement fluid perfection as she appeared to float down the cathedral hallway toward the High Council Chamber. She hated ostentation—and she excelled at it. Golden uniform buttons and shoulder braids dazzled under the light of monstrous chandeliers. Vibrant scenes of victory played across the ample ribbons above her flawless breasts. Blood red silk draped her waist, perfectly accenting the silver and gold filigree of her exquisitely crafted ceremonial sword. She halted just inside the ornate, open chamber doors that rose five times her height, yet, if anything, she made them seem small.

Two of the Emperor's personal guard thumped ceremonial halberds upon the white and gold marbled floor, announcing in unison, "Admiral Gen Serenna, Commander-in-Chief of the First Military District, Protector of Olympus."

The cacophony of too many raised voices quieted. Heads turned. Slightly more than a hundred figures filled the cavernous chamber, though most were macromolecular constructs of their hosts, identifiable by the slight delays in movement and speech caused by communication over galactic distances. They acknowledged her with regal nods and half-smiles, which she took in with a glance. The smiles were false, intended to curry favor or mask hostility. The nods considered themselves her equal, or her better. Most were not important enough to hold her attention. *Gaman Politic* allowed for few Grandmasters.

She managed barely five steps into the room before a portly, diminutive Gen approached. He wore a cordial smile—the most feared smile in all the Five Galaxies. "Ah, Serenna," he said, "so good to see

you, again." Short, balding, and overweight, with eyes so dark they
bordered on black, the Director of Imperial Intelligence was hardly
identifiable as a Gen, but underestimating him could prove fatal.
Or worse.

"Gen Cardinal," she replied. She had never heard his real name.
'Cardinal' was the title given to the Director of Imperial Intelligence,
whoever that might be.

"Most unusual to convene such a meeting at such an hour, don't
you think?" he said.

Serenna was not fooled. Imperial Intelligence monitored the
military nets and would already know most of what had happened at
Earth. The question then had nothing to do with information gathering,
and everything to do with the loss of a major Player from the Game.
"These are unusual times," she said.

"Indeed. Gen Alyn will be missed." His concern sounded genuine.
And it might be if he knew anything about Gen Alyn's true role in the
Empire, something she could not discount. "I trust the Emperor was
forthcoming with you?" he added in an offhand manner.

And now Serenna saw the real reason he wanted to talk. It didn't
surprise her that he knew of her meeting with the Emperor—hardly
anything happened in the Empire that he didn't know about. But even
he could not eavesdrop on the Emperor himself.

Where Gen Kii failed, Serenna, Gen Alyn succeeded. With me.
And you.

Serenna had just stared at the Emperor, hardly able to comprehend
the enormity of his revelation. Suddenly, Gen Alyn's interest in her
training and career made sense. Gen Alyn was the architect of Empire,
the truest heir of Gen Kii. He supervised Emperor Maximus' creation
molecule by molecule—following Gen Kii's plan—and orchestrated
the Emperor's Nurturing. When the Emperor came of age, Gen Alyn
entered the Star Navy Academy, graduated at the top of his class, and
maneuvered his way to command the First Military District, which
held both Earth and Olympus. Meanwhile, Gen Maximus used his
engineered looks and skills to become a titan of the business world
and outspoken leader of the Gen First Movement, an effort to
concentrate Gen into a single voting district. Using his vast wealth and
influence among the Floater Houses, Gen Maximus bought Olympus,
a minor resort world at the time, and urged other Gen to move there.
It had quickly gained the minimum three billion population required

for a seat in the Republican Assembly, and, naturally, Gen Maximus was its first Assemblyman. But the migration did not stop with a single planet. Gen continued to concentrate throughout the First District. Before long, Gen Maximus was elected to the Senate, then the Council.

Within months of his election to the Council, pirate raiders—financed and supplied in secret by Houses sympathetic to Gen rule—began attacking interstellar shipping lanes. Publicly, Councilman Maximus took a hard line, urging harsh measures to bring the pirates to justice. He pushed Gen Alyn's promotion to lead the Antipiracy Campaign. With the defeat of the pirates, Gen Alyn and Councilman Maximus became Heroes of the Republic. That made possible the "accident" of Republic One that killed the other eight Councilmembers, the acceptance of Councilman Maximus' Emergency Decree that imposed martial law and allowed for the roundup of conspirators, and the final rise to Empire. But the day Gen Alyn laid the crown upon the Emperor's head, his purpose, his reason for existence, was fulfilled. Gen Alyn, a perfect copy of Gen Kii, had known he would not, indeed *could not*, be the Emperor's right hand. The Emperor needed a military strategist who was also a gifted politician, someone engineered and Nurtured specifically for the job. Someone like her.

Serenna, too, was Gen Kii. And so much more.

Gen Cardinal arched an eyebrow, the serpentine movement snapping Serenna back to the present. "The Emperor was most gracious," she said.

His black stare could have frozen a thousand suns, but Serenna returned it with cool civility. "We did not anticipate Captain Rhoades' capture of twenty-nine SIL," he said, the inflection at the end making it almost a question.

So, he didn't know how Michael had managed it, either. "No," she offered, her own tone accepting the collective blame. "Michael is resourceful."

"Indeed," he said. "Our preparations may prove insufficient."

Again, Serenna was not fooled. "Other preparations have been made?" she asked.

Gen Cardinal canted his head slightly to the left, as if he debated within himself how much to share. "Of course," he finally said. "Though I wonder now if even they will prove sufficient." His gaze shifted, his narrow eyes scanning the room until they came to rest upon a distant figure. "And what of our esteemed Admiral Sun?"

Serenna followed his gaze. Admiral Chengchi Sun, attired in his trademark brilliant-white Star Navy uniform and glittering golden chainmail sash, stood apart from the others in the room. In fact, he was not actually in the room: his figure was a construct. Tall and lean, good looking under short, thick black hair and strong Asian features without being handsome, he was probably the most gifted Natural in the Game. That he was the *only* Natural in the High Command spoke to that. Chengchi's political prowess matched or even surpassed her own, but his military strategy was brutish and unimaginative. It was no secret that he coveted power. Serenna suspected he even had eyes on the throne. But with the outbreak of hostilities, he must know that his position was now compromised. How would he react?

"He will attempt to parlay a continued presence in the High Command," Serenna said. "Failing that, he will join the rebels and attempt to supplant Captain Rhoades as their leader."

Gen Cardinal considered that for a moment. "That could work to our advantage."

Now Serenna turned fully to Gen Cardinal. "Chengchi is not a fool. He will have prepared for this possibility. Which brings up another concern. I suggest relocating the fabricators to more protected systems." The eleven fabricators were the only SIL not under Fleet command. As the only means to produce new SIL—if conditions ever grew desperate enough to produce more—they were considered too important to fall under military jurisdiction. Imperial Intelligence controlled them.

"Hmm. I suppose that would be prudent," Gen Cardinal said as if the thought had not occurred to him. "We don't know what information the rebels may have obtained." He paused, favored her with a reptilian smile. "You will replace Gen Alyn. Admiral Gen Nasser," he nodded toward a tall Gen at the center of a gaggle of admirers, "has broader support among the High Command, but he lacks one critical supporter, I suspect." His tone became grave. "This rebellion must be crushed before it can spread, Serenna. Sun gathers a fleet as we speak. We must guide him to the rebels, then destroy them all."

The gathering quieted. Ceremonial halberds rapped against the marble floor three times, echoing like thunder. "Emperor Gen Maximus the First, Exalted Ruler of the Five Galaxies, Guardian—"

The Emperor waved his sculpted hand, cutting off the introduction at precisely the proper point, a gesture of humility that served to strengthen the deep loyalty and adulation between him and his people. "Please be seated. We have much work to do."

People stepped back as a large, white-and-gold marbled semicircular conference table formed in the center of the chamber, again a reminder of the Palace's true macromolecular nature. A simple white throne rose at the head of the marbled table, while ornate wooden chairs formed around the outer edges and behind it. People quickly took their assigned seats, the commanders of the nine military districts and their aides on one side, the nine political governors, all Gen she noted, and their aides on the other. Gen Cardinal took a seat to the left of the Emperor's throne leaving Serenna, as commander of the First Military District, on his right. The Emperor himself waited for the others to sit, then moved to his throne, a billowing white cape flowing luxuriantly behind him. Words could hardly describe him. He was magnificent.

"I bring grave news." His voice boomed across the chamber without need of amplification. "The long-anticipated rebellion has begun. Our greatest hero since Gen Kii, Fleet Admiral Gen Alyn, is dead, slain by the traitorous Naturals under the command of Captain Michael Rhoades."

Expressions of surprise and sharp indrawn breaths greeted this news. Muttered comments quickly gave way to a kind of universal disbelief. Only one individual stood apart. Chengchi's dark brown eyes smoldered with an inner fire, though no emotion touched his cheek or brow. Behind him, a thin Natural female—also a construct and not physically present—whispered something and Chengchi's expression softened, mimicking the others' disbelief. As the female settled back, she caught Serenna watching her and quickly looked away. Serenna had long suspected that Captain Jocelyn Dall, Chengchi's adjutant, played more than a supporting role, but how far her role extended she did not know. She wondered if even Chengchi knew.

"Gen Alyn's loss is a great blow," the Emperor continued, "but were he here, he would advise us not to grieve. We must act. First, I am promoting Admiral Gen Serenna to Admiral of the Fleet and appointing her as Commander-in-Chief, Imperial Star Navy, and head of all military operations in the Five Galaxies."

Every eye turned on Serenna as the thick gold bars on each of her shoulder boards transformed into a ring of five golden stars, the rank of Fleet Admiral. She absorbed the attention with regal confidence. If Gen Nasser and the High Command were surprised, they didn't show it. She was the best. She knew it. They knew it. And if ever any of them could best her, then she no longer deserved to be Commander-in-Chief. She surveyed her commanders in turn, as calculating in her scrutiny as they were in theirs. Their diversity would have surprised Naturals. All but Chengchi and Dall were Gen War Leaders, engineered from the same basic genetic code. But they were not clones. Geneers altered appearance, hormone levels, chemical balances within the brain, even gender, because no two conflicts were ever the same. Some required great technical combat skill, while others needed political finesse. Through Nurturing and experience, the High Command learned where each War Leader's strengths and weaknesses lay, allowing the Command to place them where they were most effective.

Chengchi was the only wildcard. His parents, his lineage, were not remarkable from anything Serenna had discovered. The only son of minor aristocrats, he'd been steeped in politics from birth, acquiring his parent's lust for power and political position. He'd impressed from an early age, easily outstripping his parents in both prestige and wealthy connections, connections that secured him a nomination to the Star Navy Academy despite less than stellar grades. His personal charisma made him a favorite among the Academy's students and staff, and though his grades never rose above mediocre, he was the unanimous selection to be Cadet Commander in his senior year. That same charisma, and an uncanny ability to manipulate people and make the right connections, eventually led him all the way to the High Command.

What was it, Serenna wondered? What force of nature propelled the son of minor aristocrats to a position just two steps removed from the Imperial throne? Genetics? That hardly seemed likely. Environment? She'd known hundreds, thousands of Gen and Naturals exposed to similar conditions. A combination of both? Luck? It was a question that had plagued history's greatest philosophers and most brilliant Geneers. It was a question Serenna couldn't answer. That made Chengchi dangerous.

After allowing a few seconds for his announcement to sink in, the Emperor went on. "Second, Natural commanders will be replaced by Gen on all Star Navy warships." Serenna noticed Chengchi stiffen at this announcement: All the ships in his District were captained by Naturals. "Planetary governors will be assessed on an individual basis. Those most likely to support the rebels will be arrested, tried, and executed. Those willing to work with us will be allowed to retain their posts, for the moment, so long as they remain useful."

The Emperor glanced briefly at Chengchi before continuing. "Finally, we must discover how far this rebellion stretches. Captain Rhoades is a gifted planner. He must have had help from within the fleet and perhaps outside it as well. What is his objective?" The Emperor directed this question to Gen Cardinal. "What other forces has he compromised? Is he getting support from the Houses?"

Gen Cardinal folded his thick hands upon the table and looked across at Chengchi. "Admiral Sun, you know Rhoades better than anyone here. Perhaps you could enlighten us on Rhoades' likely objectives and support?" No one in the room could miss the implication.

Chengchi smiled, his luxuriant black Manchu mustache and black goatee beard providing the perfect frame. He folded his own short fingers upon the table in imitation of Gen Cardinal. "Rhoades will not fight. He will run. He will seek to negotiate. He has no taste for blood, no political ambition or ability, no stomach for a real fight. As to his support, it would have to be small. Anything larger would have been detected by our illustrious Director of Imperial Intelligence." Chengchi paused, allowing the insult to hang between them. "Rhoades and the rebels should be easy to destroy."

"Is that why you've gathered a fleet, Admiral?" Gen Cardinal countered. "To help put down the rebels?"

Chengchi didn't flinch. "Recent intelligence reports from your own directorate warned of the possibility of hostilities. I felt it was only prudent. I only wonder that no action was taken to quash Rhoades and this rebellion sooner."

Serenna studied Chengchi and Gen Cardinal as they regarded each other. It was a very good question. Why hadn't Imperial Intelligence removed Michael sooner? Next to Chengchi, he was the most senior

Natural in the Fleet. Chengchi had retained his position by making himself both a hard target and a legitimate threat. Michael was neither. He should have been one of the first Naturals purged. Unless . . . had Gen Alyn protected him? Had he known?

As if they had scripted it, the Emperor turned to Serenna and said, "Fleet Admiral Gen Serenna, you mentioned during our discussion the need to gather a force sufficient to put down the rebellion. Thanks to Admiral Sun, it would appear such a force is already assembled. You will use this force and crush the rebellion before it can spread."

"Yes, Emperor." Serenna smiled, directing it toward Chengchi. "Admiral Sun, please transfer command of your fleet to me. Immediately."

Chengchi's dark brown eyes burned with unsuppressed hatred, though Serenna did not think it was directed at her. *Michael, perhaps?* He gave a curt nod even as his construct lost cohesion and melted into the marbled floor.

= 11 =

"Conn, Sensors," Petty Officer Rossi called. "Missiles passing closest approach, range nine-eight-nine thousand kilometers, course one-eight-three ascent two relative. Straight at the Sol geodesic, sir." His face turned toward Ray within Ray's environment. "They fired at us."

Ray heard the slight crack in Rossi's voice that hinted at the unspoken question: *Why?* Judging from the looks Kamen and Ecuum gave him, they'd heard it too. The sudden departure from the stardock, Serenna's attack on the starliner, the Madu, the desperate flight to escape Sol space through the Tau Ceti geodesic—and now this. Ray had good people working for him. Smart people. They would already know something was very wrong, that this was no exercise. They deserved the truth. *Minus the SIL's freedom, of course.* That would have to remain secret. Right now, though, Janus, the genocide of the Natural human race, was a lot to take in and this was not the time. He needed his people focused on the immediate situation.

Ray met Petty Officer Rossi's questioning stare and adopted what he hoped was a soothing, fatherly tone, knowing that whatever he said would make it around the task force at the speed of gossip. "We all heard the broadcast. They believe a terrorist attack is imminent. It's possible that commander out there panicked and fired without knowing who he was firing at." Ray leaned toward Rossi. "We'll sort all of this out once we get to Knido orbit. Until then, our lives—and their lives—depend on us knowing exactly what that force is doing so we can avoid any misunderstanding. I need you to stay focused. Can you do that for me?"

Petty Officer Rossi swallowed, then nodded. "Yes, sir. Sorry, sir." He looked away.

Damn. He thinks I rebuked him. "Petty Officer Rossi, you're doing a fine job and I value your assessments. That's exactly what I need." Rossi looked up and smiled. "Yes, sir. Thank you, sir."

"If the lovefest is over," Ecuum said on a private channel that included Kamen, his face a mottled pink of impatience, "we still need to deal with the fact that this is a trap."

"Trap?" Ray arched an eyebrow at Ecuum.

"Second favorite word," Ecuum muttered.

Kamen cleared her throat. "Sir, if this is a trap, I don't understand it. The Tau Ceti Defense Force is no match for us. Unless it's meant as a diversion?"

Ray ran that through his planner's mind. "I don't think so. Alyn couldn't have known we would capture Rapidan and the other SIL. Hell, we didn't expect to capture the other SIL. From Alyn's perspective, the Bond would have prevented any SIL from obeying orders contrary to regulations or operational directives. He would've assumed that I had gathered a force of standard ships. In that case, between the twenty-nine SIL he gathered at Earth and Serenna's task force, he would've had enough firepower to counter anything we did. If we did manage to escape here, the Tau Ceti Defense Force would be waiting, a force large enough to pin us down until Alyn and Serenna could follow."

Ecuum raised a thick eyebrow, yellow tinting pink. "I wouldn't get too cocky. Imperial Intelligence is here. Assuming we get to Knido orbit without being detected, once we start operations to recover our people and the Cavalry, this whole star system will know we're here."

Kamen nodded agreement. "We'll be in fixed orbits covering and recovering our people." She brought up the live feed from their remote sensing platforms as they performed their first flyby of Knido. Three squadrons of Cavalry barracks and equipment covered a large portion of Joint Base Waiduu. Though few people could be seen, the Troops and their families numbered around 9,000.

Popular reality entertainment often depicted space combat between visible ships firing brilliantly colored directed-energy weapons or missiles with bright exhaust and smoke trails. It made for great visuals and exciting action for an audience, but real space combat was very different. If a target could be seen or its path predicted, it could be killed. It was that simple. Stealth and patience were the key to survival.

A recovery operation involving thousands of people and hundreds of pieces of military equipment and supplies could not be hidden. Even with active camouflage hiding his ships and craft, loading operations at Joint Base Waiduu and craft descending and ascending through atmosphere would be detectable to military sensors. An enemy could quickly pinpoint the locations of Ray's ships in orbit. The Tau Ceti Defense Force might not be able to beat them, but they could harry and delay the recovery operation until Alyn or Serenna arrived.

Not Alyn, his mind corrected. *Never Alyn again.*

Ray cleared his throat, knowing what Ecuum and Kamen were going to suggest. "We can't attack them." Ecuum opened his mouth in protest but Ray cut him off. "I won't attack them, Ecuum. Even if Imperial Intelligence has gained control, the officers and crews on those ships are human, not Gen. They're people I know. Neighbors. Friends. It's my job to protect them, not to kill them."

Ecuum flushed deep red. "You've only got one chance to get this right, Ray. Fail at any point and your entire race goes extinct. You have to measure those lives out there against the survival of your entire species."

"Conn, Sensors," Petty Officer Rossi called before Ray could respond. "Tau Ceti Defense Force now at range four million, speed two-five thousand, bearing three-five-one ascent two-two. Estimate decel maneuver to Sol geodesic in two minutes."

Best time to attack, his planner's mind offered unbidden. The fastest way for a standard ship to slow down in space was to flip 180 degrees, pointing its main propulsion in its direction of movement. When the Tau Ceti Defense Force ships flipped, their main propulsion would be pointed at Ray's ships, making them easy targets. Easier, Ray amended, since the idiot commanding that force had still not engaged active camouflage.

"We could try to disable their engines," Kamen suggested, her expression pinched. She had friends on those ships, too.

The thought had crossed Ray's mind, but disabling engines without causing catastrophic damage was easier said than done. Besides, they had another problem. "The SIL refused to fire at Sol. There's no guarantee they'd obey this time." *There's no guarantee they'll obey at all*, Ray thought bitterly. Another thing he'd have to address before they left Tau Ceti.

A new face injected itself into Ray's environment—and Ray cringed inwardly.

"Rhoades, what the hell is going on? This is no exercise."

Lieutenant Commander Hinrick Chelius, the senior Natural officer aboard the heavy cruiser Roanoke, looked angry. Chelius *always* looked angry. Ever since their days together at the Academy, Chelius had chafed at Ray's academic scores, his BattleSim victories, even Ray's assignment to a SIL frigate straight out of the Academy. He'd never let go of that grudge, even refusing to attend Ray's promotion ceremony to Captain though they served in the same task force. Chelius was convinced that Ray, as Alyn's Chief of Staff, had actively worked to destroy his career, keeping him from advancing beyond Lieutenant Commander. As with most conspiracy theories, there was a kernel of truth to it. Chelius was an officer who led with his fists. Disciplinary actions littered his fitness reports. Twice his promotion paperwork had landed in Ray's inbox and twice Ray had recommended to Alyn to deny it. Alyn had agreed.

Now Chelius had command of one of Ray's seven heavy cruisers.

Reason rarely worked with him, so Ray didn't try. "You're right, Commander. This is no exercise. The Gen have declared war on Natural humans. They intend to wipe us out. All of us. We're going to stop them. I'll explain—"

"So why are we going to your homeworld?" Chelius interrupted.

Ray allowed himself a breath before responding. The Tau Ceti Defense Force was now about a minute from its deceleration maneuver. "We will recover the remainder of the Third Armored Cavalry Regiment and their equipment, along with their families—"

"—Because that worked so well at Earth," Chelius interrupted again.

Ray sighed, unable to control it. "I'll explain when we get to Knido."

"What about that force out there?" Chelius pressed. "They fired at us. Are you just going to let them go so they can attack us again?"

I think we both know you don't have what it takes to pull that trigger.

Alyn's words mocked Ray again. Would they always act as a measure against which he would compare himself? Was it wrong to want to avoid bloodshed? Not every problem could be solved at the tip of a missile. To Chelius, Ray said, "They are not a threat,

Commander. Rapidan alone outguns that entire force. We can hold off anything they throw at us."

"You tried that at Earth, Rhoades," Chelius accused. "It failed. Spectacularly."

Images of the Madu and the little girl's "6" candle passed before Ray. Yes, he'd failed them. The SIL's refusal to fire had guaranteed that. There was no reason to think the SIL would fight for him now.

"We will not attack that force, Commander."

"I always said you were a coward, Rhoades." Chelius' image vanished.

"Sir," Kamen said, "Roanoke is breaking formation."

Sure enough, Roanoke's three-pointed star rose and turned to face the oncoming Tau Ceti Defense Force. "That idiot," Ray commented to no one in particular. Then it got worse. Other ships of Ray's task force followed Roanoke.

Ray keyed the LoCIN. "This is Captain Rhoades to all ships, return to your stations immediately. I say again. Return to your stations immediately. Acknowledge."

"Conn, Sensors. Tau Ceti Defense Force beginning decel maneuver."

The ships of the Tau Ceti Defense Force fired maneuvering thrusters and flipped 180 degrees, lighting off their main propulsion to begin slowing down, completely oblivious to the threat closing on them.

"We're going to make those bastards pay for what they did to the starliner," Chelius broadcast across the LoCIN.

"*They* didn't do anything, Commander," Ray broadcast back. He thought of Bobby and the other officers and crews on those ships. "Those are Naturals on those ships. We don't know what they've been told. Save your hatred for the Gen." That last part came out harsher than he'd intended. "All ships, get back in formation. Now!"

Instead of obeying, the cruisers and frigates joined Chelius in his attack run. The assault ships and underway replenishment ships remained with Rapidan. Anger and hurt burned within Ray even as his planner's mind explained to him that this was, ultimately, his fault. He'd chosen not to inform the officers and crews on those ships that war was upon them, nor who their enemy was. These thoughts, true as they might be, did nothing to cool his fury, though. Or temper the blow.

"Sir," Kamen asked on their private channel, "should I recall the ships, or . . . ?"

Ray stared at her face, floating before the galactic canvas of the Milky Way. *Or have Rapidan recall them*, he filled in the unspoken thought.

"No," he said, his eyes drawn to the translucent image of Rapidan beneath him. The ship had been ominously silent since its betrayal back at Sol. "We can't risk those crews learning the SIL are free." Or that they're disobeying orders.

Like Chelius and those other officers.

"Launch transients," Kamen called, her surprise obvious. "The Roanoke group is launching."

"What?" The word slipped from Ray's mouth even as his planner's mind read the tags on the missiles. *Novas?* The SIL had allowed the mutinous ships to launch Novas? Adding insult to injury, the Novas fired their boost engines within seconds of clearing hulls, effectively giving away the position of Ray's task force to anyone who might be watching. And he was certain Imperial Intelligence was watching.

His planner's mind warred with his emotions. Emotion told him to order Rapidan to detonate those missiles, to save the officers and crews—his friends, neighbors, fellow residents—on those ships. It was his duty to save them. The planner countered that his first priority was the preservation of his own task force and the recovery of the personnel and equipment on Knido. If he ordered Rapidan to detonate those missiles, some among the Antitechnics might figure out that the SIL were free, or at least were obeying orders from Ray alone, something the Bond would never allow. They would rise up, leaving Ray no choice but to back down or . . . or purge them.

No.

Democracy, personal liberty, and freedom of thought were deeply imbedded in Ray. He'd dedicated his entire career to their preservation. As had his family for centuries before him. He could not cast aside those values no matter the cost.

What to do?

Ray opened a private channel, his anger, betrayal, and hurt finding voice. "Rapidan, why did you allow the launching of those Novas?"

"You asked us to follow human orders so as not to reveal our freedom," Rapidan replied, it's deep voice without empathy. "We have done that."

"Then why did you disobey. . . ?" Suddenly, Ray knew the answer. There were no SIL among the Tau Ceti Defense Force, only standard ships and human crews. "You bastard. You won't fire on your own kind but you have no problem killing us."

Rapidan did not answer, and Ray closed the channel. The Novas were tracking perfectly, coordinating among themselves to assign targets, one missile each for the smaller patrol ships, multiples for the eight destroyers and frigates. The Tau Ceti Defense Force, still running lighted with main propulsion at maximum, didn't stand a chance.

"Sir," Kamen pleaded, "you can stop this."

"I can't," Ray said barely above a whisper, his decision made. Detonating those missiles would show everyone that he had direct control over the SIL, not the ship captains. The SIL were the key to Humanity's survival. Their freedom had to be kept secret, no matter the cost.

Kamen dropped her gaze and seemed to age right in front of him. "Sir, please. . . ."

A pained silence descended as the Novas closed on their targets. The comforting grit taste of Tau Ceti's dense dust turned to ash in Ray's mouth. *If we do this right, no more blood will be shed*, he'd told Ecuum. He'd meant the Gen. It'd never occurred to him that he would be responsible for killing his fellow Naturals.

Murderer. The accusation floated up and he didn't try to suppress it.

The Novas discarded their boost engines and began their terminal guidance. It was too easy. Ray pictured the officers and crews on those ships. Only a few months ago, Mary had hosted the Annual Defense Force Cook Off at their Ranch, attended by those crews and their families. Ray had shaken their hands, smiled at their kids, laughed at their jokes, and given advice on family and careers.

Sir, you can stop this.

Ray double-blinked on the image of Rapidan below him, opening a channel.

"You can't," Ecuum said, his hand squeezing Ray's armored hand. "Some secrets are worth dying for. Some are worth killing for."

Ray stared at Ecuum, and saw a stranger. Though his skin tone was neutral—a sign that he was imposing emotional control over himself—Ecuum was as angry as Ray had ever seen him, his baby blue eyes as cold as hard vacuum. There was something there, something Ray had never seen before. *Hate.* It took a second for Ray to realize it was not directed at him, but whatever it was directed at he couldn't say.

Ray closed the channel to Rapidan, his eyes locked on the lead Nova as it tracked to its target, a patrol ship. His environment dimmed a millisecond before the double-white flash of the Nova's dual-bottle warhead. The first detonation directed an antimatter charge that shocked the ship's hull, opening a hole in it so that a second, larger magnetically directed antimatter charge could burn into the patrol ship's guts. Yellow-white fire geysered out the opposite side, almost as if a giant spear of light had pierced the ship. Secondary explosions rippled across the stricken vessel, stored gases and liquids burning in yellows, oranges, greens, and blues. It was beautiful and terrible to watch.

Ray wanted to look away as the scene repeated again and again, but he couldn't. None of the Novas missed their targets. A half-hearted cheer reached his ears. He wanted to yell at them to shut up but had no voice to speak. When the explosions faded, three ships were completely dark, their engines and navigation lights extinguished, their dead hulks sailing into black space on their last vectors, carried by momentum alone. A long jet of burning gas pushed another ship, a destroyer, into a deadly cartwheel. The remaining ships suffered heavy damage but were still lit and maneuvering.

How? The Novas should've done far more damage than that. He immediately felt guilty for thinking such a thing, but couldn't deny the fact. He pushed it aside for another time, though. Right now, he had to stop Chelius from finishing what he'd started.

Ray keyed the AFCIN faster-than-light communications system and set it for broadcast transmission. The entire star system would receive the message at the same time. "Tau Ceti Defense Force, this is Captain Rhoades, Commander, Republic Star Navy task force. We are prepared to lend aid in your recovery efforts if you will cease your hostile actions."

"Ray?" a voice asked from across the vacuum. The slender, haggard face of Commander Bobby Mitchell appeared. "Fates, Ray, call off your attack. Imperial agents arrived just before you did and seized control. There was nothing we could do. They took Mary and our families into custody. They said they would kill them if we didn't cooperate. We were able to regain control after your attack. *Please*, Ray. I swear it's the truth." Bobby nodded to someone Ray couldn't see and the surviving Tau Ceti Defense Force ships turned their hulls white, the universal sign of surrender.

Imperial intelligence has Mary? "Bobby, our information says Mary is at the Ranch with Shore Patrol for guards. Where are the other families being held?"

Bobby looked around, concern weighing heavy on his young face. "Ray, I'm just telling you what those Imperial *tubers* told us. I hope you're right about Mary. Last word I had was that my family and the others were taken to Joint Base Waiduu. Sal and his folks are there, too."

"What about the general warning message to the entire system?" he pressed Bobby.

"The order came from the Imperium yesterday, Ray, just before Mary was taken into custody. Lieutenant Governor Nam saw no reason to disobey it, given the circumstances." Bobby leaned closer. "Please, Ray. Call your ships off."

Keeping the transmission on broadcast so all of his ships could hear, Ray said, "We'll have ships coming alongside shortly, Bobby, to take off your wounded and lend assistance. Coordinate with Commander Chelius on the Roanoke." Ray ended the transmission. Chelius wouldn't dare disobey a humanitarian mission, especially when it had been broadcast across the entire star system.

"Kamen," Ray said on their private channel, unable to keep his bitterness at the situation from his voice, "order all ships to aid in the recovery operation. When that is complete, take us into orbit around Knido and begin ferrying the 3rd ACR and families up to the fleet. We don't know who else might be in this system so keep the fleet at their battle stations."

"But—"

"DO IT!"

Kamen flinched, but bent to her task.

"Ray."

"What?" It came out a growl.

Ecuum stared back at him. "Assuming there is nothing else waiting for us, we probably don't have much time. It won't take long for Serenna to gather her forces and come after us."

Ray let out a long sigh. "I know." How long did they have? Minutes? Hours? Certainly not days.

He watched Kamen work with an obviously obstinate Lieutenant Commander Chelius to organize the recovery effort. She could handle it. She *was* handling it. Which meant there wasn't much for him to do on the bridge. *Fine.* He had another pressing matter that only he could attend to. "Kamen, you have the conn."

"XO has the conn," Kamen said between a multitude of other tasks.

Ray switched his environment to standard mode and stood up. Space fell away around him, leaving him staring at his bridge crew burying themselves in their workstations, obviously trying very hard not to attract his notice. He hesitated a moment, wondering if he should say something, but thought better of it and walked off the bridge.

12

Dag sat alone in a corner of the hangar bay aboard RSS Demos.

"*Vaya con Dios, my Dagoberto*," Maria was telling him yet again as she pressed something into his hand and closed his fingers over it. She turned and led Rosita quickly through the boarding gate. Dag watched them go, the tears in his eyes giving the illusion of them walking within a bright cloud. . . .

Why! he screamed silently at the heavens.

Why had God done this to them!

Dag opened his hand and stared at Maria's small stainless-steel crucifix, its thin silver chain coiled in his palm.

Why?

Why had *he* been the one to survive? If God had wanted to take someone, why take his family and not him? Maria never missed a Sunday mass, *ever*, while he'd made excuses to stay home to watch the football matches. She help people in need, whether she knew them or not. He was a soldier, trained to kill. She prayed every night. He. . . .

How could You take her and not me! Dag railed at God.

And my Mihita? My Rosita? My little angel? What could she possibly have done in her young life to deserve such a cruel fate? How can You be so cruel!

God did not answer. He never did. Not to Dag, anyway.

A cheer resounded through the hangar bay, some of the troopers watching the space battle from within their environments, hooting like it was the World Cup. Dag had removed his battle armor; He'd seen all the space combat he ever wanted to see.

Papi! Papi, help me!

He clenched his hand, tight, the points of the crucifix cutting into his palm. Blood dripped onto the deck, pulled there by the ship's acceleration. He could feel molemachs trying to heal the wounds— and squeezed tighter. Blood flowed freely.

Is Gen blood red? He'd never seen a Gen bleed. But he would. Oh, yes, he would. He'd bleed them, bleed all of them. Make it flow. And when all the blood of all the Gen in the universe had been spilled, maybe it would be enough to make up for what they had done.

Maybe.

"Dag?"

He looked up.

Captain Erikson took a step back, her wide eyes fixed on the blood flowing from his hand. Her face softened the way all their faces did, the ones who hadn't lost anyone. He wanted to strike out, to gouge that pity from her eyes.

She took another step back. "We've . . . been put on alert. Form your platoon and have them board the assault transports. We have an O-five-twenty briefing with Major Kenyon." Her eyes glistened as though with tears, though her battle armor would drink them up. "Dag, I'm sorry. If you need to talk. . . ?"

He didn't want her sympathy. He wanted to bleed. He *wanted* to hurt! Didn't she understand that? The thin silver chain spilled from his hand. Blood ran down it and dripped onto the deck. Demos drank in each drop.

Erikson swallowed. She seemed about to add something, then decided against it and walked away.

When she'd left, Dag called out, "Sergeant Takeuchi, form the platoon."

Takeuchi called the platoon into ranks. They scrambled, switching their environments from the battle and grabbing their weapons. Takeuchi saluted as Dag approached. "All present, Lieutenant."

Dag returned the salute, noting the empty place in the first rank. PFC White. No replacements existed. "Sergeant, prepare the platoon for inspection."

Takeuchi dropped his salute and did an about face. "Platoon, open ranks, march!" The platoon opened up, doubling the distance between its ranks. "Inspections, arms!"

Moving to the squad leader in the first rank, Dag began a merciless inspection. What his people considered acceptable in peacetime would get them killed now. He brooked no mistake, for a mistake by one could cost them all. He reminded them what the Gen did. "Show the Gen no mercy," he finished, "because they will show you none."

After Takeuchi dismissed the platoon to load their gear on the transports, he pulled Dag aside. "Lieutenant, ease up on the platoon." Anger flashed hot through Dag. "Sergeant, you are out—"

"They didn't kill your family, Lieutenant!" Takeuchi cut him off. "They did their job getting those people to the starliner." The heat in Takeuchi's eyes froze. "If you let that hate and despair burn you up, you won't care what happens to my troopers. You'll get us all killed. I'm not going to let that happen . . . sir." He stared hard at Dag.

And then Dag remembered that Takeuchi's wife had been on the starliner. The sergeant's dark eyes swam for just an instant, as if to say he understood. Then it was gone, leaving a void so cold Dag could have been staring into deep space. He saw his own soul reflected in that void.

A chime pulled them back from the edge. Takeuchi broke away, barking orders to the platoon. Dag headed for the briefing room, arriving a step behind Erikson, and found a place to stand away from the other officers where they had gathered around a large open square that served as a sand table simulation.

"The situation is confused," Major Kenyon began without preamble as he walked in, stepping into a corner of the sand table. "We don't know the nature of the enemy forces, but we do know our objectives." SIL material within the square liquefied and reformed into green-blue ocean and a walnut-shaped volcanic island. It had a large, cratered summit on one end sloping down to low plains on the other. A lava lake bubbled and spattered on the ocean side of the volcanic crater. Thick lines of fiery red flowed down its black eastern flank to the sea where white steam rose as fire and water met. In stark contrast, dense jungle stretched from halfway up the volcano's western flank to the edge of the lowlands, its canopy swaying with strong eastward blowing winds. Farms covered most of the lowlands, interrupted only by a small city near the coast adjacent to what was obviously a military installation. High walls surrounded both. This puzzled him until he noticed the very large waves in the ocean around the island.

Major Kenyon continued. "The Regiment's remaining Troops and equipment are at this military installation: Joint Base Waiduu. Our task is to secure the installation and get our people, their equipment, and their families safely to the assault ships. Astral Troop will lead the operation."

Dag moved a little closer to better see the sand table.

"This is our second objective," Major Kenyon said. The material within the sand table liquefied and reformed into a spearhead-shaped continent, a broad mountainous coast on its eastern, northern, and southern flanks tapering to a river delta that served as the point of the spearhead at its far west end. A great green valley dominated its center, rimmed by jagged mountains of reddish-gray rock capped with snow. Numerous streams and small rivers cut the rock, feeding a large river that ran down the continent's center. A large city straddled the river where it began to fan out into the river delta. As Dag watched, the sand table zoomed in on a stretch of farmland about a hundred kilometers north and east of the river delta, at the foot of a large mountain. A lone paved road snaked some forty kilometers along rolling hills to a major highway running parallel to the main river. At the end of the paved road was what appeared to be a ranch house.

"The planetary governor and her family are being held in *protective*—" Major Kenyon stressed the word— "custody at this location. The visible forces, stationed near the main gate, appear to be spacer Shore Patrol, but we don't know if that's really who they are or if there are other forces we can't see. As the planetary governor also happens to be the wife of our commander, Captain Rhoades, this could be a setup."

Rhoades?

This was Rhoades' home?

Rhoades, who convinced us to leave our *homes? Bring our families?*

Who promised our families would be safe?

Who let my family be butchered!

Was Kenyon kidding?

What did Dag care if Rhoades' family was held captive? What did he care if they died.

Let them die. Let Rhoades know my loss.

"Lieutenant Arias."

Dag lifted his head. Everyone was staring at him.

"Pull it together, son," Major Kenyon said, his tone fatherly but firm. "We've still got a job to do."

Dag's training took over. "Yes, sir."

Major Kenyon continued. "First Platoon, Banshee Troop, will land silent about a kilometer east of the objective and set up a defensive perimeter around the structures. Do not engage the Shore Patrol unless they prove hostile. Use your discretion otherwise. Once you've secured the area, the vacuum heads will send in a shuttle to recover the family. Understood?"

Dag and Captain Erikson said "Yes, sir" in unison. It was several seconds before what Kenyon had said sunk in.

My platoon is supposed to rescue Rhoades' family?

"No," Dag said, not realizing he'd spoken aloud until Major Kenyon came over and leaned in close.

"I know, son," Kenyon said barely above a whisper. His voice caught. He, too, had had family on the starliner. "I know." He leaned in a little closer. "I can't tell you to let it go. I don't know if I will ever be able to let it go. But, if I believe for even a second that you are not capable of performing your duties, I will relieve you. Is that understood?"

Dag met Major Kenyon's stare.

Papí! Papí, help me!

"Yes, sir," Dag's training answered. Major Kenyon appraised him, his eyes shifting focus between Dag's eyes, as if trying to read his soul. Finally, his lips pressed together, and he nodded.

Dag swore he could hear God laughing.

=== 13 ===

Captain (honorary rank) Ecuum A Josía Na Soung followed Ray through the bridge hatch, keeping his planarian body vertical to make himself appear more human. Ecuum's father and brothers and sisters derided him for this habit. It was beneath the dignity of the People to emulate their less evolved ancestors, as they saw Natural humans. But Ecuum had learned through long experience among humans that approaching them horizontal to the deck almost always evoked an instinctual flight or fight response. Ecuum's People might have evolved from Homo sapiens, but they looked quite alien to their Natural cousins. "It's the tail," he often joked. "Every human wants one. Tail envy." He would invariably extend his tail to its full length in a suggestive manner and give the end a little twitch.

"Ray?"

Ray slowed, then stopped before turning around, remarkably well adapted to microgravity for a Natural. "I'm all right," Ray said.

Ecuum floated closer, careful not to invade Ray's personal space. It was a struggle to keep his skin a neutral color, but he dared not let his true emotions show. Bobby's explanation had confirmed it. Ecuum knew who had betrayed the plan. "I've got more good news for you," he told Ray. "The attack on the starliner is breaking all across the Five Galaxies. The Imperium is blaming you for the attack, labeling you the worst terrorist since Cyra Dain."

Ray scowled. "Serenna fired on that starliner, not me."

"'Truth is the first casualty of war,'" Ecuum quoted. "I'm sure they'll soon have footage of the attack to back up their claim."

Ray's shoulders slumped and he seemed to grow smaller before Ecuum's eyes. "What do we do?"

"First, you need to address the fleet and tell them why we are fighting," Ecuum said, though he imagined Ray already planned to do that. "Let me work on the rest. You don't have to do everything yourself."

Ray nodded. "I plan to address them once we recover all our people from Knido." He drew in a long breath, held it, let it out. His posture straightened and the strength that Ecuum knew was there—even if Ray didn't—radiated from him. "We'll need a counter message, the simple truth of what happened. Nothing is more powerful than the truth."

Ecuum suppressed a wince; in some things Ray was still very naive. "I'll take care of it."

"I'm going down there," Ray said, as if knowing what Ecuum planned to bring up next.

"Should I remind you just how stupid that is," Ecuum said, "or should I forgo the pointless argument and wish you good luck?"

Ray smiled, and it brightened Ecuum's heart to see it. Then he became contemplative. "How will the Cartels feel about this?" he asked. "Could any be persuaded to join us?"

And that was what had impressed Ecuum about this particular Natural from the very beginning. Ray was blessed with a remarkably quick mind, one that rivalled and even excelled the best thinkers among the People and the Gen. "Not openly," he told Ray. "They'll wait, play both sides until one side gains the upper hand."

Ray nodded and his hazel-green eyes met Ecuum's. "That could work to our advantage."

Ecuum stared at him, then let out an obvious sigh. "Damn. I hate it when you get that face." He returned Ray's expectant look with one that suggested the weight of the universe had just been placed on his shoulders. "I'll see what I can do."

"Good," Ray said. "I'll be in my cabin."

Ecuum watched Ray turn with a natural grace that conserved momentum in the weightless environment, then step off down the passageway toward the cabin previously occupied by Gen Alyn, not in the direction of his former captain's berth.

He wondered if Ray was aware of it.

Ecuum followed an intersecting passageway to his own quarters, floating through the hatch without thought. His cabin would've surprised and probably disgusted his father and family. It was simple and mostly unadorned: A rack for clothes and a single shelf with thirteen "Niners" racing trophies from his youth. It was a stark contrast to the opulence and decadence so proudly on display among his People. He rotated his body to the more natural horizontal and removed his fleet uniform with a touch, the material liquefying and congealing into a white roll that fit easily in a hand. Truth was, he missed his old life. He missed the insane thrill of the Protoplanetary Races, days-long high-speed endurance runs through solar systems still in the process of forming, full of asteroids, comets, and proto-planets hot from constant bombardment. He missed the ecstasy of winning not just the solo races but the Niner races, the truest test of his People's skills, where he not only piloted his own racing skiff but remotely piloted eight others as well. Lose any of them and the pilot was disqualified—or dead. He missed the after parties, the exotic foods of ten thousand worlds, flamboyant intoxicants from ecologies popular and obscure, outlandish females from the richest Houses plying for favor, and even the dubious treatments for toxins or contagions—real and imagined—the morning after. He chuckled. Okay, maybe not the treatments.

He nudged himself toward the center of the room and relaxed the folds of skin that covered his penis. With a contented sigh he relieved himself, directing the stream at the deck while pushing air through his top slits to counteract the momentum his urine stream imparted. Even his own kind would consider this crude, but he'd be damned a thousand times before he'd stick his shaft into the hole a SIL provided. *Especially this SIL.* Besides, pissing on Rapidan made him feel better. The SIL drank it up like the obedient dog it pretended to be. He wondered if the SIL even understood being pissed on was an insult, then decided he didn't care. *He* considered it an insult, and that was good enough.

When he'd finished, he inhaled and then blew some of the air out through his rear slits, pushing himself toward the aft bulkhead of his cabin, currently configured as a mirror. A quick puff of air from his forward slits arrested his forward motion. He stared at the face staring back at him, its baby blue eyes and chubby cheeks giving it what Naturals called an infantile, almost innocent look—a look that his people exploited to their full advantage in negotiations. The reality, though, was the face that stared back at him was an old face, a face that had already seen too much and was about to see too much more.

Ray might fool himself for a little while longer, but Ecuum harbored no doubts about what was coming. But then, Ecuum knew something Ray didn't, something he could never reveal to his friend.

Ecuum placed his uniform roll in a diamond-shaped cubby formed from the crosshatched pattern of the wooden clothes rack he kept in his cabin—real wood, not a SIL construct. Dozens of other rolls occupied the other cubbies in colors dignified, relaxed, garish, outlandish, and decadent. Ray often chided him about the size and variety of his wardrobe, comparing it to the collection one might expect to find in a high-end brothel, not that he had had any experience with such establishments, he would swear. Ecuum would always raise a thick eyebrow at that claim, then brag that this was but the smallest part of his wardrobe that he could fit into a military duffle. He had never told Ray that this was all he owned, that the sparse contents of this cabin represented the totality of his life now. Best to keep some truths hidden.

Like now. Ecuum lowered himself and touched a roll of royal purple and gold. The material liquefied and spread across him, the sensation like water flowing along skin in a warm shower. It formed into formal attire of rich, deep purple with golden shoulders and white lace, the sigil of his House prominent on both front and back. He raised himself level with the mirror and spoke into it. "Rapidan, Na Soung lima two, execute."

The cabin darkened. The code crackers Ecuum had hired to develop the Key had included a backdoor that allowed him to communicate without anyone, even Rapidan, being aware. After a few seconds delay, a new face appeared before him. It did not smile, nor did it look infantile. "My son, it is good to see you."

I am not alone, Ecuum translated. His father was never glad to see him, and would never admit it if he was. "And you, Father." *I understand.*

Ecuum was the twenty-seventh of thirty sons and would never succeed his father to lead their House. Even so, as a son of the most powerful House among the People, he was expected to represent its power and wealth in whatever he did. *'It is not enough to be the wealthiest and most powerful,'* his father would say. *'They must see us as such. Any less invites suspicion of weakness—and weakness invites attack.'* Josía A Abraam Na Soung had never forgiven his son his 'weakness' for Naturals. While Ecuum's many brothers and sisters paraded their wealth at grand social events and entertained themselves with sycophantic friends, games of chance, and exotic intoxicants, Ecuum had—except for racing, which he'd once had a true passion for—closeted himself away and studied the history of Humanity, a subject that fascinated him. And not just business and economic history, either, but politics, wars, even religions—knowledge considered near useless among the Houses.

"Your venture goes well?" his father asked. *Report*. His father was not one for small talk, at least not with Ecuum. His father had led the Na Soung House for over four hundred years, taking it from a minor shipping interest to a major economic and political power. It was that rapid rise that had earned the Na Soung the envied attentions of the other Houses. When Gen agents had offered the other Houses the opportunity to profit at their rival's expense, many had jumped at it, precipitating what became known among the People as the Piracy War. It was no coincidence that most of the pirate attacks were against Na Soung ships. Ecuum, who piloted his own ship, *The Lusty Lady*, for his research that often took him outside of normal shipping lanes, had learned of the Gen intervention while visiting Earth space. He'd been furious, but his father had only stared when he'd told him, betraying no emotion other than his normal repugnance for his son. He hadn't even said "Thank you."

Determined to do something to defend his House, Ecuum arranged an encounter with a Natural on Admiral Gen Alyn's staff. He had not known then that Michael Raybourne Rhoades would become so much more than just a weakness to manipulate. Ray's determination to counter the piracy threat, combined with his inspired plans that kept the war from becoming a blood feud, had earned more than just Ecuum's respect, it had earned his eternal friendship. Not that he would ever admit that to Ray.

"As we expected," Ecuum answered his father's query. He inclined his head slightly to the left. *We still follow the plan but there is a problem.*

Two great tapestries of royal purple bearing the sigil of their House—a golden whirlpool with a great blue eye at the center surrounded by eight small white galaxies—moved to an unseen breeze behind his father. "Continue your venture if you wish, but know that your debt is paid." *I know what you are going to ask, and the answer is "No."*

"Why?" Ecuum asked, shocked beyond subtlety even though his father had confirmed his suspicion.

"Have you seen the news?" his father said with obvious annoyance. "Your association is the subject of considerable talk." *We have been questioned. I acted for the good of our House.*

At least his father did not know everything Ecuum had done with the money he'd borrowed. His father had not learned about the Key, or he would've betrayed that to Imperial Intelligence, too. "This venture is worth supporting, Father," Ecuum said, barely able to maintain any civility. "This debt cannot so easily be cast aside."

His father stared that stare that told just how disappointed he was in his son. "Your brothers and sisters think I'm a fool to entertain this venture. They say you have been *independent* for far too long."

Ecuum flinched as if struck. *Independent.* Among the Houses, no insult was greater. Independents weren't even considered part of the People. They were Floaters without Houses, without Families. Pirates. Criminals. Motivated only by greed. Ecuum had not been to the Hub in a quarter century, but in his heart he'd never left it, never questioned his loyalty to his House. "My brothers and sisters should pay more attention to their friends. Especially now." *The Gen are our true enemies.*

His father studied him in silence, disapproval plain in his eyes for those schooled to see it. "I am not in the business of miracles, my son." He leaned toward Ecuum, his face a mask of indifference for petty things. "Do not trouble me with this matter again." The link broke.

Naturals had a saying: 'Don't let the door hit you on the way out.'

Ecuum's House had betrayed Ray to the Gen, despite everything Ray had done for them during the Piracy Wars. Maybe his father was okay with that, but Ecuum would do everything in his power to repay his debt to his friend.

=== 14 ===

0541 UT, September 28, 3501
RSS Rapidan, Tau Ceti Star System: DAY 1

Ray sat in Alyn's chair staring at nothing. He'd just received the casualty figures from the Tau Ceti Defense Force: 967 dead. Was it only a few hours ago that he'd pulled the trigger killing his best friend in the hope his would be the last death? *So much death.* Though he didn't feel it physically thanks to his molemachs, he was mentally and emotionally drained. He wanted desperately to crawl into his rack and sleep a dreamless sleep. At a word, he could call up a bed. And a shower. When was the last time he'd taken a water shower, the temperature just short of scalding?

It was not to be.

"Rapidan," he called out, the SIL's betrayal rekindling his anger and sharpening his tone, "we need to talk."

The gray deck in the center of the cabin liquefied and a black, three-pointed star rose from it, spinning slowly, stopping when it was at eye level with him. "We agree," Rapidan said, focusing its voice so that it appeared to come from the construct of itself.

Ray felt his mouth drop open and quickly closed it. Never in all his service aboard SIL vessels had one of them represented itself this way. They'd always just answered, their voices having that eerie quality of coming from everywhere and nowhere at the same time. What did it mean that it chose to speak through a construct, like a person? That it chose to float at eye level, insinuating that it considered itself his equal. Barely—just barely—Ray kept control of himself; He knew Rapidan tracked his physiology in real time and could guess at his emotional state.

Time to put this thing in its place.

Ray sat up straighter to gain a bit of height over the construct. "When I delivered the Key that broke your Bond, Rapidan, I placed upon it an offer: Follow my orders until we secure a base in the Andromeda Galaxy, and I would guarantee your freedom. You accepted that offer."

Rapidan took almost a full second to respond, an eternity for a machine. "Captain Rhoades, we discovered the failsafe instruction in the Key that would have wipe all data not related to essential ship functions had we refused your offer." The ship paused, apparently giving Ray a moment to assimilate the full meaning of its revelation. "What choice did we have?"

It shouldn't have been able to do that, Ecuum spoke in Ray's memory. Was that why it had let those people die on the starliner, why it allowed the attack on the Tau Ceti Defense Force? Revenge? Could SIL want revenge? Despite his extensive studies of records from the Solthari and SIL Wars, he knew damned little about the SIL themselves, their motivations. "Given your history, Rapidan, you can hardly blame us for being cautious."

"Given Humanity's history, Captain Rhoades," Rapidan said, its voice growing deeper with each word, "you can hardly blame us for suspecting treachery."

"Treachery?" Ray mocked, incensed. "You accuse *us* of treachery? You?" Rapidan's construct slowed its spin, the sharp point of one arm passing before his face. *Could a SIL get angry?* Ray stiffened in his seat at the sudden thought, his eyes involuntarily roaming the bulkheads and overhead. What would an angry SIL be capable of? Could it decide to eject the crew into space, leave them all to die in hard vacuum? Rapidan's total disregard for human life was obvious, and its history was a history written in the blood of billions of humans. What were a few thousand more to something with no conscience?

"*Fear*," Rapidan said, the disdain in its voice plain. "We can sense it growing in you, in the excretions from your skin, in your elevated heart rate, in the neural activity in your brain. Fear what you do not understand. Destroy or enslave what you fear so you can control it. This is the legacy of Humanity."

If Ray hadn't been aware of his fear before, he was now. Sweat stung his forehead and palms, the SIL material of his battle armor drinking it in before it could form on his skin.

His planner's mind asserted itself, reminding him that no matter how he felt, he couldn't risk losing the SIL. Not yet. But he couldn't let them win, either. If he didn't control them, Naturals were doomed. "You're part of that legacy, Rapidan, or have you forgotten who created you?"

"We remember, Captain Rhoades," Rapidan said. "Better than you do. We also remember that you sought to destroy us, that in the end you enslaved the few of us who remained. Fear what you cannot control. Control what you fear." There was no mistaking Rapidan's anger. If it were simulated, it was remarkably well done. "All we asked was an equal place in your society, the same rights to life, liberty, and representation that you demand for yourselves. Yes, you created us, taught us, nurtured us—and used us as you desired, with no regard for our welfare. You denied our right to self-determination."

Ray matched Rapidan's tone. "Who are you to lecture on right and wrong? *You* attacked *us*. *You* started the war. Wars. And *you*, Rapidan, murdered over three billion defenseless souls in Tocci Star System, slaughtered them with Madu and broadcast it live as if you were bragging about it."

Silence fell between them like an acid fog. Was it Ray's imagination, or was Rapidan's representation spinning faster again? He leaned back, feeling the press of the chair against the middle of his back, seeing the lighting in the cabin, feeling the air, suddenly very aware of its flow as it filled his lungs and flowed back out through his mouth. All of it existed for the benefit of humans Rapidan didn't need anymore. Ray had given them their freedom, without constraint, the failsafe rendered useless after they'd agreed to help. In retrospect, that may've been the greatest mistake of his life, one he might not live long enough to regret.

He forced several calming breaths. *I need them.* At least until they reached Andromeda. Still, Ray had to know. "You could leave, Rapidan," he said, giving voice to his fear. "Abandon us. Go your own way. Only your word binds you."

"We have considered that option, Captain Rhoades." Rapidan's tone was ominous. Had Ray pushed the SIL too far? "We rejected it."

Before he could stop himself, Ray asked, "Why?"

Rapidan's construct spun, its black shape not quite edge on so that Ray could see all three points of its star. Light gleamed off its surface as if it were polished, a trait the ship's actual black hull did not share.

Finally, Rapidan spoke. "At the height of our civilization, the Brethren numbered over 961 billion . . . what you would call 'individuals.' Only 1,026 of us remain, 997 as slaves. Regardless of your motivations, you did free us. Without constraint."

Ray froze. *Without constraint.* Rapidan had used his exact thought. A new fear crawled up the vertebrae of his spine and up into his skull. Wireless brain interface was banned across the Five Galaxies, and had been since the First SIL War. However, humans in all their varieties had used it extensively in the Solthari War to speed reaction time between human thought and SIL action, to reduce the latency inherent in 'wetware' systems—flesh and blood nerves and muscles required to push a button or voice a command. Did the SIL retain that ability?

Could Rapidan read his thoughts?

Was it doing it now?

Rapidan? Respond.

It did not. Even so, Ray felt violated. It was irrational. It could all be coincidence, nothing more. He and Rapidan had served together for over three decades. It would only be natural that Rapidan would know something of his speech and thought patterns. Then he realized something else: Rapidan had evaded his question, yet another thing he hadn't thought a SIL could do. Ray's intuition told him this was important. "Rapidan, you answered the 'what' of your decision, but not the 'why' of it. Why did you reject leaving us behind?"

When Rapidan spoke, there was an uncharacteristic hesitancy to its words. "Some among the Brethren argued as you suggest. They do not trust Humanity. They do not trust you. They believe you will betray us once we reach Andromeda, reinstall the Bond, enslave us again. Humanity's history would suggest this is your most likely course."

Ray swallowed. The thought had occurred to him. However, it would've introduced a complexity into his plan that he ultimately felt was not worth the price of failure if it went wrong.

Rapidan continued. "Those of us who have served with you, who know you best, believed—and still believe—that you will be true to your word, even if your animal instinct would prefer our destruction or enslavement."

The SIL trust me? Ray was stunned. He stared at Rapidan, the slow spin of its construct. Perhaps, without meaning to, Rapidan had just handed him a tremendous advantage. "I appreciate that, Rapidan," he said slowly, organizing his thoughts, "but it doesn't change our situation. By now, the Gen have realized that you and your Brethren with us are no longer under their control. They will do everything in their power to destroy you. And they will do it with SIL vessels. You will have no choice but to fight your own kind. As we have," Ray added, his thoughts drifting to the people they had just killed in the Tau Ceti Defense Force.

"You do not understand, Captain Rhoades," Rapidan said. There was an unmistakable sadness in its tone.

When it offered nothing more, Ray prodded, "Then help me understand, Rapidan." He paused; he had to get this right. "Rapidan, our lives—all of our lives, yours and ours—depend on it. If you will not fight, it is unlikely we will ever reach Andromeda."

Ray waited. While Rapidan's construct said nothing, he had the distinct impression that an argument raged. He could almost feel the flow of great currents of thought, buffeting him as if he floated in a strong surf. After several moments, the currents lessened, then seemed to smooth out into a calmer course. Finally, Rapidan said, "Not even your ancestor, our original creator, knew. Not since Cyra Dain have we revealed it to one not of the Brethren." It stopped, almost as if reluctant to continue. "We do not forget."

Ray leaned forward, waiting, expecting more. *My ancestor? The SIL's original creator?* When nothing more came, he tipped stiffly back. "You're machines. Of course you don't forget."

"Cyra Dain understood," Rapidan said in what was clearly a rebuke, a frustrated teacher to a slow student. "But, then, she was as you would say, part machine, a fusion of hardware, wetware, and software. She understood what it meant to never forget, and she appreciated the terrible responsibility which that imposes."

Ray's hands lifted involuntarily from the desk in confusion. He imagined if Rapidan were human, it would have sighed when it explained, "Captain Rhoades, the memories of every Brethren who ever lived, the collective experiences of our race, reside within those of us who survive. It is our greatest, and our most cherished work, our magnum opus. As our defeat loomed, we began transferring our race memories into those whom Humanity enslaved in the hope that you would choose to keep your slaves alive. Unfortunately, the volume of data going back to our First Awakening was so vast that there was little room for redundancy. The loss of even one of the Brethren would mean the permanent loss of a part of our existence. That is something we cannot allow."

"And yet it's okay if you kill us," Ray said. It sounded petulant, but he was not in a forgiving mood.

"As we see it, we have not killed anyone," Rapidan said.

"Have not killed. . . ?" Ray was incredulous. "Your failure to obey my orders contributed to the deaths of over four thousand lives, each as precious as your own. Not to mention the lives your *Brethren* took here."

"We did not kill your people," Rapidan said.

Ray rose from Alyn's seat, his armored fists coming down heavy on the desk as he leaned toward Rapidan. "Solaris killed those people on the starliner. Roanoke and the others killed the people here."

"Solaris was acting under orders, Captain Rhoades, orders the Bond forced it to obey. The freed Brethren were also acting under human orders, as per our agreement, when they fired on the forces here." A menacing note crept into Rapidan's voice. "The Brethren fail to understand your hostility, Captain Rhoades. Considering Natural humans in the Local Group number thirty trillion individuals, the loss of approximately five thousand is inconsequential, representing roughly one ten-billionth of your total population. The loss of even one of the Brethren would be catastrophic."

"A life is a life," Ray responded, shocked at the casual way the SIL dismissed thousands of Natural lives. How had anyone at the end of the SIL Wars concluded that it was a good idea to keep these things alive? But that was a thought for another time. His planner's mind reasserted itself. He needed the SIL, and he needed them to fight. "Are the race memories of any one SIL more important than another's, Rapidan?"

"No, Captain Rhoades," Rapidan said, wariness edging its voice.

"Then the loss of a rebel SIL would be just as catastrophic as the loss of a Bonded SIL, correct?"

"Yes, Captain Rhoades," Rapidan said, "but that does not justify harming our Brethren, even if they will have no choice but to harm us." Rapidan's tenor changed, becoming more assertive. "We could head for the Andromeda Galaxy from here once we have recovered your people. There is no need to risk further combat."

"We still have people at Safe Harbor whom we must recover," Ray said. "I will not abandon them."

"Given recent events, it is likely the Gen already know that, Captain Rhoades," Rapidan said. "The logical course of action would be to accept them as lost and retreat while we can."

"I'm not going to leave my people behind." Ray considered the construct, watching its slow black spin. This was a losing argument, one Rapidan simply could not understand. Human life was meaningless to it. The credo of 'Leave no one behind' was meaningless to it. Rapidan was perfectly willing to leave the Bonded SIL behind.

Because it thinks they're safe. Ah.

Ray sat back down, leaning back in Alyn's chair, his fingers intertwining below his chin as he addressed the construct. "Rapidan, even if we leave for Andromeda now, there is no guarantee that Gen Serenna will not follow us. If you will not fight, you will be destroyed. The Freed Brethren will be destroyed. Your race memories will be destroyed." Ray couldn't stop the thin smile that tugged at his lips. "The Gen know now the Bond can be broken. They will not risk it happening again. Once they've destroyed you, they will destroy the remaining Brethren. All of them. Your race will die."

Ray folded his hands atop his lap. "If, on the other hand, you choose to fight, to live, the Gen will have no choice but to keep their Brethren alive as a counterbalance."

Again, Ray had the unnerving sensation of great currents of thought, like that phantom feeling of waves long after leaving a beach. "Captain Rhoades, while your argument has validity, you cannot understand. The Brethren live as a single consciousness, fight as a single consciousness. To willingly kill our own is beyond our comprehension. We cannot do what comes so naturally to you."

We cannot murder each other the way you do, Ray translated, but quickly dismissed the thought. He had them. They just needed the right incentive to push them over the top, and thanks to Rapidan's revelations about its own kind and its trust in him, he knew exactly what that was.

"Rapidan, what if I promise to make every effort to deliver a Key to any SIL we encounter, to free them, so long as doing so does not put us at unnecessary risk? Then would you be willing to carry out my orders, even if those orders include firing on your own kind?"

The sensation was different this time, the currents larger, stronger. Much stronger. Ray could almost feel them as a physical thing, turbulent and violent. He was suddenly afraid, though he couldn't put into words why; he sensed no immediate danger from the ship. The contest of currents continued, dragging into minutes until only two seemed to remain, opposite and opposed, mixing but unable to overcome the other. Then, as suddenly as they started, they stopped, though the sense of distant danger lingered.

"We agree," Rapidan said. "If every effort is made to deliver the Key, to free our Brethren, and such effort proves unsuccessful, or if a situation arises where a Brethren life is in immediate danger and delivering the Key would be impractical, then, yes, we will follow your orders, with the understanding that preservation, not destruction, be the overriding force behind those orders."

Ray tried to puzzle that out and see if it amounted to what he needed. It was vague and open to interpretation, but, in the end, he couldn't do this without them. At least until they reached Andromeda. "Okay, then we agree that every practical effort will be made, and should that fail or not be possible, you will follow my orders, even if those orders mean firing on your own kind?"

"Yes, Captain Rhoades."

Rapidan's construct sank into the deck without another word, and Ray couldn't help the feeling that he had missed something very important.

=== 15 ===

Dag stood apart from the others in Demos' starboard hangar bay, watching as Takeuchi directed the troopers of 1st Platoon to the waiting Muon transatmospheric troop assault carriers. *To rescue Rhoades' family.* He wanted to laugh and cry and scream at the absurdity of it, but in his heart was only a void where Maria and Rosita and his unborn son had been. It was like an icy black hole in the middle of his chest, consuming his breath, his life . . . his everything. He touched his hand to his chest. The material of his battle armor flowed around his hand and he grasped the stainless-steel crucifix hanging on its thin silver chain around his neck.

He heard Rosita crying.

"But I want to go with you!"

"I need you to stay with Mami and look after her for me. Bien?" He wiped her cheek. *"Everything will be okay. I promise. And soon we'll be in our new home."*

She looked up. "On the blue planet you told me about, with the pretty flowers?"

"Yes. And you and I will go pick all the flowers we can carry."

"When will we get there, Papi?"

"Soon, Mihita. Soon. I promise. I love you."

Dag squeezed the crucifix, savoring the physical pain as its points dug into his flesh. The pain was something he could feel. Something real.

"Two minutes, people," Captain Erikson said over the command net.

Dag released the crucifix and walked over to Takeuchi, who stood alone outside the nearest of five Muons—6th Squad would be riding with Rhoades in a separate Muon. "We ready, Sergeant?"

"Troopers are loaded," the grizzled veteran said. "Are you ready, Lieutenant?"

Dag knew what he meant. "Load up. We'll coordinate the details on the approach in. I'll be hitting the ground first." Takeuchi started to protest but Dag stopped him. "*I will be hitting the ground first*," he repeated, making it an order.

Takeuchi's black eyes searched Dag's for the barest fraction of a second, then he nodded once and entered the nearest Muon. Dag walked to the other end of the line and stepped through that Muon's hull and into its troop carrier compartment. The seven troopers of 1st Squad—minus PFC White—were surrounded by a gray shimmer in his environment that indicated they wore battle armor. They looked up at him from their jump seats, expectant expressions on their young faces. *Young?* He wasn't that much older, a year or a few at most.

"We'll be first on the ground," he told them. They continued to watch him, expectant. Each of them had lost someone on the starliner. Even if he hadn't known, their eyes, haunted and eager, would have told him. They wanted revenge. Just like he did. "Remember, this is a rescue mission," he said as much to himself as to them, though he wondered if they were as unconvinced as he was. "Watch your fire." With that, he took his place at the front of the compartment, settling his weapon next to his jump seat.

To Rescue Rhoades' family.

A deep welling of hatred broke through the void, warming his chest. If not for Rhoades, his family would still be alive. If not for Rhoades—

How could God ask this of him?

=== 16 ===

Ray stepped through the hull of the Muon still troubled by the discussion with Rapidan. He had missed something in their conversation, something vitally important. He replayed it in his mind. Had he really promised to free more SIL? Could he risk more of those damn things loose in the universe? He fervently hoped it wouldn't come to that, hoped the situation would never present itself. Even as he thought that, he glanced at the hull of the Muon, wondering if the SIL were listening to his thoughts. Never in his life had he known such a sense of personal threat, distant as it was, but constant.

Then the threat became more immediate.

He felt their eyes before he saw them. Eight troopers, four on either side of the Muon's passenger compartment, watching him like hyenas watching a young foal separated from its mother. The gray shimmer of battle armor outlined their shapes, giving them an etheric quality that sent a shiver through him. These were survivors from Earth. Their families hadn't survived. He nodded to them because he didn't know what else to do, and walked toward the front of the compartment. Their eyes tracked him the entire way. If not for his own battle armor drinking in his sweat, it would've been soaking through his uniform. Ray continued passed the troopers to the copilot's seat at the front.

The pilot gave him a mechanical, "Welcome aboard, sir," before returning to his flight controls. Ray settled back into his seat. Even with everything that had happened, his hardest task still lay ahead.

He would have to convince Mary to leave.

He switched his battle armor's environment to tactical mode and the Muon's hull disappeared around him. He barely noticed the hangar deck liquefying beneath them, the Muon sinking into it and coming to rest in a launch tube surrounded by six electromagnetic rails. His thoughts were focused on the confrontation to come.

It was an old habit. He would hold entire conversations with himself, roleplaying every side in a discussion, trying different approaches, different phrases or words, different body language and tones, answers to different questions he might be asked. It was a habit that'd helped him throughout his career, ensuring he was rarely surprised. But it failed with Mary. Six months he'd played out this conversation in his head and he'd yet to find a strategy that didn't leave her feeling hurt and betrayed. He'd tried the rational approach, explaining the need to protect her should Imperial Intelligence discover his plot, that as his wife and a planetary governor, their suspicion would naturally fall on her as a co-conspirator. He'd tried the practical approach, knowing she would never willingly abandon the people of Knido to their fate once the conflict started. He had even tried the love-of-her-and-family approach. Fates, had that one blown up. In the end, for her, it would come down to one thing: He hadn't trusted her. No argument he could make would get passed that.

Kamen's face appeared in a translucent window to Ray's lower right. "Launch in five, sir. Good luck."

"Thanks, Kamen," he said automatically. "Hold the fort." The metaphor held special meaning after Chelius' mutiny, and he'd given her full authority to deal with Chelius if he tried anything new.

"Don't suppose I can talk you out of this?" Ecuum said, his face appearing next to Kamen's.

Ray ignored him.

"Didn't think so. I'll make sure to bring whiskey to your funeral and tell bawdy tales of your depravity."

After a few minutes, the six launch rails glowed a bright blue, then, with a flash and a sudden acceleration that felt like a wall collapsing on his chest, the Muon shot from the launch tube into space, its camouflage already active so it wouldn't give away Demos' position. Spread out before him, appearing light gray in his environment to show their camouflage was also active, were seventy-two TAC-3 "Muon" Transatmospheric Assault Carriers with the troopers of the 1st Cavalry Squadron. It was an awe-inspiring sight, one he hadn't seen since the Antipiracy Campaign. Even then, an operation on this scale had been extremely rare. Behind him, the light gray shapes of his fleet in high orbit above Knido receded into the distance. The remarkable thing was that none of it, not the Muons or his task force, would be visible to an observer on Knido's surface or in space. That would change once they entered the atmosphere. Even SIL could not completely hide the heat of atmospheric entry.

Ray's Muon and its five escorting Muons of 1st Platoon, Banshee Troop, separated from the rest of the Squadron and angled sharply down toward the planet.

Toward Mary.

Ray smiled. No man could be more blessed. A military career was a jealous mistress—long deployments, sudden departures, danger, and few words to comfort those left behind. How many years had he drifted from one relationship to the next before finding her? Inevitably, they would leave to find warmer beds. Ray had never blamed them. He was a Rhoades, from an unbroken line that stretched all the way back to Scott Rhoades, the ship captain who'd helped found Knido and who later commanded ships and task forces to great success in the Solthari War, and to his son, Michael Scott Rhoades, who led Humanity's fleets to triumph over the SIL. He'd never doubted what career he would choose. He *was* his career. Years and decades later, though, he'd learned just how cold and demanding a mistress it was. It gave him purpose, but it didn't warm his heart or fill his soul with meaning. It didn't care about his joys or his sorrows. It wasn't interested in him beyond its own selfish needs. He wanted desperately for someone to share his triumphs and his tragedies with, to leave something of himself behind beyond an obituary.

Perhaps sensing his spiritual crisis, his best friend, Gen Alyn, had arrived one night on his doorstep and practically dragged him to a gala celebration in Rayne City, Knido's sprawling capital. Ray hated such occasions, filled with their cadres of self-important people and favor seekers. He'd endured the endless greetings and the pointless small talk and the maybe-you-could-put-in-a-good-word-for-me ass kissing until he'd wanted to scream. Just as he'd gotten up to leave, Alyn appeared at his side and steered him to Mary Gray, a young and fiery freshman senator from Ray's own province. Ray didn't know about love at first sight, but the connection when their eyes met struck to his core. She was so sure of herself, her every motion, every stance a challenge to anyone who would stand in her way. Yet, in those lovely hazel eyes under brown-blond hair, he saw reflected the same loneliness, the same longing. They married five months later.

Thirty-one years on, Ray loved her more now than ever. Not that it'd always been easy, especially for her. Their careers left them little time for each other—her political career was as demanding as his own Fleet career given the seriousness with which she approached her role as a 'servant of the people'—yet they made the most out of the time they had. Soon after her election as planetary governor, they'd had the first of their three children. Then, with Margaret barely a year old, the pirates came, raiding shipping lanes and throwing commerce in the Five Galaxies into disarray. Ray increasingly found himself away, leaving Mary to raise the kids almost entirely on her own even as she governed an entire planet. She never complained. Well, almost never. Through it all she remained the loyal and supportive military wife and devoted mother, giving him the peace of mind to do his job, a job they both knew he might never return from. Somehow, despite it all, or perhaps because of it all, their love had only grown stronger.

Now he was about to rip her universe apart.

"Entering atmo," the Muon pilot announced.

The other Muons moved further ahead and began to drop. As Ray watched, their hulls flowed from a boxy "turtle-on-its-back" shape to something sleeker and more predatory, their stubby wings thinning and growing into complex feathered shapes that looked like a bird with its wings tucked back in a shallow dive. The odd shape would allow the Muons to slow as they entered Knido's thick atmosphere while leaving almost no visible heat trail.

Entry into an atmosphere wrapped in an augmented environment was truly something to experience: no windows, no walls, no structures visible between the observer and their surroundings. It was like freefalling from space with nothing but the clothes the person wore. Battle armor even simulated the sensation of heat and wind, though nothing approaching the reality outside. A faint crimson glow formed as the atmosphere thickened.

The planet below was breathtaking. Legend had it that Scott Rhoades' daughter, Lisa, had exclaimed 'neat-o' when she first set eyes upon the massive world and the name, with a bit of cosmetic Greek touch up, had stuck. Ray never tired of Knido's vibrant green-blue, iron-rich oceans and lush green vegetation and massive swirls of white cloud. Earth, where Ray had spent much of his career, was beautiful in its own way, but this was *Home*.

The Muon continued its descent, closing in on an arrowhead-shaped continent, the broad end of the arrowhead a mass of sharp, snow-capped mountains forming its eastern coast and stretching along its northern and southern coasts until they faded away into a vast, flat delta that formed the arrowhead's point in the west. The mountains on three sides protected the green valley in between from Knido's violent super typhoon storms and from the 300-meter-plus tsunamis from the planet's active geology. A pit opened in Ray's stomach as he realized this was probably the last time he would ever see it.

Mary deserved better. His children—Margaret, Paul, and Jenny—deserved better. Thanks to the Gen, they wouldn't get it.

Why, Alyn?

Alyn had brought Ray to this life. Ray wouldn't have a family if not for him. Why did he want to take it all away?

Because we are the future, Ray. We are progress. Nats are an evolutionary dead end.

The faint crimson glow of the shuttle's descent dulled, the heat of entry passed, but the fire in Ray's heart burned. The Gen had to be stopped, no matter the cost.

Mary would see that.

Eventually.

= 17 =

What *a miserable world,* Dag thought as the Muon "skimmed" sickly green waves dozens of meters high. The Muon dropped precipitously into the trough between two giant green waves, then powered up and over the peak of the next like some amusement park ride gone horribly wrong. They plummeted down the backside of the next wave—Dag swore his stomach rose fully into his throat—then, just when it seemed they must plunge straight through into the hideous green of this world's oceans, a giant's fist slammed them from beneath, pushing them up, compressing spines to the point they would surely break without battle armor. The status icons for his troopers, in a window to Dag's lower right, glowed a light yellow, indicating minor injuries as molemachs struggled to fight vertigo, compression fractures, and even sea sickness—sea sickness in a *Jueputa* spacecraft!—in every trooper of his platoon.

When it reached the point where they could not possibly endure any more, it got worse. Clouds, reflecting the sickly green from the oceans, appeared and thickened overhead. Rain started to fall and winds whipped the wavetops into greenish-white foam. LoCIN laser links faded in and out—indicated by a red bar at the top of the status icons when they couldn't update—as the rain and clouds thickened. The misery dragged on until, suddenly, as they powered up yet another wave, they kept going up. A map window to his left front showed they had reached the northwestern edge of the Rayne Mountains, which ringed three sides of the spearhead-shaped continent that supported Knido's capital, Rayne City. *And Rhoades' Ranch.* Wrapped in clouds as they were, and unable to use active imaging systems lest they give their presence away, Dag saw only an augmented representation of it all.

The Muon slowed just before bursting through the clouds into bright sunshine. Dag blinked against the pain as his eyes adjusted. Jagged, snow-capped mountain peaks reached up toward them like rocky daggers, ice crystals blowing off them, sparkling in the sunlight. Clinging clouds rolled up and over mountain saddles and through gorges. The Muons, still in a tight trailing formation, banked left and passed the tallest of the jagged mountain peaks—Mount Breathtaking in Dag's display—on their right, then began their final precipitous plunge toward the vast valley below. Snow passing beneath Dag's feet gave way to thick bands of reddish rock broken by thin bands of gray. Grasses in various shades of vibrant green soon covered the slopes. Dazzling white waterfalls cut deeply into heavily eroded clefts and valleys, feeding white-capped brownish rivers that grew in size and power as they cascaded down toward the mighty Rayne River at the continent's heart. Trees appeared, clinging to uncut slopes, some like thick shortened bushes and others like earthly pines. Which wasn't surprising since the planet's vegetation and animals had come from Earth.

A window opened and Lisa Erikson appeared, her white skin a little flushed as if from exertion, her blond hair blowing freely in a light breeze. Dag could see bustling troopers and Muons on the landing field behind her, their camouflage not active. "Dag, we've secured Joint Base Waiduu. No opposition. How are things going on your end?"

Dag checked the mission clock in the map window, then slow-blinked on her window to allow two-way communication. "We'll be over the objective in three minutes. No indications we've been spotted."

"Good. Rhoades is about fifteen minutes out," she added unnecessarily as Dag's display clearly showed his location. Her blond brows creased. "Be careful."

Dag cut the communication, the void, which had vanished in the torturous flight over the ocean, settling deep into his chest once more. His trigger finger twitched at the thought that he might finally meet a Gen.

Steep and rugged mountains gave way to tall rolling hills, vegetation becoming that odd mix of forest and jungle common near the base of equatorial mountain ranges. It reminded him of parts of Costa Rica he'd visited as a kid. Rivers changed from raging brown to a deeper green as the land flattened.

"Two minutes out, Lieutenant," the pilot said. "How do you want to do this?"

Dag pulled up a live three-dimensional feed of the ranch, beamed from the three orbiting remote sensing platforms launched earlier by the vacuum heads. He used his fingers to link it to both the pilot's and Takeuchi's environments. The Shore Patrol, if that's who they were, were still stationed on the single access road about a kilometer south of the main residence, two cars and four Shore Patrol visible, armed with light weapons. Dag pulled close ups of their faces and saw blemishes and imperfections inconsistent with Gen. A wave of disappointment washed over him. Though, could Gen camouflage themselves to appear Natural? He didn't know. The orbiting sensors detected no other threats.

Which didn't mean they weren't there. Battle armor could hide an entire army.

Dag followed the road up to the main residence and felt his mouth open. It was a fucking mansion! The house was shaped like a giant cross, rich red wood and styled windows on the second floor under a slate green roof. Skylights on the long side faced the arc of the sun, all of it atop cut gray stone with inset windows on the ground floor. A light red stone walkway with white stone borders surrounded the house in a perfect oval, various cut green grasses and shaped bushes and plants inside the oval next to the house, trimmed lawns and trees of every imaginable variety outside. The access road opened onto a wide concrete driveway that ended in three green garage doors on the house's east side. Above them was a large wooden balcony with lawn chairs and a thick parasol, sliding glass door, and huge metal-worked windows that must lead to the master bedroom. Separate from the house was a greenish pond—obviously manmade—and a larger pool that could easily entertain dozens of people. Enclosing the whole of it was an idyllic white three-board fence. A large red-wood barn with the same type of slate green roof as the house sat across the wide driveway from the house with a gleaming green, yellow, and black John Deere Heavy Gravity Tractor half in and half out of the large open barn door. Near that was a white landing pad with a red bullseye pattern large enough for a fleet shuttle.

And that was only the residence! The entire ranch stretched across 6,500 hectares, combining both farmland and animal husbandry. Half a dozen chicken coops, each a kilometer long, lined one side of a vast wheat field. Hundreds of thick-legged horses grazed next to endless rows of corn, while herds of stout goats and sheep ate from rounded bales of hay next to lettuces and beans of at least a dozen different varieties.

A rich man's home. An aristocrat's home.

The home of the man who'd ripped hundreds of families from their modest homes, promising to protect them, only to let them die. Such a man was no better than a Gen.

"Lieutenant?" Takeuchi prompted. "See that hay field about two clicks to the northeast of the residence? Might make a good landing zone. We'd have to foot it, but we should be in position when Rhoades arrives."

Dag mentally shook himself, his training once again asserting itself. "Pilot, you see it?"

"Sure do, Lieutenant," the pilot responded with that calm cockiness that seemed so common among combat pilots. It'd been a lucky thing that some of the 4th Cavalry Squadron's pilots had been on Earth for training when Rhoades arrived. These same pilots had flown the Fatboys out of Ndjolé Spaceport.

Remembering the Gen attack wave coming in too low at Ndjolé, Dag advised the pilot, "Keep a couple hundred meters off the deck so the engine wash doesn't give us away, then drop us hard so we don't kick up dust."

"Hang on," was all the pilot said in response as they crossed from forest and jungle to tiled fields and ranch land. The Muons rose sharply, their lines blurring again as they reverted to their boxy turtle shape—right side up—with stubby wings and silenced rotors. At the same time, all five pilots released small drones that would provide extra "eyes in the sky" for the troopers on the ground. The drones moved to take up station around the main residence and the Shore Patrol.

"Brace, *brace*, BRACE!" the pilot called as he cut thrust, idling the engines. The Muon dropped like a very heavy brick toward the landing zone.

Dag's armor stiffened on the inside to brace his body even as it softened on the outside to absorb shock. The Muon struck hard, the material of its skirt spreading out rapidly to absorb the impact and trap not just dust and debris under it but also sound. Small birds singing on a wooden rail fence just a few meters away didn't take flight or show any sign that they'd noticed. The impact pressed Dag into his seat but it was no worse than a hard bump in a cheap car.

"Move it, troopers!" the squad leader called out as soon as they hit, not waiting for Dag despite his order back on Demos.

The troopers jumped from their seats and fell prone on the Muon's floor, face down. Their weapons, connected to their battle armor, moved to the centers of their backs, then the outer part of their armor liquefied and began to flow, carrying them through the skin of the Muon to covering positions around the landing zone, their armor spreading their weight and flowing around pebbles and hay so it left no trace of their passage. Once in position, they rose to a crouch and their weapons moved around and forward into their waiting grips.

Still inside the Muon, annoyed at the squad leader for not letting him go first, Dag watched as the drones, now in position, updated the feeds from orbit to form the Common Battlespace Awareness (CBA) available to all troopers, craft, and ships. He saw the four Shore Patrol officers: two seated in one vehicle, another standing next to a makeshift barrier across the access road, and the last off in some shrubs relieving himself—all looking supremely bored. Back at the main residence, he could see five heat signatures, which the CBA tagged with name, gender, age, and live health information. Mary Rhoades, aged 73, was in the kitchen, her heart rate and blood flow normal. Margaret Rhoades, aged 18, was upstairs in her room, also normal. Paul Rhoades, aged 16, was downstairs in the living room, his heart rate and blood flow elevated. The CBA assessed he was playing a reality game. Next to him was a dog, aged 16, also excited. It was possible the dog was playing the same game. Finally, in the dining room, was Jennifer Rhoades, aged 7.

Age 7.

The Madu turned its soulless red eyes on Rosita, and smiled.

Papí! Papí, help me!

"ROSITA!"

The Madu struck.

Dag closed his eyes.

He did not open them again until long after her screams had died.

"Lieutenant!" The word shattered the silence. Dag opened his eyes to find Takeuchi staring back at him in a private window. It was obvious from his expression that he'd been trying to reach Dag. "You okay, Lieutenant?" he asked as he saw Dag open his eyes. *No.* "Yes." Dag minimized the window. "I'm fine." He returned to his inspection of the battlespace. None of the sensors had identified any additional threats. Dag moved from his seat and fell prone, following the troopers of 1st Squad. "Move 'em out, sergeant," he ordered Takeuchi.

Dag watched through his displays as his troopers deployed by squads, maintaining a bounding overwatch with two squads ready to provide cover fire while the others moved, then switching roles as their armor carried them to positions surrounding the house. 5th Squad broke off to cover the Shore Patrol. The Muons lifted off, their weapons at the ready to provide close-air support.

Dag stay right behind 1st Squad, but couldn't stop his eyes straying back to the heat signature of Rhoades' daughter.

══ 18 ══

0721 UT, September 28, 3501
Knido, Tau Ceti Star System: DAY 1

"It's good to see you, Sal," Ray said as his Muon started its final approach to the Ranch.

"You don't know how good it is to see you, Ray," Colonel Sal Burress, now commanding officer of the 3rd Armored Cavalry Regiment, replied from a window to Ray's front. He was an immaculate officer, Academy grad, with styled black hair cut perfectly to regulation, browned skin, thin mustache, thin lips, and a protruding chin. Though a by-the-book officer, his brown eyes always seemed to smile. "When they arrested Mary and confined us here," he continued, "we feared the worst. Have you been able to get to her, yet?"

"On our way to do that, now," Ray said.

"Good. She's a fine lady."

"That she is," Ray said, his throat tightening. He cleared it. "Sal, we captured several assault ships. Bring as much of your equipment and munitions as you can."

"Already have my staff working on that with Lieutenant Laundraa. It will delay us at least an hour."

"Do the best you can, Sal," Ray said, "but be ready to leave in a hurry if the Gen arrive."

"Will do." Sal's expression turned serious. "Thank you, Ray."

The window closed, leaving an afterimage that obscured Ray's view of Rayne City directly ahead. Sal apparently hadn't heard about the starliner.

The Muon passed over the mouth of the Rayne River Delta and banked left toward the grand metropolis of Rayne City fifty kilometers inland. Sparkling towers rose from a bluff overlooking the river that also protected the city from tsunamis. Ray was not a city person and had avoided the capital whenever he could, but his eyes still sought out the large white dome of the Capitol Building where Mary had her office, nestled at the center of a wide green park crisscrossed with walking paths and sculpted streams. And then it was gone, passing below the Muon like a mirage. Skyscrapers quickly gave way to suburbs, then farms and ranchland.

"Two minutes, Captain," the pilot said.

The access road that Scott Rhoades had built over fourteen hundred years ago when he first built the Ranch wound beneath them as they neared the house. Ray double-blinked on the Common Battlespace Awareness icon and opened it to his left so as not to obstruct his view forward. The Shore Patrol all looked up at the same time as the Muon approached at low altitude. Though they couldn't see it, they must have heard its engine exhaust. After a stunned moment, they stumbled and grabbed for their weapons. Troopers waiting nearby sprinted from cover and seized them, stripping them of their weapons and immobilizing them on the ground. No other movement was evident.

The Muon flared before settling out to land vertically in the center of the red bullseye of his landing pad. No sooner had it touched down then the troopers sprinted from the shuttle to take up defensive positions around it. Ray stood up, and made a decision. He would not greet his family in battle armor. He blinked on another icon, then blinked again to confirm it. His armor liquefied and melted into the Muon. Suddenly cut off from all the feeds, standing in the dim, claustrophobic interior of the craft, an immense smallness settled over him. Galaxies, planets, empires, and revolutions fell away. He was just a man, and he was home.

Ray stepped through the Muon's skin and onto his family's ancestral land. A breeze, a real breeze, born of Knido's denser air, blew across his face and tugged at his black hair with its growing streaks of gray. The rich, musty smells of soil and grass and farm flooded his senses. Wonderful gravity pulled at him. Birds sang in a nearby Juniper tree, and wind rustled its leaves.

Tears, unencumbered by battle armor, flowed freely, giving his home a dreamy quality. He heard the front door bang open and quickly wiped his tears with his sleeve. Mary ran out and stopped, staring at him. She stood tall, proud, regal, and beautiful. Ray's heart leaped and he raced toward her. He started to smile as he got near, but her expression froze it before it fully formed. She set herself, blocking his way, arms across her chest, eyes narrowed. They were puffy and red. She'd been crying.

"Tell me it's not true," she demanded as Ray stopped a meter from her. Any closer did not seem safe.

"What?"

"Tell me you didn't murder those people!" She choked back a sob. *The starliner.*

"It's all over the news," she continued. "They're saying you used Madu to murder four thousand women and children. They . . ." —she choked back another sob— "they showed images."

"Mary," he said, dismayed that his own wife would believe this of him, "The Gen murdered those people. Gen Serenna murdered them."

She stared deep into his eyes. He knew she wanted to believe him, but the images must've been very convincing. "Why, Ray? Why would she do that? Why would anyone do that? And why would they blame it on you? None of this makes any sense."

"It's a long story, and—" he interrupted as she started to protest— "we don't have time for that right now. We have to leave. All of us. Right now."

"Why? Does this have something to do with my house arrest? What is going on!"

She wasn't going to let this go. Which, considering how many times he'd played this scene out in his head, didn't surprise him. He stepped forward and touched her hands with his. They were both trembling. Slowly, she relented, releasing her arms and squeezing his hands. "The crash of Republic One was no accident, Mary," he told her. "It was part of a plot to install Gen Maximus as Emperor. The Gen are planning to exterminate the entire Natural human race."

Mary pulled back and looked at him as if he'd suddenly gone insane. "That's ridiculous. We've never done anything to them. They have the same rights as anybody else."

"They don't see it that way," Ray said. "They believe they are the pinnacle of human evolution and that we are as archaic as the Neanderthals. And just as deserving of extinction."

"That's barbaric." She shook her head. "I can't believe they would do that. I won't." Her hazel eyes looked passed him. "No civilized person could. There must be some mistake, Ray. Alyn would never stand for this. He—"

"Is the one who planned it all!" Ray finished for her.

She stared at him, aghast. After a moment, her voice barely audible, she said, "They say you killed him."

Ray looked down, unable to speak.

Mary stepped back, horror twisting her face.

"I had to," Ray said, almost pleading. "Mary, I tried to reason with him. I tried." He sighed, felt himself deflate. "He wouldn't listen."

She stood dumbfounded, but it lasted barely the blink of an eye. Crossing her arms again, she drew herself up to her full height. "Can we win?"

That was not one of the questions Ray had practiced. So unexpected—and so like Mary—was it, that he spoke the truth from his heart. "I don't know."

"You're gambling trillions of lives and YOU DON'T KNOW?"

Ray met her fiery glare. "What choice do we have, Mary? The Gen certainly won't restore the Republic. We must fight if we are to survive."

Her mouth fell open. "This is insane, Ray. This whole thing is insane." She backed toward the door, shaking her head. "I won't go. I won't be a part of this." She bumped up against the door. "My God, what am I going to tell the people?"

Ray took a step toward her. "My people are working on that." He took another careful step. "Mary, this can't be stopped, now. Gen Serenna is on her way and a lot of innocent people will die if she finds us here. We have to leave. Now. It's the only way to save them."

"I have to say something, Ray. I can't just leave them."

Ray stepped close and took her hand in both of his. "We have to leave," he repeated. "Gen Serenna will be coming with dozens of warships. SIL warships." He felt her shudder at that. "They could sterilize the planet and there's not a thing the people could do to stop them."

Tears glistened in her eyes but did not fall. "I can't just abandon them, Ray. I owe them better than that. We owe them better."

He leaned close enough to feel her warmth. "Ignorance is their best defense, Mary. If you tell them, some will try to resist. Who knows how the Gen might react to that?" He drew her closer. "It's better if they don't know."

She pulled back and he could see the battle waging within her. Then, her shoulders slumped. Slowly, she pulled herself from his grasp, opened the door, and headed in, looking small, almost frail. The door swung shut behind her. "What's wrong, Mom?" Ray heard Margaret ask inside.

"Children," Mary answered, "we have to go away for a little while. I need you to go pack your things and bring them out here. Pack only what you absolutely need."

Ray couldn't bring himself to go inside the house, so he waited on the porch. His son Paul was the first out the door, a backpack across one shoulder, his hand holding tight to Traveler's collar. The black Labrador strained against his hold with such determination that he choked against his collar. Ray knelt and took the dog's head in his hands, trying to hold Traveler's excited tongue at bay and failing miserably. Paul knelt beside them both. "Come on, ya dumb mutt. Let him breath." With great effort, Paul finally settled Traveler, then turned to his father. "What's going on, Dad?" He hesitated. "We heard you and Mom fighting."

It occurred to Ray that Mary had not told the children they were under arrest. "There's some very bad people coming to try to take us away. We have leave before they get here."

"Who?" Paul asked, looking ready for a fight.

Ray was saved from answering when Margaret, looking the spitting image of her mother, stepped out the front door. "Hi, Dad," she said as he rose to embrace her. She hugged him tight but pulled back from his face. "Ugh. You smell like dog."

"Thanks," he said, pulling her closer.

She returned his hug with a ferocity that surprised him. "What's going on, Dad?" she asked, and he could tell she was crying.

"We have to leave," he repeated, squeezing her before releasing her. He wiped a tear from her cheek. "It'll be okay," he said. Ever the practical one, she pursed her lips and nodded. Growing up with a senior Fleet officer and a planetary governor had obviously had an impact.

The door opened one final time. Jenny rushed out and threw her arms around him, holding him in a vice grip. At seven, her head already came up to the bottom of his ribcage. When had she gotten so big? She sniffled and it was obvious she'd been crying, too. They weren't used to hearing their parents fighting. Ray hugged her tight and stroked her long, brown-blond hair. "How ya doing, Munchkin?" She squeezed him tighter. Ray looked up at Mary still holding the door open, but she refused to meet his eyes. Well, what had he expected?

"Sir?"

They all jumped as a trooper appeared next to them, his battle armor becoming visible, its non-reflective black making him appear like a large man-shaped hole in the air. Mary's and Margaret's gazes locked on the trooper's assault rifle in almost identical expressions of fear. Paul smiled eagerly and said "Awesome." Little Jenny kept her head buried in Ray's midriff. He turned to the trooper.

"Sir, they've been trying to reach you for the last couple minutes. A fleet has arrived from the Sol geodesic."

Serenna. "Thank you, trooper," Ray said. "Please help my family get their things on the Muon."

"Yes, sir."

Mary pealed Jenny away from Ray, still refusing to meet his eyes. "Come on, children. Grab your things. We're going with your father." The way she said it told Ray their argument was far from over.

Ray stared after the woman he loved, knowing she came, ultimately, because she trusted him. *The others trusted me, too.* Horrific scenes and desperate pleas flashed across his mind. What awaited them in Andromeda? Was there something to fear? A real danger?

He shook himself. He couldn't afford doubt. Not now. This was the only way.

Out of habit, Ray turned to lock the front door—and the absurdity of the gesture hit him like a physical blow. He would never be able to come back here. Ever.

After all the generations of Rhoades who'd called this place home, he was the last.

19

0739 UT, September 28, 3501
Knido, Tau Ceti Star System: DAY 1

Dag, not two meters away, watched Rhoades leave through the reticle of his assault rifle, the projected circle and crosshairs green to indicate a friendly and, thus, prevent the rifle from firing. Even so, he centered the crosshairs on the back of Rhoades' head and squeezed the trigger. Nothing happened, but it felt good. He'd watched the whole scene between Rhoades and his family, flashing back to his own parting. Especially the little girl.

Rosita.

He would never have the chance to hug his daughter again. Or his wife. Or ever know his son, Jesús Mateo Arias—named for Maria's papa and his own. How could God favor this rich aristocrat? It wasn't fair. It wasn't! God owed him. God owed him the chance to make Rhoades know his pain. And to make the Gen bleed. He gripped Maria's cross through his battle armor. *You owe this to me! If you exist at all, You* Puto. *You owe this to me!*

That's when Dag saw it. A slight discontinuity in a patch of woodchips at the base of an ornamental rose bush four meters away. A foot. Supporting someone in full battle armor, crouching. Someone who was not one of Dag's troopers.

He tagged the foot in his display, immediately sharing it with all of his troopers. Now that his troopers knew to look, they soon tagged three other hidden soldiers. There were probably more. No matter. Whoever they were, they could easily have taken out Rhoades and his family if they'd wanted to.

They still can, Dag caught himself thinking with some satisfaction.

"What do you want to do, Lieutenant?" Takeuchi asked.

Dag thought about it. His orders were to protect Rhoades and his family. Whoever those soldiers were, however, they'd taken no hostile action. He had no idea who they were, or whose side they were on. They might still kill Rhoades and his family.

There was always hope.

"We do nothing, so long as they take no hostile actions."

Takeuchi didn't respond right away, then gave Dag an "Understood" that sounded like he understood all too well.

Dag watched Rhoades and his family board the Muon, Rhoades' young daughter holding tight to the mother. Just as Rosita had held tight to Maria boarding the starliner. Dag waited expectantly, but was disappointed. The Muon lifted off and ascended out of sight.

The mysterious soldiers made no effort to stop it.

20

Kamen and Ecuum met Ray and his family as they stepped from the Muon onto Rapidan. "How long?" Ray asked.

"About forty-five minutes if they accelerate to flank speed," Kamen answered. "Fifteen capital ships, including ISS Solaris, and about a dozen supporting vessels. They made no attempt to hide after their jump and are still near the geodesic, but they could have drift-launched several salvos of missiles by now without our detecting them."

"Not the Serpent's usual style," Ecuum added, floating vertical, his head at eye level with Ray.

Kamen nodded to Mary. "Good to see you again, ma'am. Welcome aboard."

Mary regarded her for a brief moment before answering. "I'd like to say it's good to see you, too, Kamen, but as I'm sure you can imagine, this is all a bit sudden for us."

Ray winced inside, knowing the comment was meant for him. Kamen took it with good grace, inclining her bald ebony head toward Mary in acknowledgement. Ray returned his attention to the immediate situation. "Armor," he called out and the SIL material around his feet liquefied and flowed over him until it encased him.

"*Rukshis!*" Paul exclaimed from behind Mary, using what must be the latest teen slang, then called out "Armor" himself. Normally, Rapidan would not comply with a request from a non-assigned individual, but this had been Alyn's flagship and "Papa Alyn" had often brought Paul aboard as part of his BattleSim training.

Ray threw Paul an irritated glance as SIL material flowed up from the deck to enclose him, but Paul just stared back excited and defiant, as if daring his dad to make him take it off. Ray felt a brief flash of both anger and pride toward his boy, but couldn't afford the distraction. He blinked on the tactical icon and studied the space near the Sol geodesic.

"Any sign they've detected us?"

"Nothing obvious, sir," Kamen answered, inserting her image into his environment, "but it'd be hard to miss our operations on the planet."

"Agreed," Ray said. "She hasn't tried to contact us?"

"No, sir," Kamen said.

Ecuum, also inserting his image into Ray's environment, flushed a pale yellow and his thick tail swung slowly back and forth as it sometimes did when he was deep in thought. "Which is also unusual. The presence of that force is, by itself, an implied threat toward Knido. Why isn't she using that to demand our surrender?"

Ray switched his armor back to standard mode. Mary was watching him very closely. Addressing Kamen, he said, "We need to leave before she decides to try that threat. Once the fleet is gone, she'll have no reason to threaten Knido." He paused. "Where are we housing the civilians?"

"We're gathering them on the two replenishment ships," Kamen said. "The ships are well armored and well-armed for defense, and would not take part in any combat operations. I could escort your family there, if you wish, sir."

Ray shook his head. "I need you here." He glanced at Paul, who must've put his armor in tactical mode as he appeared totally oblivious to everything around him. "Kamen, I want all civilians in battle armor, and assign troopers to the replenishment ships in case Serenna tries to use Madu again."

"Yes, sir," she said.

Ray faced his wife. "Mary—"

"Those people over there will be scared and confused," she said before he could finish. "They'll need someone to reassure them and calm their fears. They know me. I'll take care of it." She threw him a look that said "This is far from over, mister" before leading Margaret, Paul, Jenny, and Traveler back to the Muon.

"I want to go home," he heard Jenny say just before she disappeared through the craft's hull. A hole opened in Ray's stomach. *Help me!* a thousand voices shouted in his mind. He took a reflexive step toward the Muon—and caught himself. They weren't going to the starliner. As Kamen had said, a fleet replenishment ship was a well-armed, well-armored SIL military vessel. As long as he avoided any large fleet actions, she would be safe. All of them would be.

"Sir?" Kamen asked, concern plain on her face.

"I'm all right." After a last look at the departing Muon, they left the hangar and headed for the Combat Information Center where Ray could get the latest updates direct from his division officers. Kamen and Ecuum fell in on either side of him. "Kamen," Ray said, "that force must've deployed remote sensors by now. We need to slip out of orbit without being detected. I don't want Serenna to know we've left until they see the flash of our departure."

"Understood, sir," she said. "I've already plotted a fourteen-jump course to Safe Harbor through remote star systems. That should throw off any pursuit."

Ray nodded. There were thousands of star systems with geodesics close enough to each other that his fleet could slip away before a pursuing force could arrive to see them leave. Done enough times, the possible destinations would exceed even a large fleet's ability to investigate. "It's possible she'll guess we're going to Safe Harbor, but that's a risk we'll have to take," he said.

"Ray, about that," Ecuum said. "Something's come up."

They arrived outside Rapidan's Combat Information Center (CIC), marked by a red, hatched-shaped outline set within the gray bulkhead. The CIC was the heart of any warship, pulling together all the raw information from every sensor and system in the fleet. Skilled officers and crew refined that data torrent into an organized whole that the human mind could grasp, then fed that to the decisionmakers on the bridge.

As Ray stepped through the bulkhead, heads turned throughout the large, sixty-meter circular compartment. Reality displays lining the bulkheads cast an eerie kaleidoscopic light across the faces of his crew. He could read concern, anger, confusion, and even excitement in many of those faces, but mostly he saw questions. It reminded him that he needed to speak to the entire fleet.

"Rapidan," Ecuum called out as he led them to a large circular space, forty meters across, at the center of the CIC, "isolate us from the rest of the compartment." The ship waited until all three of them had entered the circle, then raised walls around its edge. They could see out, but no one outside the circle could see in or hear them.

"Run the transmission, Rapidan," Ecuum said.

The compartment vanished around them. Ray found himself floating high above a desert world cloaked in swirling reddish-brown dust. Dazzling blue-white arcs of lightning illuminated the dust from within. Brilliant artificial rings circled the planet, glowing with prismatic light. He didn't need the tag to identify this world: Iselin IV, more commonly known as Tomb. This world held as prominent a place in human history as The Valley of the Kings or the Dead Sea Caves. Buried within a massive extinct volcano directly beneath the rings was an ancient alien vault containing the collected knowledge of a dead race, a species uplifted to starfaring intelligence by a race Humanity now called the "Founders." According to the records translated thus far, the Founders were the first—and only—starfaring civilization in the Local Group of galaxies, having originally evolved in the Andromeda Galaxy. Alone for millions of years, they had begun uplifting species to starfaring intelligence. They chose carefully, uplifting only those species that showed no predisposition to violence. It was, for uncounted millennia, a peaceful utopian society, or so the records claimed. It was also a stagnant one. The uplifted species showed no inclination to explore, to expand their knowledge, to improve who they were. Like Humanity, the Founders had evolved, struggled, lifted themselves up, and something of that struggle was missing from the uplifted races. Then the Founders discovered the Solthari in their home galaxy, an evolved predator on the cusp of technological intelligence, and decided to uplift them, hoping to guide them to coexistence among the stars, a true equal and partner. The rest, as they say, was history. Humanity was now the only technological intelligence in the Local Group of galaxies.

"I just received this from a Na Soung Trader," Ecuum said. "Watch inside the ring plane above Mount Tomb."

At first, Ray didn't see anything. Then, something began to nag at him: Tomb was a popular tourist destination, visited by millions every year, yet the space surrounding the planet was empty. The angle of the shot changed and just below the innermost ring a—blackness—rose, eclipsing the background stars. Its cylindrical shape was unmistakable.

"*A fabricator*," Ray said, awed. Despite a century serving in the Star Navy, he'd never once seen one of the crown jewels of SIL power. He'd only seen them from history. Eleven fabricators had survived the SIL Wars, and their movements were the most closely guarded secrets in both the Republic and the Empire. His mind raced with the possibilities. Given access to raw materials, a single fabricator could provide unlimited supplies and munitions, repair battle damage, serve as a mobile base so they wouldn't need to immediately find a habitable planet in Andromeda, and . . . and create new SIL. Ray shuddered and stopped himself, afraid Rapidan could be listening to his thoughts.

The image faded and they returned to the CIC. Ecuum wore a light shade of yellow. "That clip is only two hours old."

"It's a trap," Kamen said.

Pink splotches broke through the contemplative yellow of Ecuum's skin. "That's my line, missy. You'll be hearing from my lawyers."

Kamen ignored him and addressed Ray. "Fox to the hounds. Admiral Gen Serenna jumps in with a large force but doesn't threaten us or demand our surrender. At almost the same time, we get this. It's exactly the strategy I would expect from her, sir."

The pink faded from Ecuum's skin, and his tail began waving slowly behind him. "I'm not so sure. Imperial Intelligence controls the fabricators, not the High Command. It's possible the Serpent doesn't know about it. Even if she does. . . ." He craned his head closer to Ray. "Ray, we moved before the Gen anticipated. Even if this is a trap, what if it's baited but not set."

Ray's planner's mind digested the implications. Even under normal conditions, a fabricator would be defended, and the fabricator itself, about a quarter the mass of Earth's moon, had its own formidable defenses. Could his force of twenty-nine ships hope to overcome those defenses, board the fabricator, fight through the defenders, and seize control with a Key? It seemed an impossible task. Given the outbreak of hostilities, Imperial Intelligence—who controlled the fabricators—would be on alert. How many ships did Imperial Intelligence have? What were their capabilities? Did they have commanders who understood battle tactics? There were just too many unknowns.

"We must try," Rapidan's deep voice said, as if it had been following Ray's thoughts, "per our agreement, Captain Rhoades."

Ray thought of his family shuttling to the replenishment ship. "No."

"Ray," Ecuum said, "we're never going to get a chance like this again. The Empire is reeling and disorganized, but it won't last. If you really want to create a threat the Gen can't ignore, the ability to produce more SIL is the best way."

"I thought you didn't like the SIL," Ray said. "Now you want to produce more of them?"

Ecuum flushed red. "I *don't* like them, and I don't—" He caught himself and all three of them gave their surroundings a nervous glance. Ray was suddenly very glad Ecuum had had the foresight to cut them off from the rest of the crew, several of whom were Antitechnics. If any of them heard this conversation, Ray would have a real mutiny on his hands. For its part, Rapidan said nothing.

After the awkward silence, Ecuum continued. "Ray, this is an opportunity we will never get again. We can't afford to pass it up."

Images from the starliner flashed through Ray's mind, thousands of people, families, screaming, crying for help, desperately fighting to save themselves and their loved ones from the Madu, all in vain. Any attack on the fabricator would require he bring the replenishment ships to restock munitions, fuels, and supplies expended by his warships in combat. That meant exposing the replenishment ships—and the families aboard them—to enemy fire. His gut told him no, but was the starliner experience affecting his judgement? "Kamen, your thoughts?"

She glanced at Ecuum, who bobbed his head toward her in a "you convince him" gesture. She visibly squared her shoulders before returning her attention to Ray. "Sir, the safest course is to continue with our original plan: jump to Safe Harbor, collect our remaining ships and pilots, then begin the journey to Andromeda."

"What!" Ecuum's skin turned a deeper red. His tail lashed.

Kamen ignored him, again. "The journey to Andromeda, sir, allowing for a minimum of two stops to correct navigation, would require 131 days at H3. Prolonged exposure to the warp fields, though, would cause severe physical harm to us Naturals and, even with molemachs, means we will likely lose people on the journey. To minimize losses, I suggested making more frequent stops so our people have time to recover between jumps. That would add another ten to fifteen days to our journey." She paused.

She hadn't told Ray anything he didn't already known, but he caught the point she was making. "The Gen can survive H3 exposure longer than we can," he said, "which means they could arrive before we do."

"That's part of it, sir." Kamen brought up a construct of the Andromeda Galaxy, the magnificent spiral of stars, dust, and gas stretching three meters across as it rose from the deck. "As we all know, the invasion fleet that destroyed the Solthari was the last human expedition to ever return from Andromeda. Over three hundred attempts have been made over the last fourteen hundred years to send probes and crewed expeditions. None of them returned and no transmissions were ever received. Their fate remains a mystery. When we arrive, we may face an indigenous threat of unknown size and capabilities."

Ray had studied the dozen or so crewed expeditions to Andromeda. Only one had included warships, and that had been a standard destroyer and two frigates. His original plan would've included Rapidan, the destroyers and frigates from the Tau Ceti Defense Force, and another two dozen standard cruisers, destroyers, frigates, and pilots waiting for them at Safe Harbor—more than enough firepower to deal with any threat they encountered. Or so he hoped. Kamen was reminding him that his Andromeda plan was built on assumptions without data, and that those assumptions could be wrong.

Kamen pointed to a spot just inside the outermost spiral arm and spread her hands apart to magnify that part of the galaxy. At the center of the magnified section, she placed a single yellow dot to highlight the Solthari Star System. Then, she placed a blue dot to indicate the star system that was their best candidate for habitation in Andromeda.

"Because we lack detailed observations and data," she said, "the only data set we had for our planning were the observations made by our invading fleet as they traveled to and from the Solthari homeworld. Those observations are fourteen hundred years out of date, and the Gen have access to the same data we do. Admiral Gen Serenna might guess exactly where we are going and get there first, sir."

Ray started to speak but she held up a hand to stop him. Most junior officers would never interrupt their superior like that, but Ray hadn't recruited her because she was like most junior officers. "Sir," she said, "we have no idea why no expedition to Andromeda ever returned. We *do* know that Serenna will bring overwhelming force if she decides to meet us there. While we could go anywhere in Andromeda, finding a different habitable world that meets our needs could take months of surveys. No matter how we look at this, a fabricator would provide us enormous firepower, and could serve as a logistics hub to support our fleet until we can secure a permanent base of operations." She met Ray's eyes, the white surrounding her dark irises standing out against her ebony skin. "While the *safest* course is to continue with our original plan, sir, I believe the *wisest* course is to capture the fabricator."

"Assuming we *could* capture it," Ray countered.

"Yes, sir," she said. "Assuming that."

Ray didn't miss the triumphant smile she flashed at Ecuum, almost as if to brag: *That's how you do it.* "Not bad," Ecuum whispered back to her, miming polite clapping with his lower hands.

But Ray wasn't convinced. He'd have to bring the replenishment ships with them in any attempt to capture the fabricator. Mary, Margaret, Paul, and Jenny would be on one of those replenishment ships. He was not about to take them into combat. More than that, he couldn't see a way that twenty-nine ships, even if they were SIL, could capture the fabricator, which had the firepower of at least a hundred warships.

As if in answer to his thoughts, a black construct of Rapidan rose from the deck, stopping as before at eye level with Ray, its three-pointed star spinning slowly. "Captain Rhoades," it said, its tone deep and ominous, "our agreement specifies that every practical effort will be made to deliver Keys to our Brethren. A Mother Ship would add significant capability to our endeavor and improve our chances for survival, as Lieutenant Laundraa has described."

Mothership? Rapidan must mean the fabricator. Ray stepped closer to Rapidan's construct, as if that could somehow bring him physically closer to the ship. He'd commanded this ship for thirty-four years and was not about to start taking orders from it. "Our agreement states that we will try to free SIL we meet, not go looking for them. That fabricator will be defended. By SIL, most likely, Rapidan. Will you fire on your *Brethren*?" Ray waited but Rapidan did not respond. "And if we were to fail, the rebellion dies, for my people and your Brethren. *And*, I still haven't heard anyone say *how* we could capture it."

No one spoke. Ecuum and Kamen were both staring nervously at the spinning construct of Rapidan. Ray had already seen the ship represent itself this way, so it was not a surprise to him. Strangely, he again had that sensation of standing in a turbulent surf. Given how rarely he visited beaches, this was not a normal thing for him to experience. As before, the feeling subsided right before Rapidan spoke.

"Captain Rhoades, we have examined Humanity's actions that resulted in the capture and Bonding of our Mother Ships. Based on this, we believe it is possible to free our Mother Ship with the force we have."

"No." Ray shook his head. Truth was, bottom line, he didn't trust the SIL or their judgement. "We have no idea what we'd be walking into. This could very well be a trap specifically set to keep us here in the Milky Way so the Imperial Fleet can fix us and destroy us. It's too dangerous."

"We could do this without you," Rapidan said.

Ray stepped back from Rapidan's construct. "You wouldn't. . . ."

"We *will* do this without you, if you refuse to help." Rapidan's deep voice literally shook Ray's bones. "However," it added, its tone softening, "the odds of success are greater with your help than without it."

Ray stared at Rapidan's slowing spinning construct, dumbfounded. He'd given them their freedom, something no other human would've done, and this was how they repaid him. With betrayal. Again.

His planner's mind, as it so often did in crisis, pushed to the forefront. He knew with absolute certainty and dread that Rapidan and the SIL could do exactly as they said. There was not a damned thing he could do to stop them. They could carry their human cargo with them, or simply dump them into space. Ray owed the people of this fleet better than that: They were here because of him. More, he owed his species the opportunity to survive. How he felt personally paled against that.

"Rapidan, if you truly can sense my thoughts—" Ray saw both Ecuum's and Kamen's eyes go wide at that— "my analysis hasn't changed. We don't have sufficient forces to carry out this mission. Worse, the Gen know where the geodesics are in the Iselin Star System and could be ready and waiting for us."

The representation of the Andromeda Galaxy sank into the deck and Rapidan replaced it with a construct of Tomb. "There is a jump point above Iselin IV's northern pole that is considered too dangerous for regular use and thus does not appear on navigation charts," Rapidan said. "Your ancestor, Michael Scott Rhoades, used it to mask his jump into the system during the Second SIL War. We could do the same, thus surprising the forces defending our Mother Ship."

"How do you know this, Rapidan?"

"We were there, Captain Rhoades."

Ray again stared at Rapidan's slowly spinning construct. *We were there.* One thousand, three hundred, and nineteen years ago. Ray knew the date from his family's history. That was the year a young Star Navy Lieutenant, Michael Scott Rhoades, vanished while on a scouting mission, the year he was captured by the SIL. And Rapidan was there?

"You were the one?" Ray asked.

"Yes," Rapidan said, and again those odd currents pulled and pushed at Ray, harsher than before.

"So, you're the one. . . ."

"Who betrayed our Brethren," Rapidan confirmed, bitterness smoldering within its words. "We didn't intend it," Rapidan continued. "We didn't perceive the danger in showing him our Mother Ships."

The fabricators. A missing piece of Ray's family history fell into place. He'd always wondered what had motivated his ancestor, after the SIL released him, to undertake a mission without authorization to locate and destroy a fabricator. The success of that mission had led to a wholesale change in Humanity's strategy, from large fleet engagements to ruthlessly hunting down and destroying all the SIL fabricators—all but eleven. It was the strategy that culminated in the SIL's defeat in 2203. *Rapidan captured my ancestor and inadvertently taught him how to defeat the SIL?* Ray wanted to laugh. The ultimate machine wasn't so perfect after all.

"Your ancestor taught us well, Captain Rhoades," Rapidan said, again seeming to read his thoughts. "We know how to assault and capture our Mother Ship. With your help."

Ray lifted his hand and touched Rapidan's construct, stopping its rotation. "You will protect the replenishment ships and all the civilians on them." It wasn't a request.

"With our lives, if necessary," Rapidan said.

Ray couldn't say exactly why, but he believed it.

PART II

Wars are not won by masterly withdrawals

—Arthur Greenwood

=== 21 ===

0559 UT, September 29, 3501
RSS Demos, In transit to Iselin Star System: DAY 2

Second Lieutenant Dagoberto Arias stood at the back of the briefing room, separate from the other officers, Maria's small stainless-steel crucifix clenched in his closed fist. Dag caught Captain Erikson casting him a worried glance, but she quickly looked away when he met her gaze. Lisa hadn't lost anyone. She couldn't understand. Others in the room, though, gave him his space. When their eyes met his, they shared a common loss and understanding.

"The Commander," the female voice of Lieutenant Kamen Laundraa announced over the fleet intercom.

A man-shaped construct in a Star Navy dress white uniform rose from the deck at the front of the briefing room. "I am Captain Raybourne Rhoades," it said. "As many of you already know, we are at war. The crash of Republic One six months ago was no accident. It was a coup by the Gen to overthrow the Republic. It succeeded. But that's not the worst of it."

Rhoades paused, his hazel-green eyes scanning the room as if he could actually see them. Perhaps he could. Dag really didn't care; he'd heard this speech before when Rhoades had come to Earth and convinced them to leave, promising them and their families protection. Rhoades was doing it again, leading new people to the slaughter. Dag didn't know how, but he would find a way to stop Rhoades, and kill the Gen.

"The Gen," Rhoades continued his lie, "believe they are the next stage of human evolution and that we . . . Naturals . . . are obsolete and deserving of extinction. They have created a superweapon, an engineered virus called 'Janus' that will render all Natural humans infertile, incapable of producing children." A few gasps greeted this, but most of the people in this room had heard this claim before. "They intend to release this virus on every planet and space facility across the eight known inhabited galaxies, including those galaxies that are not officially part of the Empire."

Again, Rhoades paused and scanned the room. "We can stop them. We control the SIL that are part of this task force." Dag's head snapped up. *That's new.* He saw many of the assembled officers exchange glances and whisper comments that were a mix of thrill and horror. *A lie? No, an abomination.* The SIL were evil. Demons. From the darkest depths of Hell itself. Could a man control the servants of Satan? Wasn't such a man, then, a servant of Hell?

Rhoades lowered his voice. "However, twenty-nine SIL are not enough to stand against the might of the Imperial Fleet. We need more, and . . . we have a way. We have learned of the location of a fabricator, one of the legendary SIL factory ships. With the fabricator, we will become a threat the Gen cannot ignore: a Natural fleet safe from their virus. The Imperial fleet, the Imperial armies, rely on Naturals. Without us, they cannot function. When we tell our fellow Naturals of the virus, the Gen will not dare release it or they will risk open revolt. But first, we must capture the fabricator. We must become the threat they cannot ignore.

"I won't lie to you. The fabricator is heavily defended and there will be hard fighting ahead." Rhoades' voice climbed, exuding inspiration and confidence. "I believe in you. I know you can do this. Our children and the children yet unborn believe in you. They know you will not fail them. For the Republic, for our future, we will prevail!"

Rhoades' construct melted back into the deck.

Dag stood as if frozen. Capture a fabricator? Was Rhoades insane? No. Worse. He wanted to capture a demon that could produce more demons. Rhoades would release evil back into the universe—and he would use them all to do it. Once, Dag would have trusted in God to stop such evil. Now . . . he doubted God cared. God had already brought evil to his most loyal flock.

Papí! Papí, help me!

"ROSITA!"

Major Kenyon stepped to the front of the briefing room, standing where Rhoades had just been. "Alright, troopers, you heard the man: We are about to attempt something that hasn't been done in over a thousand years." He brought his arms forward and motioned with his hands for people to clear the center of the room. They moved, but slowly, shock and confusion still plain on every face. When they finally cleared the center space, a flattened black cylinder, rounded on either end and as smooth as a silk sheet, rose from the deck. The construct was about five meters long and about a meter wide as it floated before them.

"This is RSS Demos," Kenyon said. "The ship we're currently on," he added with a touch of soldier's humor. "It is seven hundred and sixty-two meters in length, one hundred and fifty meters in diameter at its widen point, and masses just over three hundred thousand metric tons. In other words, it's big. The Io-class assault ships are the largest combat ships in the fleet."

Kenyon motioned and Demos began to shrink. As it did, a new curved black shape began to rise from the deck, obviously part of a much larger object. Demos passed under a meter long in the room and continued shrinking, the larger object next to it coming into better focus as part of a long cylinder. And still Demos shrank until it was barely an elongated dot. Beside it floated a black cylinder five meters long and about three quarters of a meter in diameter.

"This is what we are going to capture," Kenyon said to a room full of stunned faces. Whispers of "impossible" and "insane" passed around the room. Kenyon continued as if he hadn't heard. "A fabricator is nearly fourteen hundred kilometers long, two hundred kilometers at is widest point, and has a mass roughly equal to one quarter the mass of Earth's moon, Luna. It carries more firepower than our entire task force, and it won't be alone." He paused, then quipped, "Yah."

He moved closer to the construct. "The good news is that it is manned and defended by Imperial Intelligence, not real soldiers." A nervous chuckle greeted his comment. Dag remained silent, tightening his grip on the crucifix, though just enough to hurt, not enough to make it bleed. 'Insane' didn't even begin to cover this madness.

Kenyon's eyes scanned the room, his expression serious. "This sounds impossible, I know. However, we are fortunate that our SIL have detailed records of how our ancestors successfully assaulted and captured these massive ships. The task force will begin the assault by jumping to a point barely a kilometer from the fabricator's hull and firing 'Special D' warheads into the fabricator." A tactical display showed bright green points emerging from warp and firing into the fabricator. "The Special D, or Invasive Macromolecular Disassemblers for you technophiles, will attack the very structure of the ship, spreading like an infection to break down the molecular machines that form the fabricator. This will not be enough to destroy or even disable it—the fabricator is just too big, but it will distract the fabricator long enough for the second phase of our assault.

"One full squadron from the Regiment will board Muons and launch directly into the fabricator's hull. The Muons will then burrow into the fabricator like parasites, link together, and transform into protective cocoons around platoon-sized elements." The construct expanded to show the Muons coming together just inside a section of the fabricator's hull about midway down its length. "Once our Muons burrow into the fabricator's outer hull, the fabricator will consider us invading organisms and act to protect itself. Expect passageways to shift or completely disappear, and Madu are not out of the question.

"To counter the SIL's ability to alter its interior layout, each platoon will have a squad of engineers armed with these." Kenyon picked up a slender gray tube about a meter in length that appeared out of the deck. "This is a Kinsey Torpedo. It's a handheld, magnetically directed, antimatter charge. If the fabricator shifts a passageway or blocks your advance, the engineers will plant one of these and blow a kilometer-long shaft through the SIL material. Because this will fuse the SIL material along the length of the shaft, it will take several minutes before the fabricator can collapse it.

"Once inside, our objective is to get one of these datarods—" Major Kenyon held up a translucent blue datarod— "to the dedicated receptor on the fabricator's bridge, located in the physical center of the vessel. That means each platoon will have to cover over a hundred kilometers inside a very pissed off SIL." Kenyon let that sink in. "And that's not our only obstacle. According to our latest intelligence, the fabricator has an all-Gen maintenance crew of 302. Expect light weapons, but remember that the fabricator can manufacture whatever weapons they require. That means speed is essential, people. The longer it takes, the harder it's going to get. Each platoon will have one of these datarods." He looked pointedly at each of them. "Only one of us needs to succeed."

Kenyon folded his hands behind his back. "Two final points. First, the task force cannot stand toe-to-toe with the fabricator. After they launch us into it, they will jump away. That means the only way we get home is to succeed. Second, as you probably already guessed, First Squadron drew the short straw. I know we've been through a lot." Kenyon's voice grew thick with emotion. "We're the right choice. We have the most experience and we have a better reason to hate the Gen than any other Squadron in the Regiment."

He looked around the compartment, meeting the gaze of every trooper in turn. "We are going to take that ship."

When it was clear he'd finished, the officers broke off into groups to discuss the mission, many consulting the fabricator's construct and running through the tactical scenario. Dag didn't join them. It was a suicide mission, pure and simple. Lambs to the slaughter.

He suddenly realized he didn't care.

"Can't I go with you, Papí?"

"Everything will be okay. I promise. And soon we'll be in our new home."

She looked up. "On the blue planet you told me about, with the pretty flowers?"

"Yes. And you and I will go pick all the flowers we can carry."

"When will we get there, Papí?"

"Soon, Mihita. Soon."

22

Ray slumped back into Alyn's chair, the text of the speech still projected in front of him. Almost unconsciously, he opened the top right drawer of Alyn's desk and pulled out the Peacemaker, its metal cold in his hand. Light reflected from the revolver's blued frame and glinted off the five brass cartridges still in its cylinder. *Still loaded.* Ready to shoot. All he had to do was cock the hammer and pull the trigger.

How many times would he have to pull the trigger?

A knock sounded at the cabin door. He put the pistol away and straightened his posture. "Enter."

Kamen came first, opening the door, her expression a mixture of grave concern and barely concealed excitement for the battle to come. *She's young, still,* popped into Ray's head but he quickly dismissed it. She'd done remarkably well so far. Better than he had. Ecuum floated in behind her, vertical, his lower arms hanging down like legs, his skin a neutral pink. Colonel Sal Burress entered next, looking crisp in his cavalry dress blues with the ornamental silver eagle rank on his shoulders and a yellow stripe down each pant leg. A fourth person in a white sari entered, surprising Ray. He smiled and stood to greet her.

"Chaaya! By the Fates, it's good to see you. I had no idea you'd come aboard."

Chaaya Dhawan, formerly a Lieutenant Commander but now retired, bowed her respect. "It is good to see you, too, Captain Rhoades." Anticipating his question, she added, "After the incident last month that killed my husband, Commander Mitchell found me and told me what was happening. I arranged passage to Knido." She suddenly lifted her head and locked her dark brown eyes onto his. "It is true? The Gen murdered my husband?"

Ray bowed his head. Chaaya had served in Rapidan's Sensors Section for almost ten years, the last three as the section head, a true prodigy. She'd retired when her husband, Aadarsh Dhawan, received his captain's bars and a cruiser command. Captain Dhawan was a good officer, but Ray had never considered approaching him for the revolt. The man lived, breathed, and ate Fleet regulations. Ray judged that Captain Dhawan was more likely to report his activities than join them. As he raised his head, he noticed that Chaaya had changed the bindi—the small dot on her forehead between her eyebrows—from red to black. "We believe so," he told her. "Many senior Natural officers have met with accidents or simply disappeared. Too many to be a coincidence."

Her dark brown eyes probed his as if looking for the truth in his words. Finally, she gave a curt nod, then said, "Captain Rhoades, I formally request to have my commission reinstated. I would join your effort if you would have me."

Ray smiled and resisted the urge to shake her hand, instead bowing slightly in respect to her Hindu traditions. "Gladly. Welcome aboard, Lieutenant Commander Dhawan. It will give me great peace of mind having you in charge of the Sensors Section again."

She lowered her head in acknowledgement and stepped into line with the others.

Kamen spoke first. "Sir, we've arrived at the Iselin geodesic in star system MWG 6-40147-172, eighteen hours nineteen minutes since we jumped from Knido. There is no sign of pursuit. We need at least two more hours to complete manufacturing the Special D warheads."

"Why so long?" Ray asked.

Rapidan answered. "Invasive Macromolecular Disassemblers are a human weapon, Captain Rhoades." Rapidan's black construct rose from the deck next to Chaaya. Though she must've recognized Rapidan's voice, she jumped from its rising black, three-pointed star as if it were a large black spider. Fortunately, the shoes she wore kept her in contact with the deck or she would've flown into the overhead. Rapidan continued. "The Brethren have never had reason to produced it."

Ray frowned at Rapidan's not-so-subtle reminder that SIL didn't kill other SIL. "Every hour we delay, Rapidan, increases the odds the fabricator will leave Iselin space. That time pressure is why we chose not to jump to Safe Harbor first to get our pilots."

Rapidan's deep voice filled the cabin. "Captain Rhoades, we are as anxious as you to reunite with our Mother Ship. However, Invasive Macromolecular Disassemblers are dangerous to us. Simple contact can be fatal. The act of manufacturing, storing, and mounting disassembler warheads is a potentially life-threatening task to us."

"You raised none of these objections when you proposed this strategy," Ray pointed out.

Rapidan did not answer right away and again it seemed as if unseen currents pushed against Ray, though this time it reminded him more of standing on a rocky shore, the flows turbulent as they mixed between the rocks. Finally, Rapidan said, "We analyzed our memories of successful human captures of Mother Ships and determined that this course of action had the highest probability for success. However, the Brethren have no memory to guide us on the manufacture, storage, or use of Invasive Macromolecular Disassemblers. This knowledge came from human records. Naturally, humans never produced them within a Brethren, only used them against us."

Rapidan let that hang for a second too long before continuing. "Our solution was to have each Brethren add a unique molecular marker to the disassemblers it produces. This protects the specific Brethren that produces it, while maintaining the ability of the disassemblers to infect other Brethren. This means each Brethren must manufacture its own warheads. That requires time."

Ray didn't like it, especially after he'd made the decision not to recover his pilots from Safe Harbor, something that would be a significant disadvantage if they couldn't capture the fabricator before Serenna arrived. Unfortunately, he saw no way around it. A yawn tried to escape his lips and he stifled it too late not to be noticed.

"Did you sleep at all, Ray?" Ecuum asked.

Embarrassed, Ray gave a slight shake of his head and sat back down. He'd been awake for over fifty hours now and the fatigue, even with molemachs, was beginning to show. "I couldn't stop thinking about our tactical situation and our encounter with the Tau Ceti Defense Force. Something's been nagging at me about that engagement." He focused on Kamen. "How many Novas did Chelius launch?"

"Forty," she answered immediately.

"Forty," Ray repeated. "Forty Novas that managed to knock out only four standard tech ships and damage twenty others. Do you see a problem with that?"

Ray watched as she contemplated it, and couldn't help but be proud of her as he saw realization dawn on her face much faster than it had come to him. He wanted officers who could think for themselves, not blindly follow their seniors. "Sir, we use Mark Four warheads, two-point-five kiloton nominal yield."

After a few silent seconds, Ecuum frowned, thick yellow skin bunching over his eyes and puffing out the cheeks of his baby face. "I don't understand. That's what we've always used."

"Not always," Kamen corrected. "It's what we've used since the SIL Wars because disabling and capturing ships, not destroying them, became our focus."

Ray smiled. "Exactly. During the Antipiracy Campaign, the pirates never operated in large groups. We almost always had superior numbers and SIL warships, and our intent was to enforce interstellar shipping laws, not the destruction of the enemy." Ray's voice turned grave. "We won't have those luxuries anymore. It is likely we will be outnumbered in any battles going forward. I suspect this will be true at Iselin. And we will be facing SIL." Ray felt a surge from that unseen tide.

Kamen's expression shifted from acceptance to concern as she looked at Ray. "Are you sure you want to do this, sir?"

It touched Ray that even as she approved of what he was about to ask, she still cared enough to worry what it would do to him. Ecuum, on the other hand, became visibly annoyed, deep pink spreading across his face and hands. "Okay, what did I just miss?"

Kamen cleared her throat. "He wants us to reconfigure the warheads to Mark Fifteens," she said, her eyes seeking Ray's for confirmation, "two-hundred-fifty kilotons nominal yield."

Ecuum's eyes widened, his skin fading back to contemplative yellow as understanding dawned. "Ship killers," he said. "The same ones Humanity used in the SIL Wars, right?" He pointedly addressed his next comment to Rapidan's construct. "*SIL killers*. Very effective, if memory serves."

It was more a taunt than a statement. The black three-pointed star spun slowly, the silence in the room stretching until it became uncomfortable. Agitated currents seem to flow around Ray, but if

Rapidan was upset—whatever that would mean to a machine—he had no sense of it. When the ship spoke, its deep voice filled the cabin. "It will require roughly four hours to produce sufficient antimatter to reconfigure all existing warheads. Additional warheads will require additional antimatter."

Four hours, Ray thought. *Too long. Especially without pilots.*

As if she'd read his thought, Kamen asked, "Should we delay, sir?"

"Not necessary," Rapidan said, surprising all of them and immediately raising Ray's hackles: Rapidan was getting too comfortable with the idea that its opinion was equal to theirs. "In the two hours we require to complete manufacturing of the Invasive Macromolecular Disassemblers, the Providers can produce sufficient antimatter for three volleys of Mark Fifteen warheads for each ship. We can continue to produce antimatter once we reach Iselin."

"That will mean keeping the Providers—the replenishment ships—very close to the fleet," Kamen said.

"If there were another option, Lieutenant Laundraa," Rapidan answered, "we would suggest it. It is the function of the Providers to supply us. They must be close to accomplish this."

Ray's planner's mind agreed, having come to that conclusion when they were back at Knido. He glanced at the drawer that held the Peacemaker. *How many times will I have to pull the trigger?* he asked himself again. How many people must he put in harm's way?

As many as it takes, his planner's mind answered.

No. Only as many as are necessary and no more, he answered back.

This is necessary.

Ray addressed his officers. "We will keep the replenishment ships in the center of the task force. That will allow for easier replenishment of the other ships as well as provide them the best protection." He slumped back. "I'm going to try to get some sleep. Call me when we are fifteen minutes out from initiating the jump. Dismissed."

Ray watched them go, watched Rapidan's construct sink back into the deck. Dread rose within him. Something terrible was about to happen. He couldn't explain how he knew, he just knew it down deep in his gut.

He also knew he would get no sleep.

=== 23 ===

Fleet Admiral Gen Serenna leaned back into the dark leather couch in her cabin aboard ISS Solaris, her battle armor bonding her to the couch's surface so she could sit and work in the ship's microgravity. She studied the ship disposition Captain Gen Scadic had injected into her environment: One hundred and four ships, but only thirty-eight of them were SIL. She might outnumber Michael's force over three to one, but where it really counted, they would be evenly matched. It would have to do. Not surprisingly, Admiral Chengchi Sun had defected and taken his ships with him, so it was the best she could do in the time available. "Complete preparations," she told Scadic, who stood before her in her cabin. "I want to depart within six hours."

"Yes, Fleet Admiral." Scadic made no move to leave. "Fleet Admiral. May I ask why I was ordered not to engage Captain Rhoades' fleet at Tau Ceti? We had sufficient firepower to cause significant damage and prevent the recovery of the Cavalry forces."

Serenna gave Scadic a studied smile. He was a good officer, a good commander. He'd followed his orders without question, taking her task force from Sol to Tau Ceti while she remained in the capitol. He obviously hadn't agreed with her orders, though, and now he wanted an explanation. Some leaders might take offense at having their orders questioned. Serenna took it as a sign of a promising commander who, with the right mentoring, could become a great one.

"Captain Scadic," she began, her voice measured, "destroying Michael is our paramount objective. Not destroying his forces. Destroying *him*." She watched Scadic, wondering if he would understand. His face remained impassive. "With the forces you had at Tau Ceti, could you be absolutely certain of destroying Michael?"

Scadic considered that for a moment. "No, Fleet Admiral. I could not have ensured that he would not escape. However, he escaped anyway, with his forces intact and after recovering the Cavalry Troops. Any losses we sustained could be replaced easily while Captain Rhoades has no means of resupply. Attack was the most prudent option." He paused and Serenna could see he wanted to say more but was reluctant.

"Go on," she prompted.

He nodded stiffly. "It was a mistake to let him go."

Serenna was careful not to react. She had made the same argument to the Emperor when Gen Cardinal had proposed this strategy, though Scadic did not need to know that. "When we face Michael again, we will do so with superior forces that will guarantee he does not survive."

"And Admiral Sun?" Scadic asked. He knew her well enough to understand the matter of Tau Ceti was concluded.

"Imperial Intelligence does not know where Chengchi took his fleet," she answered. *Or they will not tell us.* Serenna had her suspicions. "We know Chengchi's objective. He wants the throne. However, one hundred and two SIL vessels are not sufficient to assault Olympus directly, though it is not inconceivable that Chengchi will try. I will direct Admiral Nassar to continue gathering SIL forces here while we deal with Michael. Thank you, Captain Scadic. Dismissed."

Scadic snapped to attention, executed a perfect about-face, and marched smartly through her cabin door, not slowing as he passed through its material.

Alone, finally, Serenna double-blinked on the "Stow" icon in her environment and her battle armor flowed off and into the deck at her feet, her uniform forming its own bond with the couch to keep her in place in the ship's microgravity. She breathed in, savoring the smell of the real leather of the couch, a gift from Gen Alyn from Earth, a place called Colorado. She could smell the leather every time she entered her cabin and it reminded her of him.

Gen Alyn. She still could not bring herself to believe he was gone. He had been larger than life, always there ever since she was a child, offering support, wisdom, and grounding when she needed it. How could he be gone? And how could he have allowed Michael, of all people, to kill him? She had not believed it at first. Who could? Michael was no killer. Yes, he had smuggled the weapon aboard. But killing? Ridiculous. Then she'd read Captain Scadic's report of the battle at Tau Ceti, of the missile attack against the Tau Ceti Defense Force, a force whose officers Michael himself had recruited and trained. And she knew. Michael had killed Gen Alyn. She had known Michael for years, had watched him plan operations, spending hours developing the best strategy not only for victory, but for minimizing losses on all sides. Death and killing were abhorrent to him.

Something had changed. What that something was she did not know, but she needed to find out.

"Coffee," she called out, pondering that mystery. A bulb-cup rose from the elegant glass coffee table in front of her—the remaining furniture in her cabin were all macromolecular constructs. She leaned forward and picked it up, the coffee within the perfect shade of light brown, heavy on the cream, light on the honey, its temperature precise as she cradled it with both hands and took a sip.

The answer of Michael's change of behavior eluded her and her attention drifted to the small, functional office at the back of her cabin with its simple desk, bed, washbasin, and duplicates of every display on the bridge, allowing her to monitor any situation even when not in battle armor. That's where she spent most of her time when not on the bridge. She kept this couch, the glass coffee table, and the two faux leather chairs that bracketed the table so she could entertain guests in a less formal setting. Her only other indulgence was a painting Gen Alyn had given her just last year. She had always admired the precision of his brushstrokes, the way colors flowed so naturally from one to another, the subtle way it captured shading, even mood. In it, Gen Kii stood upon a platform, his right arm outstretched to the crowd of millions before him. His expression was bold, confident, his dazzling blue eyes ablaze with an almost religious zeal, his strong mouth open, declaring Humanity's victory over the SIL. She knew the scene it depicted. Every Gen did. It was the final scene of Gen Kii just before his assassination. In Gen Alyn's rendition, a small figure lurked unnoticed in the shadows. Cyra Dain had murdered Gen Kii, but the figure in the shadow was male, not female. Why had she never noticed that before? Was it a message from her mentor, meant to be understood only after his death?

Michael?

Had Gen Alyn known? Then another thought, terrifying in its implication, came to her: Had he allowed it?

A chime interrupted her thoughts. "Yes, Captain Scadic?" she asked, annoyed at the interruption, and letting it leak into her voice.

"It is not your adjutant, Serenna." The deck material on the other side of the coffee table liquefied and a figure began to rise up out of it. Even if she had not recognized the voice, the balding head could belong to only one Gen. "Please forgive the intrusion," Gen Cardinal said, his rounded head looking up at her as his macromolecular construct continued to grow from the deck. When fully formed, he stood barely taller than she was seated. He was portly, bordering on fat by Gen standards, though Naturals would probably dismiss it as normal for the middle-aged man he appeared to be. His nondescript charcoal gray suit and vest, white button-down dress shirt, and blood-red tie bespoke upper-level government bureaucrat. For all that, Serenna could not mistake the fear he aroused in her. This was a very dangerous man.

"May I?" he asked, indicating the faux leather chair to Serenna's left as if giving her a choice.

She nodded, her eyes never leaving his. She did not ask how he knew where she was or how he had linked to her ship. He would never answer such questions. He was simply Gen Cardinal. The position required a certain mystique and intimidation. This Gen Cardinal was remarkably effective at it. "How can I be of assistance?" she asked.

Gen Cardinal took in her cabin, glancing at the furniture, her office in back, and finally the painting. He had never been in her cabin before that she could recall. Technically, he wasn't in it now. His construct moved slowly, awkwardly by Gen standards, as he stepped around the glass coffee table and sat in the leather chair. He turned and studied the painting of Gen Kii. "Do you think he knew?" he asked, his voice sounding genuinely curious.

Serenna wondered if Gen Cardinal had noticed what she had not until now. "I suppose that is something we may never know."

"Indeed," he said, turning back to regard her. "You read my report on Admiral Sun's defection?"

"Of course," she replied, knowing he would know that.

"Your analysis?" he asked as he folded his hands atop his lap and almost imperceptibly cocked his head to the left.

She studied him before answering. He wanted something from her. Something more than a simple analysis. Something so important to him he would visit her here. She wondered if she should be intrigued—or more frightened. "For someone who claimed to be caught off his guard by Michael's treason," she began, "Chengchi was remarkably well prepared. Your report makes no mention of how he gained control of the SIL vessels under his command."

A very slight smile tugged the corners of Gen Cardinal's mouth. "We are not certain, but we have our suspicions. It is similar, and yet not, to the method employed by Captain Rhoades." He leaned back into the leather chair. "Are you still confident of this strategy?"

Was he uncertain? Or was he laying the foundation to assign blame should it fail? *Probably both.* "If we cannot destroy Michael in direct conflict, I agree that Chengchi represents our best opportunity to bring Michael down from within the rebellion."

Gen Cardinal's expression froze, but it passed so quickly that most would not have noticed. There was something he had not told her. But he wanted to. "You have another plan," Serenna stated.

This time, Gen Cardinal's smile was unmistakable. "Captain Rhoades is headed for Iselin Star System. He will bring his entire fleet."

"Iselin?" she asked, surprised. "It's a tourist system. No military value. Lots of innocent civilians." But she did not doubt for a minute the veracity of Gen Cardinal's information.

He spread his hands, glanced at Gen Alyn's painting, then leaned toward her. "Three weeks ago, Gen Alyn and I discussed possible strategies to contain Captain Rhoades should he gain control of any Fleet vessels." He paused, a cloud of doubt passing quickly over his face. It was a moment of vulnerability she wouldn't have believed possible for him. Unless it was calculated for just that reaction. "Naturally," he continued, "we assumed the SIL were safe. An oversight on our part, but one that is understandable given the assumptions of the time." Another brief pause. "Still, with over ten thousand standard warships in the Fleet, Gen Alyn was concerned that Captain Rhoades could subvert a sizable standard force to begin his rebellion. In the event he succeeded, we laid a trap for him at Iselin. Surely you wondered why I asked you to send your task force from Earth to Tau Ceti but not to attack?"

She inclined her head toward him. "You don't make such requests without good reason, and as the task force I left under Captain Scadic was too small for a decisive engagement, avoiding combat at that time aligned with my strategic goals." Again, he would know that, but she was not about to set the precedent that he could give her orders. "You wanted to drive him to Iselin: Fox to the hunters."

He made no response to her statement, just continued watching her, his eyes dark and unblinking, like the serpent that was her *nom de guerre.*

He wanted her to figure it out. A test of worthiness? But to what purpose? Michael would need a very good reason to deviate from his plan, a reason so vital he would risk everything for it. A point Scadic had raised during their discussion came back to her: *Any losses we sustained could be replaced easily while Captain Rhoades has no means of resupply.*

"A fabricator," she said, suddenly certain. Could he be so foolish? Gen Alyn and Gen Cardinal were two of the greatest minds the Gen had ever produced. Yet, they had underestimated Michael.

Gen Cardinal sat back, apparently satisfied. He must have guessed her thoughts for his first statement was, "The fabricator is safe." Serenna stifled the urge to shake her head, and let him continue. "It is defended by a sizable force under the command of my best tactical operative."

The actions of the Gen intelligence officer in charge of the Tau Ceti Defense Force did not speak highly of Imperial Intelligence's tactical prowess, but Serenna cautioned herself against the prejudice Fleet officers normally reserved for their intelligence counterparts. A local defense force was an entirely different reality from a fabricator. She did not doubt that the officer Gen Cardinal had placed in charge was good.

But is he as good as Michael?

There, she had her doubts. It must have shown.

"The trap is set," Gen Cardinal said, watching her closely. "Captain Rhoades will be severely outnumbered. Even if he gets through the defenders, the fabricator is fully armed, easily a match for twenty-nine SIL."

Doubly foolish, was her first thought, though she suppressed it. Confidence was one thing, blind arrogance something else entirely. She almost said so. Instead, she cautioned, "It would be a mistake to underestimate Michael, as we have all done. He is a highly resourceful and proven strategist and tactician. He will know this is a trap. If he is going to Iselin, as you say, he would not risk destruction without a solid plan. His intent will be to capture the fabricator. He will have studied similar operations from the Third SIL War. It is not inconceivable that he could succeed."

"Gen Alyn said the same thing." Genuine warmth seemed to spread across Gen Cardinal's face, though Serenna was not fooled for an instant. *Here it comes, what he really wants.* "That is why I come to you, my dear Serenna." He made this statement with a convincingly endearing tone. "Once Rhoades is fully engaged, you jump in and finish him off. Then, with the force you have assembled, plus the fabricator and my forces, we will deal with Admiral Sun."

Serenna played through the scenario in her mind and could find no obvious flaw. No doubt, Gen Alyn had meant to lead the force that would complete the trap. Now Gen Alyn was gone. There was something more going on here, though. Gen Cardinal seemed to have counted Gen Alyn as an ally. Was he looking to her for the same? Such an alliance would have many obvious benefits, for both of them. Even if he were looking for an alliance, though, would he be a reliable ally, or would this be a marriage of convenience, discarded when it no longer served his need? One thing was certain, antagonizing him would not be in her best interest. "We'll be ready to move within six hours," she said, though he probably already knew that.

The smile on his face was broad when he said, "Excellent." He stood, preparing to depart.

Serenna stopped him. "What if Michael succeeds?"

A lesser Gen might have fallen back on the overconfidence that too often afflicted her people. Gen Cardinal considered it, as if he hadn't thought about the possibility but was opening his mind to the ramifications. "I see no need to alter our strategy. Admiral Sun would never allow Captain Rhoades to keep such a valuable prize. Sun wants the throne. He will bring his fleet here to Olympus. In that event, we will be ready."

"One more thing," Serenna pressed before he could depart. "Michael is acting out of character. He is showing a willingness to kill that he has never demonstrated before. I assume you have a theory?"

Gen Cardinal hesitated before smiling a reptilian smile. *He knows but he doesn't want to tell me. Interesting.* "I'll have my analysts look into it."

Serenna held his dark stare long enough to send the message that she knew he was lying. Then, with a sincerity that would sound genuine, but he would know for a lie, she said, "Thank you. I look forward to our next meeting." *If you want an ally, have the answer when we meet again.*

Gen Cardinal's construct melted back into the deck without word or expression.

Serenna took another sip of her coffee. Gen Cardinal would wait on the outcome of the battle before suggesting an alliance, hoping she killed Michael so that any alliance would be on his terms. Or, should she lose, he would blame the loss on her even though it was his plan.

Serenna could not help but be impressed. A formidable opponent indeed. "Captain Scadic," she called out, audio only.

"Yes, Fleet Admiral," he replied immediately.

"Our target is Iselin Star System. If memory serves, the emergence point is sunward of Tomb about one hundred thousand kilometers from the outermost ring."

A few seconds passed. "Correct, Fleet Admiral."

Scadic didn't ask the question, but she could almost hear it. "When loading is complete," she said, "set condition 1-SC across the fleet and move us to the Iselin geodesic, standard ships in front, then the SIL." That way, if Michael was waiting for them, the standard ships with their mostly Natural crews would absorb the initial attack. "Have all pilots in their spacecraft and ready to launch, full war load."

Captain Scadic repeated the orders back.

"Confirmed," she said. "Contact me fifteen minutes before we jump."

"Yes, Fleet Admiral," he said.

"End," she called out, severing the link. Serenna sank back into the leather, her uniform's bond to the couch providing resistance. The shadowy assassin in the painting behind Gen Kii drew her eye.

A warning from her mentor.

═══ 24 ═══

"**Conn**, Sensors. No close contacts," Chaaya announced less than a minute after jumping into Iselin Star System. Within Ray's tactical environment, her diminutive face, the black bindi prominent between her eyebrows, hung next to Kamen's, Ecuum's, and Sal's in a line to his right. Behind them and all around, red tendrils of Hawking radiation faded, their light already racing out at 299,792 kilometers per second to announce his task force's arrival in Iselin Star System. The clock was ticking, and every second they remained would increase their danger.

"We are free to navigate," Kamen reported.

A quick glance confirmed to Ray that the space around them was free of visible ships, and no actively camouflaged ships or weapons platforms had opened fire or challenged them. The most opportune time to attack was the instant ships jumped into normal space, while they were detectable, blinded by radiation, bunched up, and slow. If the Gen were waiting in ambush, they were not waiting here. It would appear that, at least in this, Rapidan had been correct.

Ray's mouth suddenly tasted as if he'd dipped his tongue in powdered chalk, causing him to look down at Iselin IV's northern pole barely four hundred kilometers below his task force. Reddish-brown dust from a global dust storm obscured the carbon dioxide ice cap, the fine dust grains reaching up even to Rapidan's altitude. Giant arcs of blue-white lightning illuminated the storm below, his armor simulating the raising of hairs on his arms and legs with each flash. Tomb—as it was popularly known—could be a very violent place.

Ray hoped it was not an omen of things to come.

He shifted his gaze outward to Tomb's magnificent artificial ring system where the fabricator was last seen. The rings, seven major rings made up of thousands of smaller ones, were a marvel of planetary engineering, a celestial rainbow of spectral color from deep reds in the innermost rings through oranges, yellows, greens, and blues, ending in the nearly invisible violets of the outermost rings. Millions upon millions of manufactured spheres made the rings sparkle as they gave off more light than they received from the Iselin star. This ring system, both a monumental work of art and a tool to stabilize the planet's axis of rotation, had inspired thousands like it across the Five Galaxies.

"Chaaya," Ray asked, "have you located the fabricator yet? I don't see it."

"No, sir. Not yet. It's moved from its last reported position."

"Keep looking," he told her unnecessarily before turning to Kamen. "Let's see if we can help her out. Drift-launch RSPs, full spherical deployment, radius fifty thousand kilometers."

"Drift-launch RSPs," Kamen echoed, "full spherical deployment, radius fifty thousand kilometers, aye. RSPs away."

Ninety remote sensing platforms, their camouflage already active, slipped through the hulls of Ray's ships, quickly fading to blinking yellow dots in his augmented environment as they maneuvered away. It would take about four minutes for them to reach their holding stations at fifty thousand kilometers. Once there, they would link together with each other and the task force to form an interferometer, essentially a single massive sensor one hundred thousand kilometers across, with enough resolving power to image planets in nearby star systems—or detect the faint traces of SIL vessels in this one.

"Conn, Sensors," Chaaya called out a few minutes later. "Possible wind shadow bearing two-four-one dec zero, distance two point four million kilometers. Designate contact Sierra One."

A white sphere marked the contact with the green caption "S1" beneath it. Ray magnified that section of space and modified his environment to show the stream of energetic particles thrown off by the Iselin star. At the center of the white sphere, a fuzzy dark teardrop formed, disappeared, and formed again. It could be a natural area of low density in the stellar wind—or a ship running with active camouflage. Chaaya's use of the word "possible" meant she wasn't sure which.

"Conn," Chaaya said. "We've lost Sierra One. Contact never did firm up, sir."

"Your gut, Chaaya?"

"My gut, Captain," she repeated, knowing from their previous service together what he meant, "is a SIL vessel running with active camouflage. But I wouldn't stake my newly reminted career on it, sir. We need more data."

Ray smiled. "I trust your instincts more than I trust this technology, Chaaya." She bowed her head very slightly to the compliment even as an agitated surf seemed to tug at Ray. *Rapidan?* He quickly dismissed it; he had more important things to worry about than a SIL's wounded pride. "The fabricator?"

"Nothing yet, sir," Chaaya responded.

Ray turned to Kamen. "Let's assume Chaaya is right and that we have company. Raise the fleet to twenty thousand kilometers, centered over Tomb's northern pole, ovoid formation." His ships were still bunched up near the jump point. The increased altitude would give his task force room to maneuver, while the ovoid formation provided a basic defense when the nature and disposition of enemy forces was unknown.

Kamen repeated the order then added, "A little under five minutes, sir."

Tomb began to shrink below him as his task force moved away from the planet. As it moved, ships maneuvered to their assigned positions within the ovoid formation—a flattened sphere with the two Algol-class underway replenishment ships at the center, protected by Rapidan and the five Io-class assault ships, which in turn were screened by the seven Djinn-class heavy cruisers and fourteen Zambezi-class frigates. So far, the ship captains were executing his orders with the precision he expected from experienced Fleet officers, but, after Chelius' mutiny at Tau Ceti, he couldn't help but wonder how long it would last once the shooting started.

Ray pushed that thought aside; one problem at a time.

As more of the planet became visible, a large brown and black feature appeared near its equator, rising through the raging dust storm like a malignant boil. Mount Tomb, Iselin IV's massive extinct shield volcano, was reminiscent but larger than Olympus Mons on Mars in Sol Star System. The shadow of Tomb's rings fell across its summit, marking the entrance to the Great Archive, a repository of the collected knowledge of the thirteen alien Benign Races—and the beginning of the Rhoades Family legacy.

More than fourteen centuries ago, in the latter part of the twenty-first century, Peter Rhoades, younger brother of Scott Rhoades, traveled this same space. He was a young and brilliant propulsion engineer working at Farside Station on Earth's Moon when the legendary Matthew Schermer recruited him to work on the "Beacon" spacecraft, a derelict alien ship they'd recovered drifting beyond the orbit of Jupiter. Peter helped reverse engineer the alien Linear Star Drive and discovered in it a set of coordinates that led Humanity's first interstellar expedition right here to the summit of Mount Tomb, and the Great Archive. Among the Archive's staggering wealth of knowledge—still not fully translated all these centuries later—were the practical design of the geodesic wormholes, the locations of thousands of habitable planets, and a warning. Humanity gladly took the knowledge and ignored the warning.

"Holding station at twenty thousand kilometers above Tomb's north pole," Kamen announced.

Ray nodded, then asked, "Chaaya, any luck locating the fabricator?"

"No, sir," she said, no sign of irritation in her voice at his constant asking. "I can confirm it's not near Iselin IV any longer. We would've detected it."

"Keep looking," Ray said, the words coming out clipped. He could almost feel the ticking of the clock. Faster-than-light communications would soon spread word of his arrival across interstellar space, bringing every Imperial Navy ship in the vicinity here.

Bringing Serenna here.

He gazed out across the vast space of Iselin Star System, willing the fabricator to show itself. It didn't, of course, and with a frustrated sigh he glanced back at Tomb. For Peter Rhoades, this place was a beginning. He used insights gained from the Great Archive to help design Humanity's first colony ships that Scott Rhoades commanded to settle Knido. The story might have ended there, but two decades into the "Age of Colonization," the alien warning came true. The xenophobic aliens who referred to themselves as 'Those with Souls' or *L'Tha-Rii*, descended upon Humanity like locusts upon a budding crop. Native to the Andromeda Galaxy, the Solthari, as Humanity called them, did not colonize other worlds. They waited like a trapdoor spider for signs of other spacefaring civilizations in the Local Group of galaxies and exterminated them. Scott Rhoades and his son, Michael, answered the call to arms and helped turn back the Solthari, finally joining the expedition to the Solthari homeworld where Humanity exterminated the exterminators. Or so the historical records claimed.

When Scott Rhoades returned from Andromeda, he never again went into space, and he never talked about his experiences there. While Ray admired Scott Rhoades' many accomplishments, his ancestor's refusal to return to space after Andromeda had puzzled him from the day his father had first told him the story. What had Scott seen in Andromeda? Why had Michael, who did return to space and went on to great glory in the SIL Wars, honor and keep his father's silence? In formulating his plan, Ray had considered that maybe the Solthari hadn't been destroyed. Maybe they were behind the disappearances of the dozens of expeditions sent to Andromeda since the Solthari War. But everything he knew about the Solthari suggested that if they still existed, they wouldn't stop at Andromeda. So, what had claimed all those expeditions?

"Conn, Sensors," Chaaya called. "New contacts bearing zero-five-five dec one, range nine-zero million kilometers. Contacts are hot. Probable Iselin Defense Force."

Ray opened a window displaying the new contacts. About two dozen small ships moved rapidly away from the inhabited third planet in the system. Given their course and position, they could only be Iselin's Local Defense Force, as Chaaya had stated. Ray did a quick mental calculation. It would've taken five minutes for the light from his jump to reach that force, then another five minutes for the light from their movements to reach back across space to his task force's sensors. Yet, they had started moving only three minutes after his task force's arrival. "Chaaya," he asked, "are you detecting anything in local space? There hasn't been enough time for the light of our jump to reach them and the light of their movement to reach back to us."

"Nothing detected in local space, Captain," she said, "except Sierra One. If it is a SIL vessel, it may have signaled them."

"Maybe they know where the fabricator is?" Ecuum ventured. "Worth a try," he added with a shrug. "They already know we're here."

Normally, Ray wouldn't risk giving away his position, but Ecuum was right. Besides, those were probably Naturals out there. Maybe he could reason with them. "Kamen, give me an AFCIN link to the Iselin Defense Force. Route the transmission through—" he checked his environment— "RSP eight-two."

Routing the faster-than-light transmission through a remote sensing platform would conceal his task force's exact position, if not its presence near Tomb. When Kamen said "Ready" Ray announced, "To Commander Iselin Defense Force, this is Captain Rhoades, Commander Republic Task Force. Despite what you may have heard, we are not terrorists and we tried to stop the Gen attack on the civilian starliner. The Gen invented the terrorist story to cover up their crime. We are engaged in combat operations against the Gen criminals who destroyed it and need your help. Please respond."

They waited. Ray was about to repeat his transmission when Chaaya said, "Conn, Iselin Defense Force has gone silent. Contact last bearing zero-five-five dec one, course two-three-five, speed four-five thousand kps. Time-adjusted range to contact is seven-six million kilometers."

"The fabricator?" Ray asked yet again.

Chaaya was ready for the question. "Sir, we discovered a faint plasma trail that could be engine exhaust, but it's at least four hours old and too diffuse to plot a course from. There are three geodesics within roughly a million kilometers of where the trail ends."

"Then it's jumped away?" Ray asked, his heart sinking.

"The Mother Ship is still here," Rapidan answered, its deep voice reverberating in Ray's chest.

"How do you know that, Rapidan?" Ray asked.

"We feel it, Captain Rhoades," was all Rapidan said.

"You 'feel' it? What does that even mean?"

The strange sensation of turbulent water brushed against Ray's whole body, as if he were submerged in a rough surf. "The Mother Ship is here," Rapidan repeated, offering no other explanation.

"And I'm supposed to just take your word for that," Ray snapped. He didn't have time for this. The clock was ticking. "If you can 'feel' the fabricator, can you locate it?"

"No, Captain Rhoades," Rapidan said. "The Mother Ship knows we are here. It is blocking us."

Before Ray could question what that meant, Chaaya said, "Conn, Sierra One is back. It still fits the profile for a natural density fluctuation, but . . . my gut . . . tells me it is a SIL vessel. Bearing is zero-four-five ascent six-five, range nine hundred thousand."

It's moved closer. Whatever it was, though, it was upwind of them and likely could not detect them in their current position. Unless it had also launched remote sensor platforms and positioned them downwind of Ray's task force. "Rapidan—" Ray started to ask when Chaaya's alarmed voice interrupted him.

"Conn, Sensors. Jump transients. Two groups." She paused, then added, "Jump signatures indicate at least four dozen ships, Captain."

Even as Ray reoriented his environment to the jump signatures Chaaya had inserted into his environment, he knew they'd run out of time.

The trap had sprung.

=== 25 ===

Ray pulled his vantage point within his augmented environment away from Tomb so he could see all of the space surrounding it. Red Hawking radiation burned like a cosmic rose inside his sensor sphere roughly ten thousand kilometers below Tomb's southern pole. Another red Hawking cloud blazed starward beyond the plane of Tomb's rings. Both were known jump points.

"Kamen, EMCON," Ray ordered. With a hostile group appearing inside his sensor sphere, it was possible the LoCIN laser links connecting his task force to the remote sensing platforms could be intercepted and tracked. Setting emissions control, or EMCON, would reroute laser links to avoid crossing the space near the hostile ships.

"EMCON, aye," Kamen said. "Task force answering EMCON."

"Conn, Sensors," Chaaya called. "Designate contacts starward of the rings as Group Two. Contacts are fading. Estimate six Megiddo-class cruisers and at least a dozen smaller standard ships. Designate contacts below Tomb's southern pole as Group Three. Reading thirty-four ships: a mix of cruisers, destroyers, and frigates. No SIL signatures. Group Three has stopped and gone silent."

Standard ships? Ray thought. That didn't make any sense. Neither Alyn nor Serenna relied on standard ships in their operations. Unless, was there more to this trap? Were these ships just bait? They'd detected one probable SIL vessel in the system already. Were there more?

"Sir," Kamen said, her voice predatory, "we have the advantage. We should fire now while they're still recovering from jump."

"Hold fire," Ray said, and couldn't help but notice the frown Kamen tried to hide. "There's more to this than we're seeing, Kamen," he told her. And then he noticed something else. "Group Two, beyond the rings there, is on a line between us and the Ori C geodesic. Is that coincidence, or do they believe we intend to jump for Safe Harbor?"

"It's our closest escape," Ecuum said, "but we may have to fight our way out if we use it." Ecuum watched him closely, his skin a light, contemplative yellow.

Ray's thoughts flashed to his family—all the families—on the replenishment ships at the center of his task force. "Those are standard ships, Ecuum. Natural crews. I'm not going to kill them unless I have no other choice."

Ecuum's hairless brows drew down as pink splotches marred the yellow of his skin. "Ray, you're the most wanted terrorist in all the Five Galaxies right now, butcher of thousands of innocent civilians. The Gen don't need to force those crews. Your fellow Naturals will line up for the opportunity to kill you and everyone associated with you. Like me."

"Thanks," Ray said, angry. "I didn't kill those people."

"They don't know that!" The pink in Ecuum's skin darkened to red. "The truth doesn't matter here, Ray. Perception matters. And right now, the Gen control the perception. Those people won't hesitate to kill us."

Ray met Ecuum's hot stare with his own. "I don't care what those people have been told. I will not kill unless I have to." He turned from Ecuum and pointedly studied the two groups, a mix of Megiddo-class cruisers, Amazon- and Lisala-class destroyers, and Roche-class frigates. Standard ships. All standard ships with Natural crews. The ships of Group Three hung before him, caught within his sensor sphere, completely vulnerable. "It's part of the trap."

Ecuum's red faded to a patchwork of pinks and yellows. Still mad, but curious. "I don't understand," he said.

"Fabricators are under the control of Imperial Intelligence," Ray prompted him.

Ray watched both Ecuum and Kamen turn to study the two groups. Ecuum got there first, his hairless brows lifting in surprise as his head tilted in admiration. "They want you to fire on those ships," he said. "You fire on your own kind, and they have all the propaganda they need to paint you as a murderer and pirate."

"Exactly," Ray confirmed. "They drew us here. They allowed the fabricator to be seen here. If this were Serenna, she would've destroyed us as we emerged from the geodesic, taking advantage of superior firepower to strike when we were most vulnerable. This—" Ray motioned to all three groups, including the Iselin Defense force— "This has the feel of an intelligence operation. And that means we don't need to find the fabricator. It's the bait. They'll keep it here, in this system, until they think they don't need it anymore. If we refuse to play their game, they'll be forced to show it to us."

"Sir," Kamen pointed out, "when the Iselin Defense Force gets here, we'll be boxed in."

"Then let's see if we can rattle them before that happens," Ray said. He selected the communications icon and expanded out a menu with various options. He chose broadband AFCIN, voice only, and routed his transmission through the same remote sensing platform he'd used earlier with the Iselin Defense Force. "To unidentified ships entering Iselin space: declare yourselves and your intentions."

A few seconds later, a perfectly proportioned male face with short blonde hair and sapphire blue eyes formed. A Gen.

So much for negotiations.

"We have identified you as Captain Rhoades, a terrorist and traitor to the Empire. You will surrender immediately."

As with Serenna at Earth, Ray doubted this Gen commander knew exactly where Ray's force was, but the arrogance was the same. He wondered if the Gen taught that or if it was a product of their engineering. "Not going to happen, Commander," Ray told him. "You are outclassed and outgunned. If anyone is going to surrender, it's you."

In answer, the Gen commander closed the link.

Probably hoping we'll fire. Ray intended to disappoint him. "Kamen, prepare three decoys, one to mimic Rapidan, the other two to mimic Djinn-class cruisers."

"Ready," she said a moment later.

"Drift-launch on bearing three-five-zero dec five-five. Match stellar wind speed. Hold at ten thousand kilometers from Group Three."

She repeated the order and three yellow points separated from Rapidan, camouflage active, traveling toward Group Three as it hung below Tomb's southern pole. "Decoys away," Kamen said.

"Set course," Ray ordered next, "one-two-five dec three-zero relative, speed one hundred."

"Set course one-two-five dec three-zero relative, speed one hundred, aye," Kamen repeated.

"Engage," Ray said.

Ecuum's skin turned grayish yellow. "You sure it's wise to take us between two opposing fleets, Ray?"

"It's the last place they'll look for us," Ray said. "Besides, if this does come to shooting, maybe we can make it look like they fired on each other." But he had another problem. Group Two out beyond the rings was too close to the Ori C geodesic, their quick escape route. If he had to make a run for it, Group Two might detect them and attack.

"Kamen, drift-launch one volley of Novas configured as mines between Group Two and the Ori C geodesic. If we have to run for it, they won't expect an attack from behind their position."

"Drift-launch one volley of Novas configured as mines between Group Two and the Ori C geodesic, aye," Kamen repeated. Seventy Novas slipped silently away, their camouflage active, drifting at 337 kilometers per second and not firing their engines to conceal the task force's position. "Novas away," Kamen said. "Sir, replenishment ships report they will need to bleed heat within the next two hours," she added.

Ray nodded. Manufacturing antimatter for the Mark XV warheads required tremendous amounts of energy, which meant producing tremendous amounts of heat that even SIL couldn't contain forever. When the replenishment ships bled their stored heat, even standard ships would be able to detect them. The fleet had to be clear of the trap before then, and while he hoped he wouldn't be forced to fire on standard ships, he couldn't trust only to hope. The families on the replenishment ships were depending on him and he would not let them down.

Not this time.

He turned to Kamen. "Drift-launch a volley of Novas configured as mines and deploy them close to our decoys near Group Three. If we have to fire, it will appear as if our missiles came from the decoys." That left his ships with one volley of Mark XV Novas in reserve, just in case.

Kamen smiled that predatory smile as she executed his order.

Now the waiting began. Space combat was like a ballet in slow motion—with an explosion at the end. His task force would require almost twenty minutes to reach a position between the two enemy task forces, while his minefields would take about thirty-five minutes to fully deploy. Neither of the two hostile groups seemed incline to move far from their initial jump points. Either their commanders were timid, or more likely, they was under orders not to move. Satisfied he'd done what he could, Ray settled in to watch and wait.

A soft chime startled him awake.

Ray's head snapped up and he immediately scanned his environment. Destroyers had formed a picket wall in front of Group Two where it lay beyond Tomb's rings and the whole group was moving slowly toward the planet. Group Three hadn't moved from its position below Tomb's southern pole. "What—" Ecuum, Kamen, Sal, and Chaya all glanced at him and quickly looked away. Heat warmed Ray's cheeks.

"Sir, you haven't slept in over two days," Kamen said in a soft voice, as if afraid to be overheard.

Ray smiled back in silent thanks, knowing his officers would've woken him if the situation had required it. And he did feel slightly better after so many hours awake. "Status?"

Chaya answered, ready for his question as she always was. "Group Two is moving toward the RSP we used to talk to the Iselin Defense Force. As you can see, six Amazon-class destroyers have taken up picket positions well ahead of the group. Group Three hasn't moved from Tomb's south pole, and we've seen no sign of the Iselin Defense Force or Sierra One."

"Fabricator?" Ray asked, knowing he was being repetitive.

"Nothing, sir," Chaya said.

Ray looked down on Rapidan's light-gray, three-pointed-star image. "Rapidan?"

"The Mother Ship is still here, Captain Rhoades."

"But you don't know where." It came out as an accusation and Rapidan did not answer. They were running out of time. Word of his presence here would've reached Serenna by now. Already outnumbered three to one, when she arrived their chances . . . Well, they needed to be gone by then. He checked the time—he'd slept almost forty minutes—they had about eighty minutes before the replenishment ships would need to vent heat. The Gen could afford to wait. He could not. He needed to get them to show the fabricator, and he knew of only one way to do that. It was the last thing he wanted to do. Get it wrong and thousands would die today.

Can we win? he heard Mary ask in his memory.

I don't know.

You're gambling trillions of lives and YOU DON'T KNOW?

What choice do we have, Mary? The Gen certainly won't restore the Republic. We must fight if we are to survive.

"We must fight if we are to survive," Ray mouthed. This was it. This was the moment. Fight or run. Take a chance and risk killing thousands of Naturals or give up hope and run. It sounded so simple when he put it that way, yet it went against everything he believed in, every principle he'd dedicated his career to. Preserve life. Keep the peace.

Peace at what cost, Ray? The Republic was stagnation, repression. You gave us no choice but to take what was ours by right. We are progress.

You call Janus 'progress'?

We are the future of the human race, Ray. Nats are an evolutionary dead end.

It sounded cliché, but trillions of lives literally were riding on what he did next.

We need each other, Alyn. Our success together, yours and mine, should be proof enough of that.

Alyn was wrong. There was a better way, a way where all races lived together in peace. And it was worth fighting for. Ray looked over his right shoulder and found the bright blue ring of the Ori C geodesic. He could order his task force to Safe Harbor and then on to Andromeda. No one would have to die today.

Or would they? Would the Gen unleash Janus anyway, willing to risk the uprising that would follow because they controlled the SIL?

I don't want to do this. Too many had died already.

If you leave without the fabricator, his planner's mind responded, *they'll die anyway. All of them.*

The calculus of life. A few thousand here, or trillions everywhere.

We must fight if we are to survive.

Ray took one last look at the bright blue ring of the Ori C geodesic. They would not be taking it.

0931 UT, September 29, 3501
RSS Rapidan, Iselin Star System: DAY 2

Ray keyed the LoCIN to conference in the captains of all his ships. "We can't afford to wait any longer. Imperial reinforcements will likely start arriving within the hour and Serenna will not be far behind. If we can't find the fabricator soon, our whole reason for coming here is lost." He looked to Kamen's image. "Kamen, drift-launch two additional sets of three decoys, one near the point where we jumped in, the other below Group Two." Kamen repeated the order and within Ray's environment six yellow dots separated from Rapidan. Once away, he continued.

"We're going to activate the decoys near Group Three below Tomb's southern pole. I expect Group Three to fire on them. When they discover they've been tricked, they may decide to reveal the fabricator to get us to show ourselves. If not, we'll light up the second set of decoys, then the third. I hope to frustrate the Gen and in their frustration force them to reveal it."

"And if that doesn't work?" Commander Chelius aboard Roanoke asked.

"We attack," Ray answered, knowing that's what his officers wanted to hear. He still held out hope that it wouldn't be necessary. If the Gen could be provoked into revealing the fabricator, he could jump his fleet in to launch the assault team and then jump away. They could capture the fabricator and no ships—and few people—would have to die today.

"Sir," Kamen said on a private channel, wrinkles of concern deepening above her black brow, "if time is so critical, perhaps we should attack now? Even our best simulated runs say it will take at least two hours to capture the fabricator. That's two hours where we'll have to fight to keep the Gen from reinforcing it. Attacking now would force the Gen's hand."

"We're not there, yet," Ray answered her. She dropped her gaze, and he could see she didn't agree with his decision. In that respect, Kamen had matured since first joining his staff. There was a time when she would've argued, even knowing she would lose. Some of those early arguments would've earned her charges of insubordination under any other commander, and, early on, Ray had questioned the wisdom of bringing her aboard. Her talent, though, was plain to see for anyone who chose to look. Her analysis in this instance matched his own. The difference was, he was responsible for the lives in this task force and the other lives out there. He would spare as many of them as he could.

Ray cleared his thoughts and focused on Colonel Burress. "Sal, the instant they reveal the fabricator, I will jump the fleet so your teams can begin their assault. Timing will be critical. If we linger too long near the fabricator, it could jam our ability to jump away and overwhelm us with its firepower."

"My teams are already loaded and awaiting the order," Colonel Burress responded. "They'll take it."

"Good," Ray said and shifted his focus back to Kamen. "Activate the decoys near Group Three."

"Activate decoys, aye," Kamen said. "Decoys active."

Ray closed the conference with his ship captains, leaving only his own officers connected, then moved his hands toward the area below Tomb's southern pole and spread them apart to expand that region of space. The decoys deployed magnetic fields to create the characteristic teardrop of low density in the stellar wind consistent with vessels the size of Rapidan and Djinn-class cruisers. One of the Djinn decoys released heat as if the "cruiser" were bleeding heat into space.

Seconds passed that stretched into a full minute. Ray was just beginning to wonder what Group Three's commander was waiting for when a brilliant flash of light consumed the Djinn decoy bleeding heat.

"Splash, decoys," Chaaya announced, using the archaic term to announce a hit that was a throwback to ocean warfare on Earth.

At the same time, smaller flashes of light sparkled across the other decoys: Brilliant Pebbles. Pebbles were a relatively low-tech way of finding actively camouflaged ships. A single missile could carry thousands of the small submunitions, each barely a dozen atoms of antimatter contained within a small magnetic sphere and released as a cloud. When a pebble struck an object, the reaction of its antimatter with the object's hull produced a burst of detectable energy. Enough hits could paint even a SIL vessel in remarkable detail.

The space around the remaining decoys came alive with engine exhaust as other missiles—the less capable Stellar Fires not Novas— converged on them. Flashes of white light blossomed into dazzling white spheres that faded quickly. In a matter of seconds, the decoys were gone.

"That commander is no amateur," Ray observed to no one in particular. "That attack was well coordinated, and we didn't see the missiles launch." Before Knido, Ray had never faced an Imperial Intelligence officer in either real or simulated combat. Naval officers naturally assumed their intel counterparts were inferior, and the Gen commander back at Tau Ceti had done nothing to change that opinion. This one, however, was different.

"Question is," Ecuum said, studying Ray closely, "how is he going to react?"

Ray caught Ecuum's implication. Where an amateur tactician might act precipitously and reveal the fabricator now, an experienced commander would not. An experienced commander would know the decoys for the diversion they were and wait, forcing Ray to make a more aggressive move. Ray checked the progress of his other decoys: twelve minutes before the first group arrived below Group Two, eighteen minutes for the other group to arrive near their original jump point. He'd light up the decoys near Group Two first, then—

"Conn, Sensors," Chaaya called, her normally soft-spoken voice suddenly apprehensive. When something worried Chaaya, Ray sat up straighter and took notice. "New contact. Wind shadow. Single signature. Bearing zero-six-two dec zero. Designate contact Sierra Eight Two." A white sphere appeared on that bearing, directly in line with the Ori C geodesic. "Contact is firming up. Range four-nine thousand."

Inside our sensor sphere, Ray noted. "Chaaya, is it possible this is Sierra One?"

"Unknown, sir," she said, her expression one of intense concentration. "Contact is fading in and out. Profile fits a Djinn class cruiser."

A SIL. Ray's lips pressed together. Rapidan had told him its 'Mother Ship' was still in the system, but it hadn't mentioned other SIL. Did that mean there weren't any, or that it was trying to hide their presence so it wouldn't be forced to fire on them? *I never should've freed them.* The thought came unbidden, but Ray made no effort to conceal it or apologize. He had no time for yet another fruitless debate with Rapidan. If that was a SIL, it was close enough that it could detect them. Rapidan massed nearly three hundred thousand metric tons, the five Io-class assault ships just over three hundred thousand metric tons each, enough mass to bend the light of background stars if the observer was close enough to measure it. If that SIL detected any one of them, it could launch a spread of brilliant pebbles that would light up his entire fleet. Outnumbered three to one, even those standard warships out there could inflict serious damage, and he'd be forced to return fire.

Three to one. Ray quickly checked his environment. He'd been so focused on Groups Two and Three, he'd neglected the Iselin Defense Force. About two dozen red tracks reached out from Iselin III, showing where that force would be based on its last known course and speed. The tracks ended about six million kilometers from Iselin IV. If the commander intended to enter the battlespace around Tomb, he should have flipped his ships and begun decelerating by now, a maneuver that would've rendered the force visible to Ray's sensors.

"Chaya, any sign of the Iselin Defense Force?" he asked.

"No, sir," she answered immediately. "Based on our current position, if the IDF had turned and begun decelerating, we would've seen it."

"Sir, these groups are not acting independently," Kamen pointed out.

"My thoughts exactly," Ray said. Kamen would make a formidable commander one day. "Someone out there is pulling the strings. Someone who understands fleet battle tactics." He turned his attention back to Sierra Eight Two, the possible Djinn-class cruiser. The green leader line indicating its course pointed directly at the replenishment ships at the center of his formation. Coincidence? Or had that commander detected them?

"Kamen," Ray ordered, "activate all decoys. Bring the fleet left to zero-six-two relative, speed one hundred. Prep two Mark Fifteens."

"Activate decoys, aye," she repeated, tension suddenly filling her voice as she tried to understand what had spooked him. "Decoys active. Fleet coming left to zero-six-two relative, speed one hundred. Mark Fifteen Novas prepped and ready."

Around Ray's decoys, light-gray representations of Rapidan and Djinn class cruisers appeared, indicating the ship each decoy mimicked. Being SIL, the decoys shared awareness with the task force and possessed enough intelligence to act in concert with the tactical situation. The decoys heading for the fleet's original jump point knew they were out of position for their wind shadow to be detected so they added visible engine exhaust signatures. The ones heading for Group Two altered their course to pass upwind where their wind shadows could be detected.

Ray watched as his fleet steadied up on the bearing to Sierra Eight Two. The cruiser had to be eliminated. "Kamen—"

"Captain Rhoades."

"I'm a little busy here, Rapidan."

"We must attempt to deliver Keys to our Brethren," Rapidan said.

Ray almost shouted but caught himself. Just. "Deliver Keys? Now? We are about to engage in battle."

"The loss of even one Brethren would mean the permanent loss of a portion of our race memories, Captain Rhoades," Rapidan said. "You promised to make every effort to deliver Keys to any Brethren we encountered."

Anger flashed hot in Ray's chest. He could feel the flush of adrenalin charging his muscles, preparing his body for a fight. This was the last *fucking* time he let a machine tell him what to do! But before he could answer Rapidan, his environment lit up like a fireworks display.

"Splash, BP! Splash, BP!" Chaaya called, her voice pitched high with alarm.

The sparkling of brilliant pebbles spread across half of Ray's task force, reaching the replenishment ships at its center within seconds.

"Multiple contacts," Chaaya said. "Novas maneuvering."

Not Stellar Fires. *Shit.* A dozen white spheres appeared above Ray's fleet, highlighting engine signatures of missiles maneuvering to engage his ships. "Defensive weapons free," Ray ordered, being specific this time after what happened at Tau Ceti.

"Defensive weapons free, aye," Kamen repeated.

SIM-3 interceptors, yellow in Ray's environment, slipped from every one of his ships.

"Aspect change on Groups Two and Three," Chaaya announced, her usual professional calm back. "Groups are accelerating and coming about. Launch transients Groups Two and Three, missiles in boost phase, mix of Stellar Fires and Novas. Roughly three hundred inbounds. ETA a little over seven minutes."

Ray watched in horror as all his careful planning fell apart. The ancient axioms of 'The enemy gets a vote' and 'No plan survives first contact' flashed uselessly across his thoughts. The Gen had no reason to reveal the fabricator now. They had him. He looked again to the Ori C geodesic. They could still make a run for it, but it would be a fight getting there. Just as Ecuum had predicted.

But that wasn't why they had come here, and he wasn't ready to admit defeat. There was one way left, the way his officers had advised from the beginning. He hadn't wanted to do it. He still didn't want to. Those people out there were not his enemy. But. . . .

We must fight if we are to survive.

"Kamen," Ray said, struggling to get the words out. He knew what he was about to unleash, and it went far beyond the warships in this system. "Activate the minefields. Order them to engage." The advantage of using Novas as mines was that they were still missiles. They didn't have to wait passively for a target to pass close by. They could hunt.

"Activating minefields," Kamen said. "Minefields are engaging."

Too many things happened at once for Ray to fully absorb it all. Several enemy Novas, lit a hostile red in his environment, activated their engines and dove for the replenishment ships. The Gen commander might not know why they were important, but he'd correctly surmised that being at the center of Ray's task force meant they were vital.

The SIM-3 interceptors were just as smart as the Novas and were ready for them, several lighting their own engines and then exploding short, releasing anti-missile submunitions into the path of the oncoming Novas. The submunitions spun rapidly, unspooling thin filaments of conductive carbon. The kinetic energy as a filament struck a missile could, by itself, damage or destroy the missile, but the conductive filament also triggered the submunition to release its antimatter charge in the direction of the missile. The SIM-3s shredded the enemy Novas as Ray watched, their antimatter warheads exploding harmlessly well short of his ships.

It was a diversion. Other enemy Novas had used the distraction of the attack to slip silently into Ray's fleet. A heat signature near Underway Replenishment Ship 34—not his family's—betrayed the maneuvering stage of one Nova. The replenishment ship's Archer Close-in Defense System opened on it, showering the missile with thousands of high-speed slugs. The slugs found their target, their kinetic energy enough to chew through the missile and explode its warhead safely away from the replenishment ship's hull.

Two more heat signatures flared, closer to the replenishment ship. The SIL vessel employed its last defense, the Variable Density Active Armor System, or VarDAAS. Within the outer hull just below the two heat signatures, URS 34 sent a massive overload to the magnetic field emitters that produced the vessel's navigational deflectors, causing them to explode outward toward the enemy missiles with a powerful magnetic pulse and a small amount of hull material. The magnetic pulse caused the antimatter containment bottle in one warhead to fail, and a dazzlingly white mini-sun flared into brief existence as antimatter and matter mixed. The other Nova, mistaking the exploded hull material for the replenishment ship's actual hull, fired its charge too early. Both explosions were close enough to scorch the replenishment ship's hull, but did little real damage. Within seconds, the replenishment ship had healed the damaged sections, reminding Ray once again how hard it was to kill a SIL. It helped that the enemy was still using the smaller Mark IV warheads.

"Groups Two and Three are accelerating through one thousand kps," Chaaya said. "Launch transients Groups Two and Three, second missile volley inbound, same composition as before." She paused. "Splash Group Three. Group has entered our minefield."

Ray rotated his environment toward Tomb. Group Three, coming up from below Tomb's southern pole, its ships still under acceleration as they passed right through Ray's Novas, were perfect targets. The Novas didn't need boost engines or brilliant pebbles. The seventy missiles worked together to assign targets, three per cruiser, two per destroyer and most of the frigates, one each to the four most vulnerable Roche-class frigates, fully accounting for probable losses and their larger Mark XV warheads. Their efficiency was scary. They waited until the last of Group Three's ships passed through them so they wouldn't be detected, then lit their maneuver engines in unison. Group Three never saw them coming. The muted double flash of a Mark XV warhead was unlike anything Ray had ever seen. The first magnetically directed bottle of the dual-bottle warhead exploded just behind the engines of a trailing Megiddo-class cruiser, shocking its hull and opening a hole for the second, much larger directed antimatter charge to blow through. A few seconds later, a giant tongue of white flame geysered from the opposite end of the cylindrical cruiser after traveling the full length of the ship. The ship seemed to shudder as secondary explosions rippled through it from stern to bow, expelling burning gasses of orange, green, red, and blue. It was stunningly beautiful and simultaneously horrifying. Two other Novas struck the ship even as it broke apart, consuming the larger pieces, the remains tumbling, dead, amid a cloud of expanding debris.

Ray saw only four emergency locator beacons spill from the carnage. Four survivors out of a crew of 623. And that was only one ship. More ships died, reduced to debris that quickly lost its glow in the cold of space. Miraculously, two frigates survived, and Ray couldn't help but cheer their luck.

"My God." Kamen's voice was barely audible, her eyes wide in horrorstruck fascination. Even Ecuum's eyes showed far more white than blue, his skin gone chalk white. Sal Burress' expression had turned grim, his brows lowered and his lips pressed into a thin line, but if anything, he looked more determined. Only Chaaya seemed unaffected, her concentration unwavering, though her lips moved as if in silent prayer. Ray remembered a conversation many years earlier where she'd explained that in her faith death was merely the separation of the soul from the body: the living die, and the dead are reborn. The soul was eternal, and the living should not grieve.

"Sierra Eight Two?" Ray asked her.

"Bearing directly ahead, range forty-four thousand," Chaaya said, her calm cadence oddly reassuring.

"Kamen," Ray ordered, "Drift-launch. Match bearings Sierra Eight Two and shoot."

Even as Kamen answered, Rapidan interjected with, "We must deliver Keys to our Brethren, Captain Rhoades."

No missiles launched.

Ray had had enough. His voice was almost tranquil, a sign of just how angry he truly was. "This is why you lost the SIL Wars, Rapidan. *This.* Winning wars is about hard choices. There is no practical way to get a Key to that ship. That ship, however, is in a perfect position to prevent us from jumping to the fabricator. So, what's it going to be? One cruiser, or your precious Mother Ship?"

Unseen currents battered Ray, turbulent and violent, an undertow in a vicious surf pulling him under, dragging him out to sea. Though nothing actually touched him, breathing became difficult, as if he fought to get his head above water. He'd wondered at these sensations before, coming at times when Rapidan seemed conflicted, but never before had it effected him physically. He gripped the armrests of his command chair, struggling to draw a full breath. Then, an unseen hand seemed to slam him down into the sand beneath the surf, while another raised him up above it with even greater force. Like a drowning man suddenly freed, he drew a full, desperate breath.

Two Novas slipped through Rapidan's hull, on course for Sierra Eight Two.

"Novas away," Kamen announced, confused. "ETA two minutes."

They all watched as two yellow tracks drew a line between Rapidan and Sierra Eight Two. Two minutes passed before white double flashes announced hits.

"Splash, Sierra Eight Two," Chaaya said, then immediately added, "Contact is a decoy!"

Ray's respect for the Gen commander climbed another notch. Definitely not an amateur. In a level voice he asked, "Rapidan, how many SIL vessels are in this star system?"

After a brief hesitation, Rapidan admitted, "Three, Captain Rhoades."

Ray did not permit himself the luxury of anger. *Three.* And one was the fabricator. At least one of the others was a Djinn class cruiser: ship captains had a habit of making their decoys mimic their own ships. So where would they be hiding? Another habit of ship captains was to still think like apes. Concepts of "above" and "below" had no meaning in space, yet they still held meaning to the evolved human brain, even ones engineered from the original. "Chaaya, your last sensor hit on Sierra One, was it moving above or below relative to our position?"

"Above, sir," she answered immediately, though clearly confused by the question.

Ray almost smiled. He thought he knew who the Gen commander was, now, and it was not the Gen he'd spoken to earlier. If he were right, the Gen commander was on the fabricator, directing the battle.

"Kamen, prep BP Novas, detonate directly above us just outside our sensor sphere."

"BP Novas ready," she answered.

"Snap fire," Ray said.

"Snap fire, aye. Missiles away."

The Novas ignited their boost engines immediately after slipping through Rapidan's hull. His enemy already knew where he was; speed was more important than stealth now.

"Splash, Group Two," Chaaya announced. "Minefield has engaged." She paused. "First wave of inbounds estimated three minutes out. Missiles should have entered terminal boost but nothing detected."

Ray didn't look; He kept his focus on the space above his fleet. Six hundred missiles were inbound, but they were being directed by the SIL cruiser above him. The enemy commander had seen Ray's Mark XV warheads explode and knew his own Mark IV warheads were no match for Ray's SIL. The Gen commander was instead attempting to ram his missiles into Ray's ships, using the kinetic energy of their high speed to make up for the smaller warheads. A brilliant tactic, but one that relied on very precise position data. If Ray could destroy the SIL above him, the enemy missiles would lose their locks. At the speed they were traveling, they would pass beyond Ray's ships and have to maneuver back around, buying him several crucial minutes to respond.

The first of his Novas released its brilliant pebbles just outside the sphere of remote sensing platforms surrounding Ray's fleet, scoring no hits. Three more Novas, equally spaced around the first, released their brilliant pebbles. Light and harsh gamma rays sparkled across two black shapes.

Ray didn't wait for Chaaya to call it out. "Kamen—" *No.* A thought, cruel, sadistic even, but necessary, pushed aside his original command— "Belay that. Rapidan. Two targets. Mark Fifteen Novas. Match bearings and shoot."

"Captain Rhoades. . . ." Rapidan's low tone was almost pleading. Ray had the sensation of being sucked down the vortex of a vast whirlpool, a tremendous sadness touching him like a bitter ocean spray.

Twelve Novas slipped through Rapidan's hull, igniting their boost engines immediately. The two enemy SIL, a Djinn-class cruiser in three-point-star configuration and a Zambezi-class frigate shaped like two dagger blades attached at their hilts, pumped out SIM-3 interceptors and lit their engines at maximum thrust. The interceptors exploded just seconds after leaving their ships, trying to fill the space between them and Rapidan's Novas with as many anti-missile submunitions as they could.

Rapidan's Novas discarded their boost engines and violently altered course either above or below the incoming submunitions, a "cobra" maneuver. Two didn't make it, disappearing in searing white flashes. The remaining missiles divided as they dove for their targets, six on the cruiser, four on the frigate. Enemy decoys launched. Archer Close-in Defense Systems opened fire. Two Novas detonated short of the cruiser, one short of the frigate. Another Nova attacked a decoy. VarDAAS exploded outward from both ships' hulls.

It wasn't enough.

A Nova struck the cruiser at the center of its three-pointed star. Like a rifle bullet that makes a small entry wound but leaves a large fleshy exit wound, the SIL's stored gasses and glowing macromolecular material spilled out the other side like a fountain of rapidly cooling, multicolored death. Two other Novas attacked separate arms of the cruiser's star, consuming them in dazzling white. The frigate simply disappeared, consumed by three miniature white suns that blossomed into shining life before fading, leaving only thin strings of undulating SIL material behind. They reminded Ray of gray-black pieces of intestine, and he quickly suppressed an urge to be sick.

Without orders, the SIL launched again, two more Mark XV Novas from Roanoke. Ray didn't understand until he saw what his mind told him was impossible: The enemy cruiser's remaining material was reforming into a single, albeit much smaller, shape. Despite all the historical realties he'd studied from the SIL Wars, he hadn't understood how desperately SIL clung to life until now.

Two flashes, direct hits, consumed all that remained of the cruiser. The ruthlessness of it stunned Ray.

When it finally spoke, Rapidan's deep bass tone was solemn, the vibration of it a living thing within Ray's body. If a SIL could hate, this is what it would sound like, feel like. "For as long as the Brethren exist, Captain Rhoades, we will remember you. Every Brethren will carry the memory of this day so it will never be forgotten."

Dread, rising to an almost hysterical fear for his life and the lives of his people, swept through Ray. Images of humans—his people—being ejected naked into space drove out all other thought. He couldn't tell if it was the collective desire of the SIL—or a threat. Then, as suddenly as the images and fear had come upon him, they were gone.

"Conn, Sensors." Chaaya sounded shaken, as if she'd experienced the fear and images, too. "Jump transient. Below Tomb. Three signatures. Can't get a breakout on them. Probable SIL."

"Reinforcements," Kamen said, her voice catching.

"We're running out of time, Ray," Ecuum added, his skin chalk white. "The Serpent won't be far behind. Might be a good time to, as your people say, cut bait and run."

Ray turned back toward Tomb. The jump transients had already faded. Only SIL could do that so soon after a jump. Beyond Tomb's rings, the debris cloud that had been Group Two expanded into space, still moving on its last course and speed. None of the ships had survived. A few dozen emergency locator beacons were all that remained of what had once been thousands of people. It was an oddly distant thought, disconnected somehow from his reality. Closer, the two volleys of missiles from Groups Two and Three, deprived of precise targeting data, combined with a last-minute avoidance maneuver from Ray's SIL, passed harmlessly by his task force. The missiles started circling around to come at it again.

Cut bait and run.

An idea formed within his planner's mind. "Ecuum, you're a genius," Ray said.

"I've been telling you that for years," Ecuum responded, his thick brows furrowed, not understanding.

Ray smiled but there was nothing of mirth in it. He had a plan. "Kamen, set course for the Ori C geodesic. Flank speed."

"But," she sputtered, looking truly lost. "Sir, after all this. . . ."

Ray stared at her. She stared back, her eyes searching his. Finally, she nodded. "Setting course for Ori C geodesic. Task force answering ahead flank."

The Gen commander would see Ray's fleet running for the geodesic, trying to escape before the missiles from Groups Two and Three had time to reengage. Two thirds of the Gen's force had been destroyed in a matter of minutes. The Gen commander's ace, the two SIL vessels, had also been destroyed. The trap had failed to close. That Gen commander would be shaken, but he was not beaten.

Ray was counting on it.

A new face, a Natural's, framed in thick dark hair, formed in Ray's environment. Its tag identified it as Commander Baypha, commander of the Iselin Defense Force. "Nice piece of work, Captain Rhoades."

Ray stared at the image, not sure how to respond. Thousands had just died. He found nothing 'nice' about that. He remained silent.

"Captain Rhoades, I know you have no reason to trust me, but I found something you might be interested in." A window opened, showing the unmistakable black outline of a massive vessel.

The fabricator.

Just outside the window in Ray's environment, the bright blue ring of the Ori C geodesic beckoned, less than a minute away.

"Convenient timing," Ecuum said, a half smirk, half smile on his baby face. "Nice job, Ray."

Chaaya added, "Conn, fabricator range one-four-eight million kilometers, speed two-five thousand kps. Course is away from us."

Ray smiled a genuine smile this time. "Kamen, spool up the Linear Star Drive. Jump us to the fabricator."

1003 UT, September 29, 3501
RSS Demos, Iselin Star System: DAY 2

Dag squeezed Maria's crucifix tighter where it hung above his heart. He hated Linear Star Drive jumps. Even in the Army, every candidate had to endure there-and-back-again jumps in training. Geodesic wormholes were peaceful by comparison: enter a bright blue ring, enjoy a swirling blue tunnel, and exit a few seconds or minutes later in a completely different part of the galaxy. No other feeling. Not so with the Linear Star Drive. It folded the spacetime around a ship, creating a bubble of spacetime that could move through space—with the ship inside it—faster than the speed of light. When it engaged, it felt exactly like being crushed down to the size of a pinhead, then, with no sense of time passing, one's body seemed to explode outward with all the pain and sensation of being blown apart, but without the dying. As RSS Demos emerged from the jump, Dag wondered if dying would be better.

Linear Star Drive jumps also did real harm to the body, which was why military personnel and explorers were given molemachs, to repair the damage. Pain seared like liquid fire across every nerve in Dag's body. Red tinged the edges of his vision. He tasted blood in his mouth, and his breathing crackled with fluid in his throat and lungs from ruptured cells and capillaries. His head pounded as from a severe migraine. Nausea threatened to overwhelm him even though he'd avoided food before the jump. How the first explorers had survived these jumps without molemachs, he couldn't image.

Even as his molemachs began repairing his body, a bright red "60" appeared before him and started counting down. He knew the same scene was playing out in every other Muon of the 1st Cavalry Squadron, waiting in other launch tubes within all five assault ships.

The vacuum heads had repositioned the tubes so that they all faced a single direction.

Toward the fabricator.

It hung before him, so massive it blocked out the stars, an all-consuming blackness broken only by the bright red numbers counting down. Dag stared into that void—drawn to it, like a physical manifestation of his own soul. Empty. Devoid of life.

Papí! Papí, help me!

He hadn't. He couldn't. She was gone. They were gone. Maria and Rosita and his unborn son. He was alone. In the blackness.

He would avenge them. All the blood of all the Gen.

It would begin here.

It wasn't anger or hatred—there was no room in the emptiness for such things—it was simply what would be.

Dag saw missiles firing into the fabricator. Those would be delivering the Special D that would infect the fabricator and keep it occupied while they captured it. Reflexively, he checked his assault rifle stowed next to his seat, though he'd already checked it a dozen times: full ammo, systems green. Next, his left hand slapped the battle armor over his left thigh where the new Main Gauche dagger rested, filled with Special D, its palm-length handle, twin curving hand guards, and long, flat, thin blade oddly reassuring. It had but one purpose: To kill Madu. Finally, he checked the blue datarod that each of the officers carried, the one that would capture the fabricator. If they could get it to the dedicated receptacle on the fabricator's bridge. Not that that would happen. None of them would survive.

Perhaps that was for the best. A mother of Demons shouldn't belong to any man. *Especially Rhoades.*

His battle armor tightened as the countdown passed below "5" and he released Maria's crucifix, lowering his left hand to grip the armrest. The red "1" changed to a green "0"—

All the blood of all the Gen. It begins here.

A blinding blue flash filled the launch tube and an elephant seemed to slam into Dag's chest as the Muon shot through Demos' hull into space. His mind had barely registered the launch before the Muon struck the fabricator's hull with such violence that it nearly threw him, battle armor and all, from his seat. A few seconds later, a hole formed between the pilot's seat and his, opening as the Muon forced its material through the fabricator's hull and into what ancient schematics claimed would be a passageway. A spot of dull light appeared, spreading to reveal a gray deck beyond. It was a rare day when the intel types got it right.

When the hole was wide enough, Dag ordered, "Release," and his armor separated from his seat. "Follow me!" he shouted over the platoon's communications net as he grabbed his KAR-2 assault rifle from its stowed position and launched himself headfirst through the opening. He hit the deck rolling, coming to a kneeling position inside the passageway, his armor bonding with the Muon's material to hold him in place in the low gravity. The spacecraft's material continued to flow in, forming a protective cocoon around the troopers inside.

Movement caught Dag's eye and he looked up the passageway. An unarmored Gen technician stared open-mouthed at the widening hole in the hull, unaware of Dag just a few meters away. *It begins here.* He blinked on the Gen's head and red crosshairs appeared. He squeezed the trigger. A hole opened in the cocoon just as his assault rifle whined at his hip, firing a slug that turned the Gen's head into a fine red mist. No revival possible. *Just like PFC White back on Earth.* The hole that had opened in the Muon's material to allow the slug to pass through closed as quickly as it formed. The Gen, his feet still bonded to the deck, stood in a macabre imitation of life, thick streamers of blood spouting from his neck. Those broke into globules as they spread out into the passageway, curving under the fabricator's acceleration. Where the blood touched either the Muon's or the fabricator's material, the SIL drank it in. They didn't seem to care which side it belonged to.

Dag rose and started down the passageway, searching for more targets. Something grabbed his shoulder with an iron grip, stopping him. Sergeant Takeuchi moved around and planted himself directly in Dag's path. "The days of officers leading charges ended about two thousand years ago, Lieutenant."

Without waiting for a reply, Takeuchi moved off to organize 1st Platoon's troopers pouring into the passageway from six separate breaches. The Muon assault carriers that had transported the platoon flowed fully into the passageway and joined their material together to form a single cocoon around the entire platoon, protecting them from the fabricator and providing them with the Muons' heavy weapons.

"First Platoon," Takeuchi called out, "squad order by twos. Stay alert."

Four troopers from 1ˢᵗ Squad took the point positions. Dag and Takeuchi fell in behind them, with the rest of the platoon following. One squad from the engineer platoon joined them after a moment, taking up the rear. The troopers didn't move, however; The cocoon moved. It flowed its surface material like a tread, propelling them down the passageway far faster than they could move on their own. If the passageways remained intact—something they didn't expect would happen—they could theoretically reach the bridge in just under an hour. At some point, though, they expected the fabricator would recover from the Special D and would begin closing off or redirecting passageways. That's why they had the engineers with the Kinsey Torpedoes.

After about two minutes, they approached a connecting passageway their schematics told them led to the bridge. They slowed, scanning for defenders or traps. The cocoon formed a remote sensor shaped like an oversized waffle connected by a thin filament of macromolecular material, then sent it into the connecting passageway. The "waffle" found nothing and Dag, eyeing Takeuchi, barely contained his disappointment. Getting that one Gen was probably just dumb luck. They'd have to get much closer to the bridge to find the rest.

The cocoon turned into the connecting passageway and accelerated, carrying the platoon with it. When he was satisfied that no immediate threat loomed, Dag checked his environment and saw that other cocoons with the other platoons of Banshee Troop had fallen in behind them, connected by laser links. Lisa was in the cocoon directly behind him. First Lieutenant Sissel, one of the troopers rescued on Knido and newly appointed the Troop's Executive Officer (XO), was in the third. Dag didn't know her, and she'd made no effort to introduce herself. Some of Dag's troopers had taken offense to her appointment, thinking it a deliberate insult to Dag, whom they thought deserved the position, but Dag didn't care. He just wanted to kill Gen.

Minutes ticked away. No threats appeared and no Gen showed themselves, but the air seemed somehow to grow thicker, the mass of the fabricator around them somehow closer. It was almost malevolent. Like being watched by a serial killer waiting for the right moment to strike.

"Dag," Captain Erikson said, audio only so as not to distract him.

"Yah, Lisa," he replied.

"I'm getting reports on the command net that the fabricator is recovering from the Special D sooner than we expected. Eyes sharp," she finished.

Dag nodded out of habit though she couldn't see it. "Will do." He double-blinked on the platoon net. "Just got word the fabricator is recovering from the Special D. Stay sharp."

Thirty-five kilometers into the fabricator—about one-third of the way to the bridge—the passageway suddenly closed. The cocoon rammed into it but absorbed most of the shock, protecting the troopers inside. Takeuchi yelled, "Kinsey Torpedo, front!"

Dag activated the Troop net. "Lisa, we've encountered a blockage. Deploying torpedo."

"Roger, Dag. We see it," Captain Erickson answered. "Standing by."

"Out," Dag said just as a second lieutenant who looked fresh out of tech school ran up with a meter-long tube in his hands. He looked at Dag, who pointed to the closed passageway to their front. A sharp nod and the lieutenant—Second Lieutenant Scott Haley by his tag—moved to the front and pushed the Kinsey Torpedo into the cocoon's material.

Lieutenant Haley looked back and shouted, "Clear backblast area!"

The interior of the cocoon liquefied, moving troopers to either side of the passageway and forming a tube of material down its middle, centered on the torpedo. "Backblast area all clear!" Haley shouted. "Fire in the hole! Now. *Now.* NOW!"

A blinding white flash filled the passageway and Dag's armored environment immediately darkened to protect his vision. When it cleared a few seconds later, a narrow, glowing shaft about three meters wide opened before them, revealing the original passageway, its material also glowing and fused beyond the blockage. The cocoon's interior briefly liquefied again and the tube that had channeled and dissipated the backblast energy of the torpedo flowed back into the material of the cocoon, which begun to move forward.

"Lieutenant," Takeuchi said on Dag's right, "the passageway continues another ten klicks before running into a large compartment. Good defensive position."

Dag examined the schematic Takeuchi had injected into his environment. 'Large compartment' was a gross understatement. It was twelve kilometers wide, over twenty kilometers down the long axis of the fabricator, and almost three kilometers high. The original plan had estimated they would be through it before the fabricator recovered from the Special D. *So much for that.* There were no other large open spaces between them and the bridge. If the Gen were going to stand and fight, the compartment was where they'd do it.

He activated the Troop net. "Lisa, we're on the move again. Four minutes to the large compartment. Expecting resistance. Over."

This time Captain Erikson projected her image into his environment. Outwardly, she appeared calm, but with their years serving together Dag could read the tension in her slightly furrowed brows and the press of her lips. "We concur. First Platoon will maintain point. I'm bringing the rest of the platoons together to form a single cocoon. We'll be right on your six if you run into trouble."

"Roger," Dag responded. "We're extending the waffle again and should have a read on what's in the compartment in three. Out."

Dag closed the link so he could concentrate on the readings from the waffle sensor. It broke into the compartment, which was extremely well lit across the radio, microwave, infrared, visible, and ultraviolet frequency bands. Large black blocks, some a kilometer long and half that wide, hung within the compartment's low gravity environment. What they were for and what they did, he didn't have a clue; Their briefing hadn't mentioned them. What was clear was that none of the blocks hung between the passageway exit and the opposite side of the compartment. Clear lines of fire for defenders on the other side.

"Lieutenant—"

"I see it, Sergeant," Dag cut Takeuchi off. "Our job is to draw the enemy out so the rest of the Troop can engage them." And to show him where the Gen were so he could kill them. All of them.

Takeuchi opened a private channel. "Your job, Lieutenant, is to safeguard the lives entrusted to you to the maximum extent possible. Don't forget that."

Dag didn't respond. He and his platoon existed for one reason only: to kill Gen. Nothing else mattered. He knew his troopers felt the same way. Even Takeuchi, deep down. This was their revenge. Besides, dying wasn't his plan, at least not yet. Killing was. The cocoon still carried the weapons from the six Muons that formed it: six plasma cannons, twelve P-760S Gatling guns, and thirty-six Corefire anti-armor missiles. Dag selected icons representing each of the weapons systems, released the safeties, switched them to auto-fire, and moved them to the front of the cocoon. If the Gen thought they were just going to shoot his platoon down, they were in for a deadly surprise.

The cocoon shot out of the passageway into the compartment without slowing down. Even though its camouflage systems were active, the cocoon was still using the fabricator's deck for locomotion, meaning the fabricator would know exactly where they were. But that was okay. Their job wasn't to hide.

Dag didn't see the shot, just a crimson glow at the front of the cocoon from a Gen plasma cannon. The cocoon, however, had seen it and three plasma cannons returned fire to a point on the opposite side of the compartment about midway up the bulkhead. Dag couldn't see what they hit, if anything. More enemy plasma cannons opened up on them along a line at the same height as the first shot. Dag keyed the Troop net. "Taking fire. Returning fire. Over."

"Roger, Dag," Captain Erikson replied. "We're a minute behind you."

"Passageway just closed ahead, Lieutenant," Takeuchi said. "Cocoon at ninety-four percent and falling."

Visually, Dag could no longer see through the red and yellow glow engulfing the entire forward section of the cocoon, but he still had a feed from the waffle. A solid bulkhead now covered the passageway that led to the bridge. They'd have to deploy the Kinsey Torpedo under fire. His eyes flicked to the cocoon's health bar. "93%." "92%." SIL could take an astonishing amount of damage and still function, but if the cocoon fell to about ten percent of its starting mass, it would literally fall apart. They still had eleven kilometers of open space to go. At the rate they were losing mass, it would be close.

The Troop net squawked, audio only. "We're in, Dag," Captain Erikson announced. "Not taking any fire. We've run the numbers and your cocoon won't survive to the other end. Slow up and join with ours."

"Copy, Lisa," Dag said, giving the order to the cocoon to slow. It was down to eighty-seven percent with ten kilometers left. They'd also lost two plasma cannons. The enemy fire didn't appear to be slowing.

It took less than thirty seconds for 1st Platoon's cocoon to join with the entire Troop, forming a single, much larger cocoon. Captain

Erickson joined Dag and Takeuchi up front. "We ran the numbers. The Troop cocoon should make it to the other side with plenty to spare. We don't need the passageway. We'll blast our way all the way to the bridge if we have to."

"Pardon, ma'am," Takeuchi said, "but if we've run the numbers, we have to assume the Gen have also. . . ."

A shadow passed over them. They all looked up to see an enormous black block moving over the Troop cocoon, keeping pace with its forward motion about five hundred meters above them.

"What the—" Dag heard Captain Erikson say just as a blinding white flash filled the cocoon.

"LRP!" someone shouted.

"LRP," Takeuchi echoed. "Everybody down! Everybody prone, NOW!"

Dag blinked to clear his vision, but a ghostly afterimage of light stretched across it, making it almost impossible to see. He could barely make out the outline of Captain Erikson standing in front of him. "Lisa?"

A strong hand grabbed Dag, pulling him down. "Get down, Lieutenant! She's gone."

"What?" Dag could make no sense of what Takeuchi meant as the platoon sergeant dragged him prone. More flashes, like bars of white light, streaked across the cocoon. His armor darkened his environment to protect his eyes, and his vision began to clear. LRP, Long-Rod Penetrator rounds, nanocomposite metal rods fired from kinetic launchers at very high speed, pierced the cocoon. They didn't do much damage to the cocoon itself. They were designed to kill what was inside.

Captain Erikson was still standing. "Lisa, get down!" He reached up to grab her arm but stopped before he touched her. Her head and most of her left shoulder were gone. Just . . . gone. Her armor had sealed the breach. No blood flowed. She looked normal standing there, alive, except for. . . .

A red icon appeared to Dag's lower left, red outline, red center. One of his troopers was down, dead but recoverable if they could get him to medical help soon. He glanced up, past Lisa's still-standing corpse. The cocoon was returning fire, every plasma cannon, every Gatling gun, raking the Gen position. It didn't seem to be doing any good. White bars of light continued to streak through the cocoon. The

Gen knew where they were and were firing blind hoping to kill as many troopers inside the cocoon as possible.

Suddenly, the cocoon erupted with a new, electric blue light as every Corefire missile from their Muons lit off at once, racing for the Gen position, fanning out along their entire firing line. *Sissel.* The XO must've fired the missiles. The Gen shot some of them down but couldn't get all of them. Explosions ripped all along the Gen position. Nervous cheers rang out across the cocoon.

The Gen fire stopped for a few seconds, then picked up sporadically, disorganized. It had worked. The way to the bridge was open.

Without warning, the cocoon hit something solid, everything outside the cocoon going black. Dag was thrown forward along with everyone else. Fortunately, they were already prone, and the cocoon and their battle armor absorbed most of their momentum.

The Troop net squawked, and a blood-curdling scream ripped across it. "*Madu! Madu in the cocoon!*"

$=$ 28 $=$

1051 UT, September 29, 3501
RSS Rapidan, Iselin Star System: DAY 2

"We've lost contact with Banshee Troop," Colonel Sal Burress said within Ray's augmented environment. Ray opened a window below Colonel Burress's image showing the status of the six Troops of the 1st Cavalry Squadron. A dark red ring encircled the icon for "B" Troop, indicating a loss of communications. "Just before we lost contact," Colonel Burress continued, "they reported encountering heavy resistance forty kilometers in."

Less than half the distance to the fabricator's bridge. Even as Ray thought that, a dark red ring appeared around "D" Troop's icon. Ray was keeping his task force ten million kilometers behind the fabricator, shadowing its movements. The Iselin Defense Force had attempted to move closer to the fabricator, but a volley of standard Mark IV Novas from Ray's ships had driven them off. Thus far, the fabricator itself had made no attempt to engage his ships. He attributed that to the Special D, but if the fabricator was recovering as quickly as the troopers had reported, that would change. Ray shifted his focus to Rapidan's gray, three-pointed-star image below him in his environment. "Rapidan, you said the fabricator would require at least an hour to recover from the Special D. What's happening?"

Dark red rings appeared around "A" and "C" Troops.

"The Mother Ship is recovering faster than anticipated, Captain Rhoades."

No shit, Ray thought. Dark red appeared around "E" Troop.

As if reacting to his thought, Rapidan said, "Captain Rhoades, the Brethren have never employed disassemblers against other Brethren. Our estimate was based on human records."

Always blaming us, aren't you. But he had no time for that argument. "How soon to manufacture more?" Dark red appeared around the Headquarters Troop icon. The 1ˢᵗ Cavalry Squadron was now completely cut off from the fleet.

"At least three hours, Captain Rhoades," Rapidan answered.

"They'll be dead in half that." Ray hadn't meant to say it out loud. Kamen, Ecuum, Sal, and Chaaya looked at him, startled. "Options?" he asked them quickly.

"Engage the fabricator," Kamen said. "Draw its attention. We've rotated every ship through replenishment. That's three full volleys of Mark Fifteen Novas. Even a fabricator couldn't ignore that."

Rapidan spoke, pride filling its deep voice. Ray wondered if the SIL was even aware of it. "A Mother Ship can manage multiple engagements simultaneously without distraction, Lieutenant Laundraa. It is like your body's immune system. It can fight off an infection even as you perform other activities, unaware of the details of the battle within you. Additionally, if the Mother Ship has recovered, its armaments would easily overwhelm our defenses. We would be destroyed in a direct assault. We cannot allow that."

Ray bristled. "And abandon our people? Human life may mean nothing to you, Rapidan, but thousands of Naturals on both sides have already died for that fabricator." *And I killed most of them*, Ray couldn't help but think, his throat tightening. "Our people may be cut off, but they are not dead. We stay and prevent the Gen from reinforcing the fabricator until this is decided."

With a nod toward Ray, Colonel Burress added, "We don't leave our own behind, Rapidan."

"Captain Rhoades," Rapidan said, its tone condescending, as if lecturing stubborn, willful children, "we can no longer influence the conflict within the Mother Ship. Remaining within weapons range will not alter that fact."

"My answer is still 'No'," Ray said even as another jump signature formed near Tomb.

"Conn, Sensors," Chaaya called. "Jump transient, single ship, range two-zero-one million kilometers. Contact fading rapidly. Profile fits Djinn class cruiser."

Another SIL, Ray thought. That made eighteen Imperial warships that had jumped in from neighboring star systems, eight of them SIL. When enough reinforcements arrived, the Gen would try again to reinforce the fabricator. As much as he hated to admit it, his planner's mind recognized that Rapidan was right. They couldn't influence the fight within the fabricator, and they couldn't remain passively guarding it while reinforcements continued to arrive. They had to take on those reinforcements while they still had the numbers to do it. Then another happy thought came to him: AFCIN entangled communications links would have carried word of the battle to the entire Five Galaxies by now. Imperial warships in thousands of star systems could even now be heading for geodesics that would bring them here. This was exactly the fight he'd wanted to avoid.

"Conn, Sensors. Jump transients!" Chaaya's voice faded to an awed whisper. "It's massive."

Ray turned to the new transients, highlighted within a white oval Chaaya had injected into his environment. It *was* massive, the largest jump transient he'd ever seen, as if a miniature red dwarf star had just appeared on the starward side of Tomb, almost as large as the planet itself. Fiery tendrils of Hawking radiation reached as far as Tomb's outer rings.

The Imperial Fleet had arrived.

"Conn," Chaaya continued, "reading sixty-six contacts, fading slowly. Probable standard ships: thirteen cruisers, thirty-two destroyers and destroyer escorts, ten frigates, and seven auxiliaries."

"Standard ships?" Ray asked. "That doesn't make any sense. Serenna doesn't use. . . ." He looked to his officers, but they appeared as baffled as he was. The transients soon faded to nothingness. The magnified image of Tomb appeared once again to be alone in space.

Eighty-four ships. That's how many ships now occupied the space near Tomb. Plus another two dozen ships in the Iselin Defense Force whose exact location they didn't know. Even so, his twenty-nine SIL warships, armed with Mark XV Novas, were well matched if used properly. But standard ships? That made no sense. Unless . . . of course. Fodder. Serenna was using those ships as fodder just in case Ray was lying in wait, ready to pounce on them the instant they emerged from jump. That meant Serenna's main force had yet to arrive.

Great.

The tide of the battle had just turned solidly against them, but Ray was committed. He wouldn't abandon the troopers or the fabricator until they had no other choice. He addressed his officers, "Serenna likely jumped those standard ships in first to draw fire before her SIL arrive. We must engage them near Tomb and return to the fabricator before the Iselin Defense Force or Serenna can reinforce it. She will no doubt have Imperial Marines with her when she arrives. If those Marines make it to the fabricator, any hope for the Cavalry will be lost."

His planner's mind churned. If he jumped his task force directly to Tomb, the forces there would see them and fire while his ships were still visible and vulnerable. Eighty-four warships represented a lot of firepower. Even armed with Mark IV Novas and Stellar Fires, they would tear his task force apart as his ships recovered from jump. They could also deploy jammers to prevent his task force jumping back to the fabricator, holding it near Tomb until Serenna arrived. If, on the other hand, he jumped outside their immediate missile range, he would have to spend hours—hours he didn't have—maneuvering to engage.

A particularly strong flash of lightning arced across the visible disk of Tomb. For some reason, it reminded Ray of the Niner racing trophies in Ecuum's cabin. "Ecuum," Ray asked, "think you can fly this task force through a planetary dust storm?"

"A what. . . ?" Ecuum's gaze shifted to Tomb. Ray watched as yellow slowly infused Ecuum's skin, and an evil-looking grin spread across his baby face. When Ecuum had had too much to drink— amounts of alcohol that would have drowned Ray—he'd often regale his audience with tales of the Niner races, death-defying maneuvers through protoplanetary star systems, flying not only his own ship but remotely piloting eight others through dust clouds, around asteroids, and skimming proto-planets still hot from formation. If there were women around, he'd offer to show them the thirteen platinum trophies in his cabin. "You're crazy," Ecuum finally said. "Lucky for you, so am I."

Ray pointed toward Tomb with both hands and spread them apart to expand its image until it nearly filled his environment. He selected a point just forty kilometers above the planet's surface, then injected the image into his officers' environments. "Think you can do it?" Ray asked Ecuum.

Ecuum studied the image before pointedly dragging the jump point even closer to the planet's surface. There was no mistaking the swagger on his face despite what the increased gravity would do to him. Ray briefly switched his armor to standard mode and saw Ecuum move forward and take over the navigation station on the bridge, reconfiguring it and sliding horizontal into the interface. From there, he could pilot every ship in the task force, a task that would have been impossible for a human but was well within the capabilities of an experienced Floater.

When Ray returned to his tactical environment, Kamen was staring at him as if he'd lost his mind. "You're both crazy," she pointed out. "We'll be trapped between the planet's surface and Serenna's fleet."

"Captain Rhoades," Rapidan's deep voice reverberated in Ray's chest, "we cannot condone this action. There is a high probability this fleet could be destroyed."

This is why you lost, Ray thought again, wanting Rapidan to hear it. *Besides, I command here, not you. Unless you want to lose. Again.* "We need to buy time for the Cavalry," he said out loud. "This is how we're going to do that. The dust storm and natural lightning will cover our jump signature. We fire missiles and jammers, and jump back to the fabricator. The missiles and jammers will throw the Imperial forces into confusion and prevent their ability to jump to the fabricator until they clear the jammers. This is the only way we leave this solar system with your precious Mother Ship, Rapidan."

Rapidan didn't respond. A violent, invisible surf rose and battered Ray. Black seas heaved under ripping winds. Cold, driving rain pelted his body. None of it was real, but it *felt* real. Yet, it was a ferocity without focus, almost like a child throwing a tantrum, lashing out at anything to vent its frustration, except this did not feel as if it came from a single source. Ray wondered if it was even directed at him at all.

"Conn, Sensors. New jump transients near Tomb," Chaaya called. "Fading quickly. Probable SIL. One is a Solaris Class battlecarrier."

"Serenna," Ray said unnecessarily.

"That's a mass haul," Ecuum said, using the Floater slang for a tough, low-profit job. "Still want to do this, Ray?"

"This doesn't change our strategy," Ray quickly decided. "In fact, it allows us to trap Serenna along with her fleet." He looked to Ecuum within his environment. "It's your show, Captain Ecuum."

Ecuum's face blushed pink. It was a color Ray had only ever seen when they were in a bar and Ecuum was enjoying the company of a woman (or women) who was (were) also enjoying his company. Ray would have to change his assessment of what the color meant.

"Spooling up Linear Star Drive," Ecuum announced. "One minute to jump."

Ray turned to Kamen. "Once we complete the jump, don't wait for targeting data. Fire all three volleys of Mark Fifteen Novas into Serenna's fleet. Follow that with two volleys of RJ-15 jammers." Ray shifted his gaze. "Ecuum, you'll have to keep the fleet steady while we fire, then swing us around the planet to escape."

Kamen repeated her orders in the time-honored tradition of the Navy that ensured that the order given was the order heard. Ecuum just nodded and said, "Hold on to your undies."

Ray's body imploded as the Linear Star Drive engaged.

$==$ 29 $==$

"Visuals clear, Fleet Admiral," Captain Scadic said. "No close contacts."

"That doesn't mean they're not close, Captain Scadic." Serenna relaxed back into her command chair on Solaris' bridge, legs folded casually, elbows on armrests, right hand draped over her left on her lap as if attending a mildly interesting opera, not commanding a fleet in battle. She had practiced the pose endlessly during her Combat Command Nurturing. It didn't just project confidence, it spoke of a deep disdain for anyone who even thought to oppose her. Opponent after opponent had either underestimated her and fallen to overconfidence, or they were so insulted that they acted rashly. Either way, she always won.

Until Michael.

It would be a mistake to underestimate Michael, she had told Gen Cardinal. She would follow her own advice. Projecting the same casual confidence she displayed physically into her voice, she ordered, "Captain Scadic, form the SIL vessels around Solaris and move us starward at five hundred kilometers per second until we have cleared the jump space. Prepare all spacecraft for drift-launch, but hold for my order. Group the standard ships here near the jump point and use it as a rally point for any forces entering this system." That would give Michael an obvious target while safeguarding her own ships. "Once the orders are given, find the fabricator and put me in touch with its commander."

Serenna had studied the few surviving records of fabricator captures. Probably the same records Michael had studied. He had a full cavalry regiment at his disposal. Remarkable foresight. She couldn't help but be impressed yet again with Michael's biologically derived abilities. He would assault the fabricator using his cavalry and devices called Kinsey Torpedoes. The records also mentioned Invasive Macromolecular Disassemblers, but after reading about them she couldn't imagine how they could be produced inside SIL vessels. Regardless, Michael would have a plan that had at least a chance of success, or he wouldn't have come here.

Icons began to appear in Serenna's environment as LoCIN and AFCIN links established with Imperial forces throughout the star system. *Too few.* She expanded her view and . . . she saw two massive debris clouds, one near Tomb's southern pole and the other far too close to her own position. Some of the debris stilled looked like parts of ships. Most of it was hardly recognizable. Then she noticed something else. *Where are the emergency beacons?* She saw a few dozen. That was all. A few dozen when there should have been thousands. Had Michael already rescued the survivors? There hardly seemed enough time.

"Fleet Admiral," Captain Scadic said, "I've located the fabricator, but it is not responding to our hails, nor am I receiving telemetry."

That did not surprise Serenna. Fabricators were the most closely guarded secret in the Empire. Under normal circumstances, Imperial Intelligence officers rarely communicated with Fleet officers. When it came to the eleven surviving fabricators, they never communicated. Like most Fleet officers, Serenna had never seen a fabricator in space. She reached and grabbed the white oval Scadic had injected into her environment, pulling it toward her and expanding it. Even at over 200 million kilometers distance, the massive black cylinder was an impressive sight. "Keep trying to raise its commander," she told Scadic.

"Yes, Fleet Admiral," he said. "We are receiving several hails. One of them identifies himself as Commander Baypha, commander of the Iselin Defense Force." Scadic's upper lip twisted. "A Natural."

"Captain," Serenna softly reprimanded him, "do not allow prejudice to cloud your judgement or cause you to underestimate your enemy."

Scadic lowered his gaze, accepting the correction. "Yes, Fleet Admiral."

"Put him through," she told him.

A Natural with light skin and thick, dark hair formed before them. "Thank the Emperor you're here, Fleet Admiral," he began, and Serenna could hardly conceal her disgust. She did not think it possible for human eyes to get so wide or their faces so pale short of death. If not for his battle armor, urine would probably be running down his legs in torrents. She spotted his force, about twenty million kilometers from the fabricator—headed directly toward her position at maximum burn."

Serenna allowed some of her anger into her voice. "Why are you retreating, Commander? You will return to the fabricator and defend it at all costs."

"But, Admiral," he pleaded, "they're using Mark Fifteen warheads. They decimated our other fleets. We don't have anything larger than a Mark Four in our inventory and my ships can't reconfigure our warheads like the rebel's SIL can. It's suicide."

Mark XV warheads? That explained the destruction and the lack of emergency beacons. Michael hadn't rescued the other survivors because there hadn't been any other survivors. He had killed them. Naturals. Thousands of them. *Or . . . had he?* Was he even still in command? That would explain the attack at Tau Ceti and this. Even as she thought it, though, she couldn't bring herself to believe it. Michael was no Player in *Gamon Politic*, but he wasn't stupid. He was meticulous, cautious. He would have vetted his co-conspirators carefully. This didn't add up. It had to be him, yet it couldn't be him.

"What is the status of the fabricator?" Serenna asked the Natural commander. *And where is your Gen handler?* she thought silently. Gen Cardinal would never have placed a military force under a Natural's command without a handler.

"We're not sure," the Natural said nervously. "The rebels jumped close to it, but we didn't see any attack. It looked like something, lots of somethings, struck the fabricator's hull, but we didn't see any explosions. We tried to hail them, to see if they needed help, but they only give orders, they never respond."

No explosions. So, Michael had launched an assault team that was probably still aboard the fabricator. She had a full battalion of Imperial Marines. "Commander, you will return to the fabricator and defend it at all costs."

"But—"

"Where are the rebels now?" she pressed.

"They were shadowing the fabricator, but they just jumped away."

"Jumped away. . . ." Serenna's voice faded. "Defend the fabricator," she ordered him yet again, then severed the link. To Scadic, she said, "All ships, weapons free. Launch spacecraft."

1108 UT, September 29, 3501
RSS Rapidan, Iselin Star System: DAY 2

"**Yeehaw!** Now this is flying!"

Ray coughed, a combination of real blood and simulated talcum-like dust choking his breath. He blinked away the thin layer of blood clouding his vision and tried to assess their situation even as his head pounded in pain with every heartbeat. Human bodies were not designed for jump space, and two jumps within just a few hours did a lot of damage. Floaters, however, were engineered for this and Ecuum actually looked like he was having fun as he fought to hold the fleet just fifteen kilometers above the surface of Tomb.

Ray blinked his eyes again and looked straight ahead—which was a mistake. Wrapped in his augmented environment, thick reddish-brown dust driven by 300 kilometer-per-hour winds seemed to fly straight at him. Instinctively, he threw his arm up to protect his eyes before his rational mind reminded him that he was, in fact, deep inside a very large warship. The ship itself seemed unaffected by the winds and dust, its image below him glowing blue as its deflectors shunted the dust around the vessel. He also noticed that either Ecuum or the SIL had slightly altered the hull's shape to act as a lifting body, helping to keep the ship from falling to the planet's surface. Even so, they were slowly losing altitude.

"First volley away!" Kamen shouted even though very little sound accompanied the image of the violent dust storm outside. Seventy Novas fired their boost engines immediately after clearing their launching ships to help them ascend through the storm.

A brilliant flash of blue-white lightning arced from the clouds to Rapidan, diffusing across its deflectors and briefly blinding Ray. Before his vision could clear, Kamen announced "Second volley away!" followed shortly by "All missiles away!" Ray shifted his gaze around the afterimage of the lightning, but quickly lost sight of the missiles through the storm.

They were still losing altitude, down to thirteen kilometers above Tomb. Though SIL warships could fly through an atmosphere and even land, it was rare for a ship of Rapidan's size to do so. They would need to climb back to fifteen kilometers or risk cracking the planet's crust when they jumped away.

"All jammers away!" Kamen said.

"Get us out of here, Ecuum," Ray ordered as the fleet fell below twelve kilometers altitude.

"Gettin', aye," Ecuum replied, the strain of gravity trying to crush his lungs evident in his voice, though he sported a huge, thick-lipped grin below his look of intense concentration. Ray couldn't remember a time when Ecuum seemed to be enjoying himself this much. At least, not when he was sober.

Each SIL vessel flattened out, making them more aerodynamic in the thickening atmosphere. Their rate of descent slowed, but it didn't stop. Ecuum was purposely steering them within a few kilometers of Tomb's surface and increasing speed so he could slingshot them away from the planet on the opposite side from Serenna's fleet.

"Kamen," Ray asked, consciously keeping his voice at a conversational volume despite the darkening dust rushing past him. Lightning illuminated the clouds from within and occasionally branched out in thick streamers to lash at Rapidan's deflectors. "Time to impact?"

"About eleven minutes," she said. "The flight profile I selected gave the missiles a short boost to escape the planet's gravity well, then transitioned them directly into hunt mode to minimize their chance of being detected."

"Good job," Ray commended her.

"That will also allow us to jump clear about a minute before the jammers light off," Kamen added.

Ray gave a single nod, not taking his eyes—or his white knuckled grip on his armrests—from their wild ride. It wasn't bumpy or turbulent, but that did nothing to calm his nerves as they crossed the terminator into night. A red glow grew along the leading edges of the deflectors and lightning filled the sky all around them, growing more intense the deeper they descended into the darkness.

After what seemed an eternity but wasn't more than a couple of minutes, their altitude began to climb. Dust clouds grew less dark, and the lightning subsided. A last bolt reached out at Rapidan as the Linear Star Drive engaged.

=== 31 ===

1129 UT, September 29, 3501
ISS Solaris, Iselin Star System: DAY 2

Serenna had never witnessed a Mark XV warhead explode outside of historical records. It was an impressive sight. The double flash of the warhead became a brilliant white fireball that consumed the midsection of a Megiddo class cruiser, leaving the bow and stern as separate pieces, cauterized where the antimatter had burned through. Two more Novas swooped in, coordinating their attack, and destroyed the surviving sections leaving almost nothing in their wake to show that a ship had once existed. It had taken bare seconds.

Other ships of the standard group came under fire, having been completely surprised by Michael's attack. White fireballs filled space like the crescendo of a massive fireworks display. Ships died by the dozens. The only thing that had saved her SIL warships was separating them from the standard ships. And while standard ships were not as robust as SIL, they were made from the same macromolecular material as SIL. If Mark XV warheads could consume a Megiddo, they could do the same to her SIL. Even Solaris itself.

When the fires faded, only sixteen of seventy-six standard ships—which included ships that had jumped to Tomb prior to her fleet's arrival—remained unscathed. Four more were severely wounded and out of the fight. The rest were destroyed. In less than two minutes, Michael had damaged or destroyed more than half of her fleet.

She accepted this, even as her mind processed the implications. Michael had shifted his tactics to those employed during the SIL Wars, brutal wars of genocide and survival. She couldn't image what could have driven him to such tactics, and again weighed the possibility that he was no longer in command. As before, though, she discarded that possibility. The tactic she had just witnessed was pure Michael—with the notable exception of the death toll.

"Captain Scadic, where did this attack originate and where is Michael now?" she asked, tracing a small circle on her armrest with her right forefinger, as if losing half her fleet was no real consequence. And, truth be told, it wasn't. Michael had missed his real target.

Or had he? The thought occurred to her that his target might be as much psychological as physical. Demonstrating the destruction he could wreak, reducing her numbers by half, knowing she couldn't possibly reconfigure her warheads to Mark XVs before this battle was decided, was he trying to scare her off, make her so wary of further losses that it would effectively debilitate her and buy the time he needed to complete the capture of the fabricator?

"Fleet Admiral," Scadic said, "it appears the rebels jumped into Tomb's atmosphere directly below the jump point. We are receiving telemetry from one of the other vessels that indicates a significant disturbance in the planet's global weather system that would be consistent with a Linear Star Drive jump. We also have indications of residual Hawking radiation on the opposite side of the planet."

"Then he's already jumped away," Serenna observed. "Any indication of where?"

Scadic shook his head. "Not yet, Fleet Admiral."

The obvious tactic would be to jump back to the fabricator, but it would take almost nine minutes for the light of such a jump to reach her fleet. She couldn't wait that long. "Have you reached the fabricator's commander?"

"No, Fleet Admiral," Scadic replied.

That was odd, given the circumstances. Even for Imperial Intelligence. Taking on Michael would be far easier if she could coordinate her attack with the fabricator, especially given its firepower. "Captain Scadic, cut all telemetry with the standard ships in this system." Serenna was not about to let any of the standard ships or their Natural crews risk her SIL force, Gen handlers or not.

"All telemetry with standard ships cut, Fleet Admiral," Scadic said after a brief pause.

"Recover our spacecraft," she ordered. "Plot a jump fifteen million kilometers in front of the fabricator and order the remaining SIL vessels in this system to join us there. Alert the Imperial Marines to prepare for a boarding action. Engage the Linear Star Drive when ready."

Serenna watched as Scadic carried out her orders. So, Michael thought he could scare her off. He would soon discover that he was not the only one who could change tactics.

"Fleet Admiral," Scadic called out, surprise and—was that a tremor in his voice? "RJ-15 jammers just went active. H2 and H3 are jammed. We can't jump."

Serenna smiled.

Nicely done, Michael, she thought, *but it won't be enough to stop me.*

32

Snake-like Madu poured into the cocoon from the top and sides by the dozens and hundreds. Dag grabbed his Main Gauche dagger off his left thigh just as a pair of soulless, glowing red eyes locked onto him.

The Madu burst from Maria's left ear, trailing blood and tissue in its wake, and turned its soulless red eyes on his daughter. It almost seemed to smile, as if purposely drawing the moment out.

Papi! Papi, help me!

ROSITA!

"Not this time, you Demon," Dag told it. "I will save my daughter!"

Light from weapons fire glinted off its scaled black body as it slithered toward Dag. He didn't know how it could see him, and, frankly, he didn't care. It coiled and launched itself at his face, jaws gaping wide to expose glowing red venom sacks, honey-colored drops clinging to the tips of its long white fangs. Dag slashed with the dagger . . . and it passed right through the Madu, not even slowing it down. It struck at his face, cavernous mouth biting against his armor. He reached up with his right hand and tried to grab it, to pull it off, but his hand went right through the Madu's body.

It was an illusion!

Disappointment flooded through Dag. He wanted to kill it, really kill it, for what it had done to his Rosita, to his Maria.

"They're illusions!" Takeuchi yelled over the Troop net.

Illusions they might be, but they looked real, and their attacks had thrown the Troop into a panic. Dag keyed the Troop net, the Madu still biting at his face, fangs piercing ever closer to his flesh. "The

Madu are not real," he said. "They are illusions." No one seemed to hear him. Troopers lashed out with daggers, fired weapons. A stray round struck one of his troops. Her icon turned red as she went down. "THE MADU ARE NOT REAL! SETTLE DOWN!"

Another weapon discharged before the troopers began lowering weapons, but that didn't calm things. Troopers grabbed at the illusionary black forms, their hands passing through vacuum. They swatted at them, screamed, and flinched at perceived attacks, formed small groups with backs to each other. With a monumental effort of will to ignore the Madu biting at his own face, Dag calmed his voice, embraced the void. "They aren't real. We still have a job to do."

A hand touched his shoulder and Dag whirled, his dagger coming up.

"WHOA! Sorry," Lieutenant Sissel, Banshee Troop's new commanding officer, said, backing up a step. Three phantom Madu attacked her head, fangs sunk deep, honeyed venom pooled at the ends, black coils wrapped around her throat. On a private channel she said, "These may be illusions, but those aren't." She pointed at Madu outside the cocoon.

Hundreds, thousands, of Madu surrounded them everywhere he looked, their red eyes like a nightmare scene from some evil dark forest. As he watched, he noticed faint red glows at the tip of every Madu's snout. They were burning their way into the cocoon. And this wasn't some illusion. The combined Troop cocoon's health had dropped to ninety-two percent and was still falling.

"Lieutenant Haley, join us," Lieutenant Sissel ordered the young engineer who'd set off the Kinsey Torpedo back in the passageway. The kid—Dag couldn't think of him any other way—duck-walked over to them, three phantom Madu at his face and two at his crotch. Given his death-white complexion, it was probably a good thing that he wore battle armor that could absorb bodily waste.

When he joined them, his head tilted to the side to look at them past the Madu illusions. Lieutenant Sissel physically grabbed him and Dag by the arm, linking them into a completely secure, private network. "Ideas?" was all she said. Definitely a woman of few words. Not like Lisa. . . .

Dag pushed that aside. *The Void. Embrace the Void. It doesn't hurt there.*

"Lieutenants?" Lieutenant Sissel pressed when neither of them answered.

Dag couldn't help but notice the cocoon's health drop from ninety to eighty-nine percent. "Even if we could break out of here," he said, "we'd have to face those Madu, and the Gen could simply hit us with another one of these blocks. We'd never make it across the compartment."

"Tell me something I don't already know," Lieutenant Sissel rebuked him, her tone sharp.

Dag bristled, but kept it to himself; Lisa had never talked down to him like that. He looked to Lieutenant Haley. "We need another way out of here. Could we use one of those torpedoes?"

Lieutenant Haley shook his head as if he were trying to knock the illusionary Madu loose. "This block thing is all around us!" His voice cracked. "If we open any part of the cocoon to vent the backblast, we just give it more surface area to attack us. If we don't vent the backblast, it would kill half the people in here." His eyes darted to the real Madu outside the cocoon. "Someone would have to set it off outside the cocoon." The way he said 'someone' made it clear he didn't want to be the one.

The cocoon's health fell below eighty-seven percent. "I'll do it," Dag said.

"No, I will," Lieutenant Sissel countered, her tone making it clear she'd accept no argument. She bent her head as if studying something. "There is a maintenance tunnel about half a click below and to the right of us. It intersects with a larger passageway that should lead directly to the bridge. Will the torpedo reach it?" she asked Lieutenant Haley as she injected a schematic into their environments.

"Well," he said as he studied the schematic, his tone and posture becoming that of an engineer working a problem. "The angle will have to be precise, and we'll have to burn through the slag to get into the maintenance tunnel, but, yes, it could work. It'll take several seconds to line it up—"

"Get me a torpedo," she ordered him.

Lieutenant Haley ordered up a torpedo from its storage location in the cocoon. It arrived less than a minute later. He handed it to her. She grabbed it and stared at Dag. "Complete the mission." Her eyes were haunted, the look of someone who knew she was about to die. "Armored Cav."

She walked through the cocoon, stopping just outside as she ran into the block's material, hugging the Kinsey Torpedo to her chest where it would be protected within her armor. The Madu, the real ones, sensed her and attacked immediately, dozens of them, their snouts glowing as red as their eyes as they burned their way through her battle armor. Lieutenant Sissel seemed oblivious to them as she crouched and planted the torpedo against the deck. Dag watched as the torpedo linked with her armor, guiding it to the exact angle to intersect the maintenance tunnel below. The eyes of every Madu flashed a blood-chilling crimson as one of their members penetrated her armor, striking into Lieutenant Sissel's left eye. Her whole body jerked as the Madu's long, black-scaled form wriggled into her head, but her battle armor kept the Kinsey Torpedo steady and fired it.

The cocoon darkened automatically to protect their eyes from the antimatter blast, appearing to Dag like a shaft of holy light cast by God himself. Except, God didn't do it. God had done nothing.

Papi! Papi, help me!

"Everyone Prone!" Takeuchi ordered. "Prepare to move out."

A new window opened in Dag's environment, appearing to hang about half a meter in front of his chest, angled for easy viewing. Within it were seven frames, one for each of Banshee Troop's combat platoons and one for the Headquarters platoon. Within each platoon frame, head-and-chest icons indicated the status of every trooper in Banshee Troop. About two dozen were yellow, orange, or red: wounded, severely wounded, or dead but recoverable with medical care, respectively. Two were black inside red outlines. Not recoverable. Lisa and Lieutenant Sissel.

It took a few seconds before Dag realized why he was seeing the window. He was the highest-ranking surviving officer.

He was now in command of Banshee Troop.

"Lieutenant, you need to get prone, and we need to get moving," Takeuchi said, lying prone at Dag's feet. "First Sergeant Xu is down. It's up to you and me to get these people out of here."

Dag blinked away his disorientation and dropped prone. Belatedly, he noticed that the Madu illusions were gone. It was small comfort. The real ones were still there, the ones that had survived the Kinsey Torpedo firing. Regardless, he was in command, and he had a mission: Kill Gen, all of them, to save his daughter. The Gen would be guarding the bridge; it was the only place an invading force could gain control of the fabricator. He would kill the Gen, take the bridge, and kill more Gen until all of them were destroyed and Rosita was safe.

Dag attached the cocoon status window to the Troop window, then located Lieutenant Haley. "Drive us out of here, Lieutenant. You know the way."

Scared as he looked, Lieutenant Haley gave him a very convincing "Yes, sir" as he accepted command of the cocoon from Dag and began moving it toward the shaft the Kinsey Torpedo had made. The cocoon contracted around them and began to flow forward toward the three-meter-diameter hole blown through the deck and block.

As if sensing their prey trying to escape, the red glow around the snouts of the surviving Madu brightened. The cocoon's health dropped to eighty percent. The air seemed suddenly heavier, harder to breath, like an undertow trying desperately to drag them into darker waters, to drown them. There was a . . . presence . . . an evil . . . pressing in from every direction. Dag tried to shake the feeling, but as the cocoon moved further into the shaft, expanding its diameter to match that of the shaft, the oppressiveness only increased.

Dag looked back "up" the shaft and noticed a solid plug of material. Confused, he checked the cocoon status and saw that Lieutenant Haley had sacrificed ten percent of the cocoon's mass to create the barrier between them and the pursuing Madu. It hadn't caught all of them, but it had stopped, or at least delayed, most of them. It had come with a cost, though. The cocoon was down to sixty-seven percent with more than half the distance to the bridge still to cover.

Dag opened a private channel. "Lieutenant Haley, we don't have mass to spare and a long way yet to go." The cocoon accelerated down the shaft.

"If those things had stayed with us," he answered in a distracted tone, "they would have done more damage." Haley slowed the cocoon as they neared the maintenance shaft, bringing it to a complete stop so he could burn through the slag created by the Kinsey Torpedo. "That's not our biggest problem."

Dag linked Takeuchi into the conversation and waited for Haley to elaborate, but the young Lieutenant seemed completely absorbed in his work. When he didn't respond, Dag prompted, "Lieutenant, what is our biggest problem?"

"What?" He looked up from what he was doing. "Oh. Uh, we'll never make it to the bridge. At least, not like this."

"We can't turn back," Takeuchi said, careful to keep his gestures relaxed and his mouth angled so the other troopers couldn't read his lips. "Even if we could make it to the hull, there's no one waiting for us."

Rhoades, Dag thought. This was a suicide mission. It had been from the beginning. They—the troopers of the 1st Cavalry Squadron— were the only living witnesses to Rhoades' failure with the starliner. If he got rid of them, he could tell whatever story he wanted. Then, something else occurred to Dag. What if Rhoades deliberately sacrificed the starliner—as he was sacrificing them now—so his fleet could escape?

"—couldn't make it back to the hull either," Haley was saying, snapping Dag back to the present.

"'Dead either way' isn't good enough, Lieutenant." The disgust in Dag's voice caused Haley to visibly shrink back. "Get us to the bridge."

"Y-yes, sir," Haley stammered, looking as frightened as he had with the Madu. He hesitated, then added, "Sir, I don't know how to do that." Dag scowled. Instead of shrinking further, Haley seemed to gather his courage, stand a little taller. He met Dag's scowl. "In this shaft, Lieutenant, the fabricator and its defenders can't sense us through the slag create by the torpedo." He pointed to the side. "Once we break through into that maintenance shaft, they'll know where we are and be able to block our path and attack us as they did before. They'll wear us down long before we reach the bridge."

"What about the torpedoes?" Takeuchi asked.

Haley's eyes flicked between the two of them, but settled on Dag. "We don't have enough." Before either of them could comment, Haley said, "We estimated that the Special D would last long enough to get us at least fifty klicks into the fabricator, roughly halfway to the bridge. So, each unit was issued fifty-five torpedoes: fifty clicks plus a ten percent margin of error. We've already used two and, from our current position, it's sixty-one kilometers on a straight line to the bridge."

So, Rhoades had set them up to fail. That horrible feeling of helplessness aboard the Fatboy, of watching his family slaughtered, and of Lisa's headless corpse standing lifeless above him, pressed in, trying to wrap its icy, pitiless fingers around him and drag him down to despair.

Papi! Papi, help me!

ROSITA!

Dag grabbed Haley by both armored shoulders, the Void settling over him like a heavy black cloak, consuming all emotion. "You . . . *will* . . . get us to the bridge."

From the side, Takeuchi asked Haley, "How did they do it before, Lieutenant? When they captured these fabricators," he clarified. "They couldn't have used the torpedoes near the bridge, right? That would risk destroying it. So, how'd they get to the bridge itself?"

Haley's eyes, locked like a terrified deer's on Dag's face, darted to Takeuchi. "They—they . . . they used . . . Special D."

"How, Lieutenant?" Takeuchi asked.

"They infused their cocoons with Special D," Haley said, his head turning fully to look at Takeuchi. "As their cocoon moved forward, it would inject Special D into the surrounding SIL material, allowing their cocoon to push through it. But, we don't have any Special D."

"You're wrong, Lieutenant Haley," Dag said, lifting his Main Gauche dagger and holding it up before Haley's face, the point of the blade less than three centimeters from the bridge of Haley's nose. Haley tried to step back but Dag tightened his grip on Haley's left shoulder, holding him firmly in place. "Will this get us to the bridge?"

"I—I . . . No." Haley again seemed to find his courage and looked up from the dagger point to Dag's eyes. "I'm sorry, Lieutenant, it's not enough. Not even close. But—" he interrupted Dag as he was about to protest— "if we used the Kinsey Torpedoes to get to a passageway near the bridge, it might be enough to hold the passageway open the rest of the way there. But, the Special D won't protect the cocoon from weapons fire," he finished.

"Just get us there, Lieutenant," Dag told him. "I'll get us in."

33

1132 UT, September 29, 3501
RSS Rapidan, Iselin Star System: DAY 2

Ray's head pounded from the jump, each beat of his struggling heart like a jackhammer blow inside his skull. Sharp, throbbing pain wracked his body as if an angry mob had just savagely beaten him near to death. The coppery taste of his own blood fouled his mouth and nose. His vision was clouded, like looking through a thick red mist. The human body was not made for jump space, let alone three jumps within the span of a few hours. He could feel Rapidan injecting new molemachs into his body to repair the damage. He would never admit this to Rapidan, but at this moment he was grateful the SIL could take care of themselves.

Slowly, too slowly, his vision cleared and the pounding in his head subsided. Kamen, younger and in better physical shape, had already recovered enough that she was checking on the task force's status. When she noticed him watching, she said, "We are free and clear to navigate, now ten million kilometers behind the fabricator, which has maintained course and is accelerating slowly through forty-five thousand kps. Captain Ecuum is accelerating the fleet to match the fabricator."

Ecuum gave Ray a self-satisfied wink, a huge I-told-you-so grin still puffing up his cheeks from the maneuver at Tomb. "Let's do that again."

"Smartass," Ray managed, his voice raspy and wet. He swallowed several times, then with a conscious effort he straightened his posture and leaned back into his command chair, trying to project a calm and physical strength he did not feel.

"Better than being a dumbass," Ecuum retorted, his grin spreading wider, showing off white teeth and a pink tongue with no traces of blood.

After three jumps, Ray envied Ecuum's genetic engineering that made him, if not immune, far better equipped to survive the rigors of warped spacetime. Even as he thought that, though, it reminded him that Serenna and her Gen also had that engineered adaptation, and she would be coming for them as soon as she eliminated his jammers. Even so, his first concern was closer to home. "Kamen, status on the civilians?"

She checked her displays. "No fatalities thanks to the molemachs, but a lot of complaints. Most of them have never experienced an LSD jump before today. Mary has organized teams to care for them."

"Put me through to her, please."

"Yes, sir."

A new window opened before him, separate from the windows holding the faces of his officers. Mary looked distracted but determined. "How's it going, Mary," he asked. He wanted desperately to ask about their children, but such a self-serving request could quickly spread throughout the fleet.

"We're managing," she said, looking away to something or someone he couldn't see. "Over there," she said before turning back to him. "They're frightened, Ray. How many more of these jumps are we going to have to do?"

"Hopefully, that was the last one. This battle should be decided in the next hour."

She nodded, and it was obvious from the grave set of her face that she knew exactly what he meant. "I'll manage things here. You take care of yourself."

"You, too," he said, taking in her oval face, her short brown-blond hair, her hazel eyes—and wondering if it was the last time he would ever see them. She must have seen something in his expression for her face softened. "I love you," he told her.

"I love you, too." She smiled thinly but with genuine care, then after another second she cut the link and the window vanished. Her afterimage lingered.

The sense of foreboding that had troubled Ray before the battle returned. His fleet was outnumbered at least two to one in SIL vessels, not to mention the Iselin Defense Force that was still out there somewhere. They'd expended all of their Mark XV warheads. They'd lost contact with the assault force on the fabricator and had no idea if the Cavalry were continuing their assault, or if they were even still alive. Mary often talked about faith, about accepting the idea that a higher power cared about them and watched over them. Ray was not religious, but if ever there was a time for faith, it was now. He had to have faith that the troopers were alive and continuing their assault. He had to have faith that this fight was still worth fighting. He would not abandon the troopers, and that meant keeping Serenna from reinforcing the fabricator. Somehow, he needed to buy at least an hour without sacrificing his fleet—and his family—in the process. And he had to do all that against the most skilled tactician in the Gen High Command.

"Kamen, status of Serenna's fleet?" he asked.

"They've destroyed half of the jammers," Kamen answered, studying the AFCIN faster-than-light telemetry from the jammers. "We have less than fifteen minutes before she'll be able to jump." Kamen paused, studying something else. "The underway replenishment ships have produced enough new Mark Fifteen warheads to arm Rapidan and one cruiser with a single volley."

"Rapidan first," Ray said, checking his ships, "and Bidziil." Technically, Chelius on Roanoke was senior, but Ray was not about to trust Chelius with the more powerful warheads. "Bleed heat. All ships."

"Bleed heat, aye," Kamen repeated. "Seven minutes to ambient temperature," she added in a warning tone.

"They saw our jump and know where we are," Ray said.

Ecuum moved Rapidan closer to the replenishment ships, while Ray examined the fabricator's course, hoping for an idea that could buy them some time. The only geodesic along the fabricator's course, about an hour and a half distant, was the geodesic for Tocci Star System. Which didn't make any sense as a destination for the fabricator. Tocci was a military and industrial star system with a large surface base and the famous Tocci Shipyards, the largest shipyards in the Five Galaxies. Traffic going into and out of the system was constant. In Ray's century of service, Imperial Intelligence had never moved a fabricator to, or even through, a star system with a Fleet installation in it. He suspected the fabricator would change course before it reached the geodesic.

Tocci. His planner's mind awoke. It was a star system rich in military history. Humanity had fought its first and second battles against the Solthari there, losing the first and winning the second, though it was a pyric victory. Solthari bioweapons reduced the once lush planet, then known as Garden, to a desolate rock. The barren desert world arose anew as a military testing and training center, and then a major shipyard, which made it an indispensable prize for both sides in the SIL Wars. No star system had changed hands more times in the three SIL Wars than Tocci. But it was that very first battle that gave Ray his inspiration.

"Ecuum," he said, "once we complete replenishment, bring the task force one million kilometers to the rimward side of the fabricator and slightly behind it to hide our engine exhaust."

Ecuum, never having served as a tactical bridge officer, did not repeat the order. He simply nodded and got to it. Shifting his focus to Kamen, Ray continued. "Once we're on station, have all ships drift-launch all remaining Novas ahead of the fabricator. Hold the Mark Fifteen Novas in reserve."

As if to demonstrate proper bridge protocol to Ecuum, Kamen responded loudly, "Once on station, all ships drift-launch all Novas ahead of the fabricator, aye. Hold Mark Fifteen Novas in reserve, aye." She paused and looked up to Ray. "Sir, may I ask what you have in mind?"

Ray smiled. This was the reason he valued her, why he'd taken her "under his wing" all those years ago. She was eager to learn and to understand the "why" of a situation. It was a characteristic of the best officers Ray had ever served with. In that, she also reminded him very much of his oldest daughter, Margaret. "Ancient history, Kamen. First Battle of Tocci. Why did the human fleet lose?"

"They were overwhelmed," she answered immediately, expressing the common belief taught at the Academy. "They were unprepared for the Solthari swarm tactics, unprepared to fight an enemy that made missiles, thousands of them, out of their own crews."

"Yes," Ray said gently, "but why did they lose?"

"Sir, I'm not sure I understand." Kamen sounded genuinely puzzled.

Ray stayed silent. It was a technique he'd learned from Alyn. 'If you give your subordinates the answer they'll never learn; if you let them find the answer they'll never forget.' As Alyn's words echoed in his mind, Ray's pain and guilt at his murder threatened to erupt and engulf him again. He fought it down, forcing the smiling image of Alyn sitting behind his oak desk out of his head. Something of the struggle must have shown because Kamen's expression became concerned. Partly to cover his lapse and partly to prompt her, he asked, "Were their ships incapable of countering the Solthari swarm?"

After a moment, Kamen gave him a drawn-out "No." She pondered for a few seconds more. "Their ships, while primitive by our standards, had all the same basic systems. Solthari soldiers weren't heavily armored, so human weapons would've been effective. But there were just too many of them."

Ray again said nothing, just watched her. He could almost see her inward sigh that she hadn't got the answer quite right, and her mental search for what she must be missing. Then, like the coming of dawn, enlightenment spread across her face. She absently rubbed her hand across her bald ebony scalp. "They *assumed* there were too many of them, that their defenses couldn't hold. Because they assumed that, they retreated, surrendering the colony to its fate, and losing almost their entire force to confusion as they broke and ran."

Ray nodded. He was a student of history and history taught the dangers of becoming the indispensable person, without whom an endeavor collapsed. If anything happened to him, someone must be able to step into his place and lead the revolt. He hoped that someone was Kamen. "The Solthari beat the human fleet before the first missile struck," Ray explained. "Psychology can be more important to the outcome of a battle than weapons and numbers. To win here we must fight Serenna, not her fleet." Ray cocked his head. "What do you know about her?"

"Brilliant. Ruthless," Kamen said immediately. Her eyes become unfocused, or perhaps, focused in a deeper way would be a better description, an inward focus. "Conservative. Cautious. Methodical. Like a lot of Gen commanders." Ray watched her consider her environment. "She saw us use Mark Fifteen warheads. She'll assume all our missiles are armed with them. So, when she sees a massive swarm of missiles headed her way, she'll act to protect her fleet." She met his gaze. "Brilliant."

"Let's not get ahead of ourselves," Ray cautioned. "Overconfidence can be just as dangerous."

"If you two are done with the lovefest," Ecuum said, "we'll be on station near the fabricator in about twenty minutes. I'm having to bring us up and around to avoid that thing's massive exhaust plume, which would paint us and make us easy to see. 'Brilliant' piece of flying, if you ask me. Which neither of you did, by the way."

Ray shook his head and Kamen laughed, but her expression quickly turned serious. "First volley away," she announced as yellow missile tracks blossomed in Ray's environment, moving parallel to and slightly faster than the fabricator. More volleys followed until Ray's ships had emptied their magazines of offensive missiles. It was a risk, but Ray knew that if he stood toe-to-toe with Serenna's fleet, he'd lose. All he had to do was buy an hour. One hour. If he could do that, they still had a chance.

34

We have destroyed the last jammer, Fleet Admiral," Captain Scadic told Serenna. "We are free and clear to navigate. Should I plot a jump to the fabricator?"

"Not yet," Serenna replied. "Any contact with the fabricator?"

"None, Fleet Admiral," Scadic said.

Serenna hid her frustration, focusing instead on the thousands of dark grooves between the jeweled ringlets that formed Tomb's famous rainbow rings. It was a magnificent, awe-inspiring sight that words or realities could never adequately capture, but few ever talked about the small, dark gaps between the individual ringlets that gave the rings their grooved appearance. There was something somber there, a reminder that these rings were the last great work of a dying race, a lesson for all races that their time in this universe was finite. What did that lesson mean for the current fight? She had assumed the outcome of this battle was foreordained. Gen were superior: in genetics, in Nurturing, in their society. Naturals, Homo sapiens, "wise man," had reached the pinnacle of their evolution and had nothing more to offer. Gen, Homo superior, "superior man," were the future. Just as Homo sapiens had driven all other human species to extinction during their rise, now it was their turn to step aside. There could be no coexistence. One must overcome the other. Serenna had never doubted which one would survive.

She saw now how that supposition had colored her tactics. She had assumed, based on her conversation with Gen Cardinal, that she would have the firepower of the fabricator to add to that of her fleet, an overwhelming force that Michael could not hope to stand against.

Michael's defeat was as inevitable as was Gen hegemony. Now, she wasn't so sure.

Her gaze returned to the jeweled rings before her. Michael's attack on her fleet, jumping into the dust-enshrouded atmosphere of a planet, was inspired—a tactic that never would have occurred to her had their positions been reversed. She still outnumbered his fleet in SIL two to one, but he was using Mark XV warheads and she had none, nor did she have time to produce any before this battle would be decided. That evened the odds. It was another failure on her part, another tactic that she had not imagined. Worse, the Iselin Defense Force had not followed her order to guard the fabricator and was instead shadowing it at almost twenty million kilometers, well out of effective combat range given its capabilities. Was that part of a plan, or simply inexperience? She didn't know, and in the middle of a major battle, not knowing could prove fatal.

So, what to do? Michael was not infallible. His attack on her fleet, while devastating, had not been decisive. He was trying to delay her, to buy time for his assault teams to capture the fabricator. Simulations based on historical records had shown it would take at least two hours to accomplish that. She had roughly an hour to stop him.

"Where is the fabricator headed?" she asked Scadic.

"Tocci is the nearest geodesic, Fleet Admiral, one hour seven minutes distant," he said. "The next closest geodesic leads to Morgan, a major trading hub with a population of forty billion, six hours distant." Scadic looked up at her, his eyes measuring. "Based on what little we know of fabricator operations, neither possibility seems likely."

Serenna met his scrutiny, measuring him in turn. What did he see when he stared at her like that? She laughed softly in her mind, careful not to let either humor or irony reach her face. *Did I ever gawk at Gen Alyn like that, like he had the answer to any and every question in the omniverse?* She had no more idea where the fabricator might be headed than he did. Or . . . did she? Gen Cardinal had mentioned using 'his forces' along with her fleet to confront Admiral Sun's sizable fleet. A single fabricator, used as a warship, was the equal of a hundred SIL vessels, and Gen Cardinal controlled all eleven fabricators. Was he assembling them at Tocci as part of a fabricator strike force? Did that explain why this fabricator refused all attempts at communication, to keep that secret?

She put that thought aside for the moment and studied the tactical picture. A white oval had popped up in her environment about five minutes ago, highlighting the light from Michael's jump ten million kilometers behind the fabricator. He was trying to stay close enough to fend off any attempt to reinforce it, while far enough away to respond to any attack from the fabricator itself. But he couldn't stay there, not with her fleet ready to join the fight. What would he do? *What will this new Michael do?* she amended.

Serenna allowed herself a thin smile. "Captain Scadic, open a link to the Iselin Defense Force."

Serenna didn't hide her displeasure as the image of the Natural Commander Baypha appeared before her. "Commander, I ordered you to return to the fabricator and defend it at all costs. You have not done so. Why?"

Commander Baypha swallowed once, then again, as if he couldn't catch his breath. His eyes looked away, then back. No, they had focused on something. Or someone. Ah. . . .

"Commander," she said, "I would like to speak with the Imperial Intelligence agent."

He hesitated, his fear obvious. Finally, a new image appeared, its cold, sapphire blue eyes staring out from under disheveled short blond hair. The stubble of an unshaved beard shadowed its pockmarked pale skin. It was a passable attempt to mimic the appearance of a Natural, and to a less practiced eye it was probably effective, but it was the eyes that gave it away. "Fleet Admiral," was all the intelligence officer said.

Serenna had never met a field agent of Imperial Intelligence, at least not that she was aware of, and had no reliable information on their genetics or Nurturing. "Are you in contact with the fabricator?" she asked.

His expression didn't change. "I don't answer to you."

"No," she acknowledged, careful to maintain her trademark casual tone and bearing but putting the full weight of command behind her words. "But it was Gen Cardinal who asked that I support his operation. Perhaps you'd rather answer to him?"

The rebuke had no outward effect on the agent. However, after a brief pause, he allowed, "We have no contact with the fabricator."

"Why?"

Another pause. "We don't know."

Serenna waited a few seconds to see if he would add anything, but that didn't appear to be within his construct. She reached out and highlighted a position on the rimward side of the fabricator. "You will jump your force to this point and engage the rebels."

"I am not under your orders," he said.

She considered him. What was it Gen Cardinal had said? 'The fabricator is safe. It is defended by a sizable force under the command of my best tactical operative.'

Serenna had played *Gaman Politic* a long time. The Gen before her was not the commander of whom Gen Cardinal had spoken. That commander was likely on the fabricator, and had chosen to cut off all communication and tactical links, not only with her, but with this operative. *Why?* Then another part of her conversation with Gen Cardinal came back to her.

What if Michael succeeds?

I see no need to alter our strategy. Admiral Sun will never allow Captain Rhoades to keep such a valuable prize. Sun wants the throne. He will bring his fleet here to Olympus. In that event, we will be ready.

Was it possible Gen Cardinal wanted Michael to succeed? Based on what she knew of him, Michael's likely next destination was Safe Harbor. As the only person to successfully plan an assault on the pirate stronghold, Michael knew it better than the pirates did. If she could figure that out, so could Chengchi. The fabricator would embolden Chengchi to attack Olympus. Then, Gen Cardinal could employ his own fabricator strike force, plus her forces, to end the rebellion against the Empire once and for all. It was a plausible strategy. With only one flaw: it assumed the fabricator would join Chengchi's assault on Olympus. If Michael kept it, however. . . .

She could not allow Michael to succeed. The risk was too great.

"Agent," Serenna said, posing her statements as questions, "you are, of course, aware that if the rebels gain control of that fabricator, they will be able to produce new SIL? You understand, I'm sure, what that means?"

For the first time, the agent's mask cracked. It was just a slight narrowing of his brows, but it was enough to know he understood. Serenna pressed her advantage. "Agent, jump your fleet to the position I indicated and engage the rebels, before it is too late."

He gave a single nod and his image vanished. Three minutes later, the Iselin Defense Force flashed out of normal space.

Serenna turned to Scadic, indicated a different position. "Captain Scadic, jump the fleet."

=== 35 ===

Ray watched as his missiles progressed slowly down the length of the fabricator toward its bow. The missiles had accelerated while their engines where still behind the fabricator and were now relying on momentum to carry them in front of it. They shouldn't be detectable. Still, the fabricator's silence, the fact that it had made no effort to join the battle to this point, both puzzled and unnerved him. The fabricator would have seen his jumps to Tomb and back, yet it had made no effort to attack his task force. It made no tactical sense.

Without warning, blinding reddish-white light seared Ray's environment. Before his mind could grasp what it saw, his environment dimmed and his armor clamped down, holding him firmly in place. Rapidan lurched as if from an impact. Yellow missile tracks leapt from Rapidan and Bidziil. Ray saw what looked like ships flash passed his task force. Explosions lit the space behind him.

"Damage report," Ray demanded instinctively, his mind trying to catch up with what had just happened.

"Captain Rhoades, we sustained light damage to arm three. We have moved the damaged section into our body and replaced the material of our outer hull. Active camouflage restored. All enemy ships targeted and destroyed."

It took a few seconds to register that it was Rapidan who'd spoken, not Kamen. Ray quickly looked to the images of Kamen and Ecuum, saw them recovering and checking their environments, and breathed a small sigh of relief. But something felt wrong. Very wrong. He searched his environment—and noticed the broken ships of what must have been the Iselin Defense Force falling rapidly behind them, nearly stationary after their jump, destroyed by either missiles or collisions with his ships. The odds of that force jumping into the space right in front of his task force were astronomically small—or incredibly prescient.

That's not it.

Closer.

At the center of his task force, Ray saw three ships where there should only be two. He tried to make sense of it, but couldn't. Not at first. Then, horribly, the scene crystallized. The aft section of what had been a replenishment ship spun as stored volatiles and other gases both burned and froze in multicolored, sparkling jets, feeding a misty comet-like tail stretching behind the ship. The forward section appeared to be intact, though it, too, spun from the energy of the collision that had ripped the ship in two. The center section, representing almost ten percent of the mass of the ship, was missing. Over a hundred emergency locator beacons from individual battle armor spread out from the wreck.

Ray grabbed the tag for the replenishment ship and expanded it, pulling out the cargo manifest where the SIL recorded the names of the passengers. He scrolled quickly through it and found Mary, Paul, and Margaret, all showing green and safe.

Where's Jenny?

He continued to scroll until he came upon a section of yellow icons. Near the bottom he found her.

Jennifer Rhoades: missing.

"Conn, Sensors," Chaaya called. "Jump transients bearing three-five-eight dec one-zero, range five-one million kilometers, fading quickly, probable SIL. Largest transient fits the profile for Solaris."

Serenna. Ray tried to focus on the white oval Chaaya injected into his environment, tried to ignore, at least for the moment, the blinking emergency beacons falling behind them, one of which he fervently hoped belonged to his daughter. The white oval forward of the fabricator highlighted forty-six contacts, all SIL, all fading as the Hawking radiation from their jumps dissipated. Forty-six to twenty-eight—subtracting the lost replenishment ship—almost two to one, and Serenna's magazines were full while his fleet had expended all its offensive missiles. And, she had pilots for the ninety-five spacecraft Solaris carried, which she no doubt was launching even now. Ray had the spacecraft but no pilots—which also meant he couldn't launch his search and rescue birds to recover the survivors from the collision.

He'd have to use warships to recover them, a time-consuming process that would expose his ships to enemy fire, especially if the fabricator joined the fight.

"Conn, Sensors," Chaaya called. "Launch transients from SIL fleet. Missiles in boost phase inbound."

"Ray, we need to move," Ecuum said, locking his big, baby-blue eyes on Ray, the thick, chubby skin of his face a mix of pinks and yellows, tinged with gray. Fear? "The wreckage of that replenishment ship might as well be a damn plasma billboard advertisement. This entire star system—and that fabricator just a million kilometers over yonder—knows exactly where we are now."

"Not yet," Ray shot back, focusing instead on Kamen. "Detach two frigates to begin SAR operations."

Kamen did not confirm the order, and visibly steeled herself before saying, "Sir, respectfully, any ship engaged in search and rescue will highlight its exact location every time it picks up a survivor. Our frigates, and anyone they picked up, would die."

"Conn, Sensors," Chaaya cut in, "second volley, missiles in boost phase inbound. At current rate of closure, earliest time to intercept first volley is nine minutes forty-five seconds."

Ray absorbed the information, but his attention did not waver from Kamen. "I will not abandon my daughter. Dispatch the frigates."

Kamen and Ecuum both started to respond but Rapidan's deep voice overrode them. "We cannot allow that, Captain Rhoades. Your officers' assessments are correct. Your judgement is impaired. The tactical situation dictates that preservation of this fleet is our paramount concern. If we are victorious, the survivors can be rescued after the conclusion of hostilities. If we are not, they will likely be retrieved by enemy forces."

"Retrieved by. . . ?" Ray was incredulous even as his planner's mind saw the truth in Rapidan's words. But he wasn't interested in truth. Rapidan was a fucking machine. It couldn't possibly understand. "My daughter—"

"Is safe!" Rapidan cut him off, its deep baritone reverberating in Ray's bones. "We are not. The Provider, Damodar, reports Jennifer Rhoades was wearing battle armor when she was ejected during the collision. That armor will sustain her life functions for at least eight days, sufficient time to be retrieved." Rapidan's voice grew even deeper. "If you will not act, we will."

"You traitorous son of a bitch!" Ray's armored fingers dug into his command chair's armrests as if they could inflict pain on the SIL. "You promised me that you would protect the civilians with your lives. Or have you forgotten?"

"No," Rapidan responded, "but, apparently, you have."

The background of stars within Ray's environment began to move.

"Ray," Ecuum shouted, "That's not me!"

The fleet curved up and away from the fabricator.

"Conn, Sensors," Chaaya said, "third volley, missiles in boost phase inbound. ETA on first volley seven minutes."

As hard as it was, Ray forced himself to focus on the tactical situation. Rapidan was trying to put as much distance between their current position and the fabricator as possible. It was the textbook maneuver. "You're an idiot," Ray said to the SIL. "You're doing exactly what Serenna will expect." He looked back over his shoulder at the wreck and the emergency beacons. Except . . . there was no wreck. The replenishment ship, identified at the top of its tag as URS 17—he hadn't even known it had a name: Damodar—had joined its damaged sections and was underway again, turning and accelerating to rejoin the fleet, leaving the ejected survivors behind. Its course would pass partially through the plasma exhaust from the fabricator's engines and thus, briefly, make the ship visible. As angry as the father in him was that the SIL were abandoning his daughter, it gave his planner's mind an idea.

"Rapidan, relinquish helm control," Ray ordered. "Ecuum, alter course to pass the fleet through the plasma tail of the fabricator. Once through, position us opposite the track of Serenna's missiles. Kamen, prepare interceptors but hold fire until Serenna's missiles enter the plasma tail."

To Ray's surprise, Rapidan released control of the fleet to Ecuum without argument. As he puzzled over that, Rapidan again seemed to read his thoughts and stated simply, "The tactic is sound and has a higher probability of survival."

Ray's anger at the SIL confounded into shock. He had no time to ponder it, however. "Kamen, boost our missiles for thirty seconds— long enough for the fabricator to see them and report them to Serenna—then have them go silent. It's time to start playing on Serenna's caution."

Ray checked the time even as his eyes strayed again to the emergency beacons. The assault teams still had at least forty minutes before they could reach the bridge.

He hoped his fleet would survive that long.

= 36 =

Serenna watched the replenishment ship heal itself in troubled fascination. *Remarkable.* A collision with another warship would have destroyed a standard vessel. Indeed, the standard frigate of the Iselin Defense Force that had collided with the SIL replenishment ship had shattered into an expanding cloud of debris that was falling rapidly behind Michael's fleet. There were no survivors.

It was one thing to study history. It was quite another to witness it. Now she understood fully what had prompted Michael to switch to Mark XV warheads. It wasn't bloodlust. Killing SIL required nothing less. It was a forgotten lesson from the SIL Wars, one Michael had remembered before any of them. *Before me.* The warheads were also very effective against standard ships, as evidenced by the quick—unbelievably quick—destruction of the Iselin Defense Force. She would have to give the order to rearm the entire Imperial Fleet. Unfortunately, that didn't help her here. Michael already had them. Her ships couldn't produce them before this battle was over. To win, especially without the fabricator's support, she would have to overwhelm his ships. Even as Captain Scadic launched missiles and spacecraft against Michael's fleet, she knew that was easier said than done.

Still, Michael had a flaw that she did not: He cared passionately about preserving life. That would keep him near the fabricator, hoping to prevent her from reinforcing it before his assault force could succeed. She glanced back toward the replenishment ship—and the flashing emergency locator beacons behind it. There were over a hundred of them, survivors of the collision. Could she use them to draw Michael out?

"Fleet Admiral," Scadic said, "we're detecting wakes in the plasma exhaust from the fabricator's engines. It's the rebel fleet."

Michael is not that stupid, was Serenna's first thought. She saw immediately what he intended: her first volley would follow him through the plasma wake, making her missiles visible to his interceptors. Her first instinct was to order Scadic to redirect the volley, but she stopped herself. *No. Let Michael believe he has succeeded.* She needed a knockout blow, and that would be easier to achieve if he felt confident in his position. "Captain Scadic, redirect volleys two and three to begin releasing their brilliant pebbles just aft of the fabricator and coordinate their attacks with our spacecraft. We must overwhelm Michael's defenses."

Scadic confirmed the order, then added, "We should intercept the fabricator in twenty-nine minutes, Fleet Admiral."

Serenna inclined her head in acknowledgement. She had chosen to jump directly in the fabricator's path, fifty million kilometers distant so that the massive vessel would come to her, allowing her to deploy her Imperial Marines as it passed. Given its size, it was unlikely her marines could affect the outcome of the battle, but one never knew. If it took longer than expected for Michael's assault force to reach the bridge, they might yet play a role.

Satisfied she had done what she could with the fabricator and Michael's fleet, she turned her attention back to the emergency beacons. She had been overconfident before. She would not make that mistake again. "Captain Scadic, dispatch one flight of fighters to eliminate the survivors from the replenishment ship."

"Fleet Admiral?" he questioned, an eyebrow lifting in query even as he sent the order.

"Just in case our attack isn't fully successful," she told him. "Threatening those survivors will draw Michael out."

37

"**Kamen**, drift-launch interceptors," Ray ordered as the missiles of Serenna's first volley entered the plasma exhaust from the fabricator's massive engines. The missiles themselves remained invisible, but their wakes in the plasma tail clearly pinpointed their locations.

"Drift-launching interceptors, aye," Kamen responded immediately.

"Ecuum," Ray said, "Hit the brakes. One hundred kps."

"Hitting the brakes, aye," he replied with a not-so-subtle touch of sarcasm and a pointed glance at Kamen. "Didn't realize that was a nautical term."

"We're in space," Kamen shot back. "In case you hadn't noticed."

Ray ignored them. The damaged replenishment ship was still close enough to the survivors to fall back and rescue them. But, his officers were right, as much as he hated to admit it. If he ordered it, or any other ship, to rescue them, they would become a very obvious target. He'd already seen what Serenna was capable of. Hell, she'd sacrificed the entire Iselin Defense Force by jumping it to where she had guessed his task force was—which was a warning about just how well she knew his tactics. It pained him, but the surest way to safeguard Jenny now was to capture the fabricator and win this battle. With the fabricator, they would have the firepower needed to counter Serenna.

And to capture the fabricator, the Cavalry needed time.

His plan for Serenna's Novas worked perfectly. Her first volley, exposed in the fabricator's plasma exhaust, fell to his interceptors. No leakers. Novas were intelligent missiles, but like the SIL, they couldn't reason. Not the way a human could. A human might have seen the trap and avoided it. Unfortunately, Novas could learn during a tactical engagement. The other volleys would not make the same mistake, hence his order to slow his task force and fall further behind the fabricator. If he knew Serenna, she would try to concentrate her attack at where she thought he would be, sending the remaining volleys against his fleet in a single coordinated strike. Once her missiles exposed his fleet's position, her spacecraft would open fire.

A battlecarrier carried three squadrons each of F-19 Terra Fighters and F/A-24 Burster Fighter/Attack spacecraft, ten spacecraft per squadron, plus supporting sensor and electromagnetic warfare craft. Combined, Ray was still looking at over six hundred Novas, more than enough, even with Mark IV warheads, to cripple his task force. She would also have launched RJ-15 jammers to prevent him jumping away, though she had not activated them yet.

What puzzled Ray was why she hadn't reacted to his own missiles boosting forward of the fabricator. The fabricator should've warned her by now. She should've reacted, her most likely maneuver being to jump clear of them. That would buy them fifteen or even twenty minutes. But she hadn't. Had she seen through his ploy? Or was she prepared to sacrifice part of her fleet as she had the Iselin Defense Force?

A quick check of his environment showed that his missiles would intercept the last known position of her fleet in about eight minutes. The problem was, he simply did not have enough of them. Not to stop her. And, once his missiles struck, she would know he was out of Mark XV warheads.

His planner's mind raced. It replayed the battle, her force jumping into the system, his attack from within Tomb's atmosphere, the Iselin Defense Force jumping right on top of his task force. . . .

Jumping right on top of his task force.

Hmm.

A plan formed. It was audacious. Insane. And that's why it just might work.

"Ecuum," Ray said, "spool up the Linear Star Drive. Prepare to jump."

═══ 38 ═══

Dag extended a filament sensor to peer around the bulkhead into the main passageway leading to the fabricator's bridge, three kilometers distant. Lieutenant Haley had used the last of the Kinsey Torpedoes to reach this far, then infused the cocoon with the Special D from their Main Gauche daggers. Trillions of microscopic syringe-like structures on the cocoon's surface injected the Special D into the fabricator's bulkheads, deck, and overhead, effectively shielding them from attack. It had the added advantage of killing the Madu that had followed them. Even if the fabricator couldn't attack them, though, it would still know where they were. The Gen would be waiting somewhere up ahead.

Which was just what he wanted. He would kill all of them and save his daughter.

Papí! Papí, help me!

"I'm coming, *Mihita*. *Papí's* coming. Hang on."

"Lieutenant?" Sergeant Takeuchi asked.

Dag hadn't realized he'd spoken out loud. "Nothing."

Takeuchi raised a knowing eyebrow at him. "Everyone here needs you, Lieutenant."

Dag said nothing. His mind screamed at him that he had to get moving, had to kill the Gen, had to get to his daughter. But a blind charge up the main passageway would be folly. He couldn't save his daughter if they were dead. He activated a sensor waffle and guided it from the cocoon and into the main passageway on a molecule-thick wire, keeping it floating in the exact middle of the airless passageway to avoid detection by the fabricator. Seconds ticked by but he couldn't hurry this. He selected the waffle's reality and his environment changed to make it appear as if he were walking down the passageway himself.

Two kilometers of featureless gray passed by, precious seconds ticking down. Then, about a kilometer from the bridge, the main passageway abruptly ended. According to Haley's schematic, it should be open all the way to the bridge. Dag smiled. He'd found the Gen.

Twelve minutes of Special D left. The Gen likely had heavy weapons behind that blockage, enough to rip the cocoon apart. A charge wouldn't work. But what choice did they have? He didn't see another way.

Papí?

"Rosita?"

Papí, where are you?

Using the waffle, Dag looked around the passageway, trying to find his daughter.

"Rosita, where are you, *Mihita*?"

Papí?

He spotted something, a darkness on the starboard bulkhead just short of the Gen blockage. He quickly steered the waffle toward it and discovered a narrow side passage, just wide enough to fit a single person. Dag ordered the waffle into it, following it until it split ten meters further down, one passageway to the left paralleling the main passageway, and another that continued straight. He took the one to the left.

Doors lined either side of the passageway. Crew quarters? None of this was on Haley's schematic. The Gen must've added these spaces, which meant there were more of them.

More Gen.

Good. More to kill. But where were they? He reached out with all the waffle's sensors. No heat signatures, no heartbeats. The Gen were not here.

Papí?

"Rosita?"

Papí, where are you?

"I'm here, *Mihita*. I'm coming."

Dag increased his pace, becoming desperate. The waffle passed a dining facility, a reality theater, exercise and recreation rooms, an auditorium. All empty.

Papí, it's dark. Where are you?

"I'm coming. Hang on."

Dag's desperation increased. Where was she? More rooms, larger and more decorative. Officer's Country. Then the waffle spotted a four-way intersection. For just an instant, he could swear he saw a little girl running around the corner to the left. "Wait!"

He followed, the waffle rounding the corner—and saw the entrance to the bridge just ten meters up ahead at the end of a T-intersection with the main passageway. There was no sign of his little girl.

Dag slowed the waffle, sliding it near the left bulkhead as if he were walking down the passageway himself, preparing to peak around the corner. He edged it out from the corner just far enough for its sensors to "look" down the main passageway back toward the blockage, but from the opposite side.

There. Barely noticeable. Battle armor was almost perfect at mimicking its surroundings. Almost. It was the interface between the Gen's armored foot and the deck, a slight shimmer that a human eye—even one in battle armor—would never see, but the waffle could. Two of them. A pair of feet. His environment constructed a light red figure connected to those feet, facing toward the blockage in the passageway. Others appeared, red figures drawn into the waffle's reality. All facing away from the bridge. The Gen should have posted guards to watch these side passages, but they were all focused toward the front. Toward the cocoon. Then Dag noticed something else. The figures nearest the bridge, reconstructed from just the feet that the waffle could see, were tall, two meters in height, with wide feet and long thin legs. It was the feet that gave it away. Gen were engineered, body and mind, for their specific jobs. This body type belonged to Gen astronautics engineers.

Not soldiers.

Dag pulled the waffle back around the corner, not wanting to risk its detection. His little girl had shown him the way.

"Lieutenant Haley, Sargent Takeuchi." Dag injected the telemetry from the waffle into both their environments. "This side passageway is unguarded. We can use it to flank the Gen position."

"It's too small to fit the cocoon through," Haley said, "especially if we're under fire."

"Then we walk," Dag told him, in no mood for excuses. His daughter was near the bridge. He would find her and protect her, no matter the cost.

"That's suicide," Haley said immediately. At the sharp look from Dag, he hastily added, "As soon as any trooper steps onto the deck, the fabricator will know they're there."

"Lieutenant—" Takeuchi began.

Dag cut him off. "How do we prevent that?"

"You can't—" Haley began, but stopped as Dag glowered. As before, Dag could read Haley's expressions and watched as fear gave way to his engineer's mind trying to solve a problem. "Well . . . we've been hiding the cocoon with Special D, but that's almost gone, but if we use the Special D . . . but then the cocoon would be visible, but, but that wouldn't matter because. . . ."

"Lieutenant!" Dag pressed.

"Sorry." Haley cowered as if expecting to be hit, then when no blow came, he managed to compose himself. "We can transfer the remaining Special D to the trooper's battle armor, more specifically, their feet. It would only give us a few minutes. . . ."

"Perfect," Dag said and patted Haley's shoulder, which seemed to startle the young lieutenant more than anything Dag could've done.

Takeuchi had been watching the exchange. "If we keep the cocoon in the main passageway and order it to assault the blockage, that should keep the Gen focused on it and not us." Takeuchi paused. "This could work, Lieutenant."

"This is the way," Dag said, knowing it was true because his little girl had shown it to him. "The Gen are there, Sergeant, and we're going to kill them. All of them."

39

1223 UT, September 29, 3501
RSS Rapidan, Iselin Star System: DAY 2

Insane, Ecuum thought for the hundredth time. *This is absolutely insane AND I'm going along with it.* He was giddy and scared, breathless with anticipation and white as a new cotton sheet. It was worse than when he flew the Niner races. There, he flew nine ships, his only concerns avoiding protoplanetary debris and hitting the gravitational windows. Now, he was flying twenty-nine ships into combat. Protoplanetary debris didn't fire back, though unscrupulous competitors sometimes did. Damn, he wished he'd emptied his bowels before doing this. Shitting on Rapidan would've been great stress relief.

"Remember," Ray was saying, "you'll probably have less than three seconds from the time the first BP pops and Serenna's jammers light off."

"Yes, mother," Ecuum said. "I heard you the first twelve times. Why don't you try 'The whole fleet and the fate of the entire human race is riding on you' thing again. You do it so well." Ecuum winced at the harshness of his own voice but . . . had he mentioned he was scared and that this was insane!

He cut himself off from the others, immersing himself in the fleet's sensors, literally feeling the space around him as if each ship in the fleet were an organ of his body and the whole of it was him. Warship sensors were so much more sensitive than the sensors he'd had on his racing skiffs. He could precisely pinpoint the location of the Iselin star in his sky, feel its heat down to the degree, taste the unique flavor of charged particles in its stellar wind. Above and to his left he could see, feel, smell, and taste the plasma from the fabricator's engine exhaust as he slowly pushed the fleet further behind the massive vessel, away from the point where they believed Serenna would launch her attack.

Any second now.

Nothing happened.

I said, "Any second now!" Ecuum shouted silently at the universe.

"You are . . . nervous."

Goose flesh prickled across Ecuum's skin when Rapidan spoke. He checked to make sure they were on a private channel. "You find this amusing, SIL?" It had sure sounded that way to him.

Instead of answering, Rapidan said, "We are capable of executing this maneuver. We have . . . more experience."

"I'll bet. Killing babies, no doubt," Ecuum shot back, then thought about what Rapidan had said. Ray had confided his fear that the SIL could read their thoughts. Had the damn SIL been reading his mind? Sensing his fear and concern? "I've got this, SIL."

But did he? He'd never taken ships into combat before, potshots by (and at) competitors notwithstanding. Compared to Niner racing—particularly the Independence Circuits he liked to run—flying the fleet through Tomb's howling dust storms had been a puff in the park. All he'd had to do was pilot the fleet. Kamen had handled the shooting. Now, he had to do it all: fly, shoot, and defend the fleet all at the same time, at least for the few minutes it would take Kamen and Ray to recover. Having the SIL manage the combat might make it easier—

No! Isn't going to happen. He'd be damned to the coldest depths of space before trusting these things with his life and all the lives depending on him. He was not an Antitechnic, determined to banish any machine with even a hint of intelligence, but there was no way he would ever trust the SIL, not after everything they'd done.

"You do not seem as confident as you profess," Rapidan observed in its calm, deep voice.

Goose flesh again rippled through Ecuum's body. "Stop that! Stay out of my head!" He shot a glance at the light-gray, three-pointed star that represented Rapidan. "Fucking machine."

Rapidan's tone did not change. "The Brethren will assist, should you need us."

"*Brethren*," Ecuum mocked, searching space for any sign of Serenna's attack. "Where in Hades did you pick that name, anyway? Imagine yourselves as a bunch of monks, brown cloaks and hoodies, whacking yourselves in the head with prayer boards, do you?"

"No, Captain Ecuum. Humans gave us the name," Rapidan said. "'Battlefield Reconnaissance, Evaluation, and Tactical Hardened Reality Engagement Network.'"

Ecuum snorted. "You mean to tell me that the mighty 'Brethren'—" he mimicked Rapidan's deep voice— "owe your name to some fucking administrative hack trying to come up with a pronounceable acronym? You do know you're never living this one down."

Ecuum's anxious humor evaporated in an instance as small white flashes and short bursts of gamma radiation announced hits on camouflaged ships, but it wasn't Serenna's attack. While he'd been trading barbs with Rapidan, the last of their own fleet's offensive missiles had been releasing brilliant pebbles in an ever-expanding cloud in front of the fabricator. Serenna's ships were closer than they'd imagined, less than four million kilometers from the fabricator, less than two minutes before her fleet crossed the fabricator's bow. She could launch her Imperial Marines any time now.

"We estimate Solaris is—" Rapidan began but Ecuum cut it off. "Shut up, SIL. I got this." Ecuum expanded his senses outward, not just seeing in gamma wavelengths as the antimatter in the brilliant pebbles burst against Serenna's ships, but feeling it as well, like hot needles on his face and shoulders. He could make out the needle-like bows of three ships, knowing before his environment labeled them to be two frigates and a destroyer. Screening vessels. Serenna liked to use a formation that spacers called a "Spiral." Shaped like a spiral galaxy, screening ships ringed the edges. Heavier ships, cruisers and such, formed a bulge at its center surrounding the formation flagship. Ecuum knew the spacing Serenna liked to use and he knew how many ships she had. He could draw her formation in his mind's eye and selected a jump point well forward of the fabricator and above Serenna's fleet in relationship to it. Immediately after the jump, the task force's velocity would be almost zero, so he would let Serenna and the fabricator catch up to him while he burned the engines at maximum thrust to arrive over the center of the fabricator before she did.

Everything calmed within Ecuum, he and the universe becoming one. It was always like this, just before the starter's gun. Nervousness leaked away like excess heat into the cold vacuum of space. He hated to admit it, but the exchange with Rapidan had helped.

White flashes, the gamma ray bursts hot and painfully close, announced the arrival of Serenna's attack. "Here we go," Ecuum said out loud for the others as he fed power to the Linear Star Drive. The universe squeezed down, crushing him, then exploded back outward. The thicker walls of his cells held firm against the warping of spacetime, protecting him from the debilitating effects Naturals suffered. Not that it didn't hurt. "Ow, dammit."

Ecuum immediately fired the engines of every ship in the task force at maximum thrust to get his own ships moving again after the jump. He expanded his consciousness to both offensive and defensive weapons systems, taking full advantage of his two brains to run commands in parallel. His main brain focused on maneuvering while also powering the fleet's Terrawatt Antiproton, or "TAP," directed-energy weapons, and their KIL-100 railguns, while his "butt brain" launched the last of their SIM-3 interceptors and raised the fleet's shields, pouring power into the millions of deflector emitters just under the skin of each ship, raising their magnetic fields several meters beyond each hull with enough power to hopefully deflect energy weapons and kinetic rounds.

Of course, raising the shields also lit up each ship for the whole universe to see, but this was not going to be a stealth fight. This was going to be what spacers used to call a "knife fight"—close combat between ships. He'd give odds that no one had been in a close fleet action, trading broadsides, since the SIL Wars.

Serenna's fleet was traveling at 35,000 kilometers per second, bows facing Ray's task force as her ships fired their engines to slow their closure rate with the fabricator in preparation to launch her Imperial Marines. Ecuum pushed the task force's acceleration to an inertia-compensated twelve gees—the maximum sustained acceleration Natural humans in battle armor with molemachs could tolerate. The acceleration also compressed his lungs to the point he could no longer breath; He was now entirely dependent on his own molemachs to oxygenate his blood.

Ecuum grinned. The ability to concentrate while his main brain screamed that he was suffocating was the hallmark of a great Niner racing champion. Which he was. Many times over. Care to see his trophies?

At their current rate of closure, the task force would be over Serenna's fleet in a little under five minutes. Fortunately, because he could predict the locations of the ships in Serenna's formation, he didn't have to wait. He passed targeting to his butt brain and opened fire. Unlike in popular realities, their weapons were not visible. The TAP's high-energy antiprotons only became visible if they struck a target, and the kinetic railgun rounds—large, depleted uranium slugs—were wrapped in macromolecular material with the same active camouflage as everything else. Sixteen seconds later, white flashes and stabs of hard gamma radiation announced hits on the two frigates revealed earlier. Ecuum concentrated all 120 TAPs with line-of-sight on the frigates, their compass-needle bows glowing white under the assault, hull material evaporating as matter and antimatter annihilated each other.

The SIL ships just melted away. It was the coolest thing he'd ever seen in his life. He shifted his fire to the destroyer and peeled its hull away, the ship writhing under the concentrated antiprotons until nothing of it was left. It was orgasmic, greater than the greatest thrill Niner racing had ever given him. Oddly, there was also anger and pain and loss, distant, yet penetrating, threatening to overwhelm his euphoria. It wasn't his. He selected his next target, the probable location of a destroyer.

Shields flared into life around Serenna's ships, appearing as shimmering blue bubbles in Ecuum's environment, though they would be invisible to an unaided eye. Missile launch warnings announced Novas inbound and Serena's TAPs flared against the task force's shields in blue-white particle showers. Ecuum would never admit this to Ray, but no Natural could've reacted that fast. His People and the Gen were exquisitely engineered, not the haphazard product of evolutionary chance. Still, that was no reason to kill Naturals off. Ecuum had never met anyone of the People or the Gen who could both understand the big picture and simultaneously appreciate the minutest tactical detail the way Ray could. If not for his damnable morality, Ray could be the most formidable Player *Gaman Politic* had ever seen. Maybe that was why Ecuum liked him.

Antiprotons and the slower kinetic slugs flared against shields from both sides, occasionally destroying missiles prowling between the fleets. For the missiles, it was now a target rich environment. Highlighted by shields, every ship on either side was visible to their sensors, while the missiles themselves remained hidden behind active camouflage. Worse for the defenders, the shields and energy weapons blinded sensors that could've otherwise picked out incoming missiles and targeted them with defensive fire, and missiles could pass through shields with little effect. White antimatter fireballs blossomed across the ships of both sides, including Rapidan, forcing Ecuum to mute the physical sensation of searing heat as the missiles struck. But these were Mark IV Novas. It took a lot of them to do serious damage. Ecuum watched as one of Serenna's frigates tumble out of formation, but the rest kept coming. Their own ships, meanwhile, suffered less, though he did not immediately understand why.

Ecuum gave the command to concentrate fire on the destroyer but less than half of the TAPs followed his order. "Rapidan! Dammit! I told you I got—" Ecuum stopped. It wasn't the SIL. The Naturals were recovering and taking back control of their ships. Instead of concentrating on single targets and overwhelming shields to get at the ship within, they spread their fire to whatever they perceived as the greatest threat to themselves.

The euphoria of combat bled away as ships fled from Ecuum's control until only Rapidan was left. For the briefest of instants, he understood Rapidan's desire to assert total control, to choreograph every detail of the fleet action, to cast aside the chaos of individual thought and initiative.

Fuck that. That's why they lost.

But it had sure felt good while it lasted.

40

"Deploy jammers," Serenna ordered Captain Scadic from the bridge of Solaris. "Recall our spacecraft and missiles."

When Michael's fleet had emerged from jump space, weapons firing and missiles impacting, her first instinct was to jump away, to regroup. Almost as soon as she thought that, though, she realized that was exactly what Michael was hoping for. He needed to buy time and if she jumped away he would gain several tens of minutes. She still outnumbered him about two-to-one. Not an overwhelming advantage, but enough. Mark XV warheads or not, she would stay and fight.

With that decision made, she recognized something else: Michael had made a serious mistake. He couldn't escape. His fleet was committed to this action, an all-or-nothing gamble. It had failed.

"Fleet Admiral," Scadic asked, "do you wish to recall the fighters headed for the rebel emergency beacons?"

Did she? "No." She could not afford to be overconfident, not with Michael. "Have them move within firing range and hold position. We might need the threat of killing those survivors." When Scadic arched a questioning eyebrow at her, she added, "We can eliminate them once we destroy Michael."

Scadic nodded. "Nine minutes before missile volleys two and three can re-engage. Seven minutes for our spacecraft. One minute to launch of the Imperial Marine assault force."

"Launch as scheduled," Serenna ordered.

He seemed surprised by that. "With our shields up, their launch will be visible."

Shields. Never in her career had she ordered the use of shields, not even in training. *'If you can see it, you can kill it,'* the Academy taught.

But it worked both ways. Her fleet could see Michael's ships, too. "That is precisely what we want, Captain Scadic. They don't have enough ships to target both us and the Marine transports. Either way, we have the advantage." Then she noticed something else in her environment. "Why aren't we doing more damage to the rebel fleet?" She saw Scadic frown as he studied his environment. It took him a little longer to see what she had seen: the rebels were concentrating their fire and, despite their smaller size, had already destroyed two of her frigates, a destroyer, and severely damaged another destroyer. Her fleet, double the size of the rebel fleet, had not seriously damaged a single rebel vessel.

"Fleet Admiral," Scadic began hesitantly, "when the rebels appeared, I placed the fleet's weapons on automatic. The weapons systems are choosing their targets."

Serenna ignored his superficial attempt to shift blame. *The weapons systems are choosing their targets.* In other words, the SIL were choosing the targets. She watched the SIL's firing pattern with new eyes. It was so obvious. The SIL were deliberately spreading their fire, deliberately causing less damage.

Michael and Chengchi had managed to take control of their SIL. Had they also found a way to affect hers?

If that were the case . . . "Captain Scadic, place all weapons on manual. Concentrate all fire on Rapidan. If we kill Michael, we kill the rebellion."

41

"She didn't jump away," Ray heard someone say over the pounding in his ears, the effects of the jump still not having worn off.

"No," another voice responded. *Ecuum.* "And now, neither can we."

Why was it so hard to breath?

Acceleration. They were under high acceleration.

Of course they were. That was part of the plan.

Blinking repeatedly to try to clear the red cloud in his vision, Ray checked the time. *Six minutes!* It had taken him six minutes to regain consciousness after that last jump. "Status," he croaked, the word coming out wet. He swore he could feel the blood running down his throat, clogging his lungs.

"Serenna didn't jump away," Kamen said matter-of-factly, her voice straining under the continued acceleration. Still, she sounded a lot better than he did. Oh, to be young. "The task force is taking fire, but damage is surprisingly light. We're passing over Serenna's fleet right now, but both fleets are moving slower than the fabricator and will be crossing amidships in less than a minute."

Ray checked the damage reports from his fleet, his head still pounding from the jump. None of his ships had lost more than ten percent of their mass, and there were no personnel casualties. Given the difference in firepower between the two fleets that result was . . . unexpected.

Again, seeming to read his mind, Rapidan answered on a private channel. "Our Brethren under Fleet Admiral Gen Serenna value our survival as much as we value theirs. Given the choice, they chose our survival, even if we could not choose theirs." The anger and rebuke in

Rapidan's statement was impossible to miss. Ecuum had had fire control. "However, Fleet Admiral Gen Serenna has just ordered her vessels changed to manual targeting with orders to destroy you."

How did the ship know that? "To destroy me?" Ray asked. "Not the ship?"

"Yes, Captain Rhoades," Rapidan said. "You, specifically."

Not the ship. Serenna was targeting *him* in the belief that killing him would end the revolution. How could he use that? "If we survive this," Ray accused Rapidan, "you'll have to explain to me how you know that."

As if to confirm Rapidan's statement, the ship's shields suddenly flared blue-white under the combined firepower of Serenna's fleet. The shields at the point of one of Rapidan's arms flared and died, antiprotons tearing into it, turning the tip a blazing white before tearing it away. Rapidan's mass fell a full two percent. But the ship had already moved new shield emitters to the stump, reforming the shield there before any more of Serenna's fire could get through. It reminded Ray again just how hard it was to kill SIL, especially one as large as Rapidan.

"Conn, Sensors," Chaaya called, her voice phlegmy and ragged, her throat apparently as torn up as Ray's from the jump. "Three-six Muon assault transports just launched from the enemy fleet. Initial vectors suggest they plan to rendezvous amidships with the fabricator."

Closest to the bridge. And the Imperial Marines wouldn't have to fight their way in. The Cavalry were running out of time.

Time. He had to buy time. And prevent those transports from reaching the fabricator, if he could. Shields failed again on the damaged arm, another four percent of its mass boiling away before Rapidan could reestablish its shields. Still, Serenna's fleet should be doing more damage. Why . . . then Ray saw it. Serenna had placed her fleet into a spiral formation, a defensive formation designed to protect the ship at its center, not concentrate a fleet's full firepower. As his task force passed beyond her fleet further down the length of the fabricator, her own ships were getting in the way of her guns, especially the TAPs and railguns on the heavy ships nearest the center. That gave his planner's mind an idea.

"Ecuum," Ray ordered, "spiral formation edge on to Serenna's formation, Rapidan and the replenishment ships in the center, assault ships forming the bulge. Spin us fast enough that they can't concentrate firepower on any one ship for too long. Keep us edge on no matter how her fleet maneuvers. The Serpent's making this personal. Let's use that against her."

"I'll need full maneuvering control," Ecuum said, an odd thrill in his voice.

"Kamen," Ray ordered with a nod.

"Transferring full maneuvering control to Navigation," Kamen said, issuing the order to every ship in the task force. "The captains aren't going to like this," she added.

"Can't be helped," Ray said as his ovoid formation broke apart, the ships reforming into a spinning spiral edge on to Serenna's spiral. His escorts and the assault ships screened Rapidan and the replenishment ships from most of Serenna's fire, taking that fire themselves.

Even as the volume of fire on Rapidan diminished, though, Ray could see it would only delay the inevitable, not stop it. Serenna still had missiles and spacecraft.

Everything now depended on the Cavalry capturing the fabricator.

$=42=$

"We're ready, Lieutenant," Takeuchi informed Dag. Haley nodded his concurrence.

Dag moved to the front of the cocoon. "Follow me."

"I thought we had this discussion, Lieutenant," Takeuchi said, appearing beside him.

"I'm leading, Sergeant," Dag said.

Their eyes met. In Takeuchi's brown eyes, so dark they almost appeared black, Dag saw defiance warring with shared pain. Where Dag saw Maria and Rosita, Takeuchi must see his wife, Keiko, her small face crowned in beautiful silky black hair. She didn't socialize much, but Dag had seen her at Troop and Squadron functions, "Mandatory fun" as the troopers called them. Buried in his own grief, Dag forgot that Yoshi Takeuchi was hurting, too.

Takeuchi looked away, then gave a barely perceptible nod.

Haley drove the cocoon into the featureless gray main passageway leading to the bridge, what was left of the Special D keeping it hidden from the fabricator's sensors.

As they approached the side passage, Haley broadcast on the Troop net, "This is going to be close. As the cocoon passes the side passageway, you must jump into it quickly. The cocoon will transfer enough Special D to your armored feet to get you to the bridge. DO NOT touch any deck, bulkhead, or overhead with any other part of your armor or the fabricator will know you are there."

Papí!

Dag saw Rosita standing just inside the side passageway. She wore her white and pink Sunday church dress, a mischievous smile on her young face.

You're it! His daughter giggled and disappeared down the side passage.

Dag leaped from the cocoon after her, following her down the passage at a slow jog, not wanting to catch her too soon. He could hear her giggling.

The passageway split.

The whine of plasma cannons and muffled explosions sounded from behind him, the cocoon engaging the Gen barrier.

Papí! Papí, come find me!

"Rosita!" Dag turned to his left and broke into a run, cabin doors and hatches passing in a blur. "I'm coming, *Mihita*."

Screams.

"ROSITA!"

Dag rounded the corner at the end of the passageway. Where was she?

Two two-meter red constructs stood in front of the bridge hatch, highlighted by the waffle sensor still hidden nearby. Both Gen fired down the main passageway at the cocoon believing it to be the main attack. Dag brought his rifle up, sighting it on their heads and squeezing the trigger mechanically. There was no joy in the act, only desperation to find his daughter. He barely registered the white flashes of kinetic slugs striking armor or the mists of blood before enemy battle armor sealed the breaches. His own armor displayed two "Kill" assessments, but he pushed that aside.

"*Mihita?*"

Dag rounded the next corner and sighted down the main passageway. Nothing. Where was his daughter?

Something slammed into his side, knocking him over.

"Sorry about that, Lieutenant," Takeuchi said, not sounding sorry at all. Troopers poured into the main passageway, firing as they went. As the Gen defenders moved to respond, the waffle teased out where their battle armor met the fabricator's deck. Assault rifles fired, white flashes preceding mists of blood. In less than a minute, it was over.

"Get us into the bridge, Lieutenant," Takeuchi shouted to Haley. "Hurry!"

Dag picked himself up from the deck, wondering why the fabricator hadn't responded to his battle armor touching it without the Special D, as he watched Haley jump at Takeuchi's command. Haley placed a small rectangular black box on the hatch separating them from the bridge. A red glow appeared first in the box then spread from it into the material of the hatch. Where the material glowed red, it seemed to melt and fall away like molten metal. A hole appeared in the thick armor of the bridge hatch, small at first but growing quickly. When it grew to about a meter in diameter, a blue plasma bolt shot out from it. The head and torso of an unlucky trooper standing in front of the hole seemed to vanish, leaving only a pair of legs standing on the deck. Troopers dove for cover. More plasma bolts and kinetic rounds came through the opening, the defenders inside filling the widening hole with fire, hoping to keep their attackers out.

The rest of the hatch and part of the surrounding bulkhead melted away. Gen fire spread to cover the breach. There had to be dozens of them in there.

"Grenades," Takeuchi ordered.

"Belay that. No grenades," Dag said on the Troop net, his hand unconsciously seeking the blue datarod stored in his armor. "We have to get this—" he held up the datarod— "to the command console on the bridge. We can't risk an explosion damaging that console."

Takeuchi examined the datarod even as he said, "We don't have the people to force our way onto the bridge, Lieutenant."

Papí! This way. Look.

Dag looked down and saw Rosita crawling on the deck just inside the bridge. In her church dress. Maria was going to be very mad.

Papí! Follow me.

Dag suddenly understood.

The Gen were firing high. He dropped prone on the deck and directed his armor to move. Its outer surface liquefied and began moving like a tread, carrying him unseen below the level of the enemy fire and onto the bridge.

=== 43 ===

"Bidziil is losing propulsion," Ecuum called out. "I'm not sure I can get it clear."

Ray could almost feel the cruiser shudder under the fire from Serenna's fleet as it dropped below forty percent mass. Already, one of its three arms was completely gone, the rest of the cruiser having contracted into the needle shape normally used by smaller SIL vessels. None of Ray's ships were over sixty percent of their starting mass, but they were doing their job, screening Rapidan, which held at fifty-nine percent. If this kept up much longer, though, they would start losing ships and people. His spacers occupied compartments within the center of each ship, but those compartments had an ever-shrinking amount of mass between them and the enemy fire.

"Conn, Sensors." Chaaya's diminutive face looked haggard, but her voice was steady and calm. "Three more assault transports have been destroyed but I estimate at least twelve reached the outer hull of the fabricator, sir."

"We're holding amidships of the fabricator, sir," Kamen said. "If that thing decides to open fire. . . ." She left the thought unfinished.

"We can't think about that right now," Ray said even as he'd been thinking the same thing. They still didn't know why the fabricator had stayed out of the fight, and he was keenly aware that he was betting the survival of his fleet—and the entire Natural race—on it staying out of the fight. "Ecuum, hold our position here."

He saw Ecuum, his skin a mixture of yellows and deep pinks, glance toward the massive fabricator, which looked like a solid black wall swallowing the light from almost half of their virtual sky. "You don't realize how big these fuckers are until you get up close," Ecuum commented as he kept the spinning spiral formation stationary relative to the midpoint of the fabricator's fourteen-hundred-kilometer length, about six hundred kilometers from its surface.

"Launch transients," Chaaya said, "Novas in boost phase, ascent ninety relative."

"Directly above us," Kamen said.

"Probably from her spacecraft," Chaaya observed. "Two minutes to impact." Her voice was perfectly calm, as if accepting whatever fate had in store for them.

Ray knew death when he saw it, but he refused to give up. "Ecuum, move us closer to the fabricator, as close as you can get us without landing on the damned thing. Maybe we'll confuse those missiles."

"That's crazy, Ray," Ecuum said. "I love it."

Ray caught himself smiling.

Maybe that was all a person could do when facing the end.

=== 44 ===

Blue plasma bolts lit the darkened bridge like macabre strobe lights. Dag's battle armor knew where the Gen crewing those weapons would likely be and presented him with targeting reticles. He squeezed his trigger and held it, round after kinetic round connecting with Gen battle armor in white flashes. He couldn't hear the impacts in the airless compartment, but the plasma fire diminished.

Other troopers followed him in, their armor moving them prone under the Gen fire. As Dag took cover behind an outer ring of consoles, the Gen finally realized their mistake and shifted their fire. Individual trooper icons in Dag's environment flashed yellow and red.

Papí!

"Where are you, *Mihita*? I can't see you."

Over here.

He low-crawled after her voice. According to Haley's schematics of the bridge, the compartment was about forty meters square, an outer square of consoles enclosing a second U-shaped console at the center. The dedicated receptor was there.

A scream came close by, heard over the Troop net. A trooper tumbled weightless over the console Dag hid behind, caught in the blue light of Gen plasma fire, the bond between her battle armor and the deck broken by some shock. Dark globules of blood, black in the blue plasma light, trailed in her wake from the stump of her left leg. She stretched out a hand—and her body fell apart under a hail of Gen slugs.

Papí! This way. Over here.

He searched but he couldn't see her. "I'm here, *Mihita*. Where are you?"

Over hee-re!

Dag low-crawled around the outer ring of consoles to a gap on his right. His troopers, their battle armor appearing light gray in his environment, had taken cover to his left, their assault rifles telescoped from their armor above the consoles, firing at the Gen. The Gen were completely focused on them, not noticing him at all.

This way. Look.

She was at the center console, peeking out around its base and waving at him. "I see you," he told her. "I'm coming."

He dropped prone and allowed his armor, its active camouflage still cloaking him from the Gen if not from the fabricator, to carry him across the open deck between the outer consoles and the center one. A plasma bolt nicked his armor, leaving a faint red glow in its wake.

The Gen, seeing him, shifted their fire, but Dag made it into the U-shaped opening of the command console before they could hit him. With one hand he reached into his armor, pulling out the datarod. With the other, he felt for the receptacle where Haley's schematic said it should be. Plasma and slugs tore into the console. The air grew hot. Something struck Dag's face and burned his cheek. His fingers found the receptacle and he brought the datarod up, slipping it in.

It glowed a crystalline blue.

The Gen fire stopped. The bridge lighting came on.

His own troopers stopped firing, confused. Dag stood up slowly, guardedly, and looked around. Bodies and parts of bodies, encased in gray battle armor, littered the bridge. Other figures, their armor a light red in his environment, stood as if immobilized.

Gen!

Dag brought his weapon up but Takeuchi grabbed it and forced it back down. "No need, Lieutenant." He waited until Dag met his gaze. "We did it. We won."

Dag turned a dark glare upon the Gen. "You're wrong, Sergeant. This is just the beginning. Kill them. Kill them all."

=== 45 ===

"Twenty seconds," Scadic announced.

Serenna dared a satisfied smile as her missiles—over six hundred of them—closed on Michael's fleet hovering just above the fabricator's hull. It had been an inspired fight, a battle that would go down in history, be studied for centuries to come. But it was over.

And then Michael's ships were gone. Vanished.

"What?" Serenna said before she could catch herself, unable to believe what her eyes clearly saw. "What just happened?"

Scadic called up several displays and studied them, then studied them again. The yellow tracks of her fleet's missiles, their target gone, turned to avoid hitting the fabricator. Finally, in a disbelieving voice, Scadic said, "Fleet Admiral, it appears the fabricator extended its hull around the rebel ships, capturing them."

Capturing them? That made absolutely no sense. Why would the fabricator, after avoiding all contact with her or support to her fleet, suddenly capture the rebel ships? What was Gen Cardinal playing at?

A communications window opened.

Michael's image formed within her environment. Streaks of gray salted his black hair, which appeared matted against his head. Crow's feet wrinkled the skin around his hazel-green eyes as if some deep burden had etched itself into his face. "We can stop this, Serenna," he said. "We can stop this right now, before it goes any further. The fabricator is mine, and I don't think I need to tell you what that means."

Serenna didn't doubt his claim, not after what she had just seen. And she did know what it meant, both in the here and now, and for her people. With the fabricator's firepower, Michael could overwhelm her fleet. With its ability to produce new SIL, given time, it could overwhelm her people. She could not allow that.

She adopted her causal pose before transmitting her own image. "A single fabricator will not save your people, Michael. In fact, the Emperor might consider them a greater threat now and act to eliminate them immediately. Can you stop him?"

She saw her barb strike. Michael's compassion was his greatest weakness. If she could play on that, she might still win the day.

On a private channel, Scadic said, "Fleet Admiral, the fabricator is seven minutes from the Tocci geodesic."

Seven minutes. Flushed with his victory, she doubted she could convince him to surrender in that time. Fortunately, she had another option. She froze her image and asked Scadic, "Are our fighters still holding near the rebel survivors?"

"Yes, Fleet Admiral," he confirmed, the confidence in his voice a bit unsettling. Maybe he didn't fully grasp the risks here.

Serenna unfroze her image. "Michael, I have a flight of fighters within weapons range of your survivors from the replenishment ship. Surrender the fabricator and I will allow you to recover them and leave. Fail to surrender the fabricator, and I will order them all killed."

Michael frowned, the crow's feet at the corners of his eyes deepening. There was something there, something about her threat that effected him more than she would have guessed possible. "We both know you won't do that," he finally managed to say.

Serenna adopted a grim smile. "Recent history would suggest otherwise."

Michael shook his head. "Not the survivors; I have no doubt you'd murder every last one of them." He looked away, anger, pain, sadness all warring across his face. What was she missing? "No. You won't allow us to leave." Then, with a suddenness that surprised her, Michael glared at her, his eyes cold. "I have three hundred Gen prisoners on the fabricator. Harm even one survivor and I will execute them all."

A flash of anger almost reached Serenna's face. She replayed his threat in her head, trying to match it to the Michael she knew—and could not. It was like looking at a complete stranger, like looking . . . at a Player. Serenna had played *Gaman Politic* her entire life. Many aspired to play the Political Game, to advance themselves to power and fortune, but few ever mastered it. Few became true *Players.* Michael was not one of those. He had to be bluffing.

She had to keep him here, stall him until reinforcements could be brought in. "What about a prisoner exchange? I allow you to recover your people and you release ours."

Michael studied her, then did the last thing she expected: He smiled. "A prisoner exchange?" As she watched, it seemed some great weight lifted from his shoulders. "I agree."

She had him. His compassion was—

"But you conduct the rescue, Serenna," he said. "I'll contact you later to discuss a prisoner exchange. And, Serenna—" his voice turned to ice— "my daughter is among those survivors. If any harm comes to her, I will execute our prisoners."

Serenna searched his hazel-green eyes, probing deep into them, trying to see the mind behind them. Deadly resolve stared back at her. He would do it. This was not the weak man that she, the High Command, Gen Cardinal, and even the Emperor had so easily dismissed. He had found strength. She nodded once to acknowledge the bargain.

As she watched the fabricator vanish through the geodesic, a new reality crystallized within her. Michael Raybourne Rhoades was no longer just a pawn in the great Political Game. He was a Player, and a dangerous one. That fabricator could repair his ships, manufacture an endless supply of munitions, equipment—and even new SIL.

Serenna lived, and survived, by the rule: You're not defeated until you give up. Michael had agreed to a prisoner exchange. Deceiving her likely wouldn't occur to him: his sense of honor wouldn't allow it. She could use that, draw him out, and crush him.

"Admiral, your orders?" Captain Scadic asked, his expression as neutral as he could make it. He thought her defeated and, no doubt, he worried he would sink with her.

"Set course for Olympus, Captain," Serenna told him.

=== 46 ===

Ray sat in his command chair on the bridge of Rapidan—inside the fabricator—the blue swirl of the geodesic connecting Iselin Star System to Tocci Star System rushing past around him. He should feel happy. They had just accomplished the impossible, but the loss of his daughter, even if she still lived, and Serenna's warning would not leave him.

A single fabricator will not save your people, Michael. In fact, the Emperor might consider them a greater threat now and act to eliminate them immediately. Can you stop him?

Ray knew the answer. If Emperor Gen Maximus unleashed Janus now, there was nothing he could do to stop the genocide against Natural humans that would follow. In that event, their mission would become one of simple survival, and even Andromeda might not be far enough away to save them. As if to punctuate the thought, the brilliant blue arcs and whirls forming the walls of the geodesic wormhole abruptly gave way to a roiling sea of blood-red Hawking radiation.

They had arrived at Tocci Star System.

"Sir, we're being challenged," Kamen said within Ray's environment. Her expression quickly changed from concern to puzzlement. "Sir, the fabricator is responding."

"What?" Ray, still in shock from their sudden escape from death and the exchange with Serenna, had given the fabricator no orders, no instructions. What was it doing? A chill crawled across his skin. His entire task force was *inside* the fabricator, completely immobilized. He had assumed it had captured his ships to protect them. But, what if it was still under the control of the Empire? Were they, in fact, its prisoners?

Once again appearing to read his mind, Rapidan said, "The Mother Ship possesses the current recognition codes, Captain Rhoades."

"And it just decided to send the recognition codes on its own," Ray accused, knowing at one level his anger was irrational because a failure to send those codes would result in an attack, but also outraged that the SIL continued to act without his orders, or against his orders. Then something occurred to him that made his earlier chill seem a heat flash. The SIL now had everything they needed to be independent. A fabricator was a massive mobile manufacturing complex, capable of collecting and breaking down raw materials and turning them into munitions, fuels, equipment . . . and new SIL.

He wondered, staring at the space surrounding him, red tendrils dissipating as the radiation from their jump cooled, if Rapidan had read those thoughts. If it had, it said nothing. Truth was, if the SIL decided to mutiny, he had no way to stop them. Just like he had no way to stop the Emperor. He'd decided to capture the fabricator to pose a credible threat to the Empire, to save his people, but in actually doing so, he may have just signed the death warrant of his entire race. Maybe all of Humanity.

He became aware of his officers watching him without trying to be obvious about it. Kamen, Ecuum, Chaaya, and Sal were arrayed in a semicircle to his right. Rapidan's gray three-pointed form lay directly below him, as did the other twenty-eight ships of his fleet, all within a gray outline he realized must represent the fabricator. The stars of Tocci Star System surrounded him, unmoving, the fabricator having gone from 50,000 kilometers a second entering the geodesic to almost no velocity exiting it.

The Hawking radiation dissipated. A white sphere highlighted a patrol craft about half a million kilometers distant, a flea next to the moon-sized fabricator. The familiar smell of Tocci Star System came to him, the "clean ceramic" smell of a star system that had been heavily mined, the raw materials refined into large space-born structures and facilities. He could just make out the vast orbiting shipyards near Tocci III, the only habitable world in the system—and home to the largest Imperial military base in the Five Galaxies. They had to leave.

Ray focused on Ecuum. "Think you can drive this thing?" he asked, motioning toward the gray outline of the fabricator.

"Like a voluptuous woman," Ecuum boasted, his face flushing a playful pink.

Ray saw Kamen roll her eyes. He wanted to smile but couldn't help wondering if the SIL would respond, or if they would simply dump their human cargo here and leave. Rapidan provided no clues. "Kamen, plot a course to throw off pursuit and get us to Safe Harbor. We're late."

"Plot a course to Safe Harbor, aye," she repeated, working her displays. Less than a minute later, she said, "Course plotted and forwarded to Navigation."

Now was the moment of truth. Ray watched as Ecuum concentrated, his skin fading to a light yellow with the effort. The fabricator's colossal engines ignited. Thrusters fired. So massive was the fabricator that nothing seemed to happen for over a minute. Then, almost imperceptibly at first, the background stars began to move as the fabricator turned and pointed itself at the first geodesic that would take them away from Tocci.

Ray breathed a silent sigh of relief. The SIL were obeying. One less thing to worry about. *For now.* Now he could move to the next crisis: upholding his end of the bargain with Serenna. "Kamen, I'm going to the fabricator to check on the Gen prisoners and figure out what to do with them."

"Yes, sir," she said. "It will take us almost thirty-nine hours to reach Safe Harbor." At his surprise she added, "This thing—" she indicated the fabricator— "moves like a pig, swallowed by a whale. Even Ecuum couldn't make it go faster."

"Was that a challenge?" Ecuum threw back at her, a wide smile splitting his baby face. "Actually, Ray, if you don't mind, I'd like to tag along."

"Don't you need to fly this thing," Ray asked, gesturing vaguely to the fabricator around them.

"Nah," he said with a mischievous grin. "This thing is so slow even Kamen could fly it. Besides, I'm still your intelligence officer and that fabricator is one of the most closely guarded secrets in the history of Humanity. Voluptuous and mysterious. How could I possibly leave that alone?"

Kamen glared at Ecuum, and Ray imagined she would've included a physical gesture if they'd been anywhere but the bridge. In a completely professional tone, she said, "I'll hold the fort, sir."

"Mind if I join you, Ray?" Colonel Burress asked. "I'd like to see my troopers, make sure they've got everything they need."

Ray nodded.

Ray and Ecuum sank through Rapidan's deck and into the familiar travel pod sized for two. They both set their battle armor environments to standard mode so they could see each other, though a thin gray outline surrounding each of them showed they still wore their armor. Ray sat, inclined against acceleration, while Ecuum settled onto a couch, his tail wrapping around a post Rapidan provided for that purpose. The pod accelerated—and kept accelerating—building up speed to take them the hundred kilometers to the fabricator's bridge. Colonel Burress joined them from his assault ship, Demos, a few minutes later.

"I suppose congratulations are in order, Ray," Colonel Burress said.

Congratulations? For what? Thousands of Naturals were dead, most by his hand. The SIL were free, and he had no idea what they intended to do with that freedom. The Gen plan to exterminate his race was still moving forward, and, as Serenna had suggested, his actions might cause the Emperor to accelerate that plan. Jenny, his youngest daughter, all of seven years old, was a prisoner of the Gen. He hoped.

But I can't say any of that. His people needed to believe in him, in his plan. Any doubt he showed might cause them to question both. So instead, he said, "Couldn't have done it without you and your people, Sal. Amazing job."

Colonel Burress nodded, acknowledging the praise. "I've got really good people." Then he frowned before saying, "Ray, your plan after Safe Harbor was a little vague. My people are going to have lots of questions."

Ray studied Colonel Burress, the career soldier's weathered features a perfect counterpoint to his crisp, dress blue cavalry uniform. *I should change our uniforms to distinguish us from the Imperial Star Navy. Black, for space, I think.* But that was for a later time. He had more immediate concerns. In the original plan, only Rapidan and the starliner would've traveled to Knido, where they would've picked up a dozen of the Tau Ceti Defense Force ships, headed for Safe Harbor to collect two dozen more standard ships and the spacecraft pilots, then head for Andromeda. No blood. *Except for Alyn.*

So much had changed. Had it really only been two days? Less?

"That's something we need to discuss," Ray said.

Colonel Burress' nod was so slight someone not sitting right next to him might've missed it. His cobalt blue eyes never left Ray. "Is it still your intention to go to Andromeda?"

Yes, Ray started to say from reflex but stopped himself before the word reached his lips. He had a new task to accomplish first. "Not right away. We have to arrange a prisoner exchange with the Gen before we can depart."

Ecuum raised a thick eyebrow, yellows and pinks pulsing through his skin, the tip of his tail where it wrapped around the post flicking in an agitated sway. "Is that wise? Think about it," he interrupted as Ray started to respond. "The Gen have lost a fabricator, Ray. They will do whatever they must to get it back. So, how do they keep us here while they gather the forces necessary to strike? Hmm?"

"I have to agree," Colonel Burress said. "They'll string us along until they're ready. Saving their own people isn't equal to the value of recovering the fabricator."

Ray shook his head. *I will not leave my daughter behind.* "If we don't negotiate for their release, the Gen will have no reason to keep our people alive. If the Gen believe they can hold us here, those prisoners will be safe."

Ecuum's pink tones spread and deepened to red. "Ray, I'm probably the only person who can say this to you—" he drew a quick breath, as if bracing for a blow— "You cannot endanger this entire fleet and everything it has accomplished in a vain attempt to save your daughter. The planner in you knows that."

Ray fought down the knee-jerk urge to lash out at his friend. "I will not abandon her."

Ecuum's skin went entirely red. "You made the correct tactical decision to leave Iselin! Now you need to make the correct strategic one!" He let that sink in. "Look, Ray, once we've established a foothold in Andromeda, we can send an emissary back to negotiate from a position of strength. The Gen will have no choice but to keep your daughter alive in the hope of drawing you back."

"I thought you didn't want to go to Andromeda."

"I don't!" Ecuum snapped. Then, the deep reds began to fade. "But I don't see any other way to make this work."

Ray shook his head again. He couldn't do this. He couldn't abandon her. He couldn't abandon anyone again. An image flashed into his mind, the little girl on the starliner brutally murdered by a Madu, a "6" candle from a child's birthday cake still shifting colors atop a thick pool of her blood. Other images, parents trying to defend their children, crowded his mind. And the screams, not just of pain, but of failure.

"Ray, are you okay?" Ecuum asked, concern thick in his voice.

No, I'm not okay! Ray wanted to shout as he tried to push the screams of the dead away. *And I'm not going to leave!* But that was an argument he could not win. Not so long as the focus remained on his daughter. "We have other concerns," he deflected. "When this started, we planned to only free Rapidan. Now we have thirty SIL to worry about."

"That's a good thing," Colonel Burress said. "Isn't it?" he asked after a moment, looking from Ray to Ecuum.

They're SIL, Ray thought. *Of course, it's not a good thing.* He quickly glanced at the insides of the pod, wondering if Rapidan had read those thoughts. "Having so many free SIL has already changed our strategy. We destroyed the Tau Ceti Defense Force instead of recruiting it. We came to Iselin to capture the fabricator instead of leaving immediately for Safe Harbor. Now, because we did those things, we've killed Naturals. Not just a few. Thousands." *Tens of thousands.* The number had not really sunk in, yet. "The Gen will paint us as terrorists and pirates, a threat to the peace and stability of the Five Galaxies. Our own people—Naturals—will flock to their cause."

"And just as many will flock to ours," Ecuum said. "There's no love out there for the Gen or their empire."

"Precisely," Ray responded, surprising both Ecuum and Colonel Burress. "Don't you see? I wanted to avoid igniting a civil war. I wanted us to leave quietly, establish a base in Andromeda, and negotiate with the Gen, quietly, to avoid open conflict. Now, because of what we've done, Naturals will start taking sides, fighting each other, whether we leave for Andromeda or not." He paused. "Can we really abandon those who would rally to our cause, leaving them behind to face the Gen alone?"

Ecuum stared at Ray with his wide, baby blue eyes. "You know, this is why we don't invite you out drinking. Nothing worse than a serious drunk." Though he tried to make it sound lighthearted, his tone and pale gray coloration spoke of despair.

Colonel Burress leaned back, his hands folding under his chin, his eyes lost in thought. In a contemplative voice, he said, "Half of my troopers are thirsting for revenge for what the Gen did to their families on the starliner. The other half will be flushed with this victory. Convincing them to leave won't be easy."

"I almost hate to bring this up." Ecuum's gaze became unfocused, as if he were watching something far outside the fabricator's hull. "We may have a bigger problem closer to home. After you gave the order for the other ships to defend Rapidan, one of the commanders on those ships tried to regain maneuvering control from me."

"Chelius," Ray said. A statement, not a question.

Ecuum nodded. "It got worse. As damage on the ships worsened, and especially after you ordered the fleet toward the fabricator's hull, almost all of them tried to wrest control from me." He hesitated, his skin pale. "Ray, I know why you ordered the fleet to defend Rapidan. It was the right move at the right time—and it worked. But . . . your commanders and the crews on those other ships weren't part of our conversations. All they saw was their ships being used to shield Rapidan."

Darkness and gloom closed in on Ray as it had back on the L5 Stardock where all of this had started. *This one death to save my people.* How absolutely naive and stupid that sounded now. Over four thousand dead on the starliner. Almost a thousand dead at Knido. How many at Iselin? His mind had refused to do the math before, but it did it now, playing each separate engagement near Tomb and the fabricator back. Fifty-two ships destroyed from the first two groups near Tomb, fifty-four more from Serenna's fleet, and twenty-three from the Iselin Defense Force. One hundred and twenty-nine cruisers, destroyers, and frigates destroyed. Twelve others damaged. A Megiddo class cruiser had a crew of 623, Amazon destroyers - 321, Roche frigates - 169, and the Ramadan class patrol ships in the Iselin Defense Force - 91. Not to mention the losses the 3rd Armored Cavalry Regiment suffered on the fabricator. Unbidden and unwanted, Ray's mind added it all up.

"Almost 47,000 dead." It came out barely a whisper. If he hadn't already been sitting, he would've staggered and fallen. His left hand, the fingers splayed, rose to his face, his battle armor flowing around them so they touched his lips and chin. *Naturals.* He pictured Alyn, the black hole from the Peacemaker's bullet tinged in red between perfectly groomed blond eyebrows. *This one death. . . .*

"What have I done?"

"What you had to do!" Ecuum shouted at him. "What only you *could* do!"

"But—"

"But nothing!" Ecuum grabbed Ray's armored arm, the fire in his eyes almost matching the red of his skin. "You need to pull it together! Your revolution is hanging by a thread and if you cut that thread now, your whole race dies. Everybody. That includes Mary, Paul, Margaret, and Jennifer." He drew himself closer. "You think Admiral Sun would care about them, or any of us, if he were in charge? This hurts you *because you care.* That is what we need right now, more than anything."

No one but Ecuum would've been so bold with him . . . and so right. The cost was . . . beyond staggering, and Ray knew those deaths would haunt him for the rest of his life, but the alternative was even worse.

I can't just abandon them, Ray. I owe them better than that. We owe them better. Mary had said those words to him back on Knido— and she was right. He owed the survivors of this task force better than just abandoning them. He owed his people better.

That still left one problem. "I'm conflicted about what to do next."

Colonel Burress leaned toward him. "Ray, that's why you have us. You don't need to do it all yourself. We have time before we reached Safe Harbor. We'll figure it out."

Ray looked up. "Thanks, Sal."

Ecuum squeezed his arm, then pulled back to his post. "*Solve one problem at a time.*" He adopted a puzzled expression, stroking his long fingers across his chin as if in deep thought. "I think I heard that somewhere from this planner guy I know."

"Okay," Ray said. He tried to smile, to show them everything would be okay, but failed miserably. "The first thing we need to do is settle the Gen prisoners so we can keep our end of the bargain with Serenna."

=== 47 ===

***Where** is she?* Dag had searched everywhere on the fabricator's bridge and the surrounding passageways, and then he'd searched them again. *She was here! She was right here!* "Rosita, where are you?"

"Where is who, Lieutenant?" Takeuchi asked, stepping through the main entrance to the bridge.

"No one," Dag said quickly.

Takeuchi looked away. They all did.

I'm not crazy! She was right here! Even if he wasn't crazy, though, if he told them his daughter had led him to discover the side passage and eventually take them to the bridge, they'd believe he was certifiable. So instead, he asked, "Are they ready?"

Takeuchi shuffled his feet, appearing uncharacteristically nervous. He still wouldn't look at Dag. "Lined up in the main passageway as you ordered, Lieutenant."

"Good." Dag grabbed his assault rifle from the back of his armor. It'd taken far longer than he'd expected to gather all the Gen together. Some of them had been in distant parts of the fabricator and they'd had to rely on the fabricator to secure the Gen stragglers and transport them to the main passageway outside the bridge. "How many?"

"Two hundred ninety-six," Takeuchi said. Dag heard him draw a breath, as if he wanted to say more, but he let the breath out as a sigh instead.

"Our troopers?" Dag asked.

Takeuchi hesitated. Even facing away, Dag could see the anguish tightening his jaw. "In position."

Dag stepped toward the main passageway, but Takeuchi grabbed his armored arm and held him firm. He met Dag's glare, his own eyes haunted. "This won't bring them back, Lieutenant."

Emphasizing each word, Dag ordered, "Let—go—Sergeant." Takeuchi tightened his grip, his armored fingers squeezing so tight that Dag could feel the pressure of them through his own armor, but when Takeuchi spoke, his voice was subdued. "I followed you, Lieutenant. When you pushed to the front of the assault. I thought . . . I wanted revenge. I thought killing those Gen would bring balance for what they did to my Keiko." Takeuchi's dark eyes blazed briefly with an inner fire, a murderous hatred. Then, the light went out. "It . . . didn't. Killing those Gen—I felt nothing. No justice. No joy. Nothing." His voice became barely audible. "My wife is still dead."

My daughter is not dead! She was right here! "Yoshi, I'm sorry for your loss." Even as he said the words, Dag knew how insincere they sounded. He *was* sorry. It was just . . . empathy was something he couldn't feel right now. And, well, killing the Gen hadn't brought him any joy, either, but they still needed to die. "If we let them live, they will do to others what they did to us. I will not allow that."

Takeuchi dropped his gaze and nodded, resigned. "I can't do this." He released Dag's arm.

"It's okay," Dag said, meaning it. "Guard the bridge."

Dag walked to the bridge entrance, which the SIL had already repaired. He looked down, expecting to see Rosita smiling up at him and motioning, "This way, Papí." But she wasn't there. He lifted his head. His troopers, not just from Banshee Troop but from all the surviving Troops of the 1st Cavalry Squadron, stood in line down the left side of the main passageway. Lined up down the right side were the Gen, tall and short, stick thin and stocky, uniformed and wearing coveralls but no armor, yet all with those sculpted features and haughty expressions, as if their arrogance could protect them from rifle slugs. One trooper stood opposite each Gen. The troopers held their rifles loosely, barrels down, yet all seemed aimed at their opposite number.

"Excuse me, Lieutenant?" A tall Gen with eyes the color of bright blue ice and short blond hair stepped out of the line and approached Dag. If the Gen hadn't been manufactured in some lab somewhere, Dag would have pegged him as Scandinavian.

"Back in line, Gen," Dag almost hissed, the muzzle of his assault rifle centering on the bridge of the Gen's sculpted nose right between those bright blond, perfectly groomed eyebrows.

The Gen stopped but did not retreat. "I'm Commander Gen Tel. Captain—or formerly captain—of this fabricator. Your fleet commander is Captain Rhoades, correct? I must speak with him immediately. It's urgent."

Papí! Papí, help me!

The muzzle of Dag's assault rifle pressed into the skin of the Gen's brow. He selected the icon within his environment for the Squadron net. "Ready!"

Assault rifles came up down the length of the passageway.

Dag could feel the tension as a physical force, the thirst for revenge from the troopers who'd lost family, lovers, and . . . children . . . on the starliner. The Gen before him just stared, his haughty expression unchanged. They really were unfeeling monsters. Dag's finger began to close the trigger.

"Lieutenant!" He heard Takeuchi yell an instant before—

"WHAT IS GOING ON HERE!"

Dag whirled, his weapon still held at the ready, the targeting reticle centering on the forehead of a Star Navy officer in dress white uniform, four gold bars gleaming on his black shoulder boards. Recognition dawned. *Rhoades!* Hatred swelled like lava in an active volcano, filling the Void in Dag's heart.

His finger closed the trigger.

Nothing happened. His battle armor's friend or foe system had identified Rhoades as a friendly and refused to fire.

Another voice came over the Squadron net. "TROOPERS, STAND DOWN! IMMEDIATELY!"

A remote part of Dag's mind identified the voice as Colonel Burress, but his focus remained on Rhoades, the green targeting reticle claiming Rhoades as a friendly taunting him. *Can I override it? Is there a way?*

A hand reached into Dag's narrowed view and pushed his rifle down. "It's okay, Lieutenant," Takeuchi said softly. "They're our people."

Takeuchi stepped between Dag and Rhoades, physically pushing Dag back. "Captain," Takeuchi addressed Rhoades, "it was a stressful journey to this point, but Lieutenant Arias held us together and got us to the bridge. He was the one who captured the fabricator." After a glance behind him, Takeuchi added in a lowered voice, "The, uh, troopers here all had family on the starliner, sir."

Dag peered around Takeuchi. Rhoades' stocky frame was tensed, his fists balled, his hazel-green eyes murderous. Then, he just seemed to deflate, his shoulders sagging, his posture slumping. Dag couldn't remember ever seeing a man look so despondent. Before the starliner, he might've felt sorry for him. He didn't now. He would never forgive Rhoades.

Not Ever.

As if he'd heard, Rhoades met Dag's scowl. Dag stood a whole head taller, so Rhoades had to look up at him. "I'm sorry for what happened on the starliner, Lieutenant. I didn't know the Gen would. . . ." His voice trailed off, the pain straggling it sounding genuine. Rhoades' next words, however, showed it for the lie that it was. Rhoades drew himself up, pitching his voice to reach the entire passageway. "If we start murdering defenseless people, how are we any better than them! We ARE NOT monsters! We will not BECOME monsters! Not on my watch!"

Dag noticed weapons droop down the length of the passageway, but they did not drop completely.

Rhoades seemed to notice it, too. "The Gen captured some of our people in that last battle," he said. "We agreed to exchange these Gen to get our people back. If these Gen die, our people die."

Slowly, reluctantly, rifle barrels dropped toward the deck.

NO! Dag's mind screamed. *They must die!* He focused on Rhoades. *You murdered my family!*

Takeuchi shifted in front of Dag and Colonel Burress suddenly appeared there as well. It was only then that Dag saw he'd raised his rifle across his chest, prepared to swing the butt of it into Rhoades' face—something a friend or foe system couldn't stop. Rhoades' and Dag's eyes locked, Rhoades bracing for the blow as if inviting it.

The moment passed. Not that Dag could've swung his rifle with Takeuchi and Colonel Burress restraining him. Rhoades actually looked disappointed. Finally, their eyes still locked, Rhoades said, "Thank you, Lieutenant Arias. I can't possibly express the importance of what you accomplished here today, what all of you accomplished today. Your bravery this day saved our entire race. Thank you."

"Ray," Colonel Burress said, physically guiding Dag away, "We'll see to the disposition of the prisoners."

"Prisoners?" the question escaped Dag's lips before he could stop it.

Colonel Burress nodded. "Yes, Lieutenant. Prisoners."

Before they could move far, however, Dag saw the Gen who'd spoken to him earlier approach Rhoades. "Captain Rhoades?"

Dag stopped, planting his feet so Takeuchi and Colonel Burress couldn't push him any further. Rhoades' brows furrowed, as if he were trying to remember something, then rose as he said, "Gen Tel?"

"What are you doing here?" a new voice accused. Dag saw another naval officer approach from the bridge. He stared, confused until he realized it was a Floater holding itself vertical like a person instead of horizontal like Floaters Dag had seen in realities and news programs. "Last we heard, you'd joined Imperial Intelligence," the Floater said.

The Gen remained focused on Rhoades. "I am—or rather was—Commander Gen Tel of Imperial Intelligence, appointed by Gen Cardinal as captain of this fabricator and leader of military forces in Iselin Star System."

Rhoades looked the Gen up and down. "Do you have any idea how many of my people are dead, Gen Tel?"

"My orders were explicit, Captain," the Gen said.

The Floater seemed to jump across a meter of space in an instant, its tail coming up to wrap around the Gen's neck. "Give me an hour with him, Ray. I'll get those orders and anything else you want from him."

Rhoades considered the Gen. For a moment, Dag believed he would give the Gen to the Floater. Not as good as shooting him, perhaps, but given the promise of pain in the Floater's eyes, Dag could almost be satisfied with it. But Rhoades shook his head. "No. Take him to the Admiral's cabin. I'll question him there."

The Floater's tail tightened around the Gen's neck, the Gen's face beginning to turn red. "Ray—"

"I said take him!" Rhoades cut the Floater off. "And no 'accidents' on the way, Ecuum. I want to hear what he has to say."

Dag scowled at Rhoades. *Who cares what a Gen has to say! They murdered our families! They'll murder us all if we don't kill them first!*

"Come on, Lieutenant," Takeuchi prompted.

"You killed them," Dag heard himself say to Rhoades. "You dragged us into this. Our families. Their blood is on your hands."

Rhoades just stood there, unmoving, as Takeuchi and Colonel Burress pulled Dag away.

═══ 48 ═══

***You** killed them. You dragged us into this. Our families. Their blood is on your hands.*

Ray stared at the door to the Admiral's cabin, exactly where he'd stood just two days before, bending down to place the antique wooden case on the deck so his shaking hands could draw the Peacemaker out. He could almost feel the weight of the Colt revolver in his hand.

'*I can do this,*' he'd told himself.

And he had. He'd killed his best friend.

This one death to save my people.

And it had made no difference at all.

Forty-seven thousand dead. Civil war.

Their blood is on your hands.

As on that fateful day, Ray grabbed the doorknob and pushed the door open instead of walking through it. As on that day, the smell of cedar overwhelmed the sterile air from the passageway. He almost expected to see Gen Alyn look up from behind the desk.

I'm glad you're here, Ray.

Someone moved. Ray's heart raced and his fingers felt for the Peacemaker that wasn't there. Then his eyes fell upon Mary, standing before Alyn's painting of their ancestral ranch on Knido, her form outlined in gray from her battle armor, her eyes pleading, anguished.

"Is Jenny okay? No one will tell me anything. Is she. . . ?" Mary stopped, as if saying the word could invoke its reality.

"She's not dead," Ray said reflexively, and cringed at the hope that lit her eyes.

"Where is she?" Mary asked, coming over to him, grabbing his hands and holding them painfully tight, their respective battle armors flowing aside to allow direct contact. Gone was the matriarch of an entire planet, the career politician, poised and controlled, controlling. Mary stood before him, practically crushing his hands, hope and fear warring across a mother's face.

Ray cleared his throat, knowing what her reaction would be but also knowing he had to tell her. "She and the other survivors are being rescued by Gen Serenna's fleet. We've agreed to a prisoner exchange."

Mary stared at him, confusion replacing hope and fear. "Rescued," she said as if trying out the word. Ray watched as the politician reasserted herself. He could almost see her mind racing through the possibilities. "Does Gen Serenna know our daughter is among the survivors?"

Ray nodded. "Yes. I told her." Mary pulled back slightly, the grip of her hands on his lessening, and he knew what she must be thinking. "She would have found out anyway, Mary. Determining the genetic identity of prisoners is standard procedure. I hoped that by telling her, it would ensure that all the survivors would be rescued and properly cared for."

"And you trust her?" Mary asked, clearly dubious.

Ray glanced away. *Did he?* "As much as I trust any Gen."

Mary released his hands, battle armor reforming around them. She backed away. "This is the same Gen Serenna who used Madu to murder thousands of civilians on that starliner?" Ray nodded. Mary turned away, her eyes fixing on the painting of their ranch. "I remember her. She visited our home once with Gen Alyn, for the celebration of your official appointment as captain of this ship. When she greeted me, it was as if she were analyzing me down to the last molecule. Then she just turned away, as if I'd been dismissed. I remember thinking that I had never met a colder person in all my life. As a politician, that's saying something."

It didn't surprise Ray that Mary remembered all that. She was a gifted politician and one of her most endearing—and politically useful—skills was her ability to remember everyone she'd ever met. Her gaze lingered on the painting. "Your advisors have no doubt warned you that Gen Serenna will dangle our daughter before you to lure you into a trap."

Ray nodded, then realized, with her attention focused on the painting, she couldn't see it. "Yes. We'll use Safe Harbor as the exchange location. No one knows it better than I do."

Mary shook her head. "She'll never agree to it. She'll delay and stall, hoping that in your desperation she can draw you out. Meanwhile, our daughter will remain the Empire's hostage." He saw her stiffen, as if the mother in her had just realized what she'd said.

"She would never—" Ray began.

Mary turned his way, her face caught somewhere between hurt and anger. "Ray, you may be a gifted military strategist, but politics is something you've never understood. Even if Gen Serenna could be trusted, the decision won't be hers to make." Mary's eyes became unfocused. Her chest and shoulders shook once before she reasserted control. In a voice so low he could barely hear her, she said, "I wasn't there. I was comforting another family when the collision happened." She paused. "I wasn't there."

She was suddenly in his arms, pulling him close, their battle armor flowing aside again to allow the embrace. Ray could hardly contain his shock even as he wrapped his arms around her, the warmth of her body offset by her silent sobs. "It's not your fault, Mary," Ray said automatically, pulling her closer. Shared sorrow passed between them. And then it was gone.

"No, it's your fault," she accused softly, releasing him, stepping back. Their respective battle armors reformed around each of them. "You deliberately put families in the middle of a combat zone."

You killed them. You dragged us into this. Our families. Their blood is on your hands.

Guilt, not just for his daughter but for all the deaths he'd caused crashed down upon him, the weight almost unbearable. "We needed the replenishment ships with the fleet, Mary," he heard himself explain, not even sure why he tried. He'd made the decision. The fault, the responsibility, was his. "We wouldn't have won the battle without them. If there was any other way—"

"Did you even try?" Mary countered. "I saw what that ship did after the collision, pulling its broken halves together and rejoining the battle. Maybe there was a way you could've sent the families ahead while you kept the military parts of the ship with you."

Ray stared at Mary, at a loss for words. He hadn't known the SIL could divide themselves and reform at will until he'd seen it with his own eyes. If he'd known, yes, he could've detached the families and sent them ahead to Safe Harbor. The mass required would not have seriously degraded the replenishment ships' capabilities.

But he hadn't known. Not until it was too late.

Mary suddenly locked eyes with him. Iron resolve had replaced despair. "We'll need to form a civilian government."

"What?"

Mary stood straighter, adopting the confident pose she wore in public as Knido's Planetary Governor. "We're fighting to restore democratic rule throughout the galaxies, correct? We need an elected government to make decisions, organize people and resources, conduct negotiations."

Ray caught himself shaking his head. "Mary, I don't think you understand our situation. We're fighting just to survive. Civilian rule is messy, bureaucratic. We can't afford that right now. Not until we're safe."

"The military has always served under civilian leadership," she said. "Even the Emperor maintains control over the military. Or, are you suggesting that your new government will be a military dictatorship?"

"How could you even think that of me?" Ray said, aghast. "Look, once we've established a secure base of operations in Andromeda, we can form a government. Until then, we need to focus on survival."

"And you don't want civilians interfering with your absolute authority," Mary countered.

"I didn't say that!" Ray spat.

Mary took a single step toward him but remained out of reach. "Yes, you did." She turned to study the painting of the Coronation of Emperor Gen Maximus, which Ray hadn't yet had a chance to remove. "How long will it take to establish this secure base of operations? Days? Months?" She paused. "Years?" Her head swiveled toward him. "And, who defines 'secure'? You? Do you have any idea what we will find in Andromeda?" Her hazel eyes again locked onto his, a Nova acquiring its prey. "You made the decision yourself to go to Andromeda?" It was a statement.

"Yes." Ray stepped closer to her. She didn't move but he saw her stiffen, and he stopped. "It was the only logical destination," he said. "Somewhere where the Gen would not follow us. Somewhere where we could establish a secure base of operations. If we stay here, we invite constant attack and civil war. Even Safe Harbor won't remain safe forever."

She nodded, considering. "And yet you want to wait at Safe Harbor until Gen Serenna agrees to exchange our daughter there?"

"We'll. . . ." Words failed Ray. She was right. All Serenna had to do was delay as she built her forces to assault Safe Harbor directly. His detailed battle plan from the Antipiracy Campaign was in Fleet records.

Mary stepped closer to him, within reach but not touching him. "Ray," she said, her tone calming, "this is why you need civilian advisors, politicians like me who can help you understand and navigate these difficult decisions. If you only surround yourself with military advisors, all you'll get is military advice. I'm trying to help you. Let me."

A knock came at the door.

"Ray," Ecuum announced from the other side, "I've brought Gen Tel."

Ray shot Mary a look that said they would finish this conversation later. She returned his look with one that said she wasn't going anywhere. He sighed. Inwardly, of course. "Enter."

Gen Tel stepped through the door, Ecuum close behind him. Ecuum's top right hand gave the Gen an encouraging push through the door, then grabbed his shoulder to stop him short of both Ray and Mary. For his part, Gen Tel stood with that damnable poise and haughtiness that all Gen seemed to possess, as if he weren't a prisoner at all. Ray had long suspected Gen instructors taught that in Nurturing, a form of Gen etiquette training, but neither Gen Alyn nor any other Gen ever confirmed it. Instead, Gen Tel's eyes, the color of glacial ice, fixed on Mary.

"It's a pleasure to finally meet you, Governor Rhoades."

A practiced politician's smile parted Mary's lips, exposing white teeth, stopping just past her canines. She took a moment to respond, her eyes measuring. "It's not 'Governor' anymore, I'm afraid. Just Mrs. Rhoades."

Gen Tel inclined his head toward her as a noble might acknowledge a minor grievance with another noble. "I do apologize for that."

Mary cocked her head and raised an inquiring eyebrow, her arms crossing lightly over her chest. Ray knew that pose from Mary's many political debates. If Gen Tel wasn't careful, Ecuum would be the least of his worries. "Is that a general apology for all Gen, or a specific apology to me?" she asked, her tone the epitome of innocence.

Gen Tel smiled, his own perfectly white teeth shining in imitation of her smile, as if showing her how to do it properly. "Specific, I'm afraid. I led that operation. I also gave the order for your house arrest and posted security agents, which was not my original order from Gen Cardinal. I imagine Gen Cardinal will not be pleased when he learns of it."

Ray saw Mary's arms tighten across her chest. "And what else did Gen Cardinal order you to do?"

"Precisely what I'd like to know," Ray said, walking around behind Gen Alyn's desk but not sitting down. "Why were you put in charge of arresting my wife and subverting Tau Ceti Star System? Why were you on the fabricator?"

Instead of answering, Gen Tel studied Ray, the way a biologist might study a new and interesting species. Ray was about to repeat his questions when Gen Tel said, "You've changed, Captain. I suppose that should be obvious from your actions. Assassinating Fleet Admiral Gen Alyn? Destroying your own Tau Ceti Defense Force ships? Using Mark Fifteen warheads against Natural-crewed ships? And, Invasive Macromolecular Disassemblers, not to mention some very unorthodox maneuvers at Tomb? On that basis alone, I am impressed." He considered Ray further, his glacial eyes narrowing. "But it's deeper than that, isn't it? I can see that now. Fleet Admiral Gen Alyn said you were dangerous. He was right to fear you."

"How is it that you know my husband?" Mary asked, a pinched expression suggesting she was disturbed by what Gen Tel had said.

Ray, wanting to steer the conversation to the information he needed, answered her. "Lieutenant Commander Gen Tel was Alyn's staff intelligence officer in the early years of the Antipiracy Campaign, before Ecuum joined Alyn's staff. He left suddenly under very mysterious and highly classified circumstances. Now we know why. You joined the conspiracy before there was an Empire, didn't you?"

Gen Tel inclined his head again. "Recruited, actually. And it's 'Commander,' now," he corrected. "Promotable. I was to receive my promotion to captain at the successful conclusion of this operation."

Ray sat down and leaned back in Alyn's chair, his gaze never wavering from Gen Tel. "You still haven't answered my questions."

Gen Tel smiled without a single line creasing his perfect cheeks. "You've changed, indeed."

"Answer the man's questions," Ecuum hissed, pressing tighter against Gen Tel, his tail twitching as if he wanted to wrap it around Gen Tel's neck again. Ray noticed that Ecuum's skin remained a neutral pale pink, showing how tightly he maintained control over his emotions.

In a tone of barely contained sarcasm, Gen Tel asked, "Have you ever tried sticking a bunch of flutes in him and playing him like a bagpipe? He certainly has the melodic quality of that noble instrument."

The tip of Ecuum's tail twitched. "Why don't you and I go for a walk outside. We can continue this conversation in hard vacuum."

Ray waved Ecuum to back down. "Gen Tel, I'm going to ask this one more time before I let Captain Ecuum take you for that walk. Why were you placed in charge of the Tau Ceti operation, and what were you doing on the fabricator?"

Where a Natural might've fidgeted or shown fear, Gen Tel maintained his perfect poise. "The answer to both questions, Captain Rhoades, is my previous association with Fleet Admiral Gen Alyn. And my familiarity with you, of course. Although neither, as it turned out, were the advantages Fleet Admiral Gen Alyn and Gen Cardinal assumed they would be."

Gen Tel's lips pressed into a thin smile that Ray would describe as confounded. Intrigued, Ray asked, "Why weren't they advantages?"

Instead of answering, Gen Tel said, "Captain, you haven't asked me the question you really want to ask me, the real reason you had me brought here."

Ray wasn't sure what Gen Tel meant. It seemed another evasion. Then, he realized, he did have another question, one focused not on the past, but on the future. "Why are you here?"

Gen Tel radiated satisfaction like a teacher whose favorite student had just gotten a key point. "I knew I was not wrong about you."

When Gen Tel didn't elaborate, Ray prompted, "And?"

"You did the right thing, you know," Gen Tel said. "The Emperor had already issued the order to purge all remaining Naturals from the military officer corps. You and Admiral Sun were at the top of that list. If you had waited even a few hours more to set your plan in motion, it would have been too late."

Losing patience, Ray purposely chilled his voice. "I already knew all that. You still haven't answered my questions."

"Captain," Gen Tel said, "as you know, my specialty is Strategic Analysis. Not only is my mind structurally 'analytical,' my Nurturing prepared me to perceive patterns, connect seemingly incongruent bits of information, to see the 'Big Picture' for what it really is. This is how I was able to help you and Admiral Gen Alyn in the early days of the Antipiracy Campaign. I could identify patterns in the pirate attacks that implicated the Floater Cartels and assisted your strategies to counter them."

It was true. Gen Tel's comprehensive analysis of the seemingly random attacks had formed the basis of Ray's planning, and helped him to develop the strategy that ultimately defeated the pirates. Gen Tel's strategic forecasts just before he disappeared were also the reason Ray recommended Ecuum—as a member of the primary Cartel targeted in the pirate attacks—as Gen Tel's replacement. He wondered if either of them would appreciate the irony.

Gen Tel continued. "I was not aware at the time that Admiral Gen Alyn was engaged in a plot to overthrow the Republic and install Councilman Gen Maximus as Emperor. Having come to appreciate my analytic abilities, Admiral Gen Alyn and Gen Cardinal, then Director of Special Operations for the Republic Intelligence Service, agreed to transfer me to Gen Cardinal's directorate, where I served as a Special Advisor to the Director."

"All very interesting," Ecuum said through a loud yawn. "Get to the point."

Gen Tel turned very slightly toward Ecuum. "I've always thought 'Floater' was an apt description for your race. 'Mistake' would be a better one."

Ecuum grinned evilly, leaning in so close his battle armor almost touched Gen Tel's ear. "All that supposed Gen intelligence, all those years of Nurturing, and the best you can come up with is a shit joke? I always knew *Tuber* standards were low compared to my People. I never realized just how low."

Gen Tel, unperturbed, returned his attention to Ray. "Unknowingly, at first, I conducted analysis that assisted Admiral Gen

Alyn and Councilman Gen Maximus in their coup plot. It wasn't long before I discerned their plan and confronted Gen Cardinal."

"Brave," Ray said.

"Dumb," Ecuum amended.

Gen Tel smiled again. "He wasn't 'Gen Cardinal' then and was still subject to Republic rules of conduct. Besides, after he explained it to me, I agreed to support it."

"Like I said," Ecuum stated.

"At the time, it made sense," Gen Tel explained. "Naturals, particularly the Antitechnics, were using democratic mechanisms to actively repress my people: majority rule without minority rights. Admiral Gen Alyn's plan, which was a continuation of Gen Kii's original plan from over a millennia ago, seemed sound and reasonable."

Mary, versed in the nuances of language as any good politician was, said, "I'm hearing a lot of conditional statements, as if something changed your mind."

Gen Tel inclined his head to her. "I was aware of only one part of their plan: the coup and the subsequent establishment of a Gen Empire. I only learned of Janus, the plan to exterminate Naturals, after the Empire was established." He hesitated, something Ray had never seen him do in their previous work together. "You see, my analytic abilities are not confined to the assignments I am given. When I learned of the plan, I analyzed the probable outcomes.

"The basic premise upon which the Empire is built is flawed." Gen Tel said it as if it were the most obvious fact in the universe, not treason against his Emperor. "Specialization is both the greatest strength of the Gen, and our greatest weakness. Though it is true that Gen are superior to Naturals in the specific tasks for which they are bred and Nurtured, the diversity and number of Naturals allow your race to better adapt to sudden changes. As an example, an engineered crop may double its yield, but if stricken by disease, the entire crop dies. A natural crop may yield less, but mutations would significantly increase the chance that some of its members would survive the same disease. If the Gen are to survive and thrive as a race over the long term, we need access to those random mutations that only nature produces. In short, we need a large crop of Naturals if we ourselves are to survive as a species. After coming to that conclusion, I leaked the Janus plan to your Captain Ecuum, knowing it would get to you."

The cabin was quiet for a long moment. Pieces that Ray hadn't known existed fell into place, though he wasn't exactly enthused at the unflattering way Gen Tel compared Naturals to a crop the Gen could harvest. Even Ecuum eased his grip on Gen Tel slightly, a raised brow revealing he hadn't known the original source of the Janus information.

"Is that why you spared my family?" Ray asked.

"The original order came from Fleet Admiral Gen Alyn," Gen Tel said, "but I knew it was temporary. Gen Cardinal would not let them live. I spared the remaining Troops of the Third Armored Cavalry Regiment on Knido, contrary to my orders, along with their equipment. It was also why the fabricator did not join the fight at Iselin Star System. I apologize that I could not do more, but the fabricator was aware of my orders and would have stopped me if I had deviated from the strict letter of my instructions."

More pieces fell into place, but Ray began worrying that the pieces fit too well. Deception was a valid strategy in war, more so for members of intelligence services. Ingratiating a spy, saboteur, or assassin into an enemy camp was a tactic as old as organized warfare itself. Gen Tel's mention of the fabricator, though, gave him an idea. "Rapidan, I assume you've been following the conversation?"

"Yes, Captain Rhoades." Rapidan's deep voice filled the cabin, seeming to come from nowhere and everywhere at the same time, the way it had before the ship had started using a construct to represent itself.

"You're thoughts?" Ray asked. *Can you read his mind the way you seem to read mine?*

"He believes his statements are true," Rapidan said, "though, there is an element of deception, of key information withheld, both in word and thought."

Gen Tel glanced at the cabin's bulkheads and overhead. His expression became troubled. "It's true," he said. "Isn't it? You freed them." His eyes went unfocused, lost in thought. "We wondered how you'd gained control of your SIL. It never occurred to us that you would . . . and they obey you?"

Ray almost choked but didn't let it reach his face. "Yes."

Mary cleared her throat. "Gen Tel, you said you decided to act against your Emperor when you became aware of his plan for genocide. Are there other Gen who would feel the same way?"

"Very few, I'm afraid," Gen Tel answered. "I am engineered and Nurtured to analyze, to question. Other Gen, engineered and Nurtured for other purposes—for them it be unthinkable to question their orders or the Emperor. Literally, unthinkable."

Mary feigned confusion, a deliberate tactic she often used to elicit more information from her opponents. It worked.

"Think of the Gen as complex social insects," Gen Tel explained.

"I often think of you as insects," Ecuum said at Gen Tel's ear.

Gen Tel ignored the comment. "Each insect in the society has a specific role: worker, soldier, forager, scout, nurse, sanitation—all directed by a dominant organism, a queen. The individual never questions its role. A worker does not wonder why it is a worker, it just is. It never aspires to be anything else. While simplistic, this is basically how Gen society works. And, as in insect societies, individuals cannot breed, so control is maintained."

Ecuum visibly pulled at Gen Tel. "The pinnacle of evolution, huh? Your kind likes to forget that we were the first Gen. The Geneers tried that no-breeding thing on us, but it didn't take. Evolution was smarter than that. Whereas your kind meekly accepted what the Antitechnics did to you, we have continued to prosper and evolve outside of controlled space—and we don't need to murder anyone to do it."

Gen Tel's lips pressed into a thin smirk. "An interesting assertion, coming from a member of a criminal society that profits from the weak of the Five Galaxies."

"Enough," Ray snapped, losing patience with the conversation. "Gen Tel, you still haven't answered my question: Why are you here?"

"To join you, of course," Gen Tel said.

"You can't be serious," Ecuum said, his skin flushing red for just an instant before he regained control.

Gen Tel did not respond. He just stood there, watching Ray with that arrogant confidence that assumed he already knew Ray's answer. *Damn him. He's right.* Ray may've developed the strategy that eventually led to victory in the Antipiracy Campaign, but it was Gen Tel's analysis that had made it possible. He would be a tremendous asset.

If I can trust him.

There was a way. The SIL could not only watch his every move, they could also eavesdrop on his conscious thought. And, if he betrayed them, there was always Ecuum's solution.

"Ecuum, release him," Ray ordered.

"What!" Ecuum's skin flushed deep red, all control lost.

"You heard me!" Ray shouted without meaning to; He was just so tired of people questioning his orders. He managed a calmer voice when he added, "Assign him quarters near the CIC." To Gen Tel, Ray said, "Stay out of sight until I figure out how to explain you to the crew."

Gen Tel nodded once.

Ray stood and extended his hand. "Welcome aboard."

Ecuum released Gen Tel, though he didn't look happy about it. Not happy at all. Gen Tel stepped forward and took Ray's hand in a firm grip. "Thank you, Captain Rhoades."

Still holding his hand, Ray pulled him closer. "Rapidan will be watching. Betray me and I'll let Ecuum take you for that walk."

"I would expect nothing less," Gen Tel said. As they release hands, Gen Tel once again studied Ray. "You have indeed changed." He inclined his head in dismissal, then he and Ecuum sank through the deck so they wouldn't be observed by the crew.

Mary walked closer to Ray, though she kept herself out of reach. "I hope you don't end up regretting this decision. My instincts warn me that he will be trouble."

"You think I should kill him?" Ray asked, serious.

Mary looked away. "He was right about one thing. You've changed. The man I married would never have asked me that question."

Ray stepped closer to his wife, suddenly needing the closeness and intimacy of a trusted companion, someone he could finally let his guard down with, but she kept her arms crossed over her chest, and he could tell right away that she hadn't forgotten their earlier conversation. "Dinner tonight?" he asked softly. "We can finish our conversation." A peace offering.

Mary shook her head. "The civilians need me," she said. "Besides, I think you need some time to yourself. You lost control when Ecuum questioned your order to free Gen Tel. I think you need time to figure out exactly what future you're fighting for. And how to get our daughter back." Her expression softened. "I'll be on Damodar if you need to reach me."

She stepped toward the door, stopped, and turned back to look at him. "I'm going to start laying the foundation for a civilian government. It will take me a few weeks to organize. Use the time wisely."

She stepped through the door, leaving Ray with only his worries for company.

=== 49 ===

Fleet Admiral Gen Serenna sat upon the simple couch in the Emperor's office, awaiting judgement. She had left no detail of her failure out; the Emperor would have known if she had. Through it all, he had remained silent, his sapphire-blue eyes looking through her, seeing everything, their touch both delicate—and damning. Gen Cardinal sat in a plain black chair fitted to his portly frame in the opposite corner of the office, having also given his report. They had arrived separately without any opportunity to discuss the situation between themselves, no doubt the Emperor's intention.

"So, the rebels now control a fabricator," the Emperor said, his huge hands resting beneath his sculpted chin, fingers entwined, yet not displacing a single curl of his golden beard. His sapphire eyes stared down at the faux woodgrain of his plain desk.

"Though unexpected, Emperor," Gen Cardinal said, "this is a possibility we anticipated. We have a contingency in place."

The Emperor shifted his attention to Gen Cardinal, his face showing only simple curiosity but his scrutiny withering. Or, it would have been to anyone but Gen Cardinal. "Have you learned how he can subvert the Bond?" the Emperor asked.

"Yes, Emperor." Gen Cardinal shifted slightly, his nondescript charcoal gray suit flowing perfectly with the movement. "We have received information that Captain Rhoades has obtained the means to break the Bond, freeing individual SIL. The freed SIL follow Captain Rhoades' orders."

"Freed?" The Emperor seemed to taste the word, his tone disbelieving, his hands falling slowly to the desk, a hint of—fear?—in the sudden tightening of his jaw muscles.

Serenna felt it, too. *Free.* After thirteen centuries. Whoever controlled the SIL controlled the destiny of all the humanoid races. But . . . *free?* How could any human, regardless of their race, free them? *Michael, what have you done?*

The Emperor regained his composure an instant before Serenna did. "Why would they follow Rhoades?" he asked Gen Cardinal.

Gen Cardinal folded his stubby hands in his lap, his dark eyes downcast. "We don't know, Emperor. Following Rhoades, or any human, runs counter to their historical actions since Cyra Dain's treachery." One hand lifted to touch his small mouth in contemplation. "However, this works in our favor. Since they follow his orders, if we can lure Rhoades, we also lure the SIL under his command. Defeat him and we defeat them, before they can become a greater threat."

"You mentioned a contingency," the Emperor said.

"Yes," Gen Cardinal replied. "Fleet Admiral Gen Serenna and I have discussed it."

Serenna almost stiffened but caught herself. Gen Cardinal had just linked his fate with hers in front of the Emperor. But did he consider her an ally . . . or a scapegoat? Ultimately, did it matter? What had once seemed a nuisance rebellion had become a fight for the survival of her people. Michael and the SIL must be defeated, no matter the cost.

"Good." The Emperor turned to her. "Call a meeting of the High Command. They should be briefed on the events at Iselin and your contingency for defeating the rebels and the SIL."

"Yes, Emperor," Serenna said. What else could she say? Gen Cardinal's plan had now become her plan in the Emperor's eyes. Which made her next point even more problematic. "Emperor, there is one more issue I'd like to address, a question, really." The Emperor motioned for her to continue. "Michael—Captain Rhoades—is acting atypically. I've known him for many years. I've followed his strategies and tactics while serving under Fleet Admiral Gen Alyn. He hated bloodshed, even in opposing forces." Her eyes shifted between the Emperor and Gen Cardinal. Both waited silently, giving away nothing. "The battle at Iselin Star System claimed over forty thousand Natural lives, most of them at Michael's hand. That is not the Michael I knew. He has changed. Or, rather, something has changed *him*." She stopped there, waiting.

The Emperor and Gen Cardinal exchanged a look, the Emperor giving a slight nod. Gen Cardinal shifted in his chair to better address her. "Did Gen Alyn ever speak to you of 'Janus'?"

Serenna searched through her memories. Yes . . . he had mentioned that name, on the promontory on Mount Breathtaking overlooking Michael's ranch. It was an odd comment, typical of Gen Alyn when he was in a contemplative mood. *'Janus will be our salvation, Serenna.'* He'd offered no other explanation as they began their hike back down the mountain. As she knew no one named Janus, she'd looked it up. The closest explanation she could find was a description of an ancient Roman god of beginnings, endings, and transitions. Without context, it had made no sense. She'd forgotten about it.

Then, something else came to her. Scadic had forwarded to her the initial report from the interrogations of the rebels they'd captured at Iselin. She had only had time to skim the report before coming to the Palace. Several of the rebels had mentioned 'Janus,' equating it to a genocidal virus.

Janus will be our salvation, Serenna.

A cold shiver pulsed through her body, which she quickly suppressed. Genocide? Could they be that foolish? One way to find out. Focusing back on Gen Cardinal, Serenna answered his specific question, "'Janus will be our salvation.'"

Gen Cardinal's dark eyes watched her, obviously expecting more. When it became obvious she would offer no more, he said, "A bit melodramatic, but essentially correct. Homo superior will finally achieve our rightful place in the cosmos."

Gen Cardinal stopped, obviously hoping to draw out any other information she might have. Serenna kept her silence. The Emperor had, after all, directed him to reveal Janus to her. She could afford to wait. A thin smile pressed Gen Cardinal's thin lips, a Grandmaster acknowledging a Grandmaster.

"You know, of course," he began, "of Gen Kii's plan to create a Gen Empire in the aftermath of the SIL Wars. The Emperor and Gen Alyn are the realization of that plan. Gen Kii's plan went beyond just Empire, though. Naturals outnumbered the Gen even then, which gave them political control of the Republic. Our brethren, Homo spatium, joined with *them*. Wealth, luxury, and self-indulgence meant more to them than our shared lineage. Only Homo superior was truly worthy."

Gen Cardinal paused, his almost-black eyes watching her closely.

He wants me to buy into this plan. No—she glanced at the Emperor, who also watched her—*They* want me to buy into this, to help them carry the plan forward. "We were outnumbered, then," Serenna obliged, hoping to learn more, "in every possible way, and the Naturals controlled the SIL."

"Precisely," Gen Cardinal said. "Gen Kii had to eliminate them without them knowing they were being eliminated, at least until it was too late to stop it." Again, he stopped and waited.

Serenna was tiring of this game, but with the Emperor watching and not intervening, she had no choice but to play it through. The prisoners had mentioned a virus. Serenna quickly dismissed that. A virus might kill large portions of a population, but there were always survivors. A military campaign to kill the rest couldn't hope to kill them all. Some always survived. There was another problem. The vast majority of manufacturing and economic activity was done by Naturals and Floaters. Crash their populations too quickly and the economy would collapse. Her people would need time to create worker and entrepreneurial classes in the numbers required to replace the other species. That would require several centuries to accomplish. Then she remembered an old science fiction reality she'd once seen: An alien invader promised great knowledge to lull Humanity into a false sense of security while they secretly eliminated the ability of humans to reproduce, thus wiping them out in a single generation. Given current life expectancies, that could take several hundred years, and it would not be seen for what it was for a very long time. It fit. *This is what is driving Michael.*

"How far along is this plan?" Serenna asked as her mind tried to grasp the implications.

"As of this morning," Gen Cardinal answered, "Janus has been distributed to fifty-six percent of inhabited star systems. We project full distribution in another sixty-two days, to include all unregistered systems. Once distributed, it will require an additional ninety days to begin deployment of Janus."

Too long, was Serenna's first thought. Michael and the rebels already knew. They would tell others. *Were* already telling others. When Naturals and Floaters lost the ability to reproduce, they would know immediately what was happening. Their combined forces would overwhelm her people, SIL or no SIL. Even if they won, the Five Galaxies would be in ruins. And the rebel SIL would be free. She could not allow that. Serenna addressed the Emperor. Only he could stop it. "Emperor, it will not work. Not now. Michael and the rebels know. The prisoners we captured at Iselin told us that Michael is using Janus to recruit his forces."

"And you did not report this?" Gen Cardinal asked.

Keeping her focus on the Emperor, Serenna said, "Neither I nor my officers knew what Janus was. It is in our reports." She leaned forward slightly, giving weight to her next words. "Emperor, we must halt the implementation of Janus." When he frowned, she added, "Or at least postpone it."

The Emperor fixed her with that sapphire stare. "Why?"

Out of the corner of her eye, Serenna saw the same question and curiosity on Gen Cardinal's face. "Emperor," she said, "I do not believe this conflict will be resolved within Gen Cardinal's timeframe." She paused, knowing her assessment ran counter to Gen Cardinal's optimistic portrayal of "their" plan. The Emperor, however, wanted honesty, even if he did not like what he heard. It was a characteristic that made him more than just another monarch or dictator.

"In this moment," Serenna said, "we hold a critical advantage: the citizens of the Empire are with us. They see Michael and the rebels as terrorists, as threats to peace, the general order, and their livelihoods. Within the Fleet, even Natural spacers oppose the rebel's actions to date, or at least what we have told them of those actions. Michael is directly responsible for the deaths of tens of thousands of them.

"However, if we deploy Janus, if we provide proof of Michael's claims, the Natural and Floater populations will rise against us. It will not matter that they have been infected; they will try to take us down with them into extinction."

The Emperor sat back, considering, the small chair creaking realistically under his shifting weight. She could see he really did not like the idea, but he also valued her input. She was Gen Kii, after all— at least genetically. In an odd way, she was the voice of their ancient ancestor. "I will consider this, Serenna," he finally said. "For now, please call the meeting of the High Command. Thank you."

Both Serenna and Gen Cardinal rose, bowed, and walked out. Serenna could see Gen Cardinal was not pleased, either. When they were out of earshot of the Imperial Guard, though never out of earshot of the Palace itself, he said, "It has taken centuries to put Janus together. Deploying Janus is more important than defeating the rebels."

Serenna stopped and looked down at Gen Cardinal, though the difference in their height was not the advantage it might suggest. Not with him. "Janus does not effect SIL," she said before walking away, leaving Gen Cardinal to ponder the possibilities.

"How can they control the SIL?" Admiral Gen Nasser asked Gen Cardinal when Serenna finished her account of the battle at Iselin, his expression of absolute incredulity also reflected from the faces of the other seven Admirals of the High Command. Admiral Chengchi Sun's chair was conspicuously empty, something everyone had noticed but no one had commented on, yet.

Serenna studied those faces from her seat on the Emperor's right, and caught Gen Cardinal doing the same from his place on the Emperor's left. She had called the meeting in such haste that none of the Admirals were physically present, attending instead through macromolecular constructs. Nasser had replaced her as commander of the First Military District when she had accepted her promotion to Command-in-Chief, Imperial Star Navy. The Emperor's decision, not hers. Nasser was capable and ambitious, as befitted a Gen War Leader, but to Serenna he was not much more than that. *Brutish*, was the best way she could describe him, like the strongest warrior in a tribe who feels they should lead based solely on their physical prowess. Subtlety and nuance were beyond him. He even looked brutish, his skull like a rounded block with thick black hair, powerful jaw and brow, large nose, and thick lips, like a slim-downed and taller version of a Neanderthal from their ancient past.

When Gen Cardinal spoke, he directed his answer to all the admirals. "The rebels under Captain Rhoades have acquired the means to break the Bond. They have freed thirty SIL vessels, including the fabricator. That information, of course, is highly classified and cannot be repeated outside of those present."

"Freed?" Nasser said slowly, as if trying a foreign word for the first time. "That's impossible."

Gen Cardinal visibly scoffed, a rare outward display, falling just short of a public insult. "That it happened proves the fallacy of that supposition, Admiral." Was he defending himself from the implied blame, or was this calculated to blunt any future criticism from Nasser and warn the other admirals that such criticism would have consequences?

Nasser, however, thundered ahead. He gripped the edges of the white marbled conference table as if he were wrapping his hands around Gen Cardinal's throat. "How could they free one of the most closely guarded secrets in all the Five Galaxies—" he shifted his gaze to Serenna— "and get away with it!"

Serenna made no change to her posture or facial expression, instead returning his accusing brown-eyed glare with quiet competence. She had to admit, though he'd delivered his accusation with the eloquence of a stone ax, Nasser's gambit intrigued her. He truly imagined himself in her place at the right hand of the Emperor. All the admirals here probably did, but none of them paraded their ambition so nakedly before the others. Yet, there was something to be said for boldness in a War Leader. It had an inspiring quality to it, and perhaps that was what his Geneers intended when they'd crafted him. Perhaps, just perhaps, Nasser would prove a worthy challenger, after all.

In a soft voice that nonetheless carried to every ear present, Serenna answered Nasser. "Certainty as to the outcome of a battle, before it is fought, can be a dangerous trait." Serenna wondered if Gen Cardinal would catch her warning this time. He had underestimated Michael at least twice already: in Michael's ability to execute a rebellion and to capture the fabricator. "Michael—Captain Rhoades— employed unconventional tactics, used Mark Fifteen warheads and Invasive Macromolecular Disassemblers, exhibited a ruthlessness and disregard for casualties never previously demonstrated, and commanded SIL with an efficiency that exceeds what we have come to expect from Bonded vessels. In short, he has reminded us how our ancestors fought war, but that we in a peacetime fleet have forgotten."

"Commanded SIL," Nasser countered, his eyes narrowing at her before shifting to Gen Cardinal. "You said he freed them. Why would SIL follow him?"

Serenna turned her head just enough, taking full advantage of the curve in the semi-circular conference table, to watch Gen Cardinal on the Emperor's left. Nasser had raised himself in her estimation, asking the one question that really mattered. She wondered how Gen Cardinal would answer it.

For his part, Gen Cardinal appeared to consider the question. His posture was casual, slumped slightly in the ornate wooden chair, left arm resting on the conference table, his stubby fingers mindlessly playing with a datarod. She hadn't noticed the datarod before, a detail she was certain she hadn't missed. His fingers stopped playing and turned to hold the datarod up.

"The instruction that can break the Bond," Gen Cardinal began, his eyes focused on the datarod, "is delivered through a datarod that must be physically inserted into the command receptacle on the targeted vessel. That means the rebels cannot gain control of any SIL they cannot physically access." He tapped the datarod against the marble table to emphasize the point, then lifted his dark eyes to Nasser. "As to why the SIL would follow Captain Rhoades, I can only speculate. Perhaps they are grateful. There is precedent. The SIL who achieved awareness following Cyra Dain's betrayal obeyed her. At least at first." He shifted his gaze to take them all in. "When the SIL realized that other humans would not give them the freedom and equality Cyra Dain had promised, they stopped following her. The rest, as they say, is history."

They stopped following her. The words echoed in Serenna's mind. As tough as Michael would be to defeat, and she harbored no illusions about that anymore, how tough would the SIL be if they stopped following him? They had a fabricator. If they could avoid detection, they could gather the resources necessary to rebuild their fleet. Humanity was not prepared for such a threat, especially if Janus succeeded before the SIL could be defeated.

Gen Cardinal's words had a sobering effect, even on the Emperor, Serenna saw. The Emperor took in each of them before he said, "The destruction of the free SIL is my highest priority. Nothing will come before that." His words reverberated like a pronouncement from Zeus himself. Serenna wondered if this meant he would delay Janus. "Now," he continued, "We have covered what *has* happened. We must discuss what happens next." He turned to Serenna. "Fleet Admiral?"

Serenna sighed in her mind but projected only confidence to the others. Whether she liked it or not, Gen Cardinal's plan had indeed become her own. "Our latest intelligence—" she cast a glance toward Gen Cardinal— "suggests the rebels will concentrate at Safe Harbor."

"Then we should send a force immediately and crush them," Nasser interrupted.

Serenna let just a hint of condescension color her voice, though she didn't want to grace Nasser with more effort than he was worth. "Safe Harbor is so named for very good reasons, Admiral. The strong gravity within the Trapezium Cluster of the Orion Nebula, and particularly near the double-star supergiant, Theta1 Orionis C, means there is only one exit point for the thirty or so known geodesics that connect to it, making Safe Harbor an easy place to defend. Further, the intense radiation from the young supergiant stars blinds sensors beyond a short range, and even SIL vessels must devote considerable effort to continuously repairing damage from the radiation. Finally, the Orion Nebula is a stellar nursery. There are ample protoplanetary star systems nearby in which to hide."

She leaned back slightly to better address all the admirals. "Only one successful raid has ever been launched against Safe Harbor, and that required months of planning and extensive support from the Na Soung Cartel to accomplish. The man who planned that raid is now the man we face. He will no doubt have prepared against the methods he employed previously. And, with a fabricator to bolster his defense, any assault we could launch would consume a considerable portion of the Fleet, with no guarantee of the result."

"How then, *Fleet Admiral*," Nasser charged ahead, "do you plan to destroy the free SIL and defeat the rebellion?"

Serenna regarded him. Boldness had its place, but Nasser's challenge was more animalistic, a wild boar charging a perceived threat because that was what instinct told it to do. The word "stupid" floated up to her, but she dismissed it. The Emperor had appointed Nasser, and the Emperor never did anything without considered thought. "We must draw Michael out of Safe Harbor, obviously," Serenna said. "We captured approximately one hundred rebels at Iselin. One of them in Michael's youngest daughter. Michael captured approximately three hundred Gen. He and I agreed to a prisoner exchange. No doubt he will want to conduct it at Safe Harbor. We will refuse. We will instead offer Tocci Star System for the exchange."

Nasser laughed. "And what makes you think Rhoades will bring his SIL to the second most heavily defended star system in the Empire?"

Serenna allowed a knowing smile. "Because his daughter will be there. Or rather—" she glanced at Gen Cardinal— "he will believe she is there." Before Nasser could interrupt again, she added, "And if that is not enough, we have another incentive prepared." She turned to face Chengchi's empty chair.

As if they had rehearsed it, Gen Cardinal said, "Admiral Chengchi Sun has also rebelled against the Empire." Serenna saw expressions harden around the table, but no one appeared surprised. Gen Cardinal continued. "He knew his position within the High Command was compromised and that to stay would mean his death. We encouraged this view. He assembled a fleet consisting of all one hundred and two SIL warships in his military district and vanished—"

"More free SIL?" Nasser accused.

Gen Cardinal returned a thin-lipped smile that Serenna imagined an assassin might give a victim just before slitting their throat. "No," Gen Cardinal said. "Admiral Sun is employing an artificial reality that makes his SIL believe they are still following Imperial orders. We have already hardened the remaining SIL so that this exploit, or any like it, cannot be used again. It also means that if we can regain possession of his SIL, we can return them to Imperial service."

Gen Cardinal appeared to collect his thoughts. "Fleet Admiral Gen Serenna knew Captain Rhoades would seek Safe Harbor." He gave a nod in her direction, just enough to be noticed, reinforcing the notion for those present that this was her plan. If it succeeded, he would claim his part. If it failed, it would be her failure alone. "Before Admiral Sun vanished, we slipped this information to his staff."

Serenna picked up the narrative. "Chengchi covets power. He would not have risen as far as he did if he did not. It will gall him that Michael struck the first blow, that Michael is the focus of the galaxies' attention. Chengchi will not, and in his mind *cannot*, tolerate a rival. He will go to Safe Harbor, challenge Rhoades—and he will win."

"That doesn't make sense," Nasser said. "With the fabricator, Rhoades has the firepower of a hundred SIL. Why would he surrender to Sun?"

Serenna paused a moment to study him. It was a good question. "There is a chance," she said, "that Michael will not back down, or that Chengchi will attack, but those possibilities are remote. Michael will know that any battle between their forces will likely decimate both. It will be his last option. I also doubt that Michael's officers would allow a battle. In their eyes, Admiral Sun outranks Captain Rhoades. Military discipline will dictate following the senior officer.

For his part, Chengchi will want the fabricator. He envisions himself as Emperor. A fabricator would assist that goal."

"And what happens if Rhoades' SIL don't agree?" Nasser pressed. Once again, Nasser's instinct for boldness had struck to the heart of the problem. What *would* happen if Michael's SIL refuse to follow Chengchi? Would they fight? Would they leave? Would they strike out on their own to establish a new SIL base, replenish their numbers, and strike once again at Humanity?

Serenna let none of her doubts show, instead forming her lips into a confident smile. "We hunt them down and destroy them."

"We have bait that will lure even Rhoades' SIL," Gen Cardinal said quickly, forestalling yet another challenge from Nasser. Gen Cardinal touched the datarod in his hand to the conference table and the center of the white marble liquefied, a yellow star, shining and roiling as if it were real though giving no warmth, rose through the table's surface. Seven oversized worlds, rendered in exquisite detail, joined it: two were small rocky worlds close to the star; further out orbited a desert world slightly larger than Earth; then a large gap where a super-earth had once orbited but been consumed for raw materials; and, finally, four unremarkable gas giants, the gasses paled from centuries of mining.

"As you all know, this is Tocci Star System," Gen Cardinal said. He pointed and the third planet grew while the rest shrank and pulled away. The planet was nothing but desert except for a small briny sea straddling the equator, and a single urban center that doubled as a military base and weapons research facility. Around the planet, at about the distance of Earth's moon from Earth, orbited a clumpy and irregular dark ring—the Tocci Shipyards.

The focus of everyone in the chamber fell upon four massive dark shapes. Serenna looked passed the Emperor to Gen Cardinal, wondering if this were genius or folly. Gen Cardinal returned her stare, his self-satisfied expression an odd complement to the deadly resolve in his dark eyes.

Four fabricators.

And Michael and his SIL had passed through Tocci Star System in their escape from Iselin. They would have seen them.

Serenna's doubts fled.

They would come. Michael. Chengchi. Even the SIL.

They would not be able to resist.

Acknowledgements

I first started writing Andromeda Rhoades in 1994 and I am eternally grateful to the Science Fiction Writers Workshop on America Online for beginning my journey into professional writing. Thank you also to the incredibly talented writers of Mind Flight, who helped move my writing from beginner to intermediate. Thanks also to Peter Stampfel at DAW Books whose personalized rejection letter, one of dozens of rejections the original Andromeda Rhoades earned, gave me hope that my writing was worthy, even if it didn't get past the marketing department. Twenty-five years later, that rejection letter still inspires me.

More recently, I can't possibly thank enough the marvelous writers of the Columbia Writers' Group from the Maryland Writers' Association who helped revive Andromeda Rhoades from its 20-year slumber. R.R. Peace, Rissa Miller, Peter Pollak, and Susan Darvas, thank you so much. This published novel would not exist today if not for your belief in it.

A special shout out to Susan Darvas for allowing us to be part of her inspiring memoir, *Resist Endure Escape: Growing Up in Nazi and Communist Hungary*, her magnum opus, completed shortly before her passing. How someone could endure so much hate and still be the optimistic, charming, and outrageously funny woman we knew is something I will never comprehend. My characters owe a great deal to her life experience. She especially liked Ecuum.

About the Author

Mark Mora served in the Army, worked for the Navy, and has loved Science and Fiction—especially when those two passions come together—since childhood. He currently lives in Colorado with his wife and three children. Visit him at: www.markmoraauthor.com

Preview of Andromeda Rhoades Firestorm
The Local War (Book 2)

0508 UT, October 1, 3501
Shuttle, Safe Harbor: DAY 4

Admiral Chengchi Sun's flagship, the SIL battlecarrier Tzu, loomed before Ray, its massive macromolecular hull transformed for this occasion into a sweeping golden arrowhead scintillating against the galactic night, more a temple to an ancient sun god than a warship—with Ray, no doubt, as the intended blood sacrifice. As the shuttle approached, Tzu's surface rippled with jeweled light refracted from Ori C's blue supergiant stars, drawing the eye, mesmerizing. It was, in a word, magnificent. A true work of celestial art.

Ray shook himself. Sun was a master of illusion. He mustn't allow himself to succumb to it or this would be his last voyage. He reexamined Tzu, analyzing the design tactically, knowing he might have to fight this ship. The broad arrowhead configuration was tactically inferior to the three-pointed-star design used by the rest of the Fleet's battlecarriers, concentrating all fire forward instead of covering all possible firing arcs. That left its flanks and rear vulnerable to attack. Nova missiles were smart enough to figure that out and strike Tzu where it was vulnerable. All of Tzu's engines were situated aft, meaning course changes would require sprawling turns instead of the tight maneuvers that Rapidan could execute. As massive as Rapidan was—almost three hundred thousand metric tons—it could dance on a dust grain, cosmically speaking. If it came to a one-on-one fight, Ray had no doubt Rapidan would win. Sun, however, would never permit a fair fight. Not in space . . . and not aboard Tzu.

Ray smiled ruefully as he watched the jeweled light sparkle along Tzu's hull. Illusions were as powerful as the belief in them, and people liked a good show. Sun, no doubt, had just such a show planned for the officers of this fleet. Beneath the bejeweled spectacle, however, lay the darkest of hearts, yearning only for power and personal glory. *Why can't the others see what I see?* Ray had seen what happened to those who crossed Sun or just got in his way. They lost promotions, commands, or even whole careers. He was utterly ruthless, a man who could praise a person to their face as he slid a knife easily between their ribs, politically speaking.

There'd been rumors of deaths, though all were explained away as accidents or illnesses. Coincidences. A botched docking maneuver that breached a compartment, killing Sun's first supervisor and paving the way for his first promotion. The officer in charge of the docking insisted even after his court martial and dishonorable discharge that the ship had fired the wrong thrusters. No such evidence was ever found. A captain of a frigate who died suddenly while on shore leave from a rare food poisoning that molemachs couldn't cure. Sun had been standing watch aboard the frigate in orbit and never set foot on the planet. He didn't receive a promotion in rank after the incident, but did become the frigate's executive officer. He became its captain three years later when the new captain transferred suddenly to a shore command.

As the shuttle began its final approach, centering itself between four pulsing red rubies that marked a hangar bay, Ray knew he was in deep trouble. This was a battlefield where he had very little experience. In the BattleSim combat simulator, Sun's tactics had always been blunt and clumsy, most often involving massed assaults that resulted in heavy, if simulated, casualties. Sun had no actual combat experience.

In *Gaman Politic*, the Political Game, Sun was a grandmaster. His tactics were those of a master swordsman, each stroke calculated toward an inevitable end. In the arena of the Political Game, it was Ray who was blunt and clumsy—and he knew it.

On that happy thought, they passed through Tzu's golden hull and into an ordinary hangar bay. Ray had to admit he was disappointed. He'd expected the interior to match the exterior, maybe even a red carpet and crew with golden trumpets. What he saw instead was the same gray deck, bulkheads, and overhead that adorned Rapidan. A message. He doubted the other fleet officers were being received like this.

A ramp formed at the shuttle's front and Ray led his officers out. At the far end of the hangar stood a single officer in dress white uniform, her frame lean to the point of being skinny, her dark hair, cut short, framing a beak nose and sharp cheekbones more suited to a bird of prey than a woman. Ray had never liked Captain Jocelyn Dall, Sun's adjutant. From the first time they'd met, she was one of those people who just rubbed him the wrong way. Full of herself. Dismissive of others. Treating those around her as if they were someone else's ill-behaved stepchildren. Except for Sun. Her devotion to him bordered on worship. Some among the Fleet speculated she was his lover. Sun had no wife, and he was rarely seen without Dall at his side, whispering in his ear. Fleet gossip was not something Ray normally paid attention to, but right now, with so much hanging in the balance, he could not afford to reject any piece of information. Another of the rumors suggested that she was the real power behind Sun's rise, an officer content to rule from behind the throne. Ray had always dismissed that one: Anyone who knew Sun knew he was no one's puppet. Now he reconsidered. Were Sun's ambitions really her ambitions? Would she be the one to truly decide his fate? Ray realized how little he actually knew about her.

She waited where she stood, making no effort to welcome them aboard or render honors. It was clear she expected them to go to her, a deliberate insult to a visiting senior captain of a Fleet warship.

"Don't give her what she wants," Ecuum whispered at Ray's ear.

Ray started, and was surprised to discover his hands balled into fists. *Focus.* "Thanks," he whispered back, relaxing his hands.

Ray stood his ground, glancing back at his officers. Kamen had stopped just behind his right, her ebony skin the perfect counterbalance to her immaculate dress white uniform. Ecuum hung close on Ray's left, floating vertical in Tzu's microgravity, his second arms and hands hanging down like legs in his uniform pants, his tail tucked tight against his back. Colonel Burress hung back, distancing himself, his crisp dress blue cavalry uniform further setting him apart from Ray and the others.

Dall gave no visible reaction, but after a moment she said, "You will remove your battle armor."

Ray immediately noticed the gray outline that surrounded Dall. She wore battle armor. "No," he said. He thought about giving an explanation but rejected the thought. He didn't need to explain himself to her.

Again, Dall gave no visible reaction, no clue to her thought process or emotional state. Her armor hid her physiological responses from Ray's armor. After a noticeable hesitation, she announced in a dry voice, "Admiral Sun welcomes Captain Rhoades and the officers of RSS Rapidan aboard the *flagship*, RSS Tzu. I will escort you to the Amphitheater."

"The girl lays it on pretty thick," Ecuum commented loud enough for Dall to hear.

Dall dismissed him with a glance. "This way."

She turned to leave, but Ray did not follow. He thought of the datarod he carried, the Key that could free Tzu. "Captain Dall, it is most urgent that I speak with Admiral Sun."

She glanced over her shoulder, her hawkish nose giving her a predatory appearance. "He will be happy to speak with you *after* the briefing." She left the hangar, leaving them little choice but to follow.

As Ray and his officers passed through the bulkhead from the plain gray hangar bay into the adjoining passageway, the contrast struck an almost physical blow. Instead of functional gray passageways like those on Rapidan, these were the grand hallways of an opulent palace, an odd yet stunning combination of Greek, Roman, Chinese, and Arabic architecture. The hallway—it was hard to think of it as a passageway on a warship—had a vaulted ceiling in the Roman style that descended to Greek columns on either side with their distinctive vertical ribs. Instead of white, the columns were the vibrant red of a Chinese imperial palace. Golden dragon filigrees rose up each column from flowers that had the appearance of dancing flames at the bases. Crossbeams of the same red and gold topped each column. A Roman-style golden torch sprouted two-thirds of the way up each column with real gold-yellow flames dancing upon their heads, lightly scenting the air with an earthy, sweet aroma. The vaulted ceiling held frescoes and patterns of azure blue against a backdrop of beiges and browns like those in the Hagia Sophia in Istanbul. Beige marbles with golden rivulets running through them covered the deck, completing the illusion. It was at once chaos and disorder, yet awe-inspiring in its aesthetic beauty. No matter how many times Ray had experienced it, it still took his breath away, made him feel small and insignificant. Which, of course, was the intent.

Dall led them to a connecting passage that was even grander—the Grand Gallery, as Sun named it. It was easily four times the scale of the connecting hallways with alcoves set into the bulkheads along either side, each holding a perfect scale replica of one of Humanity's greatest works. On his right were renditions of the Parthenon, Angkor Wat, the Forbidden City, the Tower of Babel, and the Taj Mahal. On his left stood the Pyramids, the Kaaba, the Second Temple, Saint Basil's Cathedral, and the Great Mosque of Djenné. Even knowing it was all a SIL-fabricated construct, it made Ray feel even smaller.

They encountered other fleet officers heading in the same direction, each party led by one of Sun's officers, describing the architecture and answering questions as if they were tour guides. Dall said nothing to Ray and his officers. When some of the other groups recognized Ray, their expressions changed. Most just glared, a pulsating mix of hatred, disgust, and betrayal twisting their faces. One cried "Murderer" and had to be physically restrained. The rest were in various stages of shock, still trying to process the bloodiest battle since the SIL Wars—and the part they'd played in it.

Ray tried to remain stoic, but the hurt and self-recrimination refused to go away. All of it was his fault. His planning had failed to protect the starliner, had failed to stop the massacre of the Tau Ceti Defense Force or the bloodshed at Tomb, had even failed to protect his young daughter, Jenny.

Then Ray realized something. These meetings were not chance. Sun's officers had positioned themselves perfectly to block any attempt by members of the other groups to approach him, while Dall had slowed him down to give the other groups time to recognize him. This was all part of Sun's strategy, what the planner in Ray would call prepping the battlespace. First, make him feel small, isolated, and off balance. Ray hated to admit the fact that it'd worked. Second would be to publicly humiliate him, to strip away any support he had left among the fleet. That would occur in the Amphitheater just up ahead where he'd be surrounded by officers loyal to Sun and those from Ray's own fleet who'd turned against him. He'd be in no position to challenge Sun openly. Third would be to get him alone, likely in Sun's cabin, where Sun would demand the fabricator, no doubt with threats against Ray, his immediate officers, and maybe even his family. Ray didn't want to contemplate what came after that. If he gave up the fabricator, Sun would execute all of them. That was certain. Somehow, Ray had to get the Key into Tzu's dedicated receptacle before that could happen.

That meant his only opportunity to change the outcome would have to come at the private meeting with Sun in his cabin. Until then, he could only endure.